Girls From da Hood 7

Girls From da Hood 7

Redd, Nikki-Michelle, and *Erick S. Gray*

URBAN
BOOKS

www.urbanbooks.net

Urban Books, LLC
97 N18th Street
Wyandanch, NY 11798

ISBN 13: 978-1-60162-691-2
ISBN 10: 1-60162-691-6

First Mass Market Printing April 2015
First Trade Paperback Printing June 2012
Printed in the United States of America

10 9 8 7 6 5 4 3 2 1

Distributed by Kensington Publishing Corp.
Submit Orders to:
Customer Service
400 Hahn Road
Westminster, MD 21157-4627
Phone: 1-800-733-3000
Fax: 1-800-659-2436

Love On Lockdown

by

Redd

Chapter 1

With more bodies under her belt than a murderer on death row, Candy had an "eye for an eye" attitude that often left kids wondering, "When is Mommy coming home?" and had some of the most feared gangstas pulling their own dicks out of their mouths. She was a former project chick, killing being her sixth sense. When it came to dudes coming up short on her and her husband's paper, instead of asking questions, she cashed in on their souls.

Candy and her husband, Raynail, had all of Century City in Westwood on lockdown. The drugs that flowed in and out of the city had their names on them. They were the only suppliers willing to risk their freedom transporting both marijuana and cocaine from Colombia to the U.S. by boat, making them Century City's most sought-after suppliers. They were pulling in as much as two hundred and fifty-two grand a month from the cocaine alone, with the monthly sales from the marijuana being a little less than $20,000. Normally Raynail would make the pickups while Candy counted the cash, but since he was in jail, Candy was left to make sure that everything was on point.

Candy sat in the waiting room of Men's Central County Jail, also known as the twin towers, searching through the orange jumpsuits for her husband. Each time she saw a tall, dark man with cornrows entering the waiting area from the door leading to their cells, she thought it was him. And when the third-to-last inmate in line walked in with a fade, she was shocked to see that it was her husband.

His signature cornrows were gone and re-placed with a fade. Candy didn't like his new look and had made a mental note to check him on it.

Raynail looked around the visiting area for Candy. His eyes jumped from one teary-eyed visitor to the next, until he spotted his strong queen sitting on a bench in a corner away from the savage-looking guards. Raynail strolled over to the bench and took a seat across the table from Candy.

"I see you cut your hair," Candy said, raising an eyebrow. She turned up her lip at his boyish look.

Out of habit, Raynail looked around the room at the women and children who were crowded around their father, brother, or uncle. "Yeah, I thought I would roll wit' this 'cause it's easier to keep up." He rubbed waves into the top of his head. "Ain't no bitches in here to braid my hair."

"Well, I don't like it; it makes you look soft." Candy looked at the guy to the right of her. She then trained her eyes on two rugged-looking inmates who were sitting behind Raynail. All three men had braids that were freshly done. "I guess them dudes in back of you found some bitches?"

Raynail looked behind him, stared his nemeses down, and turned his attention back to Candy. "Them dudes fuck wit' them he/shes up in here," he snarled.

Candy looked confused.

"You know what I'm talking 'bout!" Raynail sarcastically said. "Them faggots up in here. They the ones braided them dudes' head."

"So, why didn't you let 'em braid yours?"

"Are you fucking crazy!" Raynail barked. Fire in his tone silenced everyone within earshot, and sent children clinging to their parents. "I don't fuck around like that. Ain't no twisted-ass dude 'bout to run his fingers through my shit, and I know about it."

"Well, start letting your hair grow out. By the time it grows out, you'll be back in the streets." Candy's insides churned at the sight of the fade.

"Oh yeah, that reminds me." Raynail clasped his hands together. His eyes moved slowly around the room, like a gangsta sizing up his enemy. Raynail slipped two fingers into the wrists of his long-sleeved white thermal shirt and pulled out a kite. He made eye contact with Candy. And after making sure that no one was watching them, he slid the kite over to her.

Candy put her hand over the kite, and slipped her thumb beneath it. She held it against the palm of her hand while eyeing the guards. She then folded her fingers over her thumb, and, coughing, quickly slipped the kite into her purse.

Candy pulled a napkin from her purse to entertain the eyes that may have been watching them.

"There's five names on that paper, Feo's included. All them niggas set me up, so you know what has to happen?"

"But, what exactly happened, Raynail?" Candy wanted to know. "I mean, how did they set you up?"

Raynail got up and walked around the table. He sat next to Candy, and leaned in her ear. "I was chillin' at Feo's house wit' him and the rest of them cats, right. So, we all decide we want some Henney and Coke. I volunteer to go to the liquor store on the corner to get the shit. Since the spot was right on the corner, I'm like, I'ma walk. Now, Candy, you know I don't usually go nowhere if I'm not strapped."

Candy nodded in agreement.

"But, that day, I left my Glock at the crib 'cause, other than Feo's house, I really wasn't going nowhere. Anyway, so I'm going to the store and Feo pass me a nine. I look up, and I'll be damned. As soon as I get to the store, the cops rolled up on me.

"They fuckin' patted my ass down, and pulled out the nine. Threw on the cuffs and forced me into the back seat . . . Hold up!" Raynail leaned back, rubbed the thighs of his pants, and shook his head. He was tired of talking about it. He had told the same story to the police, then his lawyer, then his mother, and now Candy. "To make a long story short, the gun was reported stolen a year ago and the bitch had six bodies on it wit' one of them being a cop."

"And what made them stop you in the first place?" Candy asked.

"Oh, that's the best part," Raynail said, rubbing his chin. "They got a tip from somebody." He nodded his head. "Yeah, after I left Feo's house, somebody called 'em and gave 'em my description and everything. Told 'em what I was wearing . . . the whole nine. And get this: whoever the bitch was lied and said I was responsible for that cop getting murdered on 108th and Hoover last year!

"Man, I can't believe my boy that I been knowing since third grade would set me up like that." Raynail noticed a guard passing back and forth by their table.

"Okay, Raynail." Candy unzipped her purse. She moved her wallet and makeup kit to the side, searching for her keys. "I'ma send RayRay to your mom's house until all of this is over with. Have you heard from your lawyer?"

"Yeah, and it's all bad," Raynail replied. "Ken told me that Feo and them gonna testify against me in court. Said that they supposed to be the prosecutor's star witnesses. But the good part about it is that all they got is Feo and them word. They ain't got no real evidence showing that I'm the one responsible for them bodies on the gun. And, peep game. When that cop was murdered, I was already in jail for a traffic violation. Remember that time I went to court after they put that warrant out on me? That time I told the judge that I'd rather do the time than to pay the fine?" Candy nodded. "Well, I went to jail that Friday and didn't get out until Monday. That cop was killed that Saturday night.

"Once they realize that Feo and the rest of them sorry-ass niggas lied about my paws being on that cop's murder, maybe they'll drop all charges against me. From the looks of things, even if they don't charge me for that cop's murder, they can still charge me for the other bodies on the gun. Right now, they still searching through the police records for the file showing that I was in jail that weekend. They claim they having a hard time finding it in the computer. I don't believe that shit for one minute! Shit, sounds like they tryin'a set me up, just so they can find somebody to take the rap for their 'comrade's' death!"

"Well, maybe Ken can find out about that, too." Candy let out a long sigh.

"And, I meant to ask you about that nigga. Dude got teardrops under his right eye. You got me a lawyer that done killed before?" A look of confusion spread across Raynail's face. "But, how the hell is he a lawyer if he done killed before?"

"It's a long story, Raynail. But he ain't never served time in jail, believe that. He just good at what he do, and he gonna get you outta here."

"And what about you?" Raynail took Candy by the hand. "You gonna be able to handle Feo and them other niggas, or are you scared?" Raynail was testing Candy to see where her head was. She was a killer with her own instincts.

"Come on now," Candy said with a sour look on her face. "You know I ain't no punk. Feo *and* his buddies 'bout to bathe in a bloodbath."

"My queen!" A devilish grin formed across Raynail's face. "And the funny part about the whole thing is Feo is more afraid of *you* than he is me. Ha! Ha! That nigga is dumb. He forgot about the fact that me and you is one. I'm glad my baby ain't no punk!" Raynail smiled and licked his lips.

"Far from that shit!" Candy's thoughts trailed off to the first six bodies on her hands. It was a memory that she had fought so hard to forget but found herself reliving every time she collected a new body.

Her family's death hit her like a ton of bricks. And each time she thought about it, she found herself shedding a tear. It was something that she had always believed that she had to do in order to shield her innocence from her uncle's abuse.

When Raynail first met Candy, he had heard rumors about her killing her family but didn't know how to approach her with it. He figured that, when the time was right, she would come out and tell him herself. Raynail was right, but it took two years for his revelation to come to pass. In the middle of an argument in front of Feo, Candy angrily shared her story.

"Candy, I wouldn't be asking you to do it if I didn't think you could," Raynail said. "What's the big deal? Damn! Don't act like you ain't never killed before. I know you killed yo' family 'cause I heard you crying and talking 'bout it in yo' sleep!"

The room grew silent. Candy glanced in the living room at Feo. The intense look on his face suggested that he too had heard the story behind her family's death. She would satisfy the curiosity of both.

Candy stood up from one of the dining room chairs, and walked over to Raynail, who was sitting two seats away from her at the dining room table. She stood in front of him with her back to Feo. And with her eyes fixed on Raynail's pupils, she spoke to Feo.

"Yes, Feo, I killed before. I killed a lot of people. People who didn't deserve to live. People who thought they could hurt me and get away with it. I was a cold-ass bitch at one time. My heart was made of stone and if a nigga, his mama, or his kids tried to fuck over me, I was gunning down everybody.

"My uncle raped me while my aunt watched. My cousin stole from me, and blamed it on one of his homies. I ran to my mother and father for help, but they told me that I was lying. They're *the ones who sent me to live with my aunt and uncle so, yes, I blamed them for all the shit I was going through." Candy walked into the living room and stood between Raynail's and Feo's gazes. "My moms sent me to a psychiatrist because my aunt had managed to convince her that I was crazy. I was only sixteen: too young to have sex, but not too young to get raped. Then, to top it off, the bitch-ass psychiatrist didn't believe me when I told her what I was going through at my aunt and uncle's house."*

Raynail looked at Candy and lowered his head. When he met Candy, it took a long time for her to completely open up to him. After getting hurt by her family and the person she dated before him, it took her a long time to believe that anyone would ever truly love her. Each time Raynail tried to show her some type of affection, she would pull away. "Candy, don't . . ." Raynail got up and walked toward his queen with open arms.

"Get back!" Candy snapped. "You opened up my old wounds, might as well let 'em finish bleeding . . . right?" Candy turned and looked at Feo with a cold stare. "I killed them all, including the psychiatrist. I killed my family first. It was Christmas Eve and everybody was at my aunt's house, opening up gifts and singing

Christmas carols. They were all in the living room singing s-i-l-e-n-t night, h-o-l-y night." Wearing a crazed look on her face, Candy sang the song. "A holy night, that hours later turned into a deadly night. While everybody was in the living room, I was in the laundry room, putting together the perfect murder." She turned to Raynail. "Raynail, come have a seat next to Feo; this is the good part. You overheard me talking in my sleep, well, let me give you the full details of how I did it."

Raynail was afraid to move. At that moment, he feared Candy more than he did God.

Raynail walked around Candy to the couch and sat next to Feo.

"Did the both of you know that you could burn an entire house down using kitty litter?" Candy giggled at the thought.

Neither one of them responded.

"Well, you can. My aunt had a cat . . . I hated that cat, and when the cat died in the fire, I was all smiles. I took the kitty litter and poured it out under the pipe in back of the dryer in the laundry room. It took me a long time to unscrew the hose to the gas pipe in back of the dryer, but I did it! I did it!" Candy grew excited all of a sudden.

"*The chemical in the kitty litter was the key to it all. I didn't even need fire. The litter is made with a chemical called sodium bentonite. Once gas tops off that shit . . . boom! Everything goes up in smoke.*" She laughed hysterically.

"*The gas filled the air like evil spirits! I ran out of the back door, smiling as I thought about the gas flowing into the kitchen, where the burners were being used to keep the house warm. The cat litter alone would'a caused the house to explode, but the fire on the stove was a bonus.*"

"*Yo, Candy, how did you find out about the cat litter shit?*" Feo asked.

Raynail punched Feo in the arm. He wanted to change the subject. He never meant to hurt Candy by bringing up something that she obviously never wanted to talk about.

"Forensic Files! *I watched* Forensic Files *a lot as a kid. As a matter of fact, that's all I watched. Oh, and* The First 48. *Both of 'em had to do wit' somebody dying. My life wasn't happy, so why would I watch happy shit?*"

"*So, how did you kill yo' psychiatrist?*" Feo was really into Candy's story.

"*Oh, she was easy. You know how white people leave their windows and doors unlocked, thinking that they live in some upper-class, 'nonviolent neighborhood.' Well I showed their ass that death lingers everywhere. Not just in my neighborhood, but in theirs too. I crept up to the back of her house, and searched the walls of the house for the power box. Once I found it, I shut off all the lights in the house. I knew that once the lights went out, she would come outside to check the box. The bitch did, too. She walked right into my trap. As soon as she walked out the back door and cut the corner at the side of the house, I pulled out my switch blade and cut her across her neck.*

"You should have seen it. Blood gushing from her neck like a water sprinkler feeding the grass. She tried to grab her neck to stop the blood, but once your jugular vein is cut, it's just a matter of time before you bleed to death.

"I was never caught, never. Not for my family's murder, or that not-knowing-what-the-fuck-she-talking-'bout psychiatrist's murder. As you can see, Feo, I'm not afraid to kill."

Candy looked at Raynail, who, by then, had his head down, and in a whispered tone asked him, "So, who do you want me to kill first?"

Candy was so into her thoughts that she didn't notice Raynail waving his hands in front of her. "Yo, Candy, what's up wit' you?" The sound of Raynail's voice snapped Candy out of her thoughts.

"Yeah, well," he said, grabbing his dick, "we gonna cut this visit short 'cause a nigga gotta take a piss." He stood up, took Candy by an arm, and pulled her up with him. "Give me a hug, girl."

Candy wrapped her arms around Raynail's neck and pressed her body firmly against his. "I got a big job worth millions." She pulled away from him and smiled.

"There you go." Raynail laughed. "I hope you got a good team going wit' you."

"You know I do." Candy noticed Raynail leaning from one foot to the next. "Go use the bathroom," she told him. "I'll be back to see you soon."

"A'ight!" Raynail headed to the door that led back to his cell. He stopped in front of the door, turned around, and looked back at Candy. "Yo, Candy!" he yelled out to her. Candy spun around to face her husband. "Be safe," he told her.

Candy gave Raynail a thumbs up, and walked out of the door.

Chapter 2

An armored truck carrying millions of dollars in cocaine traveled down the I-5 freeway, heading to the desert. It was cocaine that had accumulated in the Beverly Hills Police Department's evidence room over the years.

Once a year, drugs from various police agencies were taken to the desert and burned. It was a practice that required heavy security because of the danger involved in transporting the drugs.

When Candy found out about the tight security, she contacted an artillery dealer from Switzerland, and ordered dozens of cases of bulletproof vest–piercing bullets, along with vests that even those bullets couldn't pierce. For the job, she rounded up the majority of the guys from 190 East Coast Crips, along with some of their homies from 30s. Their street knowledge would play an important role in the heist. Many of them had served time in prison for robbing banks, with most of the robberies involving explosives. Vaults were blown right out of the wall, with the money suffering little or no damage.

Candy found out about the time, date, and location of the drop through a gangsta-cop with the Beverly Hills Police Department.

A gangsta-cop was a crooked cop who stole both money and drugs from the evidence room of a police department. It normally involved several officers working the gang unit. The officers would plant "dirty guns" and drugs on drug dealers during police raids, leaving just enough to ensure long prison sentences. One of Candy's friends from her old neighborhood was a gangsta-cop, giving her the full heads-up on anything that involved a come up.

Ten Suburbans, each carrying eight Beverly Hills SWAT Team members, completely surrounded the armored truck as it traveled down the I-5 freeway at two o'clock in the morning. All freeway transitions that led to the valley had been shut down. Motorists were forced off the freeway by the California Highway Patrol and left to find alternate routes to their destinations.

Dressed in black combat gear that was equipped with hunting knives, gun holsters, a single pair of night-vision goggles, and a belt designed to hold hundreds of rounds of ammunition, Candy and her entourage waited in the desert in their Hummers for the armored truck to arrive.

Thirty Hummer H3s were parked shoulder to shoulder. The line of Hummers would serve as a shield to hide behind during the heist. Other than their trucks, there was nothing in the desert to protect them from flying bullets.

Candy looked at her watch. It was almost four o'clock in the morning. She estimated that the armored truck would be arriving soon. "Every-body ready?" she asked into the two-way radio.

"Copy!" rang out through the radio from all of her men.

"Remember what I told y'all," Candy said. "When the truck gets here, it's gonna park to the southeast of us. There should be a compass on the dashboard in front of the passenger seat; use it. If by chance we have to split up into different directions, the compass will lead you back to the freeway. Now, we tryin'a do this before they start unloading the coke. Why? Because we taking the whole truck. It's just easier to do it that way. We can split the shit when we get back to the ware-house in LA. I'm sure y'all already know that the SWAT Team ain't no joke. You know what, I ain't even gotta tell y'all about 'em 'cause many of y'all done had run-ins with 'em."

"Right . . . right," someone said through the radio. Candy looked over at Murphy, who was sitting in the passenger's seat. "Truth and Real gonna roll back wit' me in the armored truck," she told him. "You gonna be in the Hummer by yo'self."

"Candy, are you crazy?" Murphy asked her. "I ain't lettin' you roll like that. It's too dangerous, and Raynail would kill me if something happened to you. Naw, me and Real can roll the truck and you and Truth roll the H3."

"Ol' boy is right," someone chimed in through the radio. "I ain't tryin'a have Raynail on my ass!"

Candy looked down at the radio. Her fingers held down the talk button, allowing everyone in the H3s to hear their conversation.

"Murphy, trust me on this one," Candy said.

Murphy shook his head. "If something goes foul, Raynail . . . Nope! I don't even want to think about what Raynail would do to me."

"Ain't nothing gonna happen!" Candy tried to assure him.

"No, Candy!" Murphy said, standing his ground. "Too risky. It's bad enough you out here. We in the middle of the desert surrounded by nothing but hills and shit. If one of us gets popped, by the time the medic gets here, the dark angels be done dragged our souls to hell."

Truth and Real shifted in their seats at the thought of getting killed. They were well aware of the consequences that accompanied drug and blood money, but had never felt so close to death as they did at that moment. Hiding in the cut, selling coke was one thing, and robbing the law was another.

Their hearts pumped fear, but they would never admit it to Candy.

"Can't let that happen," Murphy said. "I'm rolling the truck!"

"Okay, you're right." Candy pressed the talk button on the radio. "You're all right. Me and Truth gonna roll the H3 back, and Murphy and Real gonna roll the armored truck."

High-beam headlights traveling from the southeast of them caught everybody's attention.

Candy put the radio to her lips. "All right, fellas, they're here," she whispered. Candy was a little nervous. "Put y'all night goggles on," she instructed.

Candy and her men slid their night goggles from their heads onto their eyes and watched as the SWAT Team prepared to unload the truck.

Ten Suburbans formed a wide circle around the armored truck. A wide space was left between two of the Suburbans for the armored truck to pass out of once the cocaine was unloaded. One by one the SWAT Team jumped out of the Suburbans, with each man holding an assault rifle.

Candy watched from the cut, timing their every move. She looked up from her 9 mm submachine gun long enough to tell Real, Murphy, and Truth to, "Roll down y'all windows and get out."

Going through several machine guns that she kept in a gun cache in the basement of her house, Candy had searched for a gun that the armor-piercing bullets would fit. In two hours, she had gone through over fifty guns before reaching the M11, with the bullets fitting perfectly. In order to have enough guns to accommodate all of her men, she ordered more guns from the makers themselves. She had made arrangements for the guns to be sent by boat to the Port of Long Beach, where she and several of her men were patiently waiting for their arrival.

"Keep y'all doors open as shields, and don't nobody start shooting until I say so," Candy said into the radio. One by one the doors to the Hummers swung open with each man standing with his M11 pointed out of the windows and aimed at the SWAT Team.

The SWAT Team stood with their rifles raised as they scanned the desert. Believing that there was nothing out there, they let their guns hang loose at their sides. They then walked around to the back of the armored truck.

"Now," Candy whispered into the radio. Candy and the Crips let loose on the SWAT Team. Like a blind man forced to find his way around his home without a guide stick, unable to see what lay ahead of them the SWAT Team dropped to their knees and returned fire.

"Get on the radios and call for a chopper!" one of the men from SWAT yelled as he ran for cover behind one of the Suburbans. "Why the hell don't we have night goggles?" he screamed.

Candy spotted a man reaching for the radio on his waist. "No, you don't!" She laughed. Candy raised the M11, and let her finger sleep on the trigger. With his intestines spilling from his stomach, the man flew back on top of a pile of bodies that Candy and her men had already served their death certificates to.

"If you see lips on a radio, blast the head off!" Candy yelled into the radio. She ran from behind the H3 door and dropped to her knees. "Quick! Everybody drop to yo' stomach and start crawling toward them! Do not let up on the trigger. Think about all the times you been knocked by a pig, and kill they ass!"

Like soldiers under attack, the Crips dropped to the ground, with the butt of their M11s resting on their shoulders. They crawled in different directions and surrounded their enemies.

Round after round of the armor-piercing bullets pierced the SWAT's bulletproof vests. Their efforts to return fire were useless, being that they couldn't see who they were shooting at. None of the Crips were hit, leaving the SWAT Team members who had not yet felt their wrath prey to hundreds of rounds of ammo.

The SWAT Team fell to the ground and drowned in their own blood. As the bullets danced above their heads, they looked from left to right, shooting at the unknown. The shooting lasted for less than ten minutes, with every member of the SWAT Team laid out on the ground either dead, or near death.

"Hold your fire!" Candy yelled.

The Crips continued to shoot, even though no one from the SWAT Team was standing.

"I said, hold yo' fire!" Candy repeated. "Y'all gonna mess around and kill one of y'all own men."

All gunfire ceased. The Crips rose from their positions and dusted themselves off.

"Did anybody get hit?" Candy asked.

Each man looked himself over. "We all good," Murphy said.

"Okay." Candy pushed the night goggles from her eyes up onto her head. "Let's head over there and see if there's anybody alive," she said, wiping sweat from her forehead onto her pants. Candy followed her men to the mass grave with the headstone that read SWAT.

It was a bloody scene. The bodies were piled on top of each other like a stack of red checkers. The man who was going for his radio when Candy shot him, his right hand was over his heart. *What you reaching for your heart for?* Candy laughed in her thoughts. *You should have reached for yo' stomach.* Another man's head was partially blown off with his brains scattered all over the chest of the man beneath him. Some of them lost limbs instead of their lives. The worst case was a man lying on his stomach and positioned as if he was running before being killed. His head was blown completely off and lying next to the tires of the armored truck, which was not too far from his body. Many of the men were still moving around on the ground trying to reach for their radios.

"Truth, Real." Candy turned her attention to Truth and Real, who were standing to the right of her, pointing to different body parts on the ground. "Truth, Real, finish off—"

The sound of gunfire interrupted Candy's orders. Shots rang out behind her, hitting the men who were still alive. Murphy walked out from between Candy and Truth and continued to fire on the men even after they were no longer moving.

"Murphy, Murphy," Candy screamed over the gunfire. "They're dead. You're wasting my damn ammo."

"Oh! My bad." Murphy laughed.

"Damn!" Candy sighed. Her eyes moved from Truth to Murphy and from Murphy to Real. "Truth, you rollin' wit' me in the truck," she said, heading for the armored truck. Candy looked at her men in pure satisfaction. "Y'all head back to the Hummers and roll out," she told them.

"But, Candy, we already discussed you driving the drugs back," Murphy told her. "And we decided that it wasn't gonna happen."

"They all dead," Candy replied. "We good."

"It's all good, Murphy," one of the Crips said in agreement with Candy. "But, yo, let's check out the stash before we roll out."

"No!" Candy growled. "We gotta get outta here. The sun will be out soon. We can't risk getting caught on the way back."

"True that," Murphy interjected.

"All right, it's a go." Candy continued to the armored truck, when she noticed that Truth was not with her. She turned and looked behind her. "Truth, come on," she spat.

Candy and Truth walked over to the armored truck and climbed in. "They didn't even have time to take the keys out of the ignition." Candy laughed. She started the truck and looked over the dashboard at the dead bodies that blocked her path. "How am I supposed to get around this?" Candy wondered out loud.

"Why don't you just roll over'em?" Truth suggested.

Candy looked at him like he was crazy. "Hell naw! I'm a killer, don't get me wrong, but I ain't down wit' hearing a nigga's bones poppin'." Candy got on the two-way. "Murphy, I need some of y'all to move these bodies from in front of the truck."

Candy and Truth listened to static. And by the time the static had cleared, they only caught the tail end of his message: "Over the bitches!"

Truth recognized the voice as Murphy's voice. "Murph said, 'Run over the bitches.'" He laughed. "Same thing I told you."

Truth sat back against the seat and folded his arms. From a distance, he and Candy could see the Hummers' headlights come on. They watched the Hummers head out of the desert, shoulder to shoulder. They merged into one straight line and headed to the I-5 freeway.

"So, what you gonna do, Candy?" Truth asked. "The sun gonna be coming up soon. We don't wanna be spotted by no cops on the way back," he jokingly mocked her.

Candy looked over at Truth with a smirk on her face. "Funny, real funny." She looked at the bodies. And seeing that she had no choice but to flatten the bones, she held the wheel straight, closed her eyes, and floored the gas.

The truck shook violently. The sound of the bones breaking caused Candy to flinch. "Damn!" she said, shaking her head. "I should have let Murphy drive this bitch."

Candy's foot rested on the gas until she caught up with the last Hummer to exit the desert.

The traffic on the freeway was light, allowing them to get back to LA in less than an hour. When they got to the warehouse, Murphy and Real got out of the H3, unlocked the doors to the warehouse, and pushed them open for Candy to pull the armored truck inside.

Candy and Truth climbed out of the armored truck. They walked to the open doors and looked through the windshield of the lead H3. "Come on." Candy motioned for the men to pull into the warehouse. "Hurry up!" she yelled.

One by one the H3s entered the warehouse. Seeing that the last truck outside was the truck that Murphy had been driving, Truth took Murphy's spot at the door, and held it open for Murphy to pull the H3 into the warehouse.

"Two of y'all open the back doors of the truck," Candy said and walked around to the back of the truck with all of the men in tow.

Candy slipped into the lock the one and only key that was on the key ring she had found, and went to turn it, when she found that it wasn't the right key. "Fuck!" Candy was pissed at herself for not having the right keys. *I prepared for everything but this.*

Candy looked the armored truck over. There were only four doors to the truck: the passenger and driver doors and the double back doors. A black wall separated the front of the truck from the back of the truck.

Candy placed her hands on her hips, and looked around the warehouse. "I'm gonna have to call my connect wit' the Beverly Hills PD." She puffed.

"Naw, I got this, Candy." Murphy climbed into the armored truck and took out his M11. He walked to the back of the armored truck, leaving a great distance between him and the truck. With a large grin on his face, he pressed down on the trigger, and replaced the lock with a hole the size of a ripe apple. The doors flew open, exposing dozens of pounds of cocaine stacked neatly on top of a wooden crate.

"Oooooowwweeee," Murphy yelled. "Look at what we got here."

Candy and her men stood in amazement. They had never seen so much cocaine at one time, and couldn't wait to get their hands on it.

It took nearly three hours for Candy to split the cocaine evenly among her and her men. And once everybody had their cut, they all managed to walk away with over $3 million in cocaine apiece.

"Nice workin' wit' you, Candy," one of the Crips said once he was done loading his share of the coke into the H3 he had been driving. "We droppin' the H3s off at the lot?"

"Yes," Candy replied. "Once y'all unload, wipe 'em down and return 'em. Y'all remember where the lot is?" Candy didn't wait for them to answer. "It's on National and Beverly Boulevard in Beverly Hills."

"We out," the same Crip said.

Candy turned to her most loyal workers. "Truth, Real, y'all done working wit' me?" she asked them.

"Hell naw, what we do ain't just about the money." Real answered for both of them. "You put us on when we ain't had shit! We ain't pullin' out the game until you do."

"And maybe not even then." Truth laughed.

"This was one of the biggest accomplishments ever!" Candy grinned. Her grin loosened into a serious face almost instantly. "But I got something major I need y'all to help me wit'." Candy was referring to the bodies that would lie at her feet once she ripped the souls from those responsible for her husband's demise.

Chapter 3

Candy was lying in bed when she heard loud laughter coming from outside of her bedroom window. She slid out of bed and picked her robe up from the foot of the bed. Slipping into the robe, she walked over to the window. With one hand holding her robe closed she pulled back the curtain and looked out of the window.

The laughs were coming from Feo and his boys. Feo and one of his boys were sitting on the hood of Feo's Impala smoking a blunt, while three of his other boys were engrossed in a conversation.

Since Candy lived in a two-story house and her bedroom was upstairs, Feo and his friends did not see her watching them. *Damn I wish it was dark. I'd kill all five of 'em and just get the shit over wit'.* Dismissing Feo, for the time being, she walked into her bedroom bathroom and looked at her reflection in the mirror. Dried sleep held the corners of her right eye together.

Her lips were chapped, and her hair was as all over her head.

Candy wiped sleep from her eyes on her way out of the bathroom. She could hear gentle taps against her bedroom door, followed by light laughter from her son.

"RayRay, you got your bags packed?" Candy called out to her son.

Candy watched the doorknob turn, with her son running into her room, wearing his Sesame Street pajamas, and one white sock. Tucked beneath his left arm was a Kermit the Frog stuffed animal that his father had given him for his fifth birthday, right before he went to jail.

"Huh, Mama?" RayRay said.

"Did you put your clothes in your bag?" Candy brushed past him and searched the top of her dresser for something to hold her hair back out of her face. She took a black ponytail holder off the dresser and walked into the bathroom, with her son on her heels.

"I can't pack my own bag," RayRay said as he reached for the lid to the toilet. "I'm only five." The lid met the cushioned toilet seat with a thump. RayRay sat on top of the lid and looked up at his mother.

Candy knelt before her son. "I know how old you are." She tickled him on his stomach and under his arms.

"Awwwww, Mommy! I gotta pee! I gotta pee!" RayRay laughed.

"I put your clothes on your bed last night. All you had to do was put 'em in your bag."

"But, Mama, I don't wanna leave you. I wanna stay." RayRay leaned forward and wrapped his arms around his mother's neck. "I don't like going to Grandma's house. She make me eat vegetables."

Candy laughed. "Okay, I'll tell Grandma no more vegetables for my little man."

RayRay's frown turned into a big smile. He hopped off the toilet, watched his mother as she stood in the mirror brushing her hair, and said, "I'm gonna put my Power Ranger pajamas in the bag too. Pow! Pow! Pow!" RayRay punched Kermit the Frog in the face while imitating the Power Rangers.

"Put those clothes on your bed in the bag too." Candy watched her son beat his stuffed animal to a pulp. Shaking her head, she said, "Put your other sock on. Grandma should be here soon."

Candy walked out of the bathroom and stood in front of the dresser. She glanced around the room in thought. She realized that she had not seen her pink Adidas sweat suit since the last time she wore it.

Candy searched through the dresser drawers for the Adidas suit. She moved to the walk-in closet and stood in front of her side of the closet. She first scanned the clothes for the sweat suit. She then slid the clothes on the hangers from left to right. *Where did I put that sweat suit?* she wondered.

On a whim, Candy searched through her husband's clothes. She dropped her shoulders when she spotted her sweat suit hanging between his favorite midnight-blue two-piece Bottega Veneta suit, and his two-piece Jay Kos suit.

Candy stuck her right hand into the wrist of the Bottega Veneta blazer. She missed her husband, and was eager to put in the work that would get him out of jail.

"The best false witness is a dead false witness," she whispered to herself with Feo and his boys in mind. The doorbell rang, snapping Candy out of her thoughts. Candy hurried out of her robe. She snatched the Adidas sweat suit off the hanger and slipped into it. She then walked into the closet and dragged her feet into her pink and white Adidas tennis shoes. She walked on the backs of the tennis shoes as she made her way out of her bedroom and down the spiral staircase to the front door.

RayRay ran down the stairs and pulled on the back of his mother's sweats. "Mommy, it's Grandma at the door," he said in excitement. "Can I open it?"

Candy spun around and bent forward into her son's face. "What I tell you about asking me that? Don't ever answer the door, or anybody else's door for that matter. Do you understand me?" Candy straightened her back and turned to the door. She looked through the peephole. She smiled at her mother-in-law smiling from ear to ear.

"Where my grandbaby at?" Raynail's mother asked through the door.

Like any child, RayRay had forgotten all about his mother's scorn. He jumped up and down at the sound of his grandmother's voice. He fanned himself with his hands, and continued to beat the floor with his feet, as he anxiously waited for his mother to open the door.

"Back up so I can open the door," Candy said with anger in her words.

RayRay lowered his head and walked away from the door with his lips poked out. Candy unlocked a row of five locks. She removed the chain and opened the door. RayRay ran past his mother and wrapped his arms around his grandmother's legs.

"Hello, Carolyn, how are you?" Her mother-in-law smiled. With RayRay clinging to her legs, she struggled to walk over to her daughter-in-law to give her a hug.

Laughing, Candy rolled her eyes at her son, and shook her head. She met her mother-in-law midway, and gave her a warm hug.

"I noticed the FOR SALE sign in the front yard. Did you plan on telling me you were moving?"

"Yeah, I just hadn't gotten around to it," Candy said, closing the door. "I think it's best that I move before Raynail gets out. As you know, the guys who set him up live in this neighborhood." *But they won't be living for long.* "I'm looking for a fresh start when Raynail gets out."

"Good idea." Her mother-in-law looked down at RayRay and laughed. He had wrapped his legs around her ankles, and was sitting on her joined feet.

Candy looked down at him and playfully grabbed his arm. "All of a sudden you happy to see Grandma, huh?" She laughed, smacking her lips. "What was all that stuff you was crying about a few minutes ago?" Candy met her mother-in-law's smile. "He said he didn't wanna go to your house because you make him eat vegetables."

RayRay's grandmother pried his arms from around her legs. She picked him up into her arms and walked over to the couch. She then sat down on the couch and cradled him on her lap.

"Your clothes packed?" RayRay's grandmother asked him.

RayRay pointed to a Spider-Man backpack that was lying at the foot of the staircase.

His grandmother slid him off her lap onto the couch and walked over to the backpack. She picked up the backpack and started over to the couch, when a pair of shorts, a shirt, and two rolled-up pairs of socks dropped out of the open backpack.

A loud scream of laughter erupted from Candy's soul. She was bent forward, and laughing so hard that one would have sworn she was being tickled. Her mother-in-law looked at her out of the corner of her eyes, while her son joined in on the laughter. But just as quick as her laughs had cut through the air, so did her tears.

Candy's eyes were as shiny as glass when she looked up from her laughs into her mother-in-law's eyes. Tears rolled from her eyes, down the sides of her nose. Her tears were just as uncontrollable as her laughs.

RayRay and his grandmother reminded Candy so much of Raynail. Not only was RayRay named

after him, but he looked just like him. RayRay
was dark with full lips. His eyebrows connected
just like his father's. Raynail hated that his
eyebrows connected, and would tag along with
Candy to the nail shop to get the connecting hair
waxed.

Candy cried for her husband's life. He was
facing the death penalty for crimes that he didn't
commit.

Candy could tolerate anything but betrayal.
She believed betrayal warranted death, while
thievery received mutilation. Forgiveness was
not in her vocabulary, especially if the guilty
deprived her son of his parents. It took years
for Candy to learn how to love, and she was not
about to let the system rob her husband of his
soul.

Her mother-in-law picked up the clothes from
the floor and shoved them inside of the backpack.
She walked over to Candy, who was now sitting
on the couch next to her son, and gave her a hug.

"I'll tell you what, Carolyn. I'm gonna take my
grandbaby off your hands for a while. Just until
all this stuff with my son blows over."

"But RayRay not gonna want to be away from
me that long. They already took his daddy."
Candy wept.

"But my son is coming home. He ain't killed
nobody."

Candy stared at her son. *It's gonna be okay; it's only for a little while,* she convinced herself. Raynail's fate was in her hands. She would have to become the old Candy, and she did not want to take it out on her son.

Candy and Raynail had written their own wedding vows. Her vow to be a "ride or die bitch for life" was now being tested.

Candy wiped tears from her eyes and switched into bitch mode. "Do unto others as you would have done to you," was the belief that she had always stood by and taken very seriously, even before killing her family.

Candy jumped up from the couch, scaring her son and his grandmother. "Okay, I think you should keep him for a while. Can you keep him until I call you to bring him home?" Before her mother-in-law could answer her request, Candy ran back up the stairs to her son's bedroom. She stumbled down the stairs, carrying a handful of his clothes and dragging a suitcase behind her. She dumped the clothes on the couch and ran back upstairs for more clothes.

"Hold on, Carolyn, don't get no more clothes." Her mother-in-law walked into the kitchen to the sink. She opened the cabinet door beneath the sink and pulled out a trash bag. "He got clothes at my house."

Out of breath, Candy walked down the stairs, carrying her husband's gym bag filled with her son's clothes. She dropped the gym bag on the floor. "Okay, that's all," she said as she struggled to catch her breath.

Her mother-in-law looked down at the bag and then at Candy. "You look like you sending him to live with me forever." She laughed.

"No, it's not that. I just wanna make sure he has everything he needs." She opened a closet door next to the front door, and pulled her son's North Face Denali jacket from a hanger. "Come here, RayRay, and put this on."

RayRay jumped off the couch and ran to his mother. He took the jacket from her hands and put it on.

"Go to your room and get your shoes," his grandmother told him.

RayRay ran upstairs to his room and came down carrying a pair of Nike tennis shoes.

Candy helped her mother-in-law carry the bags to her car. They loaded the bags into the trunk of the car. And as her mother-in-law walked around to the driver's door, Candy opened the back passenger door and strapped her son down in his car seat. She kissed his forehead.

"You be good, you hear me?" Candy told her son. "If Grandma calls me about anything you've done, Mama is going to spank you, okay?"

RayRay nodded.

Candy closed the door and walked around the car to the driver's door. She motioned, by pointing downward, for her mother-in-law to roll down the window.

Her mother-in-law started the car and rolled down the window. "Do something constructive to get your mind off of things," she said, reading the sorrow in Candy's eyes.

"I will, thank you." Candy leaned into the window and kissed her cheek. "I'll call you from day to day to let you know how I'm holding up." She walked around the car and onto the sidewalk. She crossed her arms and watched her mother-in-law pull off.

Candy noticed RayRay pushing himself up in his seat, waving at her. She smiled and waved back. But, after seeing Feo and his friends standing next to his Impala waving at her son and laughing, her smile was quickly replaced with the look that she gave her psychiatrist eight years earlier before she killed her.

Candy and Feo locked eyes. She showed Feo her pearly white teeth, through a fake smile. She then turned and walked up the walkway to the three steps leading to her front door. She opened the door and stood watching Feo and his friends pass a blunt. *Them bitches are dead.* She walked into the house and slammed the door behind her.

Chapter 4

Candy sat in her car in front of her new Rock-
ingham estate, going over the list of names that
Raynail had given her. Selling her old house
for less than it was worth, just to get out of the
neighborhood, she bought a house in Beverly
Hills, high in the mountains away from the city.

After asking around on the streets, Candy was
able to get the addresses of all five guys on the
list. She already knew where Feo stayed and
decided to save the best for last. Her first victim
lived in Wilmington off of PCH and Imperial,
which was an hour drive from her estate. With
Raynail's court date drawing near, Candy didn't
have a lot of time to case each house like she
normally would.

To make each death go as smoothly as possible, she figured the best time to go after them
without getting caught would be at night. Once
the sun set she would start her deadly reign.

Since it was only four in the afternoon, she decided to pay her runners a visit. Pulling off, she headed to one of her blocks.

Candy drove down Eighth Avenue in her 2012 Jaguar XK in search of Truth and Real. As she cruised down the street, she noticed that everybody who was outside either walked off their porches, or stood on the curb watching her. The limousine tint did nothing to elude the onlookers. Everyone recognized the XK as belonging to Candy.

Candy was disgusted by the site of the neighborhood. "I pay these bums to keep this shit clean and this is how they do me? Giving them my money in vain? This shit is more fucked up than it was before I put them on my payroll!"

The neighborhood was run-down, with graffiti decorating the walls and the ground. Couches and old chairs sat at the curb with children running around them playing tag. A group of girls stood in the middle of the street playing Double Dutch and, noticing Candy's car, stopped jumping and moved to the side of the street to let her through. Two dudes dressed in all red from head to toe sat on the porch of an apartment building, drinking something from a brown paper bag and passing a blunt.

Candy set her eyes on the roofs of the tallest buildings that lined both sides of the street. She smiled at the blue rags that hung from the right corner of each roof. The blue rags let the gang-stas in the neighborhood know that they were under twenty-four-hour surveillance by Candy's soldiers, and that only Candy and Raynail's drugs were welcomed on the street.

The soldiers had been personally trained by one of Raynail's homies, who worked for Westwood Police Department's SWAT Team. The soldiers were trained to shoot to kill without leaving a mess.

Dressed in camouflage and equipped with binoculars and assault rifles, the soldiers were posted on the roofs of nearly every building in the neighborhoods that Candy and Raynail had on lockdown.

Candy pulled up to a curb and called the soldier who was working the roof of the building that she was parked in front of.

The solider picked up on the first ring. "What's good, Candy?"

"You seen Truth and Real?" she asked him.

"Yeah, they inside the store on the corner," the solider replied. "They just walked in."

Candy drove to the corner and parked in front of the store. "So, how you holdin'?" Candy asked the soldier.

"Lovely," he replied through a smile. "But . . . um, when you turned on to the street back there, them two guys at that apartment building in back of you dressed in all red? They was straight scoping you out."

Candy pulled down her sun visor. She looked in the mirror at the two guys her runner was referring to. "Tell one of yo' partners to cover you. I want you to slip down there and listen to what they saying."

"I'm on it." The solider crawled away from the edge of the building on his stomach and motioned for the solider sitting behind him to take his spot. He slipped down a hole in the roof, which led into the attic of one of the empty apartment units. Too tall for the attic, he was forced to bend forward to keep from walking into loose boards above his head. He continued to the attic's opening and pushed a flat, rectangular piece of wood to the side. He then jumped down into what appeared to be a child's bedroom closet, and walked out of the closet and into the bedroom.

Broken toys lay scattered around the floor. A small pink shirt with mildew spots on the front of it hung on the doorknob of the closet. A pair of red and white kid's tennis shoes lay on the floor next to a broken Mickey Mouse watch, and the room reeked of urine.

The soldier covered his nose with his right sleeve and walked out of the bedroom and out of the apartment into the hallway.

The hallway was just as bad as the unit. The stench from a combination of urine and beer toyed with his sinuses. He tiptoed to a flight of stairs. He looked down the stairs at two bums who were camped out in front of the door that led outside.

The soldier crept down the stairs. He glanced down at the sleeping beauties. He then stood off to the right side of the door in front of a broken window and called Candy.

Expecting his call, Candy answered on the first ring. "What's up?"

"I'ma put my cell on speaker so you can hear what they saying," the soldier whispered.

"Muting my phone," Candy replied. Candy pushed mute. She put the phone to her ear when she noticed Truth and Real walking out of the store, engaged in conversation.

Candy blew her horn to get Truth's and Real's attention. She watched them look around before noticing her car. Truth and Real walked to Candy's car. Truth opened the back passenger door and climbed inside. Real walked around the front of the car to the back driver's side door. He opened the door and got in.

Truth leaned forward and slipped the top half of his body between the space that separated the driver's and passenger's seats. "Yo, Can—"

"Hold up, Truth." Candy held up a finger and silenced him, after hearing Raynail's name mentioned by one of the guys she and her soldier were eavesdropping on.

"Ol' boy facing the death penalty," she overheard one of the guys say. "Since he got knocked, his bitch been running things around here."

"I'm already knowing," said the other guy, who had a Spanish accent. "So killing the bitch and takin' her shit is gonna be easy."

Candy laughed at the guy's ignorance. "These muthafuckas don't know who they fuckin' wit'. Gotta be some some new cats, 'cause the old heads know what's up." She turned to Real and Truth and said, "Listen to these soon-to-be-dead niggas talk." She pushed speaker so that the runners could hear what the guys were saying.

"I wonder how much she holdin'. I say we follow her ass and take the shit right now," one of them suggested.

Candy pushed mute again. "Yo, Real, they wanna know what I'm holding." She laughed. "Let's see, I got a TEC-9 on my waist, a .22 in the glove compartment *and* one strapped to my ankle. Oh, and a Glock in the trunk."

"I don't think he talkin' 'bout no guns," Truth said, laughing.

"Wait, listen." Real held up a hand after hearing one of the guys mention something about hurting Candy.

"We gonna follow her out the neighborhood and force her to take us to the paper." There was a slight pause. The sound of guns being cocked echoed through the phone.

These niggas got me fucked up, Candy thought, ending the call. She reached over and pulled down the glove compartment door. She removed the .22 and passed it to Truth. "Real, let down yo' seat and crawl back there in the trunk and get that Glock."

Real moved next to Truth, and let down the back of the seat. He slipped into the trunk and pulled up a board that was covered by black carpet. He stuck his hand into the compartment, moved jumper cables and a jack to the side, and pulled out the Glock.

Real handed the Glock to Truth and slid out of the trunk. He then put the seat back up and took the Glock from Truth.

Candy took her TEC-9 from her waist and checked the magazine to make sure that it was loaded. "Call up y'all relief and tell 'em I said to get down here and fill in."

Both runners pulled out their cells and called their reliefs. They relayed Candy's message and placed their cells back on their hips.

"They on they way, right?" Candy closed her jacket and zipped it up.

"Yeah," both runners said in unison.

"Y'all 'bout to earn more stripes." Candy laughed.

Candy looked over her left shoulder. Seeing that there was no traffic traveling east or west, she pulled away from the curb and busted a clean U-turn.

"We're headed to PCH and Wilmington." Candy passed by the apartment building where the guys were seated on the porch. As soon as they spotted her car, they jumped into a Toyota Land Cruiser and followed her.

With one person scheduled to die after sunset, Candy decided to add two more bodies to the plot. It was obvious that the guys following her didn't know as much about her as they thought they did. But before the night was over, they would have figured it out.

The plan was to lead them to the house of the first victim on Raynail's list, and kill three birds with one stone. For most, the murders would appear to be difficult to pull off, but Candy wasn't among the most. She was one of the very few ride or die females who wasn't afraid to hold court in the streets, while getting the paper at the same time. And if a nigga didn't know it, he'd better ask somebody who did.

"Let me run some shit down to y'all before we do this." Candy looked in all of her mirrors at the guys who were following her. "These dudes 'bout to die, but here's the twist to the shit. The house we going to, it's a rat up in there and I got some poison for his ass."

Truth and Real looked at each other. "But how the three of us gonna pull that shit off?" Real asked. "You got two dudes in back of us and we 'bout to creep up on another one?"

Candy looked into the mirror on her sun visor at Real and smiled. "Such little faith," she said, shaking her head. "Just follow my lead."

Truth hunched his left shoulder. He turned in his seat and glanced back at the guys who were following them.

"This street don't look like it would have a stash house," the driver of the truck said, following closely behind Candy. He surveyed the middle-class neighborhood. "How many niggas you know got a stash house on the same street as a neighborhood watch?"

The houses sat far back away from the curb. And in each window was a sticker with a burglar sitting behind bars and the words NEIGHBORHOOD

WATCH written across the bottom of the picture. Rosebushes decorated the yards. The grass and bushes were neatly manicured. Each house was painted a soft pastel color, giving it a unique appearance.

"Well, maybe she going home," the passenger suggested. "Then again, she could be going to her other dude's house. That's how these bitches are these days. They wait 'til they dude get knocked, then run out on his ass."

"Look." The driver pointed to Candy's car. "She parked in front of that brown house over there."

Candy parked in front of a brown house and looked at the paper that Raynail had given her. She then looked at a separate piece of paper that she had gotten from somebody on the street, with the same guy's name and address on it.

Seeing that she was at the right house, Candy folded both papers, raised the armrest, and dropped them inside. She lowered the armrest, and turned to Truth and Real.

"Okay, this is the plan. We gonna go up to the house, acting like we know dude inside. When I knock on the door, as soon as he opens it, I'ma have my gun pointed straight at his gut. Once we get in, y'all start searching the house. If you find anything of value, bring that shit to me. If you find any niggas in the rooms, bring 'em to the living room." She removed her seat belt and felt her waist, making sure that her TEC-9 wasn't visible. "Let's go."

Candy and the runners got out of the car and walked to the front door of the house. Before knocking she took a quick glance at the truck that had been following her. The truck was parked across the street and three houses down from where she was. She noticed the passenger's arm hanging out of the window with smoke coming from his fingers.

"Yo, man, put that damn cigarette out," the driver barked. "I can still smell the shit!"

"You told me not to smoke in yo' ride," the passenger replied. "That's why I got my arm out the truck."

"Man, you's a stupid nigga." The driver stared his partner down. He then refocused his attention on Candy and her runners.

"That ain't her house," the passenger said. "She's knocking on the door. If that was her crib she would'a walked right in."

Candy knocked on the door three times, but no one answered.

"Maybe nobody's here." Real tried looking through the window to the left of the door.

"No, somebody's here. I can hear the TV." Candy leaned over to the right side of the door and peered into the window. The curtain was slightly open, and through the opening she could see a shirtless dark man walking to the door. "He's coming," she whispered.

"Yeah, who the hell is it?" the soon-to-be victim growled as he snatched open the door.

Candy pulled her TEC-9 from her waist and pressed the muzzle against his gut. "Walk backward into the house," she ordered through gritted teeth.

The guy backed into the house with his arms at his sides.

"Yo, what's up wit' this?" The muscles in his chest popped with anger. He towered five inches over Candy's five-foot-six-inch, 140-pound frame. Anger drew his eyebrows together. His nose expelled heat. His 220 pounds gave him a physical advantage over Candy and her runners, but were no match for her TEC-9.

"Sit on the couch and shut the fuck up until I tell you to talk." Candy turned to her runners. "Search the house," she ordered.

The runners drew their guns. Truth nodded in the direction of the den, while Real looked in the opposite direction. They then split up in search of another body for Candy to kill with her stone.

"So, what's been up wit' you . . . Don?" Candy kept a nice distance between her and her victim just in case he tried to rush her.

"Who the fuck are you?" Out the corner of his eyes, he watched Real walk out of a bathroom in the hall and into a bedroom next to it.

"Don't tell me you don't know who I am," Candy sarcastically said.

Don hunched his shoulders. His facial expression said, "And I don't give a fuck, either."

"You don't, do you?" Candy said.

Don leaned forward and balled his right hand into a fist. He then covered the fist with his left hand. "Look, what you want? 'Cause I got things to do."

Candy felt something brush against her ankle. She looked down at her leg. A devilish grin spread across her face after seeing that it was a cat.

The runners walked back into the living room, shaking their heads. "Ain't nobody else here," Truth said.

These bitches got me caught up in my own crib . . . straight violation. I'ma kill they ass wit' they own shit, though, Don thought, as he focused his attention on the gun in Candy's hand.

"That's cool." Candy glanced from the cat to Don. "Yo, you got some kitty litter?"

Truth and Real wore the same confused look as Don.

"Yeah, I got some cat litter." Don looked down at his cat. "Wouldn't I have some damn litter?"

"This nigga wanna be smart." Candy smiled into the eyes of her runners. "Go in the kitchen and look for the litter. Look in all the cabinets and shit 'til you find it," she told them.

"Why don't you just ask me where the shit is?" Don slyly asked. "What? You and yo' little kit-cat need to take a piss?"

"That's funny. Real funny." Candy smiled. "Yeah, um . . . where is it?"

"It's in the back in the cabinet above the washer and dryer." Don laughed. "Hurry up and get the shit before she pee on my expensive carpet."

The runners walked off, laughing.

"Since you think I'm so funny, let me tell you a joke." Candy took a seat in a recliner across from him. She bent forward and pulled the .22 from her ankle. She then leaned back and crossed her right leg over her left leg. She trained both her TEC-9 and .22 on him.

"When I was a kid, my uncle raped me and my aunt didn't believe me. The psychiatrist my mother sent me to was a bitch so you know I laughed after I slit her jugular vein." Sensing someone behind her, Candy turned her head slightly to her right. Out of the corners of her eyes, she watched her runners walk into the living room, each one carrying a bag of kitty litter.

"It was a bloody mess, but it wasn't as bad as the charred bodies that they pulled from my aunt's house." Candy laughed at Don, who was now shaking uncontrollably.

"First my mother, then my uncle," Candy continued. "I couldn't tell if the next body was my cousin or my father. All I know is that they all died that night. And you wanna know how I killed 'em?" Candy uncrossed her legs. She spread her legs apart and leaned forward. "Kitty litter," she whispered in a seductive tone.

Don now knew who she was. Fear danced across his face while his heart did a dance of its own. *Damn, so if Raynail is her husband, she could only be here for one reason,* he thought. "I ain't have nothing to do wit' Raynail gettin' knocked." Don bitched up. Sweat trickled down the sides of his face. "It wasn't me, not at all."

"Well, my husband gave me yo' name." Candy stood up and tucked the .22 in her pocket. She pulled a silencer from the same pocket and screwed it on her TEC-9. "If you ain't had nothing to do wit' it, you goin' to heaven, right?"

"Huh?" Don replied. Wrinkles creased his forehead.

Candy raised her TEC-9 and let off two shots into his chest. The bullets ripped through his heart and straightened the wrinkles in his forehead.

Candy tucked the gun in her waistband and immediately sprang into action. She walked over to Don and turned the pockets of his Dickies inside out, searching for cash.

"Real, y'all go pour that litter on the floor under the gas pipe in back of the dryer. After you do that, find some pliers and unscrew the gas pipe." Candy walked over to the window and moved the curtain to the side. She ran to the back of the house to help Truth and Real, after noticing that the guys were standing outside of the truck.

"We just gonna bust in the door," the driver of the truck said. "So make sure yo' shit is cocked and ready to go."

"I don't feel good about this, man," his partner said as they crossed the street. "We don't even know how many people up in there."

"It don't matter." The driver looked back at his partner. "The bitch can't stop us, and them boys sho ain't stoppin' shit."

"Damn, man, *think!* We don't even know what we walking into. If you ask me, it ain't worth it."

"Well, ain't nobody asked you," the driver said. "We gonna be in and out. Nigga willing to rob any damn body else but you scared to rob a bitch?"

"All right look, it's something I ain't tell you," the partner said. "The bitch got over a dozen bodies on her hands."

The driver suddenly stopped walking and turned to his partner.

"Word on the street is that she killed her fam." The partner nodded. "But that was only her first stripe. After that, ol' girl went on a killin' spree."

The driver looked at his partner in disbelief. "Man, I don't believe that shit. Don't nobody on that side of town got more bodies on they hands than me." He turned around and walked off, leaving his partner standing under a flickering streetlight.

The light continued to flicker. But once it came completely on, as if on cue, the entire neighborhood watch came to life. The porch light of each house was now on, with some of them brighter than others. An old lady looked out the window of the house that the partner was standing in front of and stared at him suspiciously. She walked outside and sat down on the swing on her porch. Her nosey eyes were glued to him.

Hearing a loud roaring noise across the street from where he was standing, the partner quickly looked in the direction of the noise. He watched a man pull a blue trash can to the curb. As the man walked back toward his house, he dug into the back pocket of his dirty-brown jeans and pulled out a pack of cigarettes and a lighter.

Nervous, the partner caught up with the driver.

"I see you finally decided to join me, dumbass," the driver said while looking over his shoulder.

They stopped in front of the house and looked it over. It was the only house on the street that didn't have its porch light on.

They walked up the walkway that led to the porch. They crept onto the porch and each took a window. The driver peered through the window to the left of the front door as his partner tightened his eyes and gazed into the window to the right of the door. The driver could see the top of a man's head pressed against the back of a couch that was positioned in front of the window.

"I think they 'sleep," he said. "This dude on the couch looks like he's knocked out." He looked through the window again. "And all the lights are out, so they all might be 'sleep."

"Man, this is bullshit," the partner barked. "We supposed to be following her to a stash house and shit. All she did was go home and go to sleep. Why are we still here?"

"It don't matter." The driver reached for the doorknob. "She got paper, and whether it's here or at another spot, we gonna get it." He turned and looked behind them, where he noticed the old woman sitting on the swing on her porch, watching them. "That bitch on that swing watching us."

"Yeah, I know. The bitch looks like a pit bull on alert."

"Let me try the door first," the driver said. "This bitch ain't white, but she in a high-class White area. These people known for leaving windows and shit open at night." He turned the knob. He then looked back at his partner and smiled. "Dis shit open! Nigga, this gon' be like taking candy from a baby," he said in a dry, hushed tone.

The creaking of the front door startled Candy and the runners. They had just stepped out of the back door, and were in the midst of closing it. They only had five minutes to get as far away from the house as possible.

"This shit is gonna make the news for real." Candy giggled.

Candy hit her keyless remote. She walked around the back of her car to the driver's side door. She then opened the door and climbed inside. She watched Truth climb into the back seat, but didn't see Real anywhere.

"Where the fuck is Real?"

"That nigga out there, hopin' to see bodies fly." Truth laughed.

Candy jumped out of the car. She looked over the top of the car at Real, who was standing on the grass, staring at the house. "Get yo' ass in," she angrily said in a low voice. Candy slid back into the driver's seat. "Bitch 'bout to blow up and he standin' right in front of the shit."

Once they were all strapped inside of the car, Candy slowly pulled off. She had noticed a few people on the street taking out their trash. She didn't want to attract any attention to herself by peeling out.

Candy stopped at a stop sign on the corner, and looked straight ahead.

It had gotten to the point where she did not have to see her destruction to know that her wrath would be felt. Instead, she listened for it. For Candy, the sound was almost like having an orgasm. It gave her a sensation that only a killer could identify with.

The runners rose up in their seats and looked out of the back window at the house. Candy opened her cell and called the soldier. Since his shift was over, she did not expect him to answer. She wanted to congratulate him on his keen observation.

Candy let the phone ring five times before hanging up. She looked at her watch and counted down the last sixty seconds to breaking her own record.

She had fifty-four bodies on her hands, with the guys from the truck pushing her up to fifty-six. *Wonder if the cat greeted them at the door.* Candy laughed in her thoughts.

The driver and his partner could not see their
right foot in front of their left, the house was so
dark. Once the driver's eyes had adjusted to the
darkness, he turned his attention to the guy who
he thought was asleep on the couch.

"This nigga must be a hard sleeper." The driver
bent forward and looked into Don's face. He
shook him. Once he pulled his hand away, Don
fell off the couch onto the floor.

"Goddamn, man, this dude is dead!" the driver
yelled.

"Ol' boy dead, but where is that bitch and the
kids?" The partner sniffed the air. "Hold up. Do
you smell gas?" he asked, turning up his nose.

They searched for the kitchen with the driver
leading the way. The closer they got to the kitchen,
the stronger the fumes became.

"What's that noise?" the partner asked as they
walked into the kitchen. "Sounds like a hissing
noise or something. You hear that?"

The driver nodded in agreement.

They walked around the kitchen in the direction of the noise. Realizing that it was coming
from the laundry room, which was right next to
the kitchen, they walked slowly inside.

The driver felt along the wall for a light switch.
Finding it, he flicked it up, but the lights failed
to come on. "Fuck this, let's roll," the driver

said. They walked out of the laundry room and headed for the front door. "Ol' boy is dead," he said, pointing at the guy on the floor, "and the house smells like gas. This shit is wild and I ain't tryin'a run into nothing else."

"Where you think the girl and them kids at?" the partner asked.

"I don't know, and I really don't care right about now." The driver looked down at Don. He then knelt down at his head. "If what you said about the girl killing her family is true, she probably killed him."

The partner went to kneel down next to the driver, when the house blew up. The blast sent their bodies flying into doors and walls, before burning to a crisp.

The explosion rocked the neighborhood like the Northridge earthquake. The houses on opposite sides of the house also caught fire, leaving residents running for their lives.

The entire neighborhood was now outside. People from blocks away walked to the scene. A police car filled with two officers was the first to arrive to the scene. One of the officers evacuated the residents on the street, while the other officer blocked off the street with yellow tape. Only fire trucks, paramedics, and other law enforcement personnel were allowed past the tape.

People could be seen standing on top of cars, trash cans, or whatever else they could find to get a glimpse of the action.

Excited, Truth and Real jumped up and down in their seats. "Damn, that was some crazy shit!" Truth laughed.

With her eyes still glued on the street ahead of her, Candy pulled off. "Look, I'ma drop y'all off at home but first I need to get the last of my money y'all holdin'. Since y'all done graduated into some real killas, I ain't passin' y'all no more coke. Plus y'all got y'all own coke to sell." Candy was referring to the coke from the heist.

"A'ight, that's cool." Truth replied. "I got yo' paper at the crib."

It was a quiet two-hour drive to Truth's house. Real and Truth had fallen asleep. It was now time for Candy to enjoy some real company.

Candy slipped The Isley Brothers CD into the CD player. She let down the driver's side window. She sang along with The Isley Brothers as they asked their lady to spend the night.

Candy turned on to Q Street where Truth lived. She noticed a coroner's van pulling away from his apartment. Three police officers stood on the stairs that led up to the entrance of the apartment. They each held a notepad in their hand.

"Yo, Truth, wake up." Candy parked behind a police car and looked in the back seat at Truth. "A coroner's van just pulled off from yo' apartment," she informed him.

Truth was half asleep. He sat up and rubbed his eyes. Yawning, he jerked his head at the sight of the police officers standing on the porch of his building.

Truth jumped out of the car and ran past them, into the apartment. It seemed like it took forever for him to make it up the stairs to his apartment unit. He worried that something bad had happened to his mother. And once he saw the yellow tape cordoning off his apartment door, his fears were confirmed—his mother was dead.

The yellow tape was an untold story of death. It let you know that somebody had died, but how they died? Only the people who put it there knew.

Truth's vision had become a mere blur. It doubled the three words, DO NOT CROSS, on the yellow tape. He peeled back tape from the door. He then removed his key from his pocket and unlocked the door.

The house had been trashed. Both the sofa and loveseat were turned upside down with the bottoms ripped apart. Books and magazines lay strewn on the floor next to the coffee table. The contents of his mother's purse made a trail leading from the living room to the kitchen floor. His grandmother's antique lamp was broken into what looked like a million pieces. And lying next to the broken lamp was a pool of blood. It was his mother's blood, and the scent of her Essence perfume lingered above it. Truth immediately recognized the smell; after all, he did give it to her as a Christmas gift the year before.

Truth couldn't understand who would want to hurt his mother. It was obvious that whoever it was was looking for something. His eyes suddenly grew wide as if a bell had sounded in his head. It was him that they were looking for, and Candy's money that they were after.

Truth ran to his room. He bypassed the dresser drawers and clothes on the floor. The mattress was pulled off of its box-spring onto the floor. It served as a canopy as he made his way to the closet.

All $27,000 of Candy's money was gone. Every shoebox that once contained stacks of one hundred dollar bills was empty.

"I don't believe this shit." Truth walked into the closet and kicked the empty boxes. Images of the house that he had helped Candy to blow up appeared in his head. But in the image, he was one of the people killed in the explosion.

Truth fell to his knees and wept. "Damn, man," he said, using the bottom of his shirt to wipe his face. "They killed my moms. Took Candy's money. How I'm gonna explain this to Candy?"

"Don't sweat that shit." Candy and Real appeared behind him. "That paper can be replaced, but yo' moms can't," Candy said, sympathizing with his loss. She reached down and rubbed his head. "Since it was my money that she got killed over, I'ma make sure yo' moms is buried proper. In the meantime, I'ma help you look for your own spot. This place is hot. Whoever killed yo' moms might come back again looking for more paper."

Truth looked up at Candy and smiled. He then stood up and gave her a hug. "That's real, Candy, thanks."

"Not a problem. Let's get outta here." Candy turned and headed for the door.

"Hold up, let me grab a few things." Truth looked around the room for an empty gym bag, but couldn't find one. "I know I gotta Nike bag somewhere around here," he said. He lifted the mattress back onto its box-spring and looked under the bed. He then walked into the closet. "Fuck it," he said, picking a pillow up from the bedroom floor, and shaking it out of its pillowcase.

"Don't sweat the clothes, just grab yo' important shit." Candy picked a gold chain up off the dresser and tossed it on the bed. "Me and Real gonna go wait in the car. Make it quick."

Candy and Real walked out of the bedroom and out of the house.

Truth walked over to the nightstand and picked up a picture of him and his mother. It was his tenth birthday and he was all smiles. "Dang, Mama, I'ma miss you. I'm too young not to have a mama." He gently placed the picture at the bottom of the pillowcase. He scooped all of his jewelry from the dresser into the pillowcase. He then walked over to the bed and picked up the chain that Candy had thrown on the bed. "It's all my fault and that's something I'ma have to live with for the rest of my life" He dropped the chain into the pillowcase and glanced around the room.

There were other pictures on the wall of him and his mother, but none of them meant more to him than the picture in the pillowcase. *Hmmm, I guess that's it.* He lowered his head and walked out of the room, into the living room.

The house was cold and quiet. Death had made its presence known. The circle of blood on the carpet looked like an entrance to hell. And since it was his fault that his mother was dead, he was afraid to go near it. A dried circle of blood the size of a CD was right next to his mother's purse. Small spots of blood were on her wallet. It was as if the devil had left a ladder to hell, patiently waiting for him to take his first step.

Truth felt the need to have his mother's wallet. He wanted her purse. But in order to get them he would have to take her blood with him.

Truth walked to the front door. He looked back at his mother's purse and wallet. He then dropped his head and walked out of the door and locked it behind him.

Chapter 5

It was going on five o'clock and visiting hours at the jail were almost over. Candy rushed through the double doors after getting past the security checkpoint. She walked to the receptionist window and said, "I'm here to see Raynail Jennings."

The guard flipped through a log book on her desk. She stopped at the letter J. She then skimmed through the list of last names until she got to Jennings. "One moment please," she said.

Candy looked around the room, sizing up each of the guards who stood watch in three corners of the room. Since she was the only visitor in the room, her and Raynail's conversation could easily be heard. She sat in the only corner that was not occupied by a guard. She then looked from the clock on the wall next to the entrance door to her watch, hoping that Raynail would be out soon. It was now four forty-five and she only had fifteen minutes to talk to him.

Raynail walked into the visiting room, pissed. "Man, Candy, that lawyer you got me is foul." He sat across from Candy. "Dude runnin' wit' Feo?"

"What! Who told you that?"

"One of these cats up in here," Raynail replied. "Dude told me about Feo and Ken hanging out and taking trips and shit together."

Candy shook her head and looked down at the table. "But, how does he know?"

"Dude know, a'ight? Fuck! I got a few of these dudes on payroll up in here. They got people on the outside finding shit out for me, and I pay 'em wit' the money you put on my book. When I first met that lawyer, I knew it was something foul about him. So, I had one of these cats up in here contact a uncle of his who happens to be a lawyer, and he peeped him up on game about Ken and Feo. Oh, and the uncle is my lawyer now. He gonna call you tomorrow. His name is Robert Taylor."

"Baby, you moving too fast." Candy took one of Raynail's hands into her hands. "How do we know they telling the truth?"

"I'ma tell you how." Raynail leaned in close to Candy and whispered, "You told me about Ken, but you never told me how much you paid him . . . right?"

Candy nodded in agreement.

"Well, that $226,000 that you gave him in cash at his office went straight to a brand-new 2012 BMW for him and a 2011 Lexus for Feo, not to mention the trips they took."

Raynail's informant was telling the truth. Candy had never told anyone, not even Raynail, how much she had paid Ken to represent him. "Damn." Candy was at a loss for words. "Okay, Raynail." She had a lot to think about and wasn't happy with the fact that she would now have to add Ken to the list of names that Raynail had given her. "The new lawyer is fine. I'll be looking out for his call. Is there anything else before I go?"

"Yeah," he replied. "I also found out that Feo and them be hanging out at the Dub Shack on Saturday nights. My informant up in here told me that Feo and them rolled up on one of our workers moms and took our stash," he said, raising his right eyebrow. "Yeah, ol' boy told me that Feo was at the Dub Shack braggin' 'bout my paper."

"Our paper," Candy corrected him. "And, yes, somebody did take our shit. And, on top of that, they killed Truth's mom."

Raynail bit his bottom lip and shook his head. "I heard about that too. It was that nigga, Dino. Damn, baby, this shit is really gettin' outta hand.

Look, I been thinkin' 'bout us cleaning up the money when I get out."

Candy stared at her husband like he was crazy. "Cleaning up?" She hunched. "But why?"

"'Cause, baby, peep game." Raynail took a deep breath. "We been doing this shit for a long time, so we got more than enough paper to laugh to the bank wit'."

Candy's facial expression let him know that she didn't agree with him.

"I'm facing the death penalty, all because my supposed homies turned against me. The respect is damn near gone," Raynail said.

"Naw, Raynail, you got shit twisted." Candy gave him a cold look. "The respect still there. Five dudes did us dirty—correction, six, including Ken—and one of them is nothing more than a lost soul searching for its shell." She thought back to the guy whose house she and her runners had blown up. "We gonna be straight, don't trip."

A lost soul searching for its shell? Raynail thought while laughing. "Girl, you are crazy. That's why I married you. Make sure you handle Ken while you handling the rest of them cats."

"Time's up," one of the guards yelled. Raynail looked at the guard. He then stood up.

"Oh, I'm gonna pay Ken a visit tomorrow night," Candy said as she stood up to leave.

"Let's go," the guard said to Raynail in a more demanding tone.

Raynail turned away from Candy. *A lost soul searching for its shell.* He continued to laugh. "My baby is real." Raynail walked off with the guard.

"Call me if you find out anything else," Candy yelled out to him. Raynail never looked back at her, but instead threw up a peace sign and nodded his head.

After her visit with Raynail, Candy decided to check out the Dub Shack. It was one-thirty in the morning and Candy and her runners sat in her Lexus truck with the headlights off. She had parked facing the entrance of the Dub Shack. She had positioned her truck so that they could see everybody that exited the Shack when it closed at two o'clock.

The Dub Shack was a club that catered to all of Cali's major suppliers. Not only were they suppliers, but they were billion-dollar stake-holders with major investments in real estate. It wasn't people's ID that got them into the Shack. They were identified by their finances. The owner was familiar with the paper of everybody who frequented the club. And if a dude wasn't pushing six figures or more, he wasn't getting in.

Expensive wine for expensive taste was all that was served at the Shack. Château d'Yquem, the most expensive white wine ever sold, was going for $56,000 a bottle. Montrachet from Domaine de la Romanée-Conti was going for $23,000 a bottle.

Even though Candy and Raynail refused to be a part of the Shack's "social elites," they were respectfully known by the owner and his workers.

Candy and Raynail didn't believe in dudes knowing how much money they were pulling in. To them, "a nigga braggin' 'bout his weight in the streets was just setting himself up for somebody to run up on 'em and take his cheese," as Raynail once said.

Candy pulled her cell phone from its holder on her waist and dialed the number to the Shack.

"Lue here, how may I help you?" he asked after picking up on the third ring. Lue was the owner of the Shack.

"This Candy, Lue, what's up?"

"Awwww, Candy, how are you?" Lue raised his glass to a couple of women who were dancing next to him.

"You spot Feo and his boys, Q-tip, Dino, or Lil John up in there?" she asked.

Lue shifted his attention to Q-tip and Dino. They were standing by the bar, laughing and joking with two women they had just met.

Lue overheard them earlier talking about the money that they had stolen from Candy and Raynail. He knew right away why Candy was inquiring about them.

"Q-tip and Dino are here but I haven't seen Feo or Lil John." Lue rubbed his chin. "Candy, please don't bring no shit to the Shack. This here is what pays my bills."

"Lue, I'd never disrespect another man's hustle, as long as he ain't disrespecting mines."

"I don't even want the cops coming my way." Lue watched Q-tip and Dino as they headed out the door. "They're walking out of the door now," he told Candy.

Candy sat up and started the truck. "What color are they wearing?" She noticed two men walking out of the Shack, but, because of the distance, couldn't make out their faces.

"One is wearing blue jeans and a blazer and the other one—"

"Is wearing all black," Candy chimed in. "Thanks, Lue."

"Hold up, Candy, you still there?"

"Yeah, I'm here." She kept her eyes on Q-tip and Dino. They were standing next to a silver 2011 Jeep Grand Cherokee.

"I'm only guessing that you're out there lying in the cut, but then again, if I know you *and* I do," he said, laughing, "I know there's gonna be lots of blood. Make sure none of that blood is yours."

"Come on, Lue, ain't nothing gonna happen to me," Candy assured him.

Lue's words had softened her heart. For the job that she was about to do, she had no room for emotions. She was born with a cold heart and bred to be a killer.

"I gotta go. I'll call you tomorrow to let you know I'm okay." Candy ended the call. She then called Murphy.

As usual, Murphy picked up on the first ring. "What's up, Candy?"

"I need you to find Lil John and kill him on sight," Candy instructed.

"I'm on it," Murphy said, ending the call.

Candy closed her cell and slipped it into its case on her hip.

Q-tip and Dino had gotten into the Jeep. Candy rolled up behind them. She followed them out of the parking lot, into the streets.

"Yo, take me by that twenty-four-hour Taco Bell before you drop me off at my crib." Dino closed his eyes and rested his head back against the seat.

"That's cool, but I'ma crash on yo' couch." Q-tip's eyes were opening and closing. "That wine got me fucked up."

"You can crash but you gotta be out by eight. My girl get off work at eight and I ain't tryin'a hear her mouth," Dino told him.

Q-tip turned into the parking lot of Taco Bell. He pulled into the drive-thru and placed his order. "Give me the number three wit' no sour cream on the two tacos, and instead of beef on the Mexican pizza, I want chicken."

"Anything else?" the cashier asked through the speaker.

Q-tip looked over at Dino.

Dino leaned past Q-tip to look at the menu. "Shit, give me the same thing he got, but I want sour cream on my tacos."

"What kind of drinks?" the cashier asked.

"Pepsi." Q-tip pulled off before the cashier could say anything else, and rolled up to the window.

Dino didn't like Pepsi and Q-tip had been around him long enough to know it. "But, I wanted a Coke," he spat.

"If they sell Pepsi, they ain't got no Coke." Q-tip smiled at the cashier as she slid open the drive-thru window. He handed her a twenty dollar bill.

"Yeah, a'ight." Dino looked around the parking lot for a place to take a piss. He rolled his window down. He then leaned his head out of the window and looked behind them. "I gotta take a leak," he said, shaking his right leg. "Roll me to that Dumpster back there." He pointed to the Dumpster behind them.

Q-tip looked behind his truck. Out the corner of his eye, he noticed the cashier holding his change out of the window. He turned around and got his change while looking in his rearview mirror for a spot for Dino to use the bathroom. "Man, just wait 'til we get to yo' crib," he told him.

"For real, dawg, I gotta drain the dragon." Dino grabbed his dick through his pants. "I gotta go, now!"

"This here is a one-way drive-thru and it's skinny as fuck. I damn near took off that side mirror over there on that damn wall." Q-tip pointed to the passenger's side mirror. He then pointed at the wall that he had narrowly missed. He looked ahead of him and then behind him. "I can either pull up there and park and you go handle yo' business or I can . . ." He looked over the steering wheel and at the ground, at a white arrow pointing north. "Or, you can get out here and I circle back around and pick you up."

"Circle back around?" Dino said. He looked at the girl in the window who was trying to get Q-tip's attention by waving with the Taco Bell bag. "Get the food."

Q-tip turned to the window and snatched the bag from the cashier.

"Just back up," Dino told him.

"I can't back up. It's a Lexus truck that just pulled up in back of us," Q-tip said, growing irritated.

They both looked behind them at the truck. The windows were tinted so dark that at night, even if the truck was sitting under a light, no one could see the faces of the people inside. All Q-tip and Dino could see were dark shadows.

"Candy, they keep looking back at us." Truth hunched down in his seat. "You think they can see us?"

"Naw." Candy smiled. "These fiberglass windows are darker than a tent. They make the car look pitch black inside, even if a nigga looking in through the front window. Them dumb niggas can't see shit, even if they tried."

"Look, Dino getting outta the truck." From the back seat, Real pointed to Dino.

"Just park up there. I'll be right back." Dino closed the door and walked toward the back of the Jeep. As he was passing by Candy's truck, he strained his eyes to look inside of the passenger window, but all he could see was his reflection.

Dino walked to the Dumpster and looked around. He was making sure that no one could see him. Believing that the coast was clear, he walked behind the Dumpster and unzipped his pants.

Truth watched Dino's every move through his passenger's side mirror. He opened his door after seeing Dino walk behind the Dumpster. "I'm 'bout to get his ass." He smiled.

"Hold on, Truth." Candy grabbed him by an arm. She watched as Q-tip pulled up into a parking space ahead of them. "You hyped right now, and I understand, but calm down and take yo' time. Here, take my nine." She pulled her TEC-9 from her waist and handed it to Truth. "Real gonna go wit' you."

Real got out of the truck and quietly closed the door.

"When y'all done, just stay there. I'ma have to circle around and pick y'all up," Candy told them.

Truth slid out of the truck. He and Real crept to the Dumpster to surprise Dino.

Truth walked up behind Dino as he was zipping up his pants. "Can I get a quarter?" he asked, sounding like an old man.

Dino never turned around. "You can't have shit, now scram!"

Truth bumped Real with his elbow and winked. "Please, mister. I'll even hold yo' dick while you take a piss."

"Bum? Are you outta yo' fuckin' . . ." Dino spun around and stared down the one eye that would take his life: the TEC-9. He cracked a grin when he realized whose hand was behind it.

"Crazy! That is what you were about to call me when you thought I was a bum." Truth licked his lips. "Yeah, I'm crazy, just as crazy as you are."

"Shouldn't you two niggas be at home, getting ready for school or something?" Dino looked past them at the truck that had just pulled up into the parking lot. The truck stopped a few feet behind Truth and Real. The lights remained on. *That's my nigga, Q, and just in time.* Dino laughed. *These niggas 'bout to die.*

"You think this shit is funny?" Real asked him after noticing the smile on his face.

"Look, kids, put the guns down 'fo' y'all hurt somebody," Dino joked.

"More than likely, my mother told you the same thing before you shot her." Truth cocked his gun.

"Yo' mom?" Dino rolled his eyes up into his head. He was pretending not to know what Truth was talking about.

"Okay, maybe you know what happened to yo' boy whose house went the fuck up in smoke . . . huh?" Real asked.

Wrinkles formed across Dino's forehead. He cracked his knuckles. He bobbed his head and stared at Truth and Real with death in his eyes.

"That got yo' attention, didn't it?" Real asked him.

Dino was no longer smiling. "You two niggas did that shit?" He wanted to know.

"It ain't funny now, is it?" Truth laughed. "Yeah, we did it . . . us and Candy." The driver's side door of the truck suddenly opened. With Truth and Real thinking it was Candy, neither one of them turned to look.

Dino watched the driver get out of the truck. The high beams blinded him, making it difficult for him to make out who it was. He strained to see past the light. He could see a circle with the word JEEP in the middle of it on the hood of the truck.

Dino smiled at the site of his boy's truck.

"Bitch, you 'bout to die tonight," Real told Dino.

"Is that right?" Dino laughed. "Well, I can honestly say, y'all caught a nigga wit' his pants down." He raised both hands in defeat. Dino watched the driver walk from the driver's side of the truck around to the front of the truck. *'Bout fuckin' time*, he thought. *These two little niggas could'a killed my ass by now.*

Candy walked down the path of light like a supermodel. She stopped behind her runners. Dino's eyes grew wide. He choked on his spit when he saw a gold chain around Candy's neck. The letter Q, made of pure diamonds, hung from the end of the chain.

Dino knew right away that Q-tip was dead.

"I hope you bought a life insurance policy wit' the money you stole from me." Candy stood between Truth and Real. "I'd love to kill you, but I can't."

Dino let out a sigh of relief.

"'Cause I promised Truth I'd let him do it." Smiling, Candy turned to Truth. "Handle yo' business." Candy walked back to the Jeep and climbed inside.

"I'm sorry, kid. Feo put me up to it." Dino looked at the truck. "Call Candy back over here, I got some info for her. Candy! Candy!" he yelled.

Candy shut off the headlights. She climbed out of the truck. Walking toward them she said, "What? You wanna tell me where my money at?" She stopped in front of Dino.

"Naw, but, peep game." Dino swallowed hard. "Feo and that dude Ken you got representin' Raynail are working together."

"Yeah, that's what I heard," she said.

"Ken been in on it since the beginning." Dino was singing like a bird. "He gave half of that money you gave him to Feo. Feo set Raynail up 'cause a cop told him that they had enough evidence to lock Feo up for that cop's murder. Feo tried to throw 'em off him by settin' Raynail up wit' the gun. It was Ken's idea, for real."

Candy was pissed. *Niggas tryin'a play me at every chance they get.* She looked at her runners. "Give him the silent treatment." She walked back to the truck and got in.

Truth raised the TEC-9 and shot Dino in the head. He stood over him and let off two rounds into his chest.

The runners ran to the Jeep and jumped in.

Candy drove through Taco Bell's drive-thru without stopping and parked next to her Lexus. She then looked in the back seat at Truth. "Look in the back and pass me something to wipe our prints off the truck."

Truth put both knees on the seat and looked over it. He almost screamed when he saw Q-tip's body with two bullet holes to the head. Q-tip was balled up in the fetal position on top of a torn sheet.

"Goddamn, Candy! It's a torn sheet back here but Q's body is on it." Truth looked around the body and noticed a white towel. "Okay, here's a towel." He leaned over the top of the seat and over Q-tip's body, being careful not to touch him.

"Rub y'all prints off of everything y'all touched and get out," Candy told them.

After wiping down their prints, the runners used the towel to open their doors. Truth then walked around to the driver's window and passed the towel to Candy through the window.

Candy wiped down the truck. Once she was sure she had covered everything that she had touched, she got out and slipped into her Lexus. She backed up and pulled out of the parking lot.

Candy took out her cell phone and called Murphy to see if he was able to find Lil John. She let the phone ring five times before hanging up. *Hmmm that's odd,* Candy thought. She ended the call and tried calling Murphy again. This time she waited until the voice mail picked up before ending the call.

"Man, I keep calling Murph to see if he handled Lil John, and he ain't picking up," Candy complained. She pushed speed dial and called his phone again. Getting his voice mail, she closed her cell. "Damn, if that nigga ain't dead, he gonna wish he was."

Chapter 6

The next evening, Murphy pulled a Blackhawk mask from his back pocket and slipped it on. With the exception of his eyes and nose, the mask covered his entire face and head.

Following Murphy's lead, his homie slipped on the same type of mask and adjusted it over his eyes and nose. He then looked down at the bulletproof vest he was wearing. He removed two hunting knives from the glove compartment and slid each one into the inside pocket of his vest.

Murphy pulled down his sun visor and looked at himself in the mirror. "Let's go," he said.

They both got out of the car and closed the doors gently behind them. Murphy walked around the back of the car to the passenger side, where his homie was bent over tying his shoes. Once his homie was done, they both made their way over to their victim's house.

Just like two thieves in the night, they maneuvered their way over to Lil John's house. As mosquitoes and moths danced under the street lights, Murphy and his homie tried their best to avoid the lights.

The house was situated in a middle-class neighborhood in Buena Park. Buena Park was fifteen minutes away from Knott's Berry Farm, where violence was not common. The homes were surrounded by tall gates, and sat back away from the curb. Every house on the street was well kept. That is, every house except Lil John's house.

Lil John and his family had terrorized the neighborhood for years. He and his wife argued all of the time. When his kids went out to play, they would often throw trash over the gate into their neighbors' yards. Their house was dark blue, trimmed in white, with chips of paint from the house decorating the grass. The grass was dead and the only time it grew was in the winter when it rained.

Once Murphy and his homie made it to the house, they hid in some bushes that sat right outside of the dining room window. They watched Lil John and his family prepare the dining room table for dinner.

"Daddy, can we have some ice cream after we eat?" Lil John's daughter excitedly asked. She sat on the edge of her chair, swinging her legs while eating a piece of chicken.

"Ask yo' moms, 'cause after I eat, I'm out. Got some business to take care of." Lil John yawned. He walked from the kitchen to the head of the dining room table. He sat down in a chair and picked up his fork.

"Shit, again!" his wife snapped as she placed the bowl of rice in the middle of the table. "Damn, John, you been gone every night for the past two weeks. Is something going on that you ain't telling me about?"

Lil John looked sadly across the table at his wife. He turned his attention to his daughter, who was sitting to his right, smiling from ear to ear. He then looked to his left at his son, who he could feel trying to kick his daughter under the table.

It had been weeks since Lil John had spent quality time with his kids. After pinning the dirty gun on Raynail, he knew that it was just a matter of time before Candy got to him.

He didn't want to risk getting his family involved. But what he had failed to realize was that Candy didn't care about his family, especially when it came to protecting hers. He had heard many stories about her killing dudes, but failed to study up on them. A long arm was what she had. And even if she couldn't lay down the wrath that fate had dealt her victims, if the bounty was on point, there were lots of dudes out there who would.

Lil John looked across the table at his wife. To avoid going through another night of questioning, he did the first thing that came to mind. "Put that chicken down, baby, so we can bless the food." He smiled at his daughter. He waited for her to put the chicken on her plate, and took her hand.

His wife looked at him like he had lost his mind. As usual, he was trying to avoid talking to her, but this time his tactic was unique. It involved God, somebody she knew, but that he knew nothing about.

"Stop playing wit' me and answer the question," his wife argued. "You tryin'a change the subject and shit but it ain't gonna work. Since when did we start praying before we ate?" His wife looked at their daughter. "Go ahead and eat that chicken."

"Let's say grace, Mama," their son yelled. He hopped up and down in his chair while banging his hands on the table.

"Yeah, I'll say it." Their daughter smiled, showing her dimples. "Let me say it."

"No, I asked first," the boy cried. "I . . . Daddy! I said it first."

His wife shot him an evil look before turning her attention to the children. "Shut up! Y'all daddy gonna say it since it was his idea." She stared at Lil John as she grabbed their children's hands. "Put y'all head down."

The children dropped their heads and closed their eyes.

Lil John looked at his wife and started laughing. "Close yo' eyes too." He lowered his head but instead of blessing the food, he prayed for God to watch over him and his family. He regretted what he had done to Raynail and wished that there was some way he could change his situation.

Lil John could tell by all the jerking and moving his son was doing that he did not have his head down. He opened one of his eyes and, just as he had suspected, his son was violently shaking his head from left to right. Lil John closed his eyes and continued to pray.

The little boy stopped moving after noticing two masked men looking through the dining room window, with one of them holding a gun. Smiling, he snatched his hand from his mother and waved at them. He giggled when one of them waved back. His mother opened her eyes. She grabbed his hand, and closed her eyes.

"Murphy, what the fuck you waving at that boy for?" his homie asked.

"It's cool, watch this." Murphy put his finger up to his mask where his lips would have been, as if to tell the boy to be quiet. He pulled a piece of gum from his pocket and held it up for the boy to see. He then reached his hand slightly into the window, acting as though he was giving it to the boy. The boy tried to snatch his hands away from his parents but they tightened their grips on his hand, and wouldn't let go. Seeing the boy trying to break loose, Murphy motioned for him to sit still by holding up the palm of his hand. He then pointed to his own head and lowered it, hoping the boy would do the same. Following Murphy's lead, the boy lowered his head. He assumed that he would get the candy once his daddy had finished praying.

Murphy looked at everyone's face at the table. He was making sure that their eyes were closed. He then screwed the silencer on his Glock and leveled it, so that the muzzle was midpoint through the window and aimed directly at Lil John's head.

The first and only shot hit Lil John in the temple. Lil John's head rested on his plate, with blood covering his rice like gravy.

Murphy and his homie hurried to the car. While driving away they both looked at Lil John's house and laughed.

"John, what the hell is wrong wit' you?" his wife asked, never opening her eyes. "You supposed to say 'amen' so everybody can open they eyes and start eating."

The little boy opened his eyes and looked at his father. "Mommy, I think Daddy went to sleep."

Opening her eyes, she noticed all of the blood on the table and the hole in the side of Lil John's head. "What the fu . . . !" She jumped up and ran over to him. "John! What the hell just happened?" She stood to the side of him and grabbed both of his shoulders. She pulled him back against the seat. "Oh, God, he's dead! He's dead . . . but how? Who killed him?" Still holding him up, she looked frantically around the dining room, trying to figure out what happened.

"I know!" The boy hopped up and down in his seat. He raised his hand like a student in school when the teacher asked the class a question.

"Who was it, baby? Who killed your daddy?"

The little boy pointed to the window. "Candy man."

Chapter 7

It had been years since Candy had been to church. As a kid, she attended church regularly with her grandmother and was a part of the Little Angels Church Choir. Candy's mother would drop her off at her grandmother's house the Saturday before, and then pick her up Sunday evening after church. Her mother never attended church but, instead, spent most of her time at their next-door neighbor's house getting drunk. On special occasions like Mother's Day and Christmas, when the children would do musical performances for their parents, Candy would beg her mother to go to church with her and her grandmother. But no matter how much she begged, her mother's answer was always the same: no.

Candy walked up the steps of St. Matthew Missionary Baptist Church and stood in front of the open double doors. She looked up at the cross that was on the roof of the church, and thought about something that she remembered her mother always saying each time her grandmother would ask her to, "Come ride with us to church."

"If I ever step foot in anybody's church, as much shit as I done did, the bitch liable to burn up," her mother would say.

Growing up, Candy never did understand what her mother meant. But once she got older and started doing dirt, her mother's words suddenly made sense.

Candy closed her eyes and bowed her head. "Lord, please don't let this church burn down, at least not while I'm in it," she prayed. She opened her eyes, took a deep breath, and walked into the church.

Candy was greeted at the door by one of the ushers. The usher looked around the church for an empty seat. Spotting one next to the mother of the church, he took Candy by the hand and escorted her to the bench.

The mother of the church recognized Candy immediately. She picked up her purse off the bench, and placed it on her lap. She sat up straight and moved both of her legs to the right so that Candy could get past her. Once Candy was seated, the mother of the church gave her a hug. She patted Candy on her right knee. She was happy to see Candy, and expressed it by clapping her hands to the rhythm of the song that the choir was singing.

Out of the corner of her right eye, Candy noticed the pastor walking into the church from an adjacent door that led from his office. He was dressed in a long red and black robe, with a cross in the center of it. His head was bald and his salt-and-pepper beard was neatly trimmed. Aside from the gray in his beard, he didn't look like he had aged a bit.

Damn, he looks good, Candy thought.

The pastor walked to his chair and took a seat. He then reached over to his right and shook the hand of the reverend sitting next to him. He turned to the reverend to the left of him and shook his hand.

Candy noticed that the church was in serious need of renovating. The gold cross above the choir stand needed to be repaired. The material on the pastor's chair was discolored. The words "Do This In Remembrance of Me," inscribed along the border of the table sitting in front of the front pews, were chipped. Two pianos sitting on opposite sides of the choir stand were out of tune.

The pianist/choir director was playing a hymn while the ushers walked up and down the aisles, passing the collection plate around the church. Candy looked over her right shoulder at two ushers who were two rows behind her with the collection plate. She dug into her purse and took out a pen and her checkbook. She wrote out a check to the church and waited for the usher to get to her row.

A man sitting to Candy's left passed her the collection plate. Candy placed the check face down in the plate, which mostly held change. She tried to hand the plate to the mother of the church. But the mother of the church looked straight ahead, as if she didn't see the plate.

But, when they used to serve food in back of the church, yo' old ass was the first to eat, Candy thought as she reached past her, and handed the plate to the usher.

When the ushers were done taking up the collection, they poured all of the money into one bucket. They then passed the bucket to the pastor, who was standing at the pulpit. The pastor placed his offering into the bucket and instructed the congregation to bow their heads.

"Lord, bless all of those who gave, and all of those who were not able to give. In Jesus' name, amen," the pastor prayed. He passed the bucket to one of the deacons who stood to his right. He then slipped on his reading glasses, and opened his Bible.

"Today's sermon is about Jesus on your caller ID." The pastor nodded.

The church erupted in a wave of "amen."

"Now, so many of us have had what I call callings. Callings from the Lord Jesus Christ, who is ahead of my life. Now, I don't know about your life, but He who is in heaven is ahead of my life."

"Amen," rang out over the church.

"And when we have these callings, instead of answering them, we push ignore. In our minds, we push ignore. Now, when I say we, I'm not talking about me, I'm indirectly talking about some of you." He pointed to the congregation. "Ain't no need to ugh . . . candy-coat it. I'm talking about you."

Candy looked surprised. It sounded almost like the pastor was talking directly to her.

"When you about to do something against God's Word and your conscience start bothering you, that's the Lord calling."

"Amen, Pastor," someone yelled.

"When you listen to the choir singing, and you start singing the words to the song with a voice that you never knew that you had, that's the Lord calling you to join the choir. When a person kills, robs, commits adultery, harms a child, set fire to the church, or just does anything against my God—against my God"—the church erupted in cheers and applause—"he or she who has done these wrongs had a calling from God before they did it. Y'all don't hear me, church. Yes, thieves have callings, whether you believe it or not. On the outside they wanna be thought of as being hardcore, feared, nothing to mess with. I know y'all know what I'm talking about."

Candy was ready to go. She still had to go after Feo and Ken and needed to keep a clear mind. She didn't have room for her conscience to be bothering her.

"But, on the inside, they just as small as the day they were born," the pastor told the church.

One of the deacons walked from in back of the church with something in his hand. He approached the pastor and handed it to him.

Seeing that the pastor was distracted, Candy stood up. She held up a finger, and slipped past the mother of the church, whose eyes were closed. Candy headed to the back of the church.

"Amen," the pastor said and looked at the paper that the deacon had given him. "I have a check in my hand in the amount of $250,000 from Carolyn Tweedy." He looked at the name for a second time. *Carolyn Tweedy? That name sounds familiar,* he thought as he looked from member to member, trying to match the name with a face.

Candy stopped walking. She looked to her right and tried to force her way through a row of seats.

The pastor noticed the commotion and, removing his glasses, looked at the back of the church. "Something wrong?"

Candy was awkwardly standing between two people sitting in the second-to-last row of benches. The pastor recognized her. He slipped his glasses back on and smiled.

"C-a-r-o-l-y-n Tweedy." He extended his right hand out to her. "Would you please join me up here?"

Candy walked out from between the row of seats. She lowered her head and took small steps toward the pastor.

"It's all right," the pastor said, sensing her nervousness. "Amen."

Candy stopped in front of the pastor. She kept her eyes on the carpet. For the first time in her life, she was ashamed of her life.

"Nice to see you again, Carolyn."

Everybody in the church sat in complete silence.

"I want all of you to meet Carolyn Tweedy. She was raised here in this church and sang in our youth's choir." He looked at Candy. "It's been a long time, hasn't it?"

Candy kept her eyes on the floor. There was something about being in church that humbled her. It was as if the Lord was on her caller ID, and instead of pushing ignore, she answered it.

"I don't even know how to begin to thank you for such a huge contribution to the church." The pastor smiled.

Candy looked up and met his smile.

"So, what is the nature of this blessing?"

"Well, I noticed that the church needed a few repairs and, since I had the money, I thought that I would help," Candy hesitantly answered.

"You have done a good deed, and I am glad that you have decided to return to church after all of these years." He folded his hands together on the pulpit and smiled. "Will I be seeing you from now on?"

Candy didn't want to lie to him, especially not in church, but she just wasn't ready to change her life around. "Normally I . . . um, work on Sundays. It took a lot for me to get today off. But . . . um, once my shift changes, I'll be here every Sunday." Candy actually meant that once she decided to change her life around, she would attend church every Sunday. "As a matter of fact, I was just about to leave."

"All right, Carolyn, but you make sure I see you soon, okay?" He walked around the pulpit and down the three steps. He stopped in front of Candy. He then took a small bottle of anointing oil from the pocket of his robe and unscrewed the top. He shook a little onto his finger and made a cross across Candy's forehead with the oil. "You mind if I pray for you before you go?"

Oh, shit! This shit is too much for me, Candy thought. "It's okay. Yeah, go ahead," she said. Candy rolled her eyes beneath her closed eyelids.

He put the palm of his hand against her forehead and closed his eyes. The congregation closed their eyes and lowered their heads.

"Dear Heavenly Father, I ask that you watch over your child, Carolyn Tweedy. I ask that you build a shield around her, protecting her from all of her enemies. Put your hands on her, Lord. I can feel evil spirits . . ."

Damn, he can even feel the shit I'm doing. Beads of sweat formed on Candy's forehead and onto the pastor's palm.

"Evil spirits have planted their seeds within this child's heart, and I only ask that you dig up those seeds, Lord, and replace them with . . ." He paused. Tears were streaming from his eyes. He took a handkerchief from his pocket with his free hand. He then wiped his face. "Replace them with the Word of God. In Jesus' name we pray, amen." He gave Candy a hug and kissed her cheek. "You be good."

Candy nodded, and turned away from the pastor. She walked up the aisle and out of the church.

Candy ran to her BMW, which was parked across the street from the church. She pushed the keyless remote, opened the door, and jumped inside. The tears that she held in while standing in front of the pastor were flowing freely. It was okay to cry now. Her car was her shield. For the moment, it was protecting her from exposing her weak side to the outside world. Her emotions were trying to get the best of her, but she couldn't let it happen.

Candy wiped tears from her eyes. Her thoughts drifted off to Raynail and the possibility of him being sent to the electric chair. Her entire attitude changed. She had one more piece of business to take care of before Raynail's trial.

Candy started the car. She glanced at the church. *Not now, God*. She shifted into drive, and headed home to get ready for a late-night snack with Ken.

It was nine-thirty at night and Candy had just scaled the six-foot wall that surrounded Ken's million-dollar home. It was a three-story brick house with vines growing along both sides of the house. Flowerbeds filled with red and yellow roses sat on both sides of the front door surrounded by blue nightlights. The windows on each level of the house had different-colored vertical blinds, with the blinds on the third level of the house being pink.

Assuming that the window with the pink vertical blinds belonged to a child's room, Candy decided to enter the home through a second-story window. It wasn't the children she wanted, but the man who fathered them.

She circled the house in search of an open window. She noticed a crack in a window on the second floor. The vertical blind was raised with a Renuzit air freshener sitting in the corner of the window. She surveyed the vines along the wall. She was thinking of the easiest way to climb up to the window. There was no easy way. Candy took a deep breath and started up the wall.

Moving like Catherine Zeta-Jones in *Entrapment,* she slipped her right foot into a circular piece of vine. She reached over her head with her right hand and grabbed for a vine that resembled a rope. She then pulled herself up, being careful not to cast even the slightest shadow on any of the downstairs windows. She dragged her left foot along the wall, searching for a place to rest it. She looked down and noticed a brick, as high up as her right knee. It was covered by vines and had small specks of bird droppings on it.

Candy wrapped the vine twice around her wrist. She placed her left hand above her right hand on the vine. She took a deep breath. She then took four quick steps up the wall of vines, until she reached a large brick that was protruding from the wall. Candy leaped onto the brick with her left foot. She slid her right leg between her left leg and the vines on the wall, and rested her right foot on top of her left foot.

She looked up at the window, which was still a great distance from the top of her head. She wondered how she would reach it. *I would'a came out better just knocking on the damn door,* she thought as she looked around for another loose vine. Even though the last climb had brought her a few feet closer to the top, it ultimately led her farther away from the open window. She had moved farther to her left, when the window was to her right.

Beads of sweat formed across her forehead and above her top lip. The vine that was wrapped around her wrist had cut through her skin. A cramp had formed in the calf of her left leg, causing her to tremble. Candy felt that at any moment she was going to fall. She had to switch to another position, and quick.

She spotted a light fixture protruding from the wall to the right of her and a few feet beneath the open window. She figured that if she could find another vine to her right, just as she had done before, then she could walk up the vines to the light fixture. She would then hold on to the light fixture and pull herself up to the window.

Candy noticed a loose vine not too far from where she was standing. The vine started at the top of the roof and ended just above a downstairs window. Even though it wasn't too far away from her, she would still need to either jump or climb to the right, in order to make it over to the vine. *I'm puttin' in all this work to get to this nigga? I swear when I get up there I'm killing his ass, for real.*

To keep from losing her balance, she twisted her wrist out of the vine. She then counted to three. Pushing off from the brick, she swung over to her right. She grabbed the vine with her left hand. She was now dangling from one arm. She could feel herself losing her grip. She held her lips together as she tried her best not to scream. She looked up at the vine that she was holding on to and reached her right hand above her head for the vine.

Trickles of sweat had found their way from above her top lip down to the crease that separated her top lip from her bottom lip. She licked her lips and looked up at the light, which was only a few feet above her head. She planted both feet against the vines. She took one step up with her left foot. She then reached her left hand above her right hand and pulled herself up. She took another step up with her right foot, placed her right hand above her left hand on the vine, and pulled herself up again. She continued at that pace until she had not only reached the light, but had passed it. She had finally made it to the window.

She reached for the window with her left hand, while still holding on to the vine with her right. Instead of pushing herself up like she so desperately wanted to, she listened for movement. It was quiet. With a sudden sense of urgency, she pushed up, while kicking at the vines to the right of her. Her left arm was now all the way inside of the window. She released the vine that she was holding. She then slipped her right arm into the window. The only thing standing between her and Ken was the Renuzit. She worried that she would knock it down while climbing into the window.

Candy braced herself with her left arm. She picked up the Renuzit and threw it outside of the window onto the ground.

Candy slid hands first into the window right above a toilet. To keep from falling on her face, she had no choice but to hold on to the toilet seat with her left hand, while holding on to the edge of the tub with her right. She then eased to the floor.

Candy stood up and wiped her hands together. She walked to the open bathroom door, and peered out into the hallway. At one end of the hallway was a closed door, and at the other end was a door that was slightly cracked. She could hear moaning coming from the direction of the open door. *This is gonna be his wife's last fuck,* she thought as she quietly followed the moans. The closer she got, the louder the moans became.

When she reached the door, she looked inside and noticed Ken lying on his back, with his eyes closed and the blanket pulled up to his chest. Beneath the blanket and between his legs was a head moving up and down. The body hung off the bed. A sheet covered everything but the feet, which were covered with white socks. *Sounds like the wifey giving mad head.* A slurping sound came from beneath the blanket. Candy frowned at the sound.

"That shit sound nasty," she whispered. Candy pulled the .357 Magnum from the inside of her bulletproof vest and pushed the bedroom door completely open.

On the floor, leading from the door to the bed, were two pairs of men's clothes. They were lying one in front of the other. A white dress shirt with one sleeve turned inside out was on the floor in front of the sock closest to the bed. To the right of the door was a makeup table with a mirror. The rectangular-shaped mirror had small light bulbs running along the perimeter of it. A chair was pushed up to the makeup table. And lying neatly over the back of the chair was a pair of men's dress pants.

Candy walked into the room. She discovered a second pair of men's pants to the left of her on the floor. She looked back at the pants hanging over the back of the chair and then back at the pants that were right next to her on the floor. All kinds of thoughts were running through her head. She looked quickly from one area of the room to the next. On the floor between the bed and the window were two pairs of men's dress shoes: one black pair and one tan pair.

Candy stood shocked after realizing what was going on.

Ken's heavy breathing grew even louder and the first words out of his mouth since Candy had walked into the room raised the antenna on her head even more.

"Suck that shit, Feo." Ken licked his lips. He grabbed for the pillow next to his head. "Awwww, shit! Put 'em in yo' mouth. Yeah, that's it. Now, come back up to the head."

Candy's eyes grew as wide as the sun. She lowered the gun. She couldn't believe what she was hearing. *Ken and Feo?* Ken's moans were starting to irritate her. She tried covering both ears with her hands to drown out the noise that he was making.

Ken pulled the blanket back, exposing Feo, who was using the back of his hand to wipe his mouth. Ken then flipped over on all fours and, just as easy as a man entering a women, Feo slid into his ass and started fucking him.

Candy had heard and seen enough. Like a leopard on its prey, she rushed up to the left side of the bed and smashed Feo on the side of his head with the butt of the gun.

Feo fell back off of Ken and cried out in pain. "Awww, my head! My head." He rolled from left to right as blood spilled from his head.

Ken pushed himself up in the bed. He rested his back against the headboard. "Candy, what the hell are you doing in my house?" he barked.

"The streets told me you was running wit' Feo, but, damn, I'm not thinkin' y'all was getting down like this." She looked at both of them in disgust.

Feo balled up, holding his head.

"Feo, shut yo' ass up and crawl up there next to yo' bitch!" Candy pointed her gun at Feo.

Feo slowly made his way up to the head of the bed and flipped over on his back.

"Ken, I been paying you to make sure that Raynail walks outta court next month"—she then looked over at Feo—"'cause some stupid-ass niggas set him up, and here you are, sleeping with the enemy?" She pointed the gun at Feo. "Feo, you and Raynail go way back to second grade." She shook her head and looked down at Ken's dick. "Pull the blanket over y'all ass," she snapped. "I ain't tryin'a see that shit."

Feo reached down for the blanket where he was met by Ken, who helped him to pull the blanket up over them.

"Feo, you and Raynail been knowing each other for a long time," she continued. "You fuckin' ruined y'all friendship. You would'a came out better settin' up one of them other dudes that was wit' y'all."

Feo held the blanket against the side of his head to stop the blood. "You right, Candy, and I'm sorry."

"Sorry," she yelled. "My husband facing the chair, and all you can say is that you sorry?"

"Candy, look. I can make one call first thing in the morning, and Raynail will be out before noon," Ken said.

"Do I look stupid to you, Ken?" she asked him. "And, why you bitchin' up all of a sudden? Nigga, you's a Fruit Town Brim. I bet they don't even know you get down like this. I wish I had a camera."

Ken sucked his teeth.

"So, where my money?" she asked Ken.

Ken looked at Candy. He then looked straight ahead, saying nothing.

"I asked you a question, Ken." She pressed the muzzle of the gun against his temple. "Where's my money?"

Feo looked over at Ken. "Man, give her the money so she can go!"

Ken wiped his nose. He looked coldly at Candy. "The money is gone." He turned and looked at Feo. "Me *and* Feo spent the shit. And, anyway, I been doing this shit long enough to know that whether I give you the money back or not, I'm still dead." He sat up straight and rubbed his beard. "I guess my time is up." Ken smiled and looked past Candy at his mother's picture on the wall. He then took his right trigger finger and ran it down the two teardrops beneath his eye.

Candy recognized the look that Ken was giving her. He was no longer Ken, but Baby Ghost from Fruit Town Brims in Inglewood.

Baby Ghost was a coldhearted killer, who never unwillingly saw the insides of a prison. And when he did, he was visiting one of his clients. Back in the day, he was the leader of Inglewood's Fruit Town Brims. The Fruit Town Brims would always be in his blood, law degree or not.

Ken cut his eyes at Feo and shook his head. He sensed Candy's displeasure. He then looked at her and smiled. Ken closed his eyes, preparing to meet his Maker.

Candy let out a long sigh. She raised the Magnum and shot Ken right between his eyes.

Ken's chin dropped to his chest. His body leaned slowly to the right, and fell over onto the floor.

"Oh, shit!" Feo jumped up from the bed with his hands raised above his head. "Please, Candy, don't do this."

Candy pointed the gun at Feo and walked around the bed. She then stopped in front of him. "It's nothing you can say, Feo. It's nothing you can say or do that will change things. I guess yo' time is up too." Candy let off two rounds in Feo's chest.

Feo fell to the floor. He looked up at Candy before taking his last breath.

Candy walked out of the bedroom and down the hall to the top of the stairs. She then walked down the stairs and stopped at the front door. Candy glanced around the house.

Pictures of Ken with his wife and daughter decorated the walls. In one picture, his wife was standing in front of Southwest Airlines dressed in a flight attendant's uniform.

Hmmm, maybe she's at work, Candy thought. *Now won't she be surprised when she gets home.*

Chapter 8

Raynail looked back at Candy and his mother, who were sitting behind him. He didn't know that all of the witnesses were dead. It had been three weeks since he had spoken to Candy during one of her visits with him in jail. And when he did see her, she was talking in code. It was a waiting game, and he only hoped that he would come out a winner.

Nervous, Raynail held his hands together in front of him as if he were praying. He then turned and looked at Candy.

"I love you," Candy mouthed to Raynail.

Raynail responded with a smile.

On the outside Candy smiled back, but on the inside she was crying. Murphy had not answered any of her calls, so she didn't know if Lil John was going to show up in court to testify against Raynail.

Candy squeezed her mother-in-law's hand. She gazed around the courtroom into the eyes of the victims' families.

*He didn't kill your husband. He wasn't even
in LA when your brother was murdered,* Candy
wanted to yell. Instead, she sat quiet as she
waited for the trial to begin.

"All rise." A deputy, standing next to the court
recorder, waited as everyone stood to acknowledge the judge's presence. "Judge Pernita Tinsley
presiding."

The judge walked out of an adjacent door that
was behind the court clerk, which led from her
chambers to the courtroom. She walked up the
side stairs of the bench to her "throne."

Once the judge was seated, the deputy looked
at everybody in the courtroom and said, "You
may be seated." Everybody, with the exception
of the camera crews, sat down.

The judge cleared her throat. She picked up a
folder on her desk. She then read from the cover.
"This is the case of the City of Los Angeles vs.
Raynail Jennings. Are both sides prepared to begin?" She removed her glasses. She then looked
from the prosecutor's table to the defense's table.

With sweat forming across his forehead, the
prosecutor stood up with a napkin in his hand.
He looked over at Raynail and his attorney.
"Request for a sidebar, please," he nervously said.

Raynail's attorney looked at him and patted
him on the back. He then stood up and walked
over to the judge, followed by the prosecutor.

"Your Honor, unfortunately my witnesses are all dead," the prosecutor whispered. He ran his hands through the top of his hair.

"Well, do you have any signed statements from your now deceased witnesses stating that the defendant is responsible for the murders?" the judge asked.

"Um . . . actually I don't." The prosecutor licked his chapped lips. "Only because the witnesses agreed to show up in court."

"Other than the witnesses, what other evidence were you prepared to submit before the court?" The judge was growing impatient. It was obvious that the case was over.

"Your Honor, I was relying on my witnesses' testimony. They were going to place the defendant at the scene of each murder and point him out as the shooter."

"I hope you realize that you have brought a case before the court—"

"But, Your Honor, I—"

"No, let me finish." The judge rubbed her temple. "This is a very high-profile case. Six people are dead, including an officer. Do you understand how important this case is?"

The prosecutor nodded his head.

"Is there anything else that you would like to tell me?"

"Your Honor, I agreed to try this case because no other lawyer would take it," the prosecutor said. "The defendant *and* his wife are killers from what I understand."

The judge looked at both the prosecutor and the defense attorney. "You both may go back to your positions."

Both lawyers returned to their tables and remained standing. Raynail's attorney tapped him on his shoulder and motioned with his hand for him to stand.

Raynail stood up. He looked from his attorney to Candy and his mother. Their faces held concern. And not knowing what was going on himself, Raynail too looked concerned.

"Will both sides please stand," the judge ordered.

Raynail and his attorney were already standing. Raynail looked at the prosecutor's table and watched a second prosecutor stand up.

"It was just brought to my attention by the prosecution that the witnesses against the defendant are deceased." Gasps could be heard throughout the courtroom. "Despite the severity of this case, the prosecution has failed to obtain any other evidence that could have led to a conviction. I am very disappointed with the prosecution for trying such an important case with such little evidence. But, I am not here to discipline them, although I should, being that there are family members of the victims who are here expecting justice to be served. Because it is the duty of the prosecution to submit either witness testimony or documentation, if not both, stating that the defendant is in fact guilty, it is my duty to dismiss this case on the grounds of *not* insufficient evidence, but *no* evidence on the part of the prosecution. The defendant is to be released immediately." The judged banged her gavel and exited the courtroom to her chambers.

With Candy and Raynail's mother being the only people in court to support Raynail, the anger outweighed the cheers. Reporters filed out of the courtroom, into the hall, where they surrounded the family of the slain officer. Since murder was common among people from the ghetto, the other victims' families walked out of the courtroom like nothing ever happened.

Raynail turned to his lawyer and shook his hand. He turned to Candy and his mother. He pushed his chair to the side, and leaned over the rail that separated the spectators from the defense's table. He wrapped his arms around both of them and gave them a hug.

"You did good, baby, real good." Raynail kissed Candy on her cheek.

"Yeah, you owe me." Candy laughed. "And I'm collecting tonight." She gave him a seductive look.

"Hey, don't talk like that in front of me." His mother smiled. "So you two can spend some time together, I'll watch the baby."

"Naw, Ma, he coming home wit' us," Raynail said.

A deputy walked up behind Raynail. He was waiting to take him to get processed out. Raynail turned around and looked at the deputy. He could feel the deputy's breath on his neck.

Raynail took two steps forward. "Yeah, RayRay gonna come home wit' us. I wanna spend some time wit' him. But what about Saturday?" The deputy cleared his throat and, sensing his urgency, Raynail cut the conversation short. "Look, let me go fill out this paperwork so we can roll out."

"Okay, we'll be waiting for you in the lobby." Candy picked her purse up off the seat. She and her mother-in-law then headed out of the courtroom.

Raynail's mother stopped and turned to look at Raynail.

Raynail, followed by two deputies, walked out of the courtroom and through a side door to the right of the judge's bench.

My baby's coming home . . . He's coming home, she thought. She turned to Candy, who was standing with the door open, and walked out of the courtroom.

Candy was in the kitchen cooking when her cell phone started going off. She picked her cell phone up from the counter. She then looked at the caller ID. She snapped off a paper towel, and wiped grease from her hands onto it.

"So you finally decided to call me, huh?"

"Yeah, um . . . I was just calling to let you know we handled that," Murphy told her.

"But, why haven't you answered my calls," Candy yelled into the phone. She looked over at the couch at Raynail and the baby. "Raynail's court date was a week ago."

"I know why you was calling," he nonchalantly said. "And there's a valid reason why I didn't answer."

"Okay, so why didn't you answer?" Candy walked over to the stove and picked up a fork. She flipped over the chicken in the skillet. She frowned after realizing that Murphy hadn't said anything. "Hello, Murphy?" He still didn't respond. *This nigga think I'm playin'. I hope he ain't tryin'a play me for my money.* "Murphy, what's the scoop!"

"Candy, I'm already knowing you was calling about that job you gave me and that's why I ain't answered the phone. I'm not about to chat about some shit like that over the wire. Plus, I specifically told you not to call me. I told you I would call you when the job was done, and I have. So, don't get all worked up 'cause a nigga didn't answer his phone, 'cause the way I see it, you shouldn't have called me anyway."

Candy didn't feel like arguing. She was just glad that it was over. The money was on point and the two most important men in her life were at home. "A'ight, Murphy, you right. I should have known when he didn't show up in court that the shit was taken care of. We cool. And, yo?"

"Yeah, what's up?" Murphy replied.

"Keep them guns loaded. I might need to use you again." Candy laughed.

"Oh, fo' sho. That's what's up." Murphy laughed before ending the call.

Candy cut the fire off beneath the skillet. She took the chicken out of the skillet and placed it on top of a napkin on a plate. She then walked over to the kitchen table and looked in the living room at her husband and son, who were asleep on the couch. Raynail was lying across the couch with one leg hanging off the couch onto the floor. RayRay was on his chest asleep with his head resting on Raynail's left breast above his heart. It was a father-and-son moment and Candy stood savoring all of it.

Candy thought back to her conversation with Raynail about going legit. She decided that the idea didn't sound so bad after all. The real estate business was booming, and she had met with the owners of several professional basketball teams, hoping to invest.

Five killings in less than a month had tired her out, but the love that she had for her family was worth it. If she had to do it all over again, she would.

Never in her five years of being in the game had she heard of a dude holding things down in the streets the way that she had. Not only did she and Raynail still have all of Century City in Westwood on lockdown, but they also had their love on lockdown.

Dangerous:

A Different Kind of
Girl from the Hood

by

Nikki-Michelle

For Nikeya & Michelle and thanks Dale.

Chapter 1

Don't bother asking my age because I'll never tell you. Don't even bother asking why I was sitting in class, daydreaming about having sex with my teacher even though he had a platinum wedding band on his finger. I never gave two shits about the woman a man had at home, not when I wanted what I wanted. And, what I wanted was him, Mr. Rodriguez. I could always get a man to do whatever I wanted. The more they told me no, the more persistent I became. Telling me no was like telling a brick wall to move. No, to me, meant yes and they just didn't know it yet. No man would ever tell me no and think that would be the end of it.

So there I sat, looking at the teacher; my eyes locked on him as they had been many days since he'd started over a year ago. Not because I gave two shits about what he was teaching, but because he was making me come where I sat. My pussy was so wet that I had crossed my legs and leaned forward to keep myself from sliding out of my desk. He was perfect. He stood all of six feet and I was longing to jump up, wrap my legs around his waist, and ride him until he was begging me to stop. His skin was kissed golden by the sun with dimples evenly placed on either side of his smiling cheeks. He was black. That was obvious. What was also obvious was that he was mixed with Spanish heritage that just made him even more appealing. His lips looked as if they tasted like butterscotch and his eye color matched that of warm, flowing honey. Yes, my teacher was sexy as all get out.

"Okay, so with that being said, who can tell me just what makes applied statistics such a hard concept for some students to grasp?" he asked the class.

"Because the shit is hard," answered a boy in the back of the class, causing a few of us and Mr. Rodriguez to laugh a bit.

"Watch your language, first off. Other than it being hard, what makes applied statistics so hard for some students?"

I raised my hand like a good student.

"Yes, Ms. Dixon."

"Because some students get intimidated by the numbers and the spreadsheets, making it harder than it needs to be."

He nodded my way with a smile. "Although I was looking for a more academic answer, Ms. Dixon laid it out for you in layman's terms. Most people are intimidated when they see what it takes to pass a class such as applied statistics, and they make it much harder on themselves by giving up before they start. Good answer, Ms. Dixon."

I watched as he walked back around his desk and picked up some chalk to write on the board. His masculine makeup from the back was just as delightful as the front.

"Tonight, I want each of you to work on the spreadsheet in workshop in one of your textbooks. Read the directions carefully before starting and do what you can to the best of your ability. This will be for a grade so be sure to turn it in. Tomorrow we will go over it in class and see how we all fared."

Just as he finished talking the ticker went off on my watch, letting me know this class was done for the day. I started to pack my belongings like everyone else and prepared to leave the class. I smiled, thinking that everything I did when it came to getting a man was a calculated move. The way I talked to them, the way I looked at them, the way I dressed: it was all a ploy to get what I wanted. Most times after I was done getting what I wanted, I left them alone, changed phone numbers, and moved on to the next.

"Vix, are we still on for tonight?"

I turned behind me to look at the female standing at the door waiting for me. She was five-eight, had long hair that sat in a natural press against her scalp, and had eyes so dark that they hypnotized you if you stared into them for too long. Her body was sickening: soft, plush D-cup breasts, beautiful chocolate skin, flat stomach, a lush ass, and beautiful hips. I smiled at her and turned back around to catch a glimpse of my teacher.

"I don't see why not. What do you have in mind?"

She stalked closer to me and allowed her breasts to brush my shoulders before standing in front of me to block my view, which kind of annoyed me.

"My place tonight at eight," she said.

I looked up at her with a smile and bit down on my bottom lip as she licked hers. "Okay. See you tonight."

She wasn't smiling as she naturally did when we saw each other. I watched as she looked over her shoulder at Mr. Rodriguez and turned back to me. For a moment she only did that: just stared at me. Her eyes were trying to figure out if I'd found another male victim to add to my list.

"Don't be late," she snapped at me, making me tilt my head and raise an eyebrow at the tone in her voice.

"Excuse me?"

She sighed and softened her facial features. "I'm sorry. I'm just saying, please try not to be late."

She'd pissed me off. One reason was because her tone of voice never sat too well with me when she was being demanding and, second, because she'd made me miss following Mr. Rodriguez as I'd wanted to when he left the classroom. I rolled my eyes and walked off. She'd be lucky to see me at all. I tried rushing down the hall to see if I could see the general direction my potential dick had gone—and nothing. That's okay. Everything happened for a reason and, maybe, it wasn't the time to make my first move yet.

The first thing I did once my classes for the day were over was pull out my iPad and look for my teacher on Facebook. He'd been there for a little over a year and I didn't want to make a move too soon, which was why I chose that moment to send a friend request. I needed to see what he liked to do, what his wife looked like, and what area of metro Atlanta he lived in. Most times people were so careless with the pictures and information they put on Facebook, and it would be too easy to find out all I needed to know. So, once I got home, I went right to my bedroom, and got to work. Finding him, I sent him a friend request and started my plan. In less than no time at all, he accepted my friend request and the first thing I did was go look for pictures of his wife. She was pretty enough. Spanish in heritage with jet-black silky hair and an okay body, if you liked stick figures with what looked to be drawn-on eyebrows.

She was making it easier than it had to be. She looked simple, looked like a basic bitch, and her husband would be under my spell in no time. I laughed to myself and shut my iPad down as I heard the front door open. My mom was home. The one thing that I hated was when she came home from work early because I knew that meant that she would be in my business. She only did that shit to annoy me. I'd moved back in with her when I let go of the last guy I was messing around with. I'd known in order to get rid of him I would have to let go of the apartment he'd gotten for me and all of the other amenities. What? You didn't think I fucked for free, did you? I would never understand how any woman ever suffered or longed for anything. As long as she had pussy between her legs, she could survive. And no man was ever going to fuck me for free. Did I outright charge by the hour? No. I wasn't a whore. I just knew that as good as what I had in between my legs was, he was going to be willing to give me what I wanted and do whatever I asked to get another piece of it.

Looking at my phone as it rang, and because I already knew who it was, I ignored it. She had rubbed me the wrong way so I wouldn't be going to see her later. I'd told her over and over again that it was my pussy and my body, and if I chose to throw it at the president, then it was my prerogative to do so.

I'd been having sex since I was twelve. We'd lived on Staten Island, in what they called Killa Hill, or Park Hill, if you wanted to find it on the map. It was the projects if you'd ever seen any, and I'd grown up always fearful of my neighborhood. The shit that I'd seen no child should ever have to see. That was another reason I sometimes hated my mother. She was so damn clueless as to what was going on right in front of her. Her best friend's husband, who lived right next door to us, was always watching me, always licking his lips and winking at me. My body had always been a conundrum to me. I never understood why I had more ass and titties than the rest of the girls my age.

I was too afraid to ask my mom because she had a hair-trigger attitude back then. My father had left her because of it, among other things. I was coming home from school one day; my mom was somewhere doing God knew what and her best friend's husband saw me coming home. Obviously he knew my mom wasn't around, but he asked if he could come in anyway.

"Yo, Vix, let me come in and chill wit' you until your mom gets back to the crib," he said to me.

It took me a minute to say yes or no. One side of my mind said no. The other side said, Well, he's cool with my mom, so why not?

"Okay. Sure."

I stuck my key in the door and he walked in behind me. He was a cute dude, no lie. Tall, he dressed nice, and he always rocked the hottest clothes and shoes. He was a little too close for comfort so I quickly turned around and pointed to the couch.

"You can sit there," I said nervously.

My young mind didn't even process what was about to happen. I looked up at him as he smirked a bit and walked over to sit on the couch. He moved like time belonged to him. It was clear to me why Shonda was always fighting girls over him. He was fine even to my twelve-year-old eyes. Even some of my friends

I hung around with were talking about how they'd wished they were old enough to catch his attention.

"I . . . I can get you something to drink if you'd like."

I watched as he chuckled. His dark-chocolate eyes looked at me while he licked his lips.

"Yo, why you always speaking all that proper shit all the time? You in the hood and shit and you the only shorty I know that speaks like she from the Hamptons and shit, ma."

I shrugged. "It's just the way I speak." I stood there, twiddling my thumbs as I talked to him.

"Is that right?" he asked as his hands went to his dick and he adjusted it right before me.

I quickly turned my head and pretended to look at the pictures that I'd seen thousands of times on my mom's wall.

"Come 'ere, ma. Sit by me. Talk to me," he said as he patted the spot beside him on the couch.

Something told me that I should have gone in my room and locked the door, but my feet moved me across the floor and there I found myself sitting next to him. I was so nervous my body was shaking because, no matter how friendly he seemed, something just didn't feel right and I found out exactly what that something was.

"You mad sexy, ma. You know that shit right?"

He'd slid closer to me and was leaning down, talking close to my ear. Something that felt like electricity shot through me and made my body jerk away from him. He pulled me back. He smelled good and when his hands found their way between my legs, I tried to squirm away from him again. His big hand squeezed my thigh hard and it hurt.

"Mike, I think you should leave. My mom isn't home—"

"Nah, shorty. You and me about to have a conversation," he said to me as he stood and pulled his coat off.

I saw the gun in his waistband and the squirming I was doing immediately stopped. I watched as he pulled the gun and laid it on the table. My eyes widened and I was frozen in fear.

"Take your shorts off," he ordered, standing in front of me with his arms folded across his chest as he stood in a wide-legged stance.

I nervously stood and did what he asked, my eyes trained on the gun he'd laid on the table. Stepping out of my shorts, I crossed my arms in front of me, trying to hide myself and not liking what I felt was about to happen. He grabbed his dick and licked his lips with a smirk.

"Take everything off, ma. Shirt, bra, panties too."

With tears burning my eyelids and threatening to fall, I did what he asked. What else could I do? I was scared shitless at that point. So there I stood, naked and scared, in nothing but a pair of Jordans and my socks.

What happened next would stick with me for the rest of my life because it was the beginnings of the makings of me. I found myself on my twin-sized bed with a full-grown man on top of me. His fingers, hands, and mouth were touching me in places that they shouldn't have been. I lay there like a statue with tears rolling down my face because, although I was scared and didn't want him to be on top of me, I could feel the tingles in my body that I couldn't explain.

He'd brought the gun in my room with us and had laid it on the lamp table next to my bed. So, while he licked and sucked on my C-cup breasts and his fingers pushed in and out of my still-virginal pussy, my eyes stayed trained on his gun. And, when he slid down and used his mouth on my pussy too, I didn't know what to do. He pushed my legs as far apart as he could and his tongue did something to me that made me close my eyes, and my legs snapped closed tight around his head as my breathing threatened to strangle me.

That's when he stood and pulled all of his clothes off, and that was my first visual of a dick. All I knew at the time was what he'd shown me scared me. As he crawled back in bed on top of me, I screamed out so loud when he tried to force his way inside of me that he quickly put his hand over my mouth.

"Yo, shorty. Shut the fuck up!" He growled that at me as he held his face close to mine.

With tears in my eyes and my voice barely above a whisper, I said to him, "It hurts. Please stop. It hurts, Mike."

He pressed his hand harder down on my mouth. "Shit's suppose to hurt. Just shut the fuck up and let me do what I do. It won't hurt after a while. I'ma let your mouth go but you bet' not fucking scream or I swear to God I'ma lay yo' ass the fuck out! You laid here and let me eat that pussy and shit and that ass came so you gone let me get my shit off too. Don't make me hurt you, Vix, feel me?"

All I could do was think about the gun lying next to me on my night table and nod, and when he pushed inside of me again, I couldn't help it, I screamed and his hand went back over my mouth. He pressed down so hard it felt as if he were going to cave my mouth in. Once he got past something that felt as if my whole pussy was going to fall apart, he fucked the shit out of me. He didn't care that I'd never had sex before. He beat my shit up and all I could do was scream a muffled scream behind his hand. I even tried to push him up off of me but to no avail. He fucked me and he fucked me, until it was only an hour before my mom was to come home. He came on my stomach, my thighs, face, and my breasts. He came anywhere he felt he could and all I could do was lie there and take it.

"Get up, shorty," he said to me as he looked at his watch. "Take yo' covers off and put new ones on, and you have to shower to clean all this blood and my seed off you."

He said all of that while hurrying to put his clothes on. I could barely walk and when I tried to stand my body crumbled to the floor.

"Damn, ma. Get the fuck up," he growled at me. "You better not say shit to nobody about what the fuck just went down, Vix. Swear to God. You hear me?"

He said that to me as he picked his gun up and put it back in his waistband. I nodded quickly and latched on to his arm as he pulled me up from the floor.

"Stop crying and shit, and act normal. Don't fucking tell ya moms shit about what just happened."

He looked scared and I felt like I was about to die. All I did was nod as he grabbed my sheets off my bed and stuffed them in his coat.

"Put some new sheets on yo' bed and fix that motherfucker back like it was. Go take a wash up or some shit too."

For the next few minutes I did everything he told me to do as he barked out orders and erased any evidence of his existence. When my mom came home, my homework was done, her dinner was cooking, and I was hiding in my bedroom, pretending to be sick.

So, what? Please don't feel sorry for me. I got taught a valuable lesson throughout that whole experience. Pussy makes the world go 'round, as they say. At least, I knew mine did. After that day, I learned to get smart. Mike kept coming around and kept doing whatever he felt like doing to my body. One day I heard Shonda and my mom talking about how a woman shouldn't be fucking for free and how they would make a man pay for it in some kind of way. So that's what I started doing to Mike. He liked to stick his big dick in me whenever he felt like it, so I made him start buying me the clothes and Jordans that I loved so much back then. You wouldn't catch me dead in a pair of Jordans now.

He always asked me what I wanted, or if I needed anything, and my young ass was forever saying no. I don't know why, but one day that all changed. I learned how to hold out until he got me what I wanted and after a while I'd learned how to play that little game well. By the time I turned thirteen he was putty in my hands. I had him taking from his wife to give to me and to make sure I had what I wanted and needed. He was a damn junky and I was his crack.

After a while, I was sure his wife caught on. As a matter of fact, I'd known she had, but instead of being mad at him the stupid bitch started to come at me. That's when she and my mom fell out. They got into a knockdown, drag-out fight right in the middle of the street. My mom dragged her ass up and down Park Hill Avenue because there was no way my mom was going to believe that her baby was fucking her best friend's husband. Ha! If only she'd known.

Chapter 2

The next day started off wrong all because of what had happened the night before. First off, my female lover and I had a fight once she realized that she wasn't going to see me like she had planned. The thing with this bitch was that she knew no matter how many times she showed her ass, I would always allow her to come back. For some reason there was no way I could say no to her for too long. She was the first woman I was with, and there were times when I hated her for that. She literally put her hands on me. Once eight o'clock rolled around and she hadn't heard from me she decided to show up at Barnes & Noble where she knew I would be. I was always there around that time of the day because I loved to read and they satisfied my hunger for knowledge.

She showed up and as soon as I saw her I knew the look on her face. In order to keep her from embarrassing us both, I quickly packed

up and met her at the entrance. I'd known what
she was upset about. She was mad because she
knew my eyes were on my teacher. I never hid
anything from her or anyone I was involved with.
Honesty had always kept me drama free, or so I
thought. I was finding out that the more honest I
was with her, the more she found a way to try to
start some shit with me.

"I don't understand why you keep doing this
kind of thing," she said to me with a scowl on her
face as we both walked back out of the store.

"And I don't understand, nor do I care, that
you don't understand. I've asked you countless
times not to question what I do. It's my business
and I don't question you."

I knew she was referring to me having a thing
for my teacher. As I moved past her, she went to
reach for me and I cringed away from her touch.
Sometimes her touch annoyed me. Sometimes it
sickened me.

"Don't touch me," I snapped at her while getting
into my car.

"I'm sorry, Vix. I didn't mean to upset you, but
what about my feelings? We were supposed to
spend the night together."

Many nights I spent in her bed, only to wake
up the next day regretting it, sick over it.

"I changed my damn mind," I said as I pressed
the button to let my window up.

I followed her all the way to her condo, our safe haven, down near midtown Atlanta. It made her feel safer. It was away from prying eyes and, being that she wanted no one to know about our relationship, it was perfect for her. She didn't even think she was gay, and who would be okay knowing the dean of a school was carrying on a lesbian affair with one of her students? Although I'd told her I'd changed my mind we both knew where we'd end up. It took us no time to get to her condo and my night went downhill from there.

"I'm so damn sick of you doing this to me, Vixen," she yelled at me once we'd arrived at her place.

The one thing she hated was to be ignored and I'd ignored her constant calls the whole ride over. Something about our relationship sickened me at times and, no, it had nothing to do with us hiding behind the guise of her being married and having a child. None of that mattered at the moment because she had called me a name that brought back many hurtful childhood memories, and I had asked her over and over again never to call me that when we were together. But, like always, she wanted to hurt me and hit with low blows.

I turned on her so fast she backed up and stumbled a bit. "Don't you ever call me that again."

She caught her balance and smirked. "Why? That's your name isn't it?" she asked.

I stormed past her and jammed my key into the lock, shoving the front door open. I threw my purse and keys on a table in the hall as I made my way up the stairs to our bedroom.

"How many times do I have to ask you not to call me that? You know damn well why, so don't play stupid."

I turned and faced her just as she was walking into the room. I should have known she wanted to badly start an argument just to keep me near her. She slammed the door before scowling at me.

"You always want me to play by your rules, while you run around here and throw pussy at any man willing to catch it. Sometimes you make me so fucking sick."

I simply stared at her with a disgusted look on my face. "Good, then you know how I feel almost each and every time I let you touch me!"

I made the mistake of turning my back on her after saying that and the next thing I felt was her hand wrapped around my ponytail and my neck being yanked back. If there was anything that I

would never go for, it was the people I allowed
to share a bed with me to put their hands on me.
She must have quickly forgotten who the hell I
was and what hood I grew up in. Fighting was in
my blood. I didn't go around starting them but I
damn sure loved to finish them. Growing up on
Staten Island in Killa Hill had afforded me the
luxury of learning how to defend myself at any
cost. I turned around and quickly reminded her
of just who the hell I was. The only difference
between her and me was that I remembered she
grew up in Flatbush. That meant I would not be
foolish enough to underestimate her. The details
of the fight I won't give. Let's just say I left there
with no intentions of ever returning and I knew I
was lying to myself.

You have no idea how much I really hated
that woman at times and, then, there were times
when I loved her. It was a complicated thing to
explain and even after all of that, I lay there and
let her pleasure herself at my expense, let her use
her tongue, hands, and fingers to bring herself
to an orgasm like only I could give her. Not even
her husband could make her come the way I
could and sometimes, most times, I didn't even
have to touch her. It's the kind of relationship
we had. I don't even think it bothered her that I
simply lay there.

All of that led to me sitting in class, frustrated, with tears rolling down my face. My lover was intent on making my life a living hell and if I wasn't careful, I would end up letting her. She had some kind of control over this situation that I didn't like. I didn't even participate in class like I wanted to because I couldn't get myself together long enough to do so.

"Ms. Dixon, can I get you to stay after class for a few minutes today?" Mr. Rodriguez asked me to my total surprise.

I looked up at him and nodded. "Sure."

"Good. The rest of you, I will see you all tomorrow and I want to thank you all for being my best class this semester."

A couple of cheers and a few students later we were all alone. I watched as he perched on the corner of his desk, one hip sitting on the desk with one foot on the floor. He looked at me with a smile, his dimples playing on both his cheeks.

"Is there any reason my best student wasn't participating in class today? I see you seem to be a little down. You've been that way for the last couple of days. Everything okay?"

I smiled to myself, and although things with my lover had been rough, I had no idea it would play the man I wanted right into my hands. I'd be sure to thank her later.

I nodded, taking the time to wipe my eyes. "Just going through some things at home, and relationship issues. You know, life."

"I understand that, but let's not let it get in the way of school. Like I said, you're one of my best students and your last two assignments have garnered you Bs when I know you could easily have As."

I watched as he stood and walked around his desk, pulling his briefcase up and preparing to leave.

"I know and I'm sorry. Sometimes, I just get so caught up in things . . ."

He looked up at me. "Is there anything with the assignments you need help on? Even though the answer is probably no, it seems as if for the past couple days you've only been doing enough to get by. I don't want those Bs to drop to Cs. I take pride in my students and my work."

I stood, grabbing my purse and my laptop bag. "Well, actually, there was this one thing that keeps confusing me —"

He cut me off as he looked at the time on his watch. "Look, right now I have to get out of here and pick my wife up, but, how about meeting me at Barnes & Noble tomorrow at seven-thirty? I meet with a couple of students in a study group to help them with homework and whatever else they need. Only thing is, you have to be there on time because once I start I don't let anyone else in. It's not fair to the other students that I have to start over because one was inconsiderate and late."

Watching him as he picked up his briefcase and ushered me out of the classroom, I made sure to get as close to him as I could. "Okay, I'll be there, and thank you again."

For the second time that day he smiled while looking down at me. "Good, and don't be late. Like I said, you're a great student and I don't want to see you fall by the wayside because of issues unrelated to school."

After a few more words of encouragement from him, our conversation ended and I smiled, knowing I was one step closer to getting my man. A few minutes later, I walked into my mother's home to her and my stepfather having one of their famous arguments. He wanted another child and she didn't. My mom was adamant about keeping her womb closed and off limits.

"I don't get it. You always say no, but you never give a clear-cut answer as to why," Frank said to her.

Frank was a nice brother, always had been, but he was not what my mother wanted and that was clear as day to everyone but him. They'd been

married for two years, and had met not long
after we'd moved to Atlanta almost four years
ago. He wooed her, pursued her, and eventually
won her over. It was easy to see why my mom
had married him. He was a walking bank, a very
respectable man, and he had a big dick. I knew
because I'd seen him naked. I told him it was an
accident, but I walked right in the bathroom on
him. The man's body was to die for and he knew
it, but, being the man he was he quickly covered
himself. I quickly pretended to be shielding my
eyes, while looking at the long, thick, chocolate
dick that hung between his legs.

"Frank, I'm not giving you no damn kids!
Having Vix damn near killed me," she said to
him as she stood.

"Tammi, that's real bull, baby. I know it is because I've heard you telling some of your friends
how she gave you no trouble at all carrying her.
Baby, you have a beautiful body so I know it will
bounce back if that's what you're worried about."

He knew my mom very well. She was very
superficial. I stopped and spoke to them before
heading to my room.

"Hello, both of you," I said.

My mom didn't speak. She walked past me
into the kitchen.

"What's up, Vix? How was your day?" Frank said to me.

I walked into the front room and bent down to give him a hug. "It was okay. You know how it is with school and all."

Before he could respond my mom walked back in with a smug smile on her face and her glass of Moscato, which she drank faithfully every night. She kept her eyes locked on me. A message that read she was watching me.

"Vix, don't let the pressure get to you. You're a good student. Your mom and I are proud of you."

I smiled in his direction. "Thank you, Frank. That's good to hear. Mom, and how was your day?"

She took a sip of her Moscato and looked at me. "It went well, baby, despite a few setbacks at the job. Other than that all is well."

She pulled her feet up under her on the sofa and leaned into Frank. I smiled and shook my head as his arms wrapped around her and she pointed the remote at the TV. My mom and I had started having a rocky relationship when I turned fourteen. She'd caught me in bed with one of her male friends and had never looked at me the same. It hurt at first, but after a while, I started to care less and less.

"Sorry to hear that, mother dear. Hope things work out better for you." Pretending to be tired I looked at my watch. "I'll be in my room if I'm needed."

I walked over and kissed my mother's jaw, feeling her slightly cringe away, and then kissed Frank's jaw close to his lips, just to piss her off, before walking up the stairs to my room. Our relationship was a tricky one. On any given day, at any given moment, we could come to blows, which was why I had to hurry and get my own place again. I could easily go out and find a job, as my resume was job ready, but I liked to have men supply my needs and wants. And, no, there was no shame in my game and there never would be. Yes, I used my body to get men to do whatever the hell I wanted them to and I was proud of it.

Walking into my room, I threw my purse on the bed and looked around. It was clean, bigger than a one-bedroom studio. All of the walls were white, minus an accent wall that was painted desert red. My cherry-wood California king–sized bed sat against the accent wall, along with my nightstand, and my dresser sat against the wall on the opposite side. The hardwood floor needed to be swept to get rid of strands of hair. It was nice, but no way could I keep bottled up in there. I had to get out of the house and make something happen. It had always been clear that many women would disagree with what I chose to do to get by, but those same women were sitting around broke with no life. Those same women had to worry about how their rent would be paid, or how their children would be fed, or even how any of their bills would be paid for that matter. Not me. At that very moment my bank account sat pretty, way over the amount of an average upper middle-class working woman. Why? Because I made sure any man willing to sleep with me would be willing to open his wallet. If I was to freely give you sex at your demand then you needed to be freely ready to open your wallet at my demand and it was just that simple.

I walked into the bathroom and turned on the shower, needing to give myself a way to relax. *Damn, I miss my old apartment,* I thought as I stepped into my walk-in shower. I smiled to myself, excited about the fact that the next day my plan to seduce my teacher would go into effect. No, he didn't have the pockets that normally attracted me to a man, but my taste was versatile. Mr. Rodriguez was finer than words could explain and I'd never had Latin dick. It would be a first.

I laughed as I turned the shower off and stepped out. Even the cold air hitting my nipples excited me. Maybe I should have gone to see a doctor. My love for sex could have easily been classified as an addiction. I shrugged and walked over to my window, pulling the curtain wide. I knew most of my neighbors had gotten used to the show I would put on for them. I was very free with my body. I didn't care who saw it, but to touch it was a different thing all together.

I squealed and jumped when my door came open.

"Oh shit. Oh. My bad, Vix. I . . . I . . . Your mother told me to come in here and get something for her. She said you were in the guest room. I'm so sorry."

I laughed to myself once I realized it was Frank. The look on his face was priceless. His eyes had bugged out and he quickly turned around like he'd laid eyes upon Jesus. I loved it. I walked from around my bedpost and leaned in front of it, still naked and wet.

"Well, what did she need, Frank?"

"Um. She said something about a black bag in the closet."

I giggled and walked over to my walk-in closet. It was fully filled with designer clothes, coats, jackets, shoes, boots, purses, and accessories,

courtesy of my female lover. I bent over and
Frank must have turned back around.

"Oh, my fucking God. Vix, put some damn
clothes on," he bellowed out.

I shook my head and walked over to him. He'd
turned his back again.

"Why, Frank? It's just ass, pussy, and breasts.
Geez. You act as if you've never seen the three
before."

I dropped the bag behind him so he'd have no
choice but to turn around and face me to pick it
up.

"Vix, put something on, okay? I've known you
since you were—"

"Since you started dating my mom." I stepped
closer and placed my breasts against his back.
"Tell me you've never thought about how good
this pussy could be," I whispered in his ear as
my hands came around and stroked his dick
through his slacks.

He gripped my wrists tight and quickly turned
around; his eyes blazed red in anger as he shook
me hard once and pushed me away from him.
I stumbled back but caught my balance, my
breasts swaying hard against gravity.

"What the fuck is wrong with you, girl?"

He looked like he wanted to hit me, but caught
himself. I watched as he snatched the black bag

up from the floor and stormed out of the room. I laughed to myself and lay back on the bed. He could pretend as if he didn't want it, but I felt the way his dick stirred around when I touched him. He wanted it. I laughed again and went to press play on my iPod. Lil' Kim's "Big Momma Thang" came blasting through the speakers. I danced around my room, window open, simply not giving a damn. I heard my mom asking Frank what was wrong and why he was angry. Next thing I heard was the front door slamming and I got to my window in time to see Frank drive off. The man next door stood slack jawed in his window as he caught a glimpse of my bouncing breasts before I snatched the curtains closed. Living in a nice neighborhood didn't mean you didn't have perverts. It just meant there were more of them.

It didn't take long for my mother to come charging up the stairs. She shoved the door open and came right for me, snatching me by my hair, slinging me on the bed. I screamed and kicked my feet to get her off of me. A kick landed in her stomach and made her fall back.

"You get your shit and get the fuck out of my house, Vix. You will not keep disrespecting me."

"I don't even know what you're talking about," I lied.

She walked over and sent my iPod crashing to the floor before going to my closet, snatching clothes out, and throwing them on the floor as she yelled.

"You're a damned liar. Frank told me that shit you pulled with him. Sick of you, Vix. You're trifling and you don't give a shit about nobody but yourself. You have to get the hell up out of here before you make me kill your ass."

For some reason, I didn't panic, because I really didn't think she would throw me out. My mom had never turned her back on me for anyone, even when we had our fights and even when she caught her male friend in bed with me before. She'd gone upside his head and, yes, she and I had fought, but she still never turned her back on me. So there was no reason for me to think she was serious at that moment, especially not after all she'd done to me.

"Mom, you're not serious right now."

"Like hell I'm not," she said as she stormed past me and opened dresser drawers, repeating the process she had done to my closet while I ran over to try to stop her.

"Mom, what are you doing? You can't put me out. I have no place to go."

She snatched away from me and pushed me back. "You should have thought of that before you disrespected me in my home. That's my damn husband!"

I looked at her in disbelief. She didn't even want Frank. She just wanted a man to have one. Frank was all for show for her perfect life. After running away from the demons of her past in New York, she came to Atlanta and made a whole new life for her and me, but still, some of those very same demons she'd run from followed us to Atlanta.

"You don't even want your damn husband and you're mad at me for wanting him? He's only here for show, to paint the perfect picture of this life you want."

"Vix, get out of my damn face before you make me hurt you." Her chest heaved up and down as her fist balled at her side.

"We both know the real reason you're mad and it has nothing to do with Frank."

She slapped me hard enough to draw tears, but I stood my ground.

"You can be mad at all you want, Mama, but sooner or later Frank is going to leave for the same reason my daddy did and, once again, you'll be all alone. Only this time, I won't be around to pick your sorry ass up and carry you."

She slapped me again, but I was used to her slaps and, although it knocked another set of tears from my eyes, I stood firm.

"You have five minutes to get what you can and get the hell out of here or else I'm going to throw you out, and don't try me, Vix. Please don't call my bluff."

She turned and stormed out of my room, slamming the door behind her. No matter how hard she ran or how far she ran she would still be a hood bitch. No matter the image she painted for the outside world, our demons would always chase us.

I quickly pulled on a tight-fitting sweat suit and slid my feet into a pair of sneakers, no socks, and grabbed what I could carry with me to a hotel. By the time I finished packing, I heard Frank walk back in the house. His and my mama's voices could be heard traveling up the stairs through my closed door as they argued. I threw my duffle bag over my shoulders, picked up my purse and cell, then made my way down the stairs. Frank's eyes were the first thing I saw. At first he averted them like I made him uncomfortable, then he kept them locked to mine. I had no idea what he was thinking and I wasn't going to stick around and find out. I walked out of my mama's home and never looked back.

Chapter 3

The next day found me in a hotel room off of Southlake. I didn't even bother to travel far. I had plans to go to my lover's place, but she'd been more of a headache than it was worth as of late. I skipped all my classes and stayed locked away in the suite I'd booked at Hampton Inn. I only needed a place to lay my head for the night before figuring out what it was I'd do next. To be honest, I never thought my mom would let me walk away, let alone kick me out. I guess Frank meant more to her than I thought, although I doubted it. She was the type that didn't want a man but wanted no one else to have him either.

I rolled over in bed and looked at the time. Realizing that I didn't want to check out, I called down to the front desk and booked the room for an extra day. Afterward I simply closed my eyes and went back to sleep, not wanting to think about the fact that for the first time I was homeless. Another reason I didn't have my old place was because I'd let my lover talk me out of keeping it. She wanted me to be done with the man I'd been seeing, period. And, because she'd told me that she'd purchased that condo for us, I'd agreed to it. I'd probably end up at her condo, but just needed the time at the hotel to clear my head and get my thoughts together.

I was young in age and had been through a hell of a lot, shit most people wouldn't survive. The one thing I'd never forget was watching my daddy try to kill my mama. That day, I'd thought he'd end her. My daddy was a good man, too. He'd never raised a hand to me or my mother, and he let me get away with anything. He'd loved my mama, too, but my mama had demons, real bad ones. Since the day Daddy found out just what my mother liked to do when she wasn't with him, he'd never been the same. He left and never looked back. He tried to take me with him, but I couldn't leave her. She begged me not to leave her and I couldn't. She'd always taken care of me, never done any harm to me, which was why I was shocked that she actually kicked me out.

My phone vibrating alerted me to an incoming text. It was my lover asking me to come see her. I ignored her. Although she claimed to love me, every time she wanted to see me, it involved sex and, not that I was complaining, but I wasn't in the mood. After her texts went unanswered she called over and over until I simply turned my phone off. I must have fallen asleep not soon after because I woke up seven hours later. I looked at the clock, realizing that I only had thirty minutes to make it to the session my teacher was having at Barnes & Noble. I quickly jumped up and got dressed. It took me fifteen minutes to get myself together. Good thing Barnes & Noble was right down the street. As I drove, I remembered his warning about not being late, but I couldn't care less. My mission was still to get him. No matter what was going on in my personal life, I wouldn't allow it to stop me.

Needless to say, by the time I got there everyone was packing up to leave. I spotted Mr. Rodriguez as students were leaving and rushed over to him. He spotted me from the corner of his eye as he sat at the table, gathering his things.

"Ms. Dixon, nice of you to show up. I didn't spot you in class today, either," he said as he looked up at me.

He was so sexy. Those honey-golden eyes looked up at me, waiting for me to give him a plausible excuse.

"I tried to get here on time, but things at home just aren't working too well for me—"

"Excuses are for people looking for a way out, Ms. Dixon. Now, I opened the spot for you in this group because you're one of my best students and because you said you needed help. There were many other students whom I told no when they asked to join after the deadline who needed to be here more than you."

I watched as he stood and grabbed his leather laptop bag and threw it over his shoulders.

"I know and I'm really sorry, but some things can't be helped, Mr. Rodriguez—"

"Still making excuses, Ms. Dixon. If you want to be here tomorrow then be here; if not, I will carry on and you will not be allowed another chance. This session is over. See you tomorrow."

And with that, he left me there looking like a fool. I sighed and shook my head. I should have just stayed in my hotel room. All of this to get some dick was not what I was used to. Usually it took me no time to hook and snare a man. I picked up my face and walked out to my car, but realized I was hungry. Quickly turning back around I went inside the café at Barnes & Noble and ordered myself a sandwich and a red velvet muffin, with a white chocolate mocha. I did all of that to get to the register and realize I'd left my damn wallet in my hotel room. Feeling embarrassed, I cursed myself and just walked away from the counter.

I wanted to scream, but just walked to my car, shaking my head, then realized I'd left my keys on the damn counter at the register. I laughed at the craziness of it all, but before I could turn around and make my way back in the store, Mr. Rodriguez called my name. I turned around and he stood there with my keys and the food I'd ordered.

"Thank you." I smiled and shook my head. "You didn't have to buy the food."

"It was nothing," he said as he passed my keys to me and the bag with my food in it.

I watched as he looked past me to my car. I'd just realized that clothes were still thrown haphazardly across the back seat. I laughed to myself at how it must have looked and was about to explain that it wasn't as it looked when I stopped myself. *Maybe this can work in my best interest if I play my cards right,* I thought.

I gave what appeared to him to be an embarrassed smile. "Have some things going on at home . . ."

"It's okay. You don't have to explain anything," he said as he looked at me and we both stood silent for a moment. "Is there anything I can do to help?"

I quickly shook my head. "No. I'll get it figured out in a couple of days."

"Are you living in your car?"

I looked up at the concern etched over his face. He'd probably go home and tell his wife about how it was sad to see one of his students live such a way. That only made me want him more. Lots of things attracted me to a man, not just his pockets.

I shrugged and looked at him while I fumbled around with my keys. "Technically," I answered. "I have a hotel room, but tomorrow is my last day, then I have to figure out my plan B."

"You have no family that could lend a hand?"

"My mom is the one who put me out. All my family that I know of is back in New York."

He put a hand in his pocket and we both pulled our jackets closed when the wind came barreling through.

"Look, I have to get going to pick my wife up from work, but look on the class Web site and take my cell down. Call me and let me know you're okay and I'll see what I can do to get you some help. You shouldn't be living in your car and you need to figure out where you'll sleep after tonight. My wife works with a women's shelter. I'll talk to her and see what we can help with."

I was surprised when he took my keys from my hand, unlocked my door, and held it open for me. I got in and took my keys when he held them out to me.

"Thank you. I really appreciate this. I'll pay you back."

"You worry about getting a roof over your head. Maybe you can go back and talk to your mom. Maybe you and she can work something out?"

I shook my head. "I'll take my chances in a hotel. Thank you again. I have to go."

I pulled my door closed and waited for him to back away before starting the car and backing out. I'd made up my mind already that there was no way I was setting foot back in my mom's home. That was her first and last time putting me out.

I made it back to the hotel and showered, all the while thinking of ways to get out of this hotel and find me a suitable place to live. I could have gone out and found me another sponsor, but I wasn't in the mood. I hadn't been touched by a man in six months and I needed to be touched badly. I always waited before jumping to another sponsor so as not to get anything mixed up. I needed to make sure one was completely out of the picture before stepping to another. While I loved men, sex, dick, and money, I was not about to possibly get caught in the crossfire of two men fighting. Yes, my pussy was just that good.

It didn't take long after I got out of the shower for my phone to start ringing.

"Hello?"

"Where are you?"

"Why?"

"Because I want to see you, Vix."

"Why? So you can start another fight?"

She sighed. "No, baby. I miss you and I'm sorry. You know I just hate to see you give my love away."

"Give it away? I'm not seeing anyone but you." I sat down on the bed and began oiling my legs.

"I know, but I see the way you look at him. He's married and he barely pays you any attention anyway, Vix. Why do you throw yourself at these men?"

"I don't throw myself at any man and even if I did, it's my prerogative."

She was silent for a moment. Her voice was beautiful, very smooth and feminine, the kind that could make any man weak at the knees.

"They'll never love you like I do."

"I don't want them to."

"Fuck you, Vix."

I'd known that would make her mad.

"You can if you want to."

Just like I knew what would make her mad, I knew what would calm her down.

"Really?"

I could hear the excitement in her voice.

"Yes, really. I'm horny and need a fix. Where are you?"

"Our place."

"Okay. Be there in an hour."

It was nothing to get her to calm down and it meant that I could get out of that hotel room. I finished oiling my skin and pulled on a sweater dress with no underwear. The wind against my yoni felt good to me. On the drive over to her place, I thought about my life. Ever since I could remember I'd been a fighter except for that first time being touched by a man. Even when I knew he was violating me, I didn't fight back hard enough and that shit always bothered me. I couldn't tell you why. I never had the urge to be a victim of my circumstances like most of the people from my hood. Most of those motherfuckers were okay forever being what they called "hood." Not me. I was so happy when my mom finished school and pulled us up out of there.

I remember one morning stepping out of the building we'd lived in. I was on my way to school, and my friends and I stepped right over a dead body. The sad part about it was we'd gotten so used to it that we stepped over it just as if it was a piece of trash in the street. Police, sirens, and crime scene tape, those were our Christmas decorations at one point in time. Used needles, condoms, and crack pipes seemed to be our Christmas ornaments. Never again would I go back to that.

My car started beeping. I looked at the dashboard and shook my head. I never remembered to put gas in my car until the last minute and it'd finally caught up with me. My car was threatening to cut off on me and before I made it to an exit I ended up having to pull over on the side of the road.

"Damn."

I looked behind me at headlights, shaking my head as other cars passed me. I was about to call my lover when I remembered Mr. Rodriguez telling me to call him. I believed in a thing called fate and I liked to think fate had something to do with the situation I was in. I'd taken the time when I got back to the hotel room to take his number from the school Web site. I dialed his number and waited.

"Hello," he answered, sounding as if he was sleeping.

"Hi. Is this Mr. Rodriguez?"

"*Sí*. Who's calling?"

Damn, that simple yes in Spanish made my yoni thump.

"This . . . this is Vix Dixon. I was calling—"

"Hold on," he said before I could finish.

I heard him speaking to someone in Spanish in the background and it sounded like covers rustling, like he was getting out of bed. I could tell he had gone somewhere quiet because I could no longer hear the TV that had been blaring in the background.

"What can I do for you, Ms. Dixon?"

I put on my best damsel-in-distress voice. "I called because you said I could if I needed anything. I'm kind of stuck on the side of the road."

"What do you mean kind of stuck?"

"My car ran out of gas. I was driving around to see if I could find a cheaper hotel and I forgot I needed gas."

I heard water running as he talked. "Still no help from anyone who could let you stay with them?"

"No, I don't have friends like that."

He sighed. "Where are you, Ms. Dixon?"

"I'm stuck on 75 North just before exit 246."

"Okay. I'll be there in thirty. Stay in the car, keep the doors locked, and turn your blinkers on. I'll call this number back when I think I see you."

"Okay and thank you."

I smiled to myself as I pressed the end call button on my cell. I was beyond excited and felt my nipples harden at the thought of him being near me. His wife had to be dumber than a box of rocks. No way would I allow my husband to come out alone and help some random woman. I pulled down my visor and made sure my lips were still glossy and my hair still had its fluff. I love the way my hair flowed down my back, and its natural auburn color always got compliments. I was only a couple of exits away from my lover's condo, but was in no hurry to get there. I looked at my cell as it rang. I ignored it and got out of the car after pushing the button to pop my trunk. Although the sweater dress was warm, it wasn't warm enough to keep out the chills.

It wasn't too long before the horns started blaring as men caught the sight of my heart-shaped ass bent over in the trunk of my car. I had to search in a few bags before I found a coat. Just as I was pulling it on, my cell rang and I rushed back around to the front seat to grab it.

"Hello?" I answered.

"Ms. Dixon, I asked you to stay in your car until I got to you. It's not safe for a woman to do what you're doing."

I saw his headlights pull in behind me and looked over my shoulders with a smile. Excitement rained over me.

"I was cold. Just got out to get a coat."

"It was still a bad judgment call, Ms. Dixon."

He didn't say anything else and a few seconds later he appeared at my driver's side door. I had one foot in and one foot out of the car as he kneeled down and immediately looked at my gas gauge.

"Start your car if you can."

I did what he asked, and it had just enough juice so he could see that I really had no gas. Him being so close to me in such an intimate way made me lick my lips as I looked down at him.

"I always do this and it finally caught up with me."

"Do what?"

"Wait until the last minute to put gas in my car."

He made the mistake of looking straight ahead and caught a glimpse of my bare essentials. I wanted to smirk, but quickly played coy by pulling my dress down and pulling my other leg into the car. The fact that it made him nervous because he rubbed the top of his head and looked away quickly turned me on. His Spanish heritage gave him black, shiny, silky hair that sat in a low cut on his head. He smelled good and he looked even better. He smelled like a spicy musk and Ivory bath soap. I was about to make my move when the horn blared from his truck. I quickly turned around, then looked back at him.

He looked up at me. "I brought my wife with me."

I wanted to laugh to myself at the way he said it. It was like he knew what I was up to and he was sending a message, but his wife I couldn't care less about. I heard a door slam behind us and looked to see a woman walking toward us with her arms folded. It was clear that she was cold even underneath her coat, scarf, and hat. Even I was surprised at how cold Atlanta's weather had gotten.

"Is she okay?" I heard her ask.

He quickly stood and walked to meet her halfway. I listened to him tell her that they would have to take me to get gas. Not wanting to be rude, I stepped out of my car to introduce myself. His wife's nice demeanor immediately faltered.

"This," she stated firmly as she pointed at me. "This is your student?"

Trouble in paradise, I thought as I walked over to introduce myself. I watched as he closed the gap between them as he talked to her.

"*Sí*, she is my student, Maria. Nothing more."

"Motherfucker, you must think I'm stupid or something?" Her Spanish accent was thick. She reminded me of the Puerto Rican chicks from back home.

"Maria, *calmar los ánimos. No hacerlo aquí.* I brought you with me. Do you think I would have done that had it been anything else?"

He was holding her arms as he spoke to her, searching her face for some hope that she believed him, but she kept her eyes locked on me. I smirked.

"Nigga, get your hands off me. You think I'm stupid, Alex? Huh? Think I'm gon' sit my ass at home this time and pretend that I don't notice your shit starting to stank?"

He stepped closer to her and, although I couldn't make out what he was saying, I could tell he was speaking through clenched teeth. Whatever he said to her calmed her down enough to stop her from talking. I waved at her and walked back to my car and a few seconds later he came back.

"I can take you to a gas station just off this exit and get you some gas. I have a container in my truck."

I was about to respond when, much to the surprise of us both, his wife started his truck and pulled off into traffic. To be honest, I didn't know whether to jump for joy or be embarrassed for him. Some women are so fucking stupid and her stupidity just put her husband right into the lion's den.

He pursed his lips and cursed in Spanish.

I sat with my mouth open in mock shock and surprise. "Oh my God! Did she just leave you out here?"

I got out of my car and walked back to my trunk. I pulled off my thigh-high boots and grabbed my Nike Shox, throwing them on.

"Look, I'm sorry about this," he said to me as he watched me. "You can sit in your car and I'll walk to get you some gas. Do you have a gas container?"

I shook my head as I pulled my coat from the car, then my purse and cell, before slamming the door closed.

"If I'd known this would have been such a hassle for you, I wouldn't have called. I could have just walked myself."

He grabbed me by my arm to turn me to face him after I hit the button to set the alarm on my car.

"Look, just relax, okay? I said I would go and get the gas for you. Stay here until I get back."

"No. It's cold, and at least when we get to a gas station I can warm up."

He looked at me for a moment and then nodded. "Okay, but walk on the inside. I don't want you to get hit."

I nodded and we began to walk. Judging by the looks of things it would be a minute before we found a gas station. We walked in silence for a while. My phone kept ringing. My lover was probably furious that I wouldn't answer the phone. In this case, she could wait. I was cold and pissed.

"I'm sorry about the thing with your wife. I didn't mean to cause any problems," I finally said to him after we'd walked a mile or so.

"Trust me, you're not the real issue," he responded. His tall frame towered over me and even with his shoulders bunched up and hands deep in his pockets, he was still sexy.

"Well whatever it is, I triggered her outburst and I'm sorry."

He looked at me as we walked, both almost frozen stiff. "It's my own issues and shit that caused that. I guess seeing you opened old wounds for her."

As cars zoomed past and some blew their horns at us in annoyance, we kept walking, having this mild conversation to taper away at the awkwardness of it all.

"May I ask why?"

He simply looked at me for a moment before sighing and shaking his head. "We shouldn't be having this conversation. I shouldn't even be out with you, but I couldn't just leave you there. I could lose my job for this and although you and your mom are at odds, I'm sure she wouldn't be pleased with your teacher out like this with you."

"Probably not, but it's not like I could have called her."

He didn't say anything after that. We turned the corner coming off of the exit and he sighed realizing we should have walked the other way, but we kept walking anyway.

"Look for a sign that may lead us back to any expressway. They usually have gas stations not too far away from them."

I nodded and kept my eyes open as we walked Pryor Street SW. It took us a while, but we finally found a Chevron after he stopped and asked a police officer. The officer was nice enough to take us to the gas station. I was damn near frozen as we slid into the police car. He allowed me to sit in the front seat and I noticed his eyes stayed on my thighs most of the drive. I sat there thinking about how I'd gotten myself into the situation. My lover kept calling and I knew she was probably pissed, but she'd still have to wait, regardless.

I got out of the car once we pulled into the station, and went into the store. I was thirsty and wanted water but needed to warm my insides, so I grabbed myself, Mr. Rodriguez, and the officer some cappuccino. I also grabbed a couple bags of chips and Snicker bars. I paid for it all along with gas and walked back to the car.

"Thank you. I appreciate it," the officer said when I handed him the cup of cappuccino.

"You're welcome. We would have still been walking and searching if it wasn't for you. So thank you."

He was an older gentlemen but it was clear that underneath his uniform he worked out faithfully. He had a deep voice, like Barry White, with a low-cut fade that made his angular face even more attractive. On any other night he would have been my next catch. My phone rang out again and again; I ignored it. I waited until Alex, as his wife had called him, finished pumping the gas into the container and handed him his cup.

"Hold it for a second. Need to run into the store for a minute."

I nodded and watched as he briskly walked while pulling out his cell. It was no secret that he was probably calling his wife. I watched as he bypassed the counter and headed for the bathroom. It wasn't all that long before he came back out and stopped at the counter, probably thinking he had to pay for the gas. I sighed and shook my head as I set the bag down and finally picked up my phone.

"Hello?"

"Where the fuck are you?"

I was silent as I watched Mr. Rodriguez walk back over to me. "You paid for the gas? You have enough money to do that?" he asked me.

I covered the phone. "Yeah, it's nothing. Thank you though. You want your cappuccino now?"

He looked at me and for the first time I realized that he was checking me out. His eyes were roaming my face and he gave me a brief once-over before taking the cup from my hand.

"Let's get you back to your car, Ms. Dixon," he responded once he realized that my eyes stayed locked on his for a little too long.

I put the phone back to my ear knowing she'd heard the whole exchange.

"Vix, for real? You playing me to the left for a nigga? Again?"

"What are you talking about?"

"I can hear the motherfucker in the background, bitch!"

"What you heard is someone helping me get gas to put in my car." I slid into the front seat of the cop car and sighed while rolling my eyes.

"You're such a liar. Why didn't you just call me?"

"Because it's your fault anyway."

She didn't say anything for a while after that. Anytime I hit her with a dose of the truth she got quiet.

"You'd better not be with who I think you're with. I heard his voice. Don't make me ruin his career because you want to be a whore."

I hung up the phone and she called right back. I ignored her. It didn't take long to get back to my car. We thanked the officer and he went on about his night. I stood by the passenger side of my car while he poured the gas in, and thought. As much as my lover claimed to love me, her words were harsh, that of a woman who just wanted to be in control of everything. She'd threatened his career when I held hers in the palm of my hand. I had no doubt she would make good on her threat, but then if she did I would turn her world upside down, starting with telling her husband about her past life and the relationship she and I carried on. It's not like I even cared for Mr. Rodriguez's wellbeing, but more so that I was tired of her having the upper hand in our relationship.

My attention was brought back to the current situation when I heard my car start. I turned and looked before walking around to the driver's side. He sat there with one foot in the car and one foot out, so I walked between his legs and stood there. He stopped looking at the gas gauge and looked up at me, scratching the bridge of his nose before getting out of the car. We were so close I could smell the cappuccino and peppermint on his breath.

"Let me tell you something," he said before putting his hands on my waist and turning us around so that my back was against the car and his back was facing traffic. "I know what you're doing."

"Excuse me."

"I know what you're doing, but I'm not going there. Understand? I'm not cheating on my wife and I'm not going to fall for the little game you're playing."

"Game?"

"Yes, game. I know your type. I know what you get off on. Been there, done that. It's not happening, so stop. The looks you give me in class, the way you claim to need help with class work when I know you don't, even this little thing you did with calling for my help when I'm sure you could have called someone else. Stop it. What you want, I'll never give. *Comprende?*"

I could have just pretended as if I didn't know what he was talking about, but why prolong the game? I took one of his hands and placed it between my legs.

"I always get what I want. Always. You're telling me that you haven't thought about it?"

He snatched his hand away. "No. Now get in your car and go."

"You're lying. Otherwise how would you know about the looks I was giving you in class."

"Get in the car, Vix."

I took his hand and placed it to his nose. "Smell good, doesn't she?" I took his same hand and licked each of his fingers. "I'm not leaving you on the side of the road. I'll take you home."

I slid in my car and waited for him to move so I could close the door. His mouth may have said one thing, but the growing bulge in his pants told another story. It didn't take him long to close my door—well, slam it—and walk around to the passenger side to get in. Once we were both buckled in, I pulled off into traffic and got off on the first exit to turn around and go back to 75 South.

"Where do you live?" I asked.

"Not telling you where I live. I don't trust you."

I laughed out loud and quickly looked at him. "I'm seriously no threat. If you say no, I can't make you fuck me."

He cut his eyes at me. "I know your kind. It's not happening and I think it would be best if you asked if you could transfer to another class. That would be in both of our best interests."

I shrugged. "Not going to happen. I told you I won't be a problem unless you make me one. If you know you have no intentions of getting between these thighs then I can't force you to do so. Problem solved."

I could feel him watching me every so often as we got off on the exit going back into Jonesboro. I made him uncomfortable for some reason and the only reason I could think of was because I was his student. Honestly, what could I do if the man I wanted didn't want to do me? Obviously, he was fighting with his own demons. I had put two and two together and figured that maybe he'd cheated on his wife before and that was the reason for her outburst.

"Where're you going?" he asked.

"To my hotel since you won't tell me where you live."

He didn't get a chance to respond since his cell rang.

"You're really tripping over nothing," he said as soon as he answered the phone. "You left me on the side of the road, and do you honestly believe I would bring you with me to help someone I was cheating with? *Ella, es mi estudiante* for crying out loud!"

The insecurities of women always worked in my favor. There she had a good man and she was

accusing him of something that he wasn't doing
and obviously had no intention of doing. Women
like his wife always pushed their men further
and further away and into the arms of women
like me. The only person's happiness I cared
about was mine. As he sat and argued over the
phone with his wife, I pulled into the back of the
hotel I was staying in. By the time I had parked
the car, he had hung up the phone. His eyes had
watered over and he was visibly angry, which
meant to me he was even sexier.

"Thanks for the lift. I'll wait at the Waffle
House for my brother to come and pick me up."

He said all of that as he exited the car and
slammed my door again. He quickly walked
away, not even giving me a chance to say thank
you or good-bye.

Chapter 4

One-thirty a.m. and my cell buzzed with a text. I assumed it was my lover because she'd been calling and texting nonstop. After a while I just stopped answering and responding. I looked at the phone and was about to turn it off until I saw who it was texting me.

What room are you in? the text asked.

I responded, giving my room number. A few seconds later a knock on my door made me jump up. I quickly walked to my door and opened it and shock registered across my face at the man who pushed past me and entered my room. I closed the door and locked it, looking at him with a bewildered frown.

"What the hell are you doing here and how did you know where I was?"

"I bought your car. It's LoJacked."

I simply looked at him like he'd lost his mind. "So what the hell are you doing here? What do you want?"

He stood there and looked at me with his arms folded in a wide-legged stance. Any other time this would have been a perfect scenario, but I wasn't so sure at the moment.

"Why do you do it, Vix?"

"Do what?"

"Why do you play these little games?"

I knew what he was talking about. Too many times I'd winked, smiled, and accidently bumped into him, giving him just enough space to feel my breasts or have my ass brush against his crotch. The week before I'd touched myself thinking about him and left my thongs in his briefcase. He'd left his briefcase in my lover's car, so I left a little gift for him.

"You came all the way over here to ask me that?" I asked as I went to get back in the bed. "I'm tired and I'm sleepy. Go home to your wife."

I pulled the covers back over me and left him standing there. I hated for any man to play games with me and the fact that he was there at that time of morning meant he was only doing it to see if he could rattle me. Or, he could have been there just to piss his wife off. If you haven't figured it out, the man who was standing in my hotel room was the dean's husband, my lover's husband. We'd been secretly seeing each other for a while too.

I turned over and kicked at him when he snatched the covers off of me and snatched me down to the edge of the bed by my ankle. He'd done a lot of fronting too and his wife had no idea that he wanted me. And he had no idea I was screwing his wife.

I kicked again, missing his thigh as he jumped back.

"What the hell is wrong with you?" I asked him with a frown on my face.

I looked up into his caramel candy–coated face while his chocolate eyes stared at me from behind his glasses. "I'm about to fuck you."

I tilted my head and frowned up at him. The whole time I'd known he wanted to. I didn't care how respectful he was when she was around. I knew men, and I'd known it was only a matter of time before he'd allow his true colors to show.

"Like hell you are," I said as I watched him unbuckle his pants, step out of his shoes, and strip his body naked.

My resolve faltered, looking at him naked up close. He took his hand and stroked his well-endowed manhood before walking closer to me; the pre-come leaking from his tip invited me to kiss it. He fisted the back of my hair as my neck stiffened and his other hand went around my throat.

"Open," he demanded as he held his dick to my mouth.

By looking at the man standing in front of me you would never be able to tell that there was this wickedly sexy side of him. I knew what I was about to do was wrong, but I opened my mouth and let him slide in. He grabbed both sides of my hair and made love to my mouth. Slow at first, then faster, harder, and more aggressive until he made me slobber all over him and he came down the back of my throat. He'd surprised me. I had no idea his sexual prowess was this wild. When he'd come and I thought he was done, he quickly flipped me over.

"Get on your knees," he demanded.

I wasted no time. I wanted to see if he knew how to use what was swinging low and thick between his legs. Once I was on my knees his big hand came up and grabbed the back of my neck, holding my face down so that there was no way I could move. There was nothing gentle about the way he entered me. It was hard and swift. I grinded my teeth and my hands gripped the covers. He grunted behind me as he used his dick to stab me over and over. To anybody else what he was doing may have been a turn-off, but to me, it had me coming all over the place.

"I knew you could take this dick," he growled out as his hand left my neck and grabbed a handful of my hair while still holding my face down.

A hard slap across my ass made me jerk and scream into the covers. His dick was wide and long and certain spots he hit hurt so good that they caused my pussy to have jerking seizures on the inside. I felt my pussy slobber and squirt all over him and the bed. His hips pumped hard and made his thighs slap against my ass. I would be sore the next morning no doubt. When I felt him swell and he was about ready to come he snatched my head up so hard it felt as if he was trying to snap my neck. His hands left my hair and gripped my waist, pulling me back into him, forcing me to catch and take his hard thrusts while slapping my ass hard at times.

"I'm coming," he sputtered out. "Turn around and swallow this shit."

I complied and quickly turned just in time to catch the geyser-like eruption as he grabbed both sides of my head, forcing me to deep throat him and take it all down. I swallowed and used my hands to caress his sacks, listening to him as his voice showed his satisfaction. I let him stroke my jaws until he was limp.

"I want you to know I hate you for what you just made me do. I've never cheated on my wife. Never had the urge to until you came along and I'm going to always hate you for it."

I looked up at him then pushed him away from me. "You're so full of shit. I didn't make you do shit you didn't want to do. When you go home and fuck her tonight, think about me."

He shook his head. "You're so damn evil, why? What the hell happened to you to make you so damn heartless?"

"Life. Now if you're done you can get out of my room."

I walked into the bathroom and closed the door before grabbing my toothbrush and turning the shower on. I could swallow come all day, but I hated the feel of it on my body. Some of his come splashed on my chest and I needed to wash it off quickly. I jumped into the shower. The water was scalding hot, but I needed to make sure it came off. I grabbed the apricot scrub and Ivory soap and got down to scrubbing my chest. Once I felt like I was clean enough, I brushed my teeth and tongue, gargled extra long with Listerine, and stepped out of the shower. Thinking that I would be alone, I walked out of the bathroom and was shocked to find him still in my room.

I stopped and looked at him. "Is there any reason you're still here?"

He was sitting in the chair by the window, still naked. He sat laidback with his legs wide and dick still semi-hard.

"I figure since you let me get some pussy I may as well taste it, right?"

He stood and walked over to me, snatching the towel away and pushing me back on the bed. Every word that left his mouth amazed me. None of his high-polished society friends would think he spoke like he had and they definitely wouldn't think he would be in a hotel room cheating on his wife with me.

"You'd better do it right or we're going to have a problem."

I was anxious to see who could eat my pussy better: him or his wife. He spread my legs and pushed them back. I watched as he smiled and licked his lips before taking his glasses off. All I remember next is my legs shaking, head jerking, back arching, and squirting all over his face. His tongue and lips put something on me I'd never had before. He had lifted my hips from the bed and had my legs in the shape of an N as he continued to eat me out. The next thing I remembered when he finally let me go was waking up the next morning. He was gone.

***

The next couple of days came and went and I was still paying for that hotel. I hated spending my own money on me so, after I'd played hide and seek with my lover, I decided to call her. Her husband and I had been seeing a lot of each other over the past couple of days and, trust me, he'd been good to me. He'd bring me food, money, whatever I needed. He even brought me pamphlets of apartments and condos to look at, but he wasn't getting me out of the hotel fast enough.

She answered on the first ring, just as I knew she would. "Damn, Vix. Where are you?"

"I'm safe. How are you?"

"I'm missing you. Look, I'm sorry about all of the stuff I said to you last time, okay? I just want to see you."

Her voice was shaky and I could tell something was wrong.

"What's wrong with you?" I asked her as I sat at Barnes & Noble, looking over homework.

"I think he's cheating on me."

I was silent for a moment. "And what makes you think that?" Knowing I already knew he was, I just wanted to hear her answer.

"He's been acting different, strange. I tried to have sex with him just to make sure I wasn't tripping and he didn't go for it. He's never turned my sex down. I know he's cheating."

I took a sip of my white chocolate mocha. "Or, maybe he knows you are."

She was quiet a moment. I could hear the noise in her background letting me know she was at work. "How would he know? I'm very careful about you and me."

I could hear the panic laced in her voice. If he knew what she and I had been doing all hell would break loose. Her husband was a prideful man and to find out about our affair would cause pandemonium in their perfectly built life.

"Maybe not as careful as you think. If I were you I'd make sure he doesn't know about the condo or our visits there."

She sighed and moved around a bit. Her voice dropped lower, which meant she was around her coworkers and wanted no one to know she was talking on the phone.

"Look, I don't care about any of that. I need you. Can I see you? Please? We'll worry about him later," she said to me.

I thought for a second and listened to the shaking of her voice. "Okay. I'll be there by eight."

"Thank you, Vix. Don't stand me up this time. Please. I really need to see you."

The pleading and sincerity in her voice made me smile. Like I said before, no matter how she talked to me and no matter the pain she caused me, I couldn't leave her and she wouldn't let me go.

As soon as I hung up the phone with her all we had said was forgotten. Mr. Rodriguez walked through the doors of Barnes & Noble. There was no smile on his face and I could tell things between him and his wife hadn't gotten any better. He was brief and easily annoyed in class. He wasn't the cool, calm, and collected teacher he'd been previously. He spotted me and his upper lip twitched in response. I watched him walk over and sit at the opposite side of the table from me.

"First things first, I'm only here because you said you needed help. You failed the test so what can I help you with?" he asked all of that while the stern look on his face said he'd rather be somewhere else.

"Stop playing. You know damn well I failed that test on purpose. I could have aced it with my eyes closed."

He leaned forward, pressing his elbows on the table. "So what the fuck do you want? Stop playing with me."

"I feel as if you're taking your anger out on me because there's trouble in paradise . . ."

"Your games caused all of this."

"The games you played along with and fell for. You could have easily told me you couldn't make it to help me. You noticed how I looked at you in class and it piqued your interest, so you stop playing."

His leg was shaking under the table as he looked at me, biting down and licking his lips in frustration. "I told you whatever you want to happen, or think is going to happen, it's not going to happen. Now stop before I have to go to the dean and report you."

I laughed. "Go ahead. It won't go the way you like."

We simply stared at each other for a minute. I already had him hook, line, and sinker and I knew it was only a matter of time before I reeled him in.

"Come on," I said to him again. "She already thinks you're fucking me. So let's make it a reality. That's all I want anyway. Trust me when I tell you I can keep secrets."

His eyes squinted and his face frowned a bit. "What the fuck is wrong with you? I think you need some help."

I laughed loudly, causing people to turn and look at us. "Why? Because I know what I want and am not afraid to go after it? What's the big deal? It's only sex right? That's all I want."

He rubbed his nose and spoke to me through clenched teeth. "I told you I am not cheating on my wife."

"Again?"

He pursed his lips and sat back. "I'm done. I'm leaving."

I watched as he stood and grabbed his laptop bag. I smiled and waved. He quickly left and never looked back. I smiled. He'd be back to see me. I was sure of it. Closing my laptop, I put it away and prepared to leave myself. Before leaving I ordered myself another white chocolate mocha and made my way to my hotel room to wait for my lover's husband. Some men were so easy to manipulate.

It didn't take me long to make it to my room, after stopping at Southlake Mall and running into Frederick's of Hollywood. I needed to purchase a few things to make me feel good about myself. By the time I made it to my room, I could tell he was already there. The shower was already running. Bags of clothes and shoes were laid around the room and in the middle of the bed lay an envelope with a key on top. I quickly dropped my shopping bags and rushed to the bed, picking up the key then opening the envelope. I squealed and jumped when I looked at the piece of paper. Fuck an apartment or a condo. This damn fool had gotten me a house on Lake Spivey.

I threw everything back on the bed, ran into the bathroom, and jumped into the shower with him, clothes and shoes still on. He held me up when I jumped around his waist.

"I take it you approve?" he asked after I'd kissed him.

"Yes. Yes. And, yes! Thank you so much. I really need to get out of this room."

"I know and I'm happy you like it."

I looked down into his face. Sexy as he wanted to be and in that moment I remembered another reason I'd gone after him. His heart was just as big as his bank account. Deciding that I needed to show him just how appreciative I was, I slid down and dropped to my knees. It didn't take me long to get him where he loved to be and I was enjoying myself too until some of his come accidently splashed on my face. My mood immediately sank when I felt it splash on my jaw and near my eye.

I screamed and stood quickly, grabbed the soap and towel, scrubbing my face. I scrubbed my face until I made it tender to the touch. He stood back and watched for a moment, not sure of what had happened or how to fix it.

"Damn, Vix, what's wrong? What did I do?"

I pushed him away from me and stepped out of the shower dripping wet. I didn't even realize

I'd been crying. I snatched the bathroom door open and stormed out, pulling my wet clothes off in the process. He came after me, still wet, dick swinging, and confusion written on his face.

"Don't you ever, ever do that shit again. Do not put your come on me."

"Why not? Where else was I to put it?"

I shoved him and he stumbled on the bag sitting behind him, but caught his balance, grabbed me by both my wrists, and threw me on the bed. Some of the shopping bags fell on the floor when I quickly got back up and tried to punch him in the face. I was no match for his brute strength I knew, but I was pissed and tried to fight him anyway. I was mad that he'd brought back a memory for me that I hated.

"You fucking asshole," I screamed as I tried to hit him again before he pushed me down, putting his hand over my mouth and the other around my throat.

"You better chill the fuck out, or I will leave your ass limp in this fucking room. Fuck is wrong with you, huh?"

The fact that I knew he carried a gun silenced me and made me stop screaming. My vision was blurry because of tears.

"Now you think if I let you go, you can talk to me and tell me what's wrong instead of acting like you've lost your damn mind?" he asked as he looked down at me.

I nodded.

"Good. You almost kicked me in my dick. I would have fucked you up if you had."

He removed both of his hands and sat down on the bed. I lay there trying to get myself together. Maybe I was wrong for coming at him the way I had, but all I could think about was when I was twelve years old and Mike had literally taken my virginity. He'd made a sport of coming all over my face and body. His dick was a gun, his come were the bullets, my body and face he made targets. Because of that, I hated for a man's semen to get on any part of my body that wasn't my vagina, which was probably why I just preferred to swallow it. I even hated the sight of come. I'd told my lover's husband as much as I lay there. He sat and he listened to me before saying anything. There were times his face frowned and he looked as if he was disgusted.

"What did your mom do about him?" he asked me.

"I never told her until about a year or so later."

"What did she do? What happened to this motherfucker?"

"He's in prison. My mom and I set him up to get caught with some of his own product and another underage girl."

"How long did he get?"

"He took a plea deal for the drugs and got fifteen years."

He sat silent for a moment as he listened. After a while he turned to look at me. "I'm sorry that happened to you and what I did won't happen again."

The expression on his face was blank as he stood and started to get dressed. I didn't even question why he was leaving. In fact I was happy he was leaving. He'd made me show a weakness and I hated to show weakness . . . to any man.

I lay there after he left, feeling like I was useless and nothing. Tears flowed out of the corners of my eyes as childhood memories started to play for me. After a while, I'd even started to hate my name. Once Shonda had gotten wind of what Mike and I had been doing, he'd started to get violent, especially during times of sex when he was high. He would call me his little vixen, his personal little slut. I was told I'd never be able to have children because of what he did to my body the last time, the time that I couldn't hide it from my mother any longer.

It was after the fight between her and Shonda had gone down. She'd come home early, but five minutes too late to catch Mike on top of me.

"Vix!" she called out to me as the front door slammed.

I wanted to answer but couldn't. I'd tried to fight Mike off of me and he punched me in my jaw so hard, it felt as if my jaw had come unhinged. I could hear her moving around in the front room as I lay in my bed, balled in a fetal position. Mike had been high and drunk; otherwise, he wouldn't have done it, nor would he have left any evidence that he'd been in my mom's home.

"Vix," she called out again.

I could hear her voice getting closer and closer as she talked to herself. "If that girl is out with those damn fast-ass girls again, I'ma kick her ass good."

I still lay there unable to move or talk. Mike had fucked me rough. He'd pushed my legs so far back I'd thought they would break. He banged and pumped, all the while I screamed, cried, and begged him to stop. It felt as if he'd knocked something loose and no matter how I tried, I couldn't move. Every time I tried, it hurt so bad that I was just forced to stay balled up. My mom finally pushed my room door open. She was about to say something until she looked at my swollen, bloodied face, the blood on the white sheets, and me looking up at her with tears in my eyes.

She screamed and ran to me. "Vix, what the hell happened? Who did this baby? Tell Mama who did this to you. Oh my God. Oh my God."

She kept screaming that over and over as she pulled the white sheet from tangled around me and pulled me up in her arms. I tried to cry out in pain but my jaw wouldn't let me. Luckily my moans and groans let her know she was hurting me. She left me there and ran to our front door. I could hear her screaming for help and I could hear people running down the hall to her. Luckily my mom was well liked around the way because she fed and kept most of the block boys' secrets.

"Call 911 for me. Somebody raped my baby," I heard her scream at someone. All I heard were feet running and scrambling, sounding like a thousand hooves of horses running for our apartment as my mom came back in the room with me.

"Who did this, Vix, baby? Who did it?"

Her face was red and soaked with tears as she looked down at me. I looked up and saw Shonda standing in the doorway of my room.

"Oh my God," she yelled out.

She and my mom had become friends again by then. I quickly looked from her to my mom, hoping she could read my eyes. I could hear the *sirens in the distance and it wasn't long before the meat wagon arrived. All the while my mom only wanted to know who'd done this to me. I looked at Shonda again and my mom's eyes widened.*

"Mike?"

I looked at Shonda and she stood there with her mouth open and shock written across her face.

"Mike did this to you, Vix?" my mom asked again and again I looked at Shonda to answer her.

The next couple of things to happen were like a whirlwind. The EMTs came in and took me away, I stayed in the hospital for seven days, and word around the block was that Mike had been taken care of.

I'd lied to my lover's husband. No way would I tell anyone what really happened when I left the hospital, or my mom would lose everything. Mike wasn't in prison. Mike wasn't even alive.

When my mom came to pick me up from the hospital we drove home. My mom didn't say anything to me the whole drive.

I said earlier that my mom had a hair-trigger temper, and she proved to me just what Flatbush had taught her that day.

We pulled in to park and walked upstairs, by-passing our apartment. I could feel something was funny. Block boys lined the hall of the fifth floor of building 260. Block boys were what we called the boys who ran the block, the dope game. They all looked at me and my mom and nodded as we passed. My mom knocked once on Mike and Shonda's apartment.

A boy I only knew as Sig opened the door and let me and my mom in. Shonda was sitting on the couch, looking as if she feared for her life. Tears and slobber ran down her face and nose. Two other block boys accompanied her on the couch as she sat with her head hanging down. When my mom walked in she looked up at me and the look on her face scared me. There was something akin to anger, resentment, and hate as she looked at me. The house was dark and quiet except for some cartoons playing on the TV and the laughter of a few of the block boys, as my mom and I walked to Shonda's bedroom. I already knew where it was because I'd been in her room and in her bed countless times.

When my mom knocked on the room door, it was opened by another block boy and there was Mike. He sat tied to a chair. His face was bloodied and he was shirtless. His whole body was drenched in blood and, judging by the looks on a few of the guys faces, they'd enjoyed beating him as he sat there. I watched as my mom laid her purse on the bed after pulling out a pair of black leather gloves.

She kneeled in front of Mike. "I want you to know that I only kept you alive this long so that my baby can be the last face you sees before you die. She told me all the shit you been doing to her. Did you think I would let you live afterward, motherfucker?"

He spit in my mom's face. "Fuck you and that li'l bitch. She liked that shit. Ask her about all of the shit I bought her. Ask her 'bout how she liked to suck a nigga dick to get what she wanted. Fuck you and that li'l slut."

He spit in her face again. She cringed back and stood. One of the boys in the room hit him so hard I swear I saw his jaw crack and move.

"Fuck this nigga up, Dullah," I heard another block boy say as the one they called Dullah punched him again.

He kept punching him until the chair fell over and Mike looked as if he was already dead.

"Sit him back up," my mom said to him.

He did what she asked but only after kicking him in the face with his steel-toe Timberlands. I watched as my mom pulled out a pair of latex gloves and handed them to me.

"Put these on," she said to me.

I didn't ask any questions. I was too afraid, but there was something else that I found out about myself that day. I found that I liked the power my mom had over all those men in the room and in the hall. I didn't have any power with Mike and my mom did. Once I pulled on the gloves, she took my hand and we stood on the left side of the chair that Mike sat in. The block boy named Dullah pulled out a gun, handing it to my mom.

"Yo, blow that nigga's wig the fuck back, Tammi," another one in the room said as others laughed and encouraged her.

My mom kept a calm face as she made me stand in front of her before putting the gun in my hand. I looked up at her, shaking my head.

"Mama, what are you doing? I don't want to do this," I pleaded with her.

"Yes, you do and you will. You will do to this motherfucker what he did to you. He violated you. Took your innocence, so you take his life. Fair exchange is no robbery."

She stood behind me. With her hand surrounding mine we placed the gun to his head. I watched as Mike came to and his eyes widened in the realization he was about to die.

"Come . . . come on, Tam," he pleaded.

His mouth and jaw were so swollen we could barely make out what he was saying after that. My mom leaned forward and spit in his face. Most of the boys in the room laughed. I stood there, feeling as if my world were tilting. It was only seconds but it felt like hours. My mom cocked the gun back and pulled the trigger using my hand. Blood splattered onto us as Mike's body slumped in the chair and Shonda's sobbing got louder. A hole sat in the left side of Mike's head as I heard someone slap Shonda across the face, telling her to shut the fuck up or she would be next. Dullah took the gloves and gun from me and my mom before he walked us out of the building.

Chapter 5

I hated to relive that part of my life because it reminded me of a time when I had no power. Never again would I allow a man to do that to me, which is why I so enjoyed the game of making a man do whatever it was I wanted him to. My lover's husband had just bought me a house, deed in my name, and handed me the key. Power. I made him cheat on his wife, something he'd never done before. Power. And only I had the power to give my power away. That's why I was so upset with him for coming on my face. It felt as if he'd taken me back to the time I had no power.

I pulled myself together after a few hours and made my way to my new house. I was pleased with the neighborhood and it made me feel like I was on an episode of *Cribs*. My smile widened when I saw that my house was the only one that sat in a cul-de-sac at the end of the street. Stone and brick made up the outside of my new home.

I was so excited I just parked my car and ran to unlock the door. Needless to say my new home was all that and more than I expected. It took me a few minutes to explore the whole house. Four bedrooms, two and half baths, big den, kitchen, and front room, it was two stories, and came equipped with a balcony and patio. And it was all mine. It took me a couple of trips back and forth to the hotel to move all of my stuff over after making sure the electricity and gas were already on. He'd already taken care of all of those things for me.

Having the house made me feel a little better about what had gone down. I was excited about it, and decided to treat myself by checking out of the hotel and staying in my new place. Before going back to the hotel for the last of my things, I shopped around for a bed and furniture, none of which would be delivered until the next day, but I was excited anyway. I purchased a couple of comforter sets and some pillows so that I could have something to lie on for the night, along with a futon. I purchased a TV and some DVDs, some food, wine, and wine glasses. I wanted to celebrate with myself. I even called my lover's husband over and we'd christened the front room by the fireplace.

After he left he called me while I was out and we talked a little more about what had happened. If I was into all of the relationship hoopla, I could've seen myself falling for him, but I wasn't into all of that. For the moment, I simply enjoyed his company, his money, his conversation, and his dick.

Looking at my watch I sighed and jumped on the expressway, heading to my lover's place. It didn't take me long to get there since traffic wasn't bad. I was prepared to go in and spend a few hours with her just because she sounded like she genuinely missed me. I parked my car in her gated community after putting in the security code and thought I'd surprise her by showing up a little early. I stepped out of the car and walked up to her door and I was the one who got the surprise. I saw her standing in the doorway, kissing another woman. For a moment, I simply stood there too shocked and surprised to do anything else. For the longest time she'd told me that I was the only woman she was with, the only woman she wanted to be with. I felt my stomach drop a bit and then my feet started to move forward. I was already halfway to them before she realized it was me and she damn near fell back inside of her condo.

She blinked rapidly and took the back of her hand to her mouth as if she was trying to wipe away the evidence of her lying and cheating. The woman stood there simply looking at me. She was a thick Asian chick with long hair, same color as mine: auburn. She was beautiful in the face and stood about three inches taller than me. Her eyes carried a smirk as she placed another kiss against my lover's lips, and moved her thick, toned thighs down the hall to exit the building.

That left me and my lover staring each other down in the hall. Part of me wanted to grab a fistful of her hair and drag her down the hall while I stomped and beat her ass. The other half of me told me to be happy because she'd finally given me a way out of this twisted bad romance we'd made. I frowned and pushed past her inside of what I'd thought was our place. *How dare she bring another woman here?*

She gently closed the door and called my name. "Vix . . ."

I dropped the bags I was holding to the floor and turned to look at her.

"How long?" I asked her.

She looked uncomfortable as she switched her weight from one foot to the other. Her long ponytail swayed behind her as she pulled her robe tighter and tried to avert her eyes from mine.

"I met her awhile ago."

"What's awhile ago?"

"About six months ago."

I slapped her so hard that when her head snapped to the side her ponytail whipped her in the face too.

"You're such a fucking hypocrite," I snarled at her. "A lying fucking hypocrite."

She looked down at me as water clouded her vision, and a plea held in her eyes.

"I met her six months ago. Today was the first day I invited her over."

I shook my head as my arms crossed over my chest. "You have sex with her?"

She took too long to answer and I turned on my heels to leave. She grabbed me from behind and lifted me from the floor, carrying me back to our bedroom while I kicked and screamed at her. Sometimes I'd forget that she was taller than me and stronger. No matter how hard I kicked and screamed she was still carrying me to the room, and when she finally got me there she dropped me on the bed. I quickly turned over, kicking and swinging at her. It made me feel good that a few of those kicks and swings connected. She was calling my name and tears were falling down her face by the time she'd gotten a hold of my wrists and pinned me down to the bed. She crawled on top of me and straddled my hips.

"Stop and listen to me," she pleaded. "It was this one time only. She and I had only been talking before today, I swear."

I guess she'd thought that was to make me feel better. I spit in her face, pissed at all she'd been taking me through, all the lies and promises that I was the only woman she wanted. I was pissed at all of the fights and all of the times she'd gotten in my face about men. She'd known all along that she was the only woman I'd ever been with and for her to lie to me in that moment made me madder at her than I'd ever been.

"You're a fucking liar and I know you're lying. You've never been good at that shit. Get off of me."

I turned my head when she leaned down and tried to kiss me. How dare she try to kiss me after she'd just been with another woman? I bucked my hips and tried to get her off of me to no avail. That didn't stop her from placing kisses against my neck and down my chest. In that moment I made up my mind that it would be my last time being with her. No matter how much she professed her love and apologized in that moment, my mind had been made up. She ripped my dress down the middle and trailed kisses until she made it to my waxed yoni. I tried to push her head away but then I stopped and remembered that I hadn't showered after having sex with her husband and his come was still scattered, smothered, and covered over my pussy. The plan had been to take a shower when I'd gotten here, but this would be better. It would be my own little brand of payback and satisfaction to have her lick off the evidence of my and her husband's indiscretions.

Soon after, I left her place and left the key on the kitchen table. By the time she would realize what I'd done, I'd be long gone. I made my way back to my side of town and stopped at the hotel one last time to pick up the bags I'd left. After completely checking out, I made my way back to my new home. I guess I'd been so caught up in my emotions and talking on the phone to my lover's husband that I didn't notice the truck following me. He'd called me to see how I was settling in for the night at my new home.

"I couldn't stay at the hotel another night, so even though I have to sleep on the floor until tomorrow I'm glad to be going home," I told him.

He chuckled in my ear and it permeated down to my gut. I guess I liked him way more than I should have, but it didn't matter to me at the moment.

"Yeah, give me your bank account information and let me put some money in there. Reimbursement for what you spent on the furniture and whatnot today. You can do it when you get in so you can pay attention to the road."

Things like that were what made it good to mess with a man with a bank account. "Thank you, but you don't have to do that. The house is enough. I can furnish it."

"I know I don't have to, but I want too. Besides, you'd better take me up on my offer because my wife accused me of cheating on her this morning. I may get pissed at you again and rescind the offer."

I was quiet for a moment as I thought about his wife. "Well, you are cheating on her, aren't you?"

He didn't answer right away. "Yes, but she doesn't know that."

"Obviously she does. Maybe you're being a little sloppy."

"There is no evidence of my cheating unless you count the fact that I've turned down her sex more than once this week."

I laughed to myself. "That's how you men always get caught. You change up your routine."

He was quiet again before speaking. It was as if he was contemplating his next answer.

"You know as well as I do my wife only married me for show."

My heartbeat sped up and my feet pressed the gas harder unconsciously. I squealed and hit the brakes as I almost hit the back of the car in front of me.

"Damn," I murmured to myself.

"You okay?"

"Yeah. Yeah. What do you mean by that?"

"By what?"

"What you said about your wife. What would make you think that?"

"I'm a private investigator, Vix. I can find out what I want."

My palms started sweating and my heart fell to my stomach.

"So what did you find out?"

"She has a condo in Midtown and the woman she was seen with today is a woman I hired to help me confirm my suspicions. Took her six months but I had to know and now I do."

"Wow."

That was all I could say. Although I felt some relief, I didn't like how close he was to finding out my secret. There was no way I could ever let him find out about her and me. No way.

"Yeah, that's the same thing I said."

I could hear him clicking and typing away as we talked and my mind raced a mile a minute.

"So what now? What are you going to do?"

"I'm not sure yet. I do love her and she's been good to me."

"But now you're cheating on her with me to pay her back for cheating on you?"

The fact that he was quiet gave me my answer and in that moment I felt used. It confused me because I'd never felt that way before. Plenty of the time I'd dealt with men who had cheated with me to get back at their wives in some way so I didn't understand why with him it hurt me a little.

"But that shouldn't bother you, right? You really don't give a fuck about anybody but you, right?"

Why did I have to always pick the lovers who seemed to be bipolar in their mood swings?

"You would be correct, but that's not the point. I feel as if you came to me under false pretenses. If all you wanted was to get back at her then you should have said so."

"And you would have let me fuck you anyway, huh?

"More than likely. And don't act like this is all because you suspected her of cheating. I saw the way you looked at me the day you and I met. You were just biding your time, waiting for the right moment."

He laughed and it grated on my nerves. "You really think you're hot shit, right? Like you're walking around here with the best pussy in the world?"

"It's good enough to keep your ass coming back."

"Naw. You suck a mean dick and that's good enough to keep me coming back."

"Fuck you."

"Not tonight."

He hung up the phone and I sat there pissed. What in the hell had just happened? I was so caught up in my emotions when I parked in my driveway that I didn't notice that same truck that had been following me had pulled in my cul-de-sac behind me. I got out of my car and slammed my door, trying to call him back, and he wouldn't answer. Ooh, I hated that man in that moment. He'd gotten the best of me again and I hated it.

I walked up to my door and turned the key, still looking at my phone, texting him the nastiest message I could think of; and when I say nasty, I mean nothing sexual. By the time I realized someone was behind me it was too late. He had pushed me into the house, making me fall on the floor, my knees hitting hard and forcing me to reach out and try to break the fall with my hands. I quickly turned around and looked up.

"Are you out of your damned mind?" I asked him with a frown on my face that showed the pain I was in.

He slammed the door. "No, but you are."

Snatching me from the floor he dragged me to my front room and pushed me down on the futon I'd purchased earlier.

I screamed and tried to jump back up. He shoved me back down. "What is wrong with you?"

He went in his pocket and pulled out a pair of my black lace thongs and a room key to the hotel room I was in.

"You thought this shit would be funny? Putting that shit in my laptop bag, Vix?"

I looked at what was in his hand and smiled. "It brought you back to me, didn't it?"

He bucked at me and made me flinch and scramble back. "You think this shit is a game? My wife found this shit."

"I know. That was the point."

In a nanosecond his hand grabbed a handful of my hair and slung me on the floor. When he'd come to Barnes & Noble to meet me, I'd put the thongs and key card in his laptop bag after he sat it on the floor. Now, Mr. Rodriguez stood in front of me with anger etched across his face. Not like I cared. I still got what I wanted. At that time I didn't know just how close to danger I was.

"You did all of this, all of this shit, because you just want sex?"

The confusion in his voice matched the confusion written across his face.

"Yes. I want the sex and the man. Not asking you to love me. Just asking for what I know we both want."

"Damn it, how else can I tell you that I don't want you?"

"Your mouth says one thing but your body and eyes say another. I saw how excited you got when I put your hand on my pussy, saw your eyes glaze over when you got a whiff of it on your fingers. Stop lying to yourself." I stood up and stumbled back because of the pain in my knee.

"You need help. Serious help."

"Yet, you're here in my front room. You followed me here and I'm the one who's crazy?" I shook my head with a smug smirk. "I think not. Be honest. Why're you here? Why did you get out of bed with your wife to come and help me?"

"Because, in that moment, I thought you genuinely needed my help. Not that you were on some bullshit all because you want me to stick my dick in you."

I threw my head back and laughed before looking back at him.

"So you followed me from the hotel to here just to confront me about this? You could have easily taken this evidence to the dean and called it a day."

He stalked closer to me, forcing my back against the wall. We stood that way and stared at each other, me looking up at him, wondering what it was he would do next.

"You know you want it," I said to him barely above a whisper as I stood on my toes and sucked his bottom lip into my mouth.

I lifted my hips from the wall, feeling his bulge on my stomach. He pushed my hips away from him as his arms caged me in and his honey-golden eyes gazed down at me. I saw his Adam's apple bob as he swallowed and leaned his head closer to my face.

"I do this and you leave me alone, understand?"

I nodded, feeling like I'd finally gotten the prize at the end of the rainbow. I'd been trying to get that man since I'd stepped foot in his classroom and I was finally about to get what I wanted. One of his hands gripped my waist and snatched me close to him as the other stayed against the wall and his eyes roamed over my face.

"You should always be careful what you ask for, Vix. One day all of this shit is going to come back and bite you in the ass. My wife put me out because she and I have been down this road before. If I were any other man I'd beat your ass right now, but you're right. The only thing that kept me from tagging this pussy was because I was trying to prove to my wife that what I'd done was a mistake, but you just fucked that all up."

"So you do like outside pussy?" I asked with a grin. "It was only a matter of time anyway."

He looked down at me and he snarled a bit, the dimples in his cheeks still visible without his smile.

"All of that posting to my Facebook wall, watching me in class, calling me to come and help you, and staying after class, all of that because you wanted me?"

I nodded. It was so easy to spot a man who was thirsty for the love and attention of his wife. Men needed women like me to stroke their egos and make them feel that all the hard work they did wasn't for naught. There stood a perfectly fine man, working hard, he wasn't a statistic. Not a negative one, at least; he had a good job, a respectable one, and all he was trying to do was prove to her that he deserved another chance. She accused him of fucking me and pushed him further to me. Women like her would always lose out, or push their men into the arms of women

like me and a woman like me would always be
waiting.

"Yes. I always go hard for what and who I want.
Best believe it. You're here now, so you may
as well make it worth your while. I mean she's
already accused you of it, right?"

"You know nothing about me. You don't know
my life. All you know is that I look good and you
want to fuck me. You don't see anything wrong
with that?"

I looked at him and placed both my hands on
his chest. "Do you?"

I moved from under him and started to pull
my clothes off, my shirt first and then my jeans.
I stood there before him naked, perfect size-ten
body. I'd known that after seeing me naked it
wouldn't take long for him to make up his mind.
I watched as he stepped out of his Polo boots and
stripped down to nothing. What surprised me
most was when he pulled out the box of Magnum
condoms after pulling his jeans off. Pulling the
cushion from the futon and then the comforter
to the floor he looked at me.

"Come here," he said as he crooked his finger
at me.

I walked over to him and joined him on the
cushion. All of the time we spent talking and I'd
just realized the main lights were still off. Only
the security lights and the dimmers were on.

"You brought condoms?" I asked him.

"Yes. My dick is selective. I'm not fucking you raw and you shouldn't want me to."

No man had ever said that to me so I was kind of shocked. I didn't know what to feel as I watched how he took the time to sheath his thick dick in the condom. His dick wasn't as long as my lover's husband's but it was thicker. I'd say it was about eight inches, but the veins and the thickness of it had me salivating from the mouth and pussy.

"After we're done, then what?" I asked him as he eased down beside me.

"Then we act like nothing ever happened. Nobody finds out about this and we keep it that way. We clear? I can't lose my job and I'm still married."

He said all of that while pulling me underneath him. Now, I didn't know what I was expecting, but I could tell you that it wasn't what I thought it would be. I'd never been made love to by any man, but that's what Alex did to me. He kissed me slow, took his time with my mouth, neck, breasts, stomach, and sides, and when it came time for him to stroke my kitty, I was done for. No other man I'd been with had ever taken the time to love my body slow. Shit, if that was what he was putting on his wife back home then I could definitely see why she was pissed.

And it wasn't just a one-time thing. He used the whole twelve pack of condoms in one night. He didn't come every time but he made sure I did. We drank my wine, ate the minimal food I had, and we talked some more. I found out he was an only child, he was from California, and his mom was still alive. He'd been married for six years and got married at twenty-two. He'd also cheated on his wife the year before with a coworker at his old job and that had caused a lot of problems for them.

"My problem was that I found out heaven was between a black woman's thighs," he said to me. "I have a thing for black women."

I looked at him as we lay side by side. "But you're black yourself."

"No. I'm Cuban and Puerto Rican, but sometimes I do identify as Black."

I nodded. "Oh. And when your wife saw me she flipped because you'd cheated on her with a black woman before?"

He nodded. I could tell his mind was on his wife. He'd check his phone every so often to see if she'd called.

"Yeah. She knows my type very well."

"So why didn't you just marry a black woman?"

"I didn't fall in love with one."

"So we're good enough to have sex with, but not good enough to love and marry?"

"I didn't say that."

"So what are you saying?"

He was about to answer, then he looked at me. "Are you really advocating for marriage when you're lying here with me, a married man?"

I laughed a little. "Not really. I'm simply confused as to why you're not married to a black woman since you love us so much."

"I can't help who I fell in love with and I fell in love with Maria."

I shook my head. He may as well have been a black man. He sure as hell had the same warped thought process as they had.

"You fell in love with her but yet you say you have this uncontrollable lust for black women." I laughed at the craziness of it all.

He pulled me on top of him after putting the last condom on. With his hand he guided his semi-hardened manhood inside of me. To be honest it was my first time ever having sex with a man with a condom. I'd been raw dogging since the first time I had sex. Don't get me wrong, after a while my mom took the time to tell me about STDs and such but, by then, it was too late. I'd already been having sex. I caught gonorrhea and chlamydia once. Had no idea what was going on until I went to my doctor. My throat had been sore for a little over a week and discharge from my vagina smelled putrid. Needless to say that when I'd gone back and told the man I was sleeping with what he'd given me, he tried to flip and blame it on me and I cut his ass good. He was lucky I didn't kill him.

Even after all of that, I still had sex without protection; I was just more careful and more selective in my choice of man. My gynecologist also saw me every three months. He'd asked me why I visited him so often and I told him the truth, I fuck a lot, and I left it at that.

"It's not how you explain it," he said to me, bringing me back to reality. "It's not that complicated. I just happened to meet and fall in love with Maria before I could meet and fall in love with a black woman. It's simple."

With his hands gripping my waist he began to slowly bounce me up and down on him until I could feel him getting harder and harder. His girth was ridiculous. It felt as if he were trying to split me open. I came immediately and kept coming. We were so caught up in each other that neither of us saw the shadowy figure watching us through the blinds.

Death had always been very close to me.

Chapter 6

Something in me must have liked the idea of a man being in my home with me day in and day out. Mr. Rodriguez and I had made a little love nest and I became completely unaware of the danger I placed both of us in. For the next couple of weeks he and I continued our little arrangement. I'd cut contact with my lover. I'd meant what I said about leaving her alone, but still she called, texted, and begged to see me. I continued to ignore her. For some reason my mom called me and said she wanted to see me.

"Am I allowed back in your home?" I asked her, being facetious.

"Yes, as long as you respect my rules."

I sighed. "There is no need for me to come back. I have my own place now. I'm good."

"Oh, really?"

"Yes, really."

She was quiet a moment. She and I had been through a lot and I guessed that she'd thought I'd be back home by then.

"So you're really not coming back?" she asked. It was a loaded question.

"No, Mom. I'm not coming back. Not to live."

I heard a door slam in her background and asked what was going on.

"Frank is mad about something. I guess because I'm talking to you and asked you to come back home. He was really pissed at you for coming on to him like that."

"No, he wasn't. He's a lying son of a bitch and he thinks he's so perfect. I'm sure he's not."

"Vix, he really sees you as his daughter and you shouldn't have placed him in that spot; not to mention, he's my damn husband. I don't even understand why you would do that."

Rolling my eyes I sighed again and looked up to see Mr. Rodriguez coming from the bathroom. He'd just stepped out of the shower and I was lying in bed naked. He grabbed one of my ankles and pulled me down to the edge of the bed, kneeling in front of me. He took his fingers and started exploring my pussy like it was a lost cavern with new life or something. He licked his finger before pushing it inside of me, twisting and turning it slowly, then bringing it out to pluck at my clitoris. I'd learned that he had a healthy sexual appetite and that I loved to feed it and him.

"Mom, you know as well as I do that you don't love Frank and he's going to pick up on that sooner or later."

I caught my breath and moaned out when his tongue wrapped around my clit and he sucked aggressively.

"Vix, what in the hell are you doing?" my mom asked me.

I'd completely forgotten she was on the phone with the smooth way he was practicing the art of oral sex on me.

"Nothing. I have to go. Talk to you later."

I clicked the end button and dropped the phone. Getting eaten out for breakfast was way better than breakfast in bed. We'd run out of condoms so fast until he just went to the store and bought a bigger box. Another thing I was starting to love about him: he wouldn't stay here without contributing something. He was lacing my pockets and buying the food to keep us fed and one of the sexiest things about him was that he was a clean man. He'd been leaving for work just before daybreak so our secret could remain so and at school we acted like nothing was going on. He'd park his truck in my garage just to be on the safe side, although almost no one knew where I lived. Only my lover's husband knew, and I hadn't seen him since Alex had gotten here.

He'd been calling and I'd been putting him off. Told him I'd been very sick and just needed time to be alone and heal. He'd sent flowers and Alex didn't seem to care one way or the other. There were times when he talked on the cell to his wife, still trying to fix that broken marriage. One time he was sucking on my pussy while talking to her and he did that shit so smoothly that I gushed all over his face and his voice never even cracked. Another time he was bouncing me on his dick as he professed his love to her. We both came while she was on the phone cursing him out in Spanish. He never broke a sweat and she had no idea.

It seemed as if we were getting off on that kind of thing because he was giving me deep, penetrated back shots while I talked to my ex-lover's husband. It seemed he was intent on making me moan. Or, maybe I was just a moaner and couldn't hold it in. I'd quickly hung up the phone. You know how they say if something is too good to be true then it usually is? Well I don't know what I'd been thinking. I'd let my guard down with Alex. He was easy to relax around and we got along well.

"I have to stop fucking with you, Vix," he said to me out of the blue as we lay in the bed.

It was raining and a thunderstorm had knocked the power out. The moonlight was the only light we had.

"Where did that come from?"

"You know we have to stop this shit before it goes too far. I can't risk falling for you any more than I already have. That shit is only going to complicate my life more."

"So you're saying because I make you happy, you have to go back home to your wife and try to fight for the happiness you wish you could have?"

He cut his eyes at me as I turned over on my stomach, rested on my elbows, and looked at him.

"You don't make me happy. Your pussy makes me happy."

"You're a liar."

"And you can't handle the truth."

"You don't know what the truth is."

"I'm going back home to my wife."

"Weak son of a bitch."

"Stupid-ass bitch."

"She can never give you what I can."

"And what exactly are you giving me besides good pussy?"

"I make you happy. You said so yourself."

"That was pillow talk after you'd just fucked me good and sucked my dick like no other woman has ever done."

I sat back on my haunches and rolled my eyes at him.

"Weak-ass nigga."

"Stupid-ass bitch."

"Go on then. Take your shit and go back to the other land. It's obvious you can't handle the motherland. That's why your simple-ass didn't marry a black woman."

His face hardened a bit as his stare cut into me. "Why you mad? You said all you wanted me for was dick anyway, right? So why you mad?"

I looked at him. "I'm not."

"You're a liar."

"And you can't handle the truth."

"You don't know what the truth is."

"Go back home to your wife."

I sat there and looked at him as his eyes stayed locked on me. Thunder shook the earth and lightning tore across the sky, lighting up the room.

"After I leave, I'm not coming back," he said after a moment.

I stood. "So the fuck what."

"Keep your end of the bargain. You said you could keep a secret."

"So you're asking me to just walk away like we didn't share secrets that probably no one else knows about us?"

"And we'll always have those memories to go back to."

"You'll be back."

"No, I won't."

Yes, we'd both shared secrets with one another about our lives. I told him about my lover. I told him the truth no one else knew about her. While telling him I watched as his eyes widened upon finding out who it was. It was the liquor that had us wagging our tongues, spilling secrets. He'd told me about how his mom had molested him until he was fourteen and able to leave home. His mom's was the first woman's body he'd penetrated. She'd force him to have sex with her.

He told me how he had to live on the street while still trying to go to school and get into college. He was a male whore once. He sold his dick to the highest bidder. He'd even gone so far as to let another man suck his dick. The man offered to pay him $5,000 and he went for it. I didn't judge him and he assured me that was the first and last encounter with a man he'd ever had. I asked if he'd busted a nut from it and he said no. I guessed that's why when my secrets spilled from my tongue. He didn't judge me for them.

"You'll be back, Alex, and I'll be here waiting. I know your secrets and you know mine. That will always bring you back."

He slowly sat up and looked at me. "Come here."

"No. You're leaving so I'd rather not have good-bye sex. Just get your shit and go."

"I'm not leaving until the morning."

"No. You can leave now."

My voice cracked and tears stung my eyes. I got emotional. That could have been the liquor, too. We'd been drinking again. I looked at the big bottle of Patrón Silver lying empty on the floor. With the demons chasing us, we had to chase them back. So we went to the liquor store and he bought the biggest bottle of Patrón they had to offer. We brought it back home and chased the demons that chased us. We both were alike.

I backed away from him as he stood and walked over to me.

"No. Don't touch me," I said to him as I tried to push him away.

We were both naked. The whole time we stayed together we walked around naked. His masculine build was what most men would kill for and I could definitely see what would make any woman pay to have a piece of him. He picked me up and put my back against the wall. His dick slid inside of me so effortlessly that all I could do was breathe. My walls stretched, and I let go of the fight I had in me. I realized for the first time he was inside of me raw and it felt so damn good, even better than before. He took me like that against the wall. He fucked me like it was his last time.

"This is the last time," he said to me as he looked up at me.

My breasts bounced and swayed in his face, causing his mouth to open and his tongue to seek out my nipples.

"You'll be back . . . You'll be back."

About an hour later, we both jerked awake. We'd been asleep on the floor near the wall he had had sex with me against. We both looked at each other, trying to figure out if thunder had just awakened us. Both of us relaxed back into each other until we heard the noise again. He jumped up so quick that it was like a flash of lightning. He grabbed my hand and ran to the walk-in closet.

"Put some clothes on," he said to me.

It sounded as if someone was trying to kick down the front door. I quickly pulled on whatever I could while he pulled on his jeans, quickly zipping them and running from the closet. Pulling a tank over my head, I frantically grabbed shoeboxes from my closet shelf until I found the one I wanted and grabbed the .380 hand gun. The kicking became louder and harder.

"Alex," I called out in a frantic whisper to him.

Tears stung my eyes and for the first time in a long time, I was afraid. I quickly walked to my kitchen, calling out to him again.

"Alex!"

The front door flew open and I almost screamed until a hand flew around my mouth and Alex snatched me back into the walk-in pantry with him. He turned me to him with a hand still over my mouth and a finger to his lips telling me to be quiet. I nodded as tears from my eyes fell over his fingers.

"Vix," a male voice called out to me.

Alex looked at me and I looked at him. I knew the voice. It was my lover's husband.

"You fucking bitch. You got another nigga in the house I bought you, fucking him? Bitch, are you fucking stupid?"

Alex looked at me again. "Who is that?" he mouthed to me. "Is that him?"

I nodded. I knew what he meant when he asked if it was him because I'd told him that I was also having an affair with my lover's husband. We could hear him running up the stairs.

His voice belted out, "I know you're in here, bitch. Don't run scared now."

"Stay in here," Alex said to me.

"Where're you going?"

"Just stay in here."

I didn't know what was more frightening: the fact that my ex-lover's husband was running through the house like a madman, or that there was no fear on Alex's face.

"He's got a gun."

"So? You just stay in here and don't come out until I come and get you."

With that he turned and left me in my pantry and disappeared and I heard my lover's husband coming back down the stairs. It was quiet for a moment and I started praying. I'd never prayed a day before in my life because I thought God couldn't give two fucks about people like me. I'd sinned too much for Him to care, but I started praying and I prayed hard. I guess I was right about God not caring for people like me because my lover's husband snatched the pantry door open, gun in his hand, and anger masking his face. Before my scream could manifest he punched me in my face and I fell back into the shelves, hitting the floor, blood spilling from my nose and lips.

"You must be out of your motherfucking mind," he snapped at me and went to pull me up from the floor.

I screamed and kicked to try to stop his assault when I saw Alex step from the shadows and do the shit I thought only Steven Seagal could do in movies. He grabbed my lover's husband by the neck with one arm pulling him back, and used his other hand to slam the pantry door on his wrist, forcing him to drop the gun. I scrambled to my feet and watched in horror as Alex used a knife and stuck it in his back while he held him.

That didn't deter my lover's husband as he promptly yelped out in pain but pivoted his hips to flip Alex over his shoulder. Alex landed on his feet and quickly pulled another knife from his back pocket. I screamed for them to stop but neither would hear me as Alex rushed for him again, the knife held in a defensive manner that only a skilled and trained fighter would know to use.

"Pussy must be good to you, nigga. She got you playing super save-a-ho," he said to Alex with a mean scowl on his face.

Alex never said a word in return, and when my lover's husband rushed him Alex did some kung fu master shit with the knife slicing his chest and arms as he ducked and blocked most of the punches being thrown at him. When my lover's husband hit the floor, Alex rushed over him and would have started cutting him if I hadn't run out and jumped in front of him.

"Please stop, Alex. Don't kill him."

Alex's face held no emotion as he looked past me. I distracted him because as much as I was grateful for Alex being there to protect me, I didn't want another dead body on my conscience. I was thankful he listened and backed away. I

turned and looked over my shoulder at the man
bleeding on my kitchen floor.

"Call the cops," Alex said to me.

There was no need to do that since the silent
alarm had been triggered as soon as the front
door flew off the hinges. I was about to tell him
that when I heard a gun cock back. Alex grabbed
me and we both hit the floor, crashing behind
the bar in the kitchen with him falling on top of
me, protecting and shielding me. I screamed out
as bullets flew around us and Alex kept his body
atop mine. We could hear the sirens coming and
all I could do was pray they got to us before we
ended up dead on my kitchen floor.

"Stupid-ass nigga gon' have pussy get you
killed."

"Just stop, please stop," I cried out after the
bullets stopped flying.

"Fuck you, bitch. You better hope this nigga is
around all the time. Let me catch you slipping
and both you motherfuckers are dead."

I heard his footsteps moving away from us
and then I could hear running footfalls as the
sirens and police lights decorated my front room.

It was another four hours before the police
left my home and after someone had been called
to give me another door. Alex and I answered
questions as they roamed all over the house col-

lecting evidence. He followed my lead and told the cops we both thought it was just someone trying to rob us. Our stories matched so they thought nothing of it. Some neighbors backed up our claim, saying they heard what sounded like someone was trying to kick the door down. Once the cops left, it wasn't long after that Alex left.

"You need to fix that. I may not be here to protect you next time," he said to me as he packed his bags. He'd told me the streets of Oakland had raised him and I saw that when he defended us.

"Have you ever killed someone, Alex?"

He looked at me and scratched the side of his nose. "You ever kill someone, Vix?"

He knew the answer to that so I guessed that gave me my answer. We were both murderers.

"Where're you going?"

"Home to my wife. It's safer there," he said as he pulled his shirt over his head and looked back at me.

I didn't say anything else as I watched him finish packing his things to leave. When he was done he walked over to me where I stood by the wall, used one hand to pull me close to him, and kissed me like he was never coming back.

"Bye, Vix."

I crawled into my bed and pulled the covers over my head. It would be the first time in a long time that I cried that way I did that night. I picked up my cell and sent a text.

Weak-ass nigga.

A few minutes later I got a response. Stu-pid-ass bitch.

I took a leave of absence from school and for a week, I didn't leave my home and barely left my bed. I answered no phone calls although I received many. Alex had kept his promise and I had not heard from him nor had he come back. I imagined he was living it up with his wife, kissing and pleasing her just as he had done me. I had something that she would never have though. I knew his secrets and in my mind that made me better than her.

A call from my lover confirmed that she knew about her husband and me. He'd come in with the scars of his infidelity like wounds from a war and had confessed in an effort to hurt her like she'd hurt him. She'd left message after message on my phone, threatening to fuck me up when she saw me. Then her husband's phone calls came and when I finally decided to pick up the phone, he apologized.

"I want you to know how sorry I am. I was drunk and you know I love you. Why do you

have to always make me regret falling in love
with you?"

"I didn't ask you to fall in love with me," I
answered. "And what does that have to do with
you trying to kill me?"

"I wasn't trying to kill you. I wanted to scare
you."

"You punched me in my fucking face and shot
at me. I'd say you were trying to kill me."

"Why you have that other nigga in the pad I
bought for you, Vix? That shit ain't kosher."

I could tell he was in his office at work. I could
hear Coltrane playing in the background and he
always played that in his office.

"So you only bought me this place to keep tabs
on me and with the stipulation of not having sex
with other men?"

"Something like that."

"You never said that to me. If you had I'd still
be in that hotel room looking for my own place."
I sighed, shook my head, and stood to go look
at my face in the mirror. The swelling had gone
down but the bruises and the pain were still
there.

"You really thought I'd be okay with another
nigga in the house I bought? Don't be stupid all
your fucking life, Vix."

I frowned at my phone and hung up. Screw him if he thought he could change me and keep tabs on me just by putting me in a house. He was fucking with the wrong one and if he thought I was stupid he had another think coming. I checked to make sure the deed was really in my name and it was. I'd embarrass his ass and take him to court if he tried to take the house away from me. It would ruin his image and the career he built. I'd make sure of it. He'd pissed me off and I felt as if I hadn't been in a good mood since Alex walked out of my place.

I pulled my clothes off and got in the shower. I felt the need to scrub, so I did. I needed to try to wash away the nightmares that had started to haunt me. I kept seeing me and my mother pulling the trigger and the hole that was left in Mike's head afterward, only this time he didn't die and his eyes stayed on mine.

"I'ma get'chu bitch. When you least expect a nigga to, I'ma get yo' ass," was what he would say to me.

I'd always jump awake, feeling for my gun under the pillow next to me. I hadn't had a good night's sleep since my lover's husband shot up my house. I was always fearful. Every bump or knock made me jump out of my skin. As I showered I thought of Alex and allowed my fingers to play.

I missed him, wanted him, and needed him to touch my body like only he could. Damn, that man did something to my body that no other man had come close to. He made me crave him, which no other man had ever done. I stepped out of the shower and went to get my phone. Standing under the water I held my phone away from the jetting stream and snapped photos of myself.

Once finished, I turned the shower off and wrapped myself in a towel. Sitting on my bed, I looked through the five pictures I'd taken. I didn't like any so I removed the towel from my body and sat spread eagle in front of my body mirror on the wall. I snapped a series of pictures, but the last one of me just sitting on the bed looking at the mirror with my hair flowing over my shoulders was the one I sent to him. Yes, you could see my breasts and my pussy, but I looked innocent. He'd told me he liked that look. He'd told me that after we'd talked about how my innocence was stolen from me on more than one occasion. In the message of the picture I put the words that would make him respond, knowing he would reply in kind.

Thinking of you, weak-ass nigga.

His mother would call him a weak-ass nigga when he would tell her no to sex. She would call him a faggot and say he was scared of pussy. I could feel his pain because anytime I'd do something wrong after a while when having sex with Mike, he'd call me a stupid-ass bitch. After he started using and drinking, that's all I became was a stupid-ass bitch. My phone buzzed and I jumped, hoping it was Alex. It was. He'd sent me a picture of him standing in front of a mirror. He was naked, same as I, and his dick was semi-hard.

His message read: You're beautiful. Thinking of you, stupid-ass bitch.

I smiled and lay back in my bed. Some things weren't meant to be understood and the way I felt for him was one of them. For the first time I was feeling something for a man that had nothing to do with what he could do for me, but that man was married. I could never have him so I'd take what I could get. Sleep came easy for me after that and no demons chased me in my dreams. I'd be remiss if I said Alex didn't have anything to do with that.

How was it that I'd lucked out and found a man just as damaged as I? Yes, I said it was luck, because it was. He understood me. We were cut from the same cloth and I would have never been able to tell just from the way he carried himself. He taught his students with a passion, and from the outside looking in, he was the perfect man with the perfect upbringing. Yet, he'd killed as I'd done. I saw a totally different man than the one who stood in front of his class and taught faithfully every day like his life depended on it. He gave me hope.

Finally waking up, I stepped out to get myself something to eat. I bobbed my head to "Kitty Kat" by Beyoncé as I drove. In that moment I realized that for the first time, I was alone. I had nobody in my corner, no man to cater to and no female lover to fight with. I smiled because it felt good actually. Although I missed the shit out of Alex, I would eventually come to terms with the fact that he may be the one who would never come back. He only came to me because his wife pushed him my way. Maybe it was meant to be that way. Maybe it was the universe's way of trying to teach me a lesson, to let me know there was another out there just as damaged as me. One who had overcome all of his demons to make something positive of himself. Maybe that was my lesson.

I stepped out of my car and walked into O'Charley's. I had called ahead of time to order my food since I didn't feel like cooking or waiting too long to eat. I grabbed my food and hopped back in my car, once again not paying attention to what was going on around me. My phone rang and I tapped my Bluetooth without looking to see who was calling.

"Hello?"

"So you really just gon' fuck my husband, huh?"

Her voice held an angry shrill. I sighed. "No I didn't fuck your husband. He fucked me."

She chuckled. "So it's like that?"

"Why do you care? You got the chick you wanted right? We can be done. I have nothing else to say to you. All of the shit you've taken me through and then for it to come to this. You're so full of shit."

I had told myself over and over that I didn't love her. I told myself that it was just sex and that our relationship would be the only one she had of our kind. I'd been fooling myself. I loved her. I could even go so far as to say I was in love with her. As much as I hated to admit it, I was. She'd had a hold on me for years. She was my first. She would always be my first and I'd hate her for it. I was so mad that the truck in my rearview mirror never crossed my mind. I got off onto the expressway as my lover yelled at me on the phone.

"Bitch, don't play me. You're the one full of shit. How dare you go for my husband? He told me how you left the thongs in his briefcase and how many times you've come after him. You just had to have it all, huh? Couldn't be just satisfied with me?"

I frowned then laughed after I hit the steering wheel. "Couldn't just be satisfied with you? Are you damn crazy? You need help. I see that now. I'm not the crazy one, you are. You didn't even want the man any damn way."

"You a ho-ass bitch and when I see you it's fisticuffs on sight."

I shook my head again. She would always be a wretched hood bitch underneath all of the prim and proper façade she put on.

"The last time you put your hands on me was the last time."

Her accent had gotten thicker and it reminded me that she was dangerous. "I'm going to fuck you up, Vix. Watch me. Damn. Why the fuck couldn't you see that I loved you? I'm the only one who's going to love you the way you need. Nobody but me!"

I could hear things crashing and falling in her background like she was throwing them around as she talked.

I calmly responded, "You're crazy. You need help. Serious help."

"Fuck you, Vix, for playing with me like this. Did he give you what I could? He can't touch you like me. You're really just determined to fuck me over, right?"

I hung up the phone and threw my Bluetooth from my ear. Lots of things ran through my mind in that moment, like if I'd really bitten off more than I could chew. My car started to jerk and a loud beep erupted and caused me to look down at the steering wheel like it could give me the answer why.

"What the hell?" I asked as it jerked harder and my cell started ringing.

A bulb clicked in my head and I looked at the gas gauge. Pissed, I cursed when I realized I was out of gas again. I shook my head and pulled over to the side of the road, cursing myself for once again forgetting to put gas in the damn car.

"Damn it."

I popped my trunk and got out of the car. Shaking my head, I pulled the trunk open and pulled the gas can out, shaking it. Nothing. I sighed and slammed the trunk closed. Cars zoomed past me as they went about their everyday lives. I was so pissed because I'd promised myself and Alex that this would never happen. I could still hear my phone ringing and knew it was my lover. I bent down into the car and grabbed my phone from the seat, causing my Bluetooth to fall to the floor. I reached for it as horns blared. I thought it was just perverts who were getting a kick out of seeing my full heart-shaped ass bent over. I had on a sweater dress and boots so I knew it was a sight for many since I only had a thong on.

I pulled my Bluetooth from the floor, put it in my ear, and stood up. Headlights blinded me as a truck came barreling at me full speed ahead. I was stuck where I stood. I tried to scream, in my mind I was screaming, but in that moment I was a deaf mute. I couldn't move. Fear gripped me and planted my feet where they were. By the time my fear caught up to my brain and screamed for me to move it was too late. The truck rammed into my car side, scraping it, hitting me, and knocked me several feet into the air. Time moved in slow motion as my body took flight, twisted, turned, and hit the ground in a hard splat. Blackness overtook me and wiped the pain out. I was broken.

A male's voice rang out in laughter close to my ear. "I told you I would get you, stupid-ass bitch."

Mike's face floated around and surrounded me in my blacked-out state. I floated on the edges of life and death as he danced around me, that hole in his head leaking brain matter and blood.

"Told yo' slut-bucket ass that I would get you when you least expected, ho," he said as he kneeled and looked at me. "See you in hell, stupid-ass bitch."

Epilogue

Machines beeped in the distance as my eyes fluttered open. Something was down my throat and every bone in my body felt broken. I could feel the puffiness and swollen nature of my face and I wanted to move but couldn't. I wanted to scream and couldn't so I just cried. I looked around the room. There was my lover and her husband; my mom and Frank were there as well. My eyes roamed the room before anyone realized I was awake and I was afraid for any of them to see that I was awake. Somebody had tried to kill me, but failed . . . So maybe there was a God. Did He save me? If so, why? There was no way he loved women like me. Women who'd murdered and whored around most of their lives.

The TV blared, and people talked around me. Somebody in that room had tried to kill me. I was sure of it. The threats that had been made on my life just minutes before my world went black made me aware of that. Both my lover and her husband had threatened me.

My mom walked over to my bed and I closed my eyes. She kissed my head and my lip twitched. That kiss reminded me of why I hated her. Reminded me of why my father had left her. She backed away and I opened my eyes again. She was looking right at me. She knew I was awake and it made me nervous. We simply stared at each other as she smiled. She was five-eight, had long hair that sat in a natural press against her scalp, and had eyes so dark that they hypnotized you if you stared into them for too long. Her body was sickening: soft plush D-cup breasts, beautiful chocolate skin, flat stomach, a lush ass, and beautiful hips.

Tears rolled down my face and my heart rate sped up. Frank walked to the edge of the bed and looked at me. There was no expression on his face, but he held his arm in a sling and the cut on his neck told of his demons as well. He'd gone home with the scars of his infidelity like wounds from a war and had confessed in an effort to hurt her like she'd hurt him. His jaw twitched as he looked at me and shook his head. I blinked slowly and looked away from him. I was ashamed of myself and fear had given me a new respect for life.

The news played in the background and caught my attention. The reporter stood in front of the

Clayton County courthouse as she talked and the wind blew her hair around.

"A Clayton College and University professor has been arrested and brought in for questioning in the attempted murder of his seventeen-year-old student. Vix Dixon was hit on I-75 as she stepped out of her car to go to her trunk. It appears as if her 2012 BMW had run out of gas when she was targeted. Alex Rodriguez was sought as a suspect when his 2011 Land Rover was found abandoned at a gas station not too far from where the hit and run occurred. This is a strange case because just hours before his truck was used, he'd reported it and his wife missing. His wife has since been found alive and well. We will have more details on this case as it develops. Another thing we would like to mention before we go is that Ms. Dixon is the daughter of the dean of Clayton College and University and it also seems as if Ms. Dixon and the professor were carrying on an affair of some sort, but as I said more details will come as we sort them out."

In no way did I believe that Alex or his wife had tried to kill me. What reason would she have had? She didn't know for sure her husband was having sex with me, right? My mind raced. I'd listened to some of their phone conversations and it seemed he had convinced her that she was overreacting and that there was no way he would be sleeping with his student, not when she'd initially accused him of it anyway.

I looked at my mother, the woman who'd become my lover just months before Mike had taken my innocence away from me. God just didn't love women like me. Women like me who'd allowed their mothers to touch them, have sex with, and have a relationship with them. That's why my dad had left. He'd come home from work on my twelfth birthday and caught my mother with her head between my legs and me just lying there, not knowing what do. He'd tried to beat her into a coma before he took me and tried to leave, but by then she'd conditioned me. I knew the story of her childhood and had known the same had happened to her. Her dad had taken her away from her mother but turned around and started doing the same thing to her. That's what kept me with her.

That's what made me tell my father no and beg him to leave me with her. My mom had known my father had warrants and she'd threatened to call the cops if he left with me. He had warrants for murder, too. So I'd come from a long line of killers and my mother turned me into one. She grabbed my hand and wiped my tears away as those thoughts berated me. I turned to look at Frank and still his eyes held no emotion.

She knew about him, but he had no idea about her. My demons had finally caught up with me and two of them were standing in the room with me.

Dirty Girls

by

Erick S. Gray

Prologue

Samson sat at the edge of his bed and stared strongly at the uniform hanging up on his closet door. It wasn't the fantasy job that he dreamed of, or was looking for, but it was a job. He sighed heavily. He wasn't too pleased about taking the job, but it was still work—much-needed employment in his predicament. Samson felt cemented to the bed. He didn't want to get up. He didn't want to don the dark blue attire and babysit a bunch of high school kids. He was an ex-marine. He did two tours in Iraq and was the best in the military—he was a soldier—infantry division. He was a sergeant. He was well skilled with guns— M16 assault rifles, the M2 Browning .50 Caliber Machine Gun, or the Mk 19 Grenade Launcher. If it fired and was lethal, Samson knew how to operate it. Samson knew how to protect himself. He had been into many firefights, or gun battles, and survived them all unscratched. He was the gladiator of his time. But, unfortunately, fate had a different plan for him.

After spending five years in the service, he found himself becoming a civilian again—back in Queens and living under his mother's roof. He survived an IED attack on the outskirts of Baghdad. It tore into the right side of the Hummer he was riding in—it ripped apart the vehicle like it was paper thin and left a crater in its wake. Samson was riding in the back, behind the driver. They were on a routine mission; it was a military convoy—the explosion came suddenly, and caught his platoon off-guard. There was a deafening explosion. The front passenger, Corporal Smith, was killed instantly from the blast. He was from Austin, Texas and had a family. The explosion tore half of him apart. Staff Sergeant Gibson was severely injured. He was seated next to Samson, and sitting behind Smith. The IED took out his right eye and left hand.

The day before, a suicide bomber blew himself up in a nearby market place, maiming and killing scores of nearby civilians. Samson was rushed to and treated at a nearby hospital. He had lost his hearing in his right ear for a few days and was in shock from the sudden explosion. The military felt that he was no longer fit for active duty or another tour, so he was given a medical discharge. That one incident, that one IED, changed his life—altered his career path. Samson loved serving in the Marines. He had dreamed about it since he was a kid. Now, he felt he had nothing but a job, having become a school safety officer at his old high school—August Martin High School in Jamaica Queens. The NYPD rejected him because they felt he had emotional issues, a temper, and his investigation decided for them that he was unfit to become a cop. So, unfortunately, the only uniform that Samson was fit to wear didn't carry a gun, or didn't put his life in danger. It was a safer gig—boring, so he thought.

It was early in the morning; the house was quiet. Samson looked at the time on the dresser. It was almost six in the morning. He was used to rising early—before dawn. It had been the routine in the service—always up before the sun. The sun was gradually peeking through the closed blinds in the bedroom, indicating morning was coming. Samson sat in his boxers. He was shirtless. His strapping physique was a marvel to those who happened to see him without a shirt. He was ripped with chiseled features that wrapped around his smooth dark skin like the night in the sky. He sported a low Caesar haircut like he always did in the military. He had dark brown eyes, was clean shaven, and was tall, and strikingly handsome. He was eye candy for the ladies.

Samson continued to sit and stare at the uniform. It had been six months since his discharge from the service. His mother was happy to see her son home. She felt Iraq was no place for her son to live. But she hated to see his heartache—the pain of being ripped away from something he loved, and knowing the love he had for joining the service.

There were a few gentle knocks at the door. Samson turned his head slightly and said, "Come in."

The door opened leisurely. Ms. Jones peeked her head inside the bedroom and caught a glimpse of her son sitting at the foot of the bed in his underwear. He looked like a statue in the dimmed room.

"Baby, are you okay?" Ms. Jones asked softly, moving farther into the bedroom.

"I'm good, Ma. Just sitting here thinking, that's all," Samson replied, his eyes focused back on the uniform that he had to wear for work in a few hours.

"You hungry?"

"I'll just have some coffee."

"Baby, you need to eat something. You can't go to work on an empty stomach on your first day," his mother said.

Samson was used to going through days on an empty stomach; there were times when staying alive was more important than eating. He was used to it. But his mother was adamant.

"I'm going to fix you some grits and eggs; it used to be your favorite."

Samson was nonchalant. He nodded.

"You nervous about work?" she asked.

"I don't know . . . it's different, Ma. How do I go from being around soldiers and killers to a damn high school?" he complained. His face cringed with just the thought of his new job.

"Baby, it's something at least. It's work. But, just thank God that you found work, and thank Sister Mary for bringing you the application. God knows you needed to finally do something, instead of moping around this house thinking about yesteryear."

"Marines won't take me back, NYPD won't hire me . . . Five years in the service, training and learning, advancing . . . for what? To babysit some damn kids at a high school. One bad road, one false judgment, and this becomes my life," Samson stated despondently.

"You're alive, Samson . . . that's what counts. You came back home to me in one piece. You came home, baby, and that's what matters right now. I feel for some of the mothers whose sons came back home in a box, or not in one piece. Every day I worried about you over there in that

272 Erick S. Gray

war . . . a senseless war that our president sent
our children over there to be slaughtered in. Our
men and women do not belong in that country,
they belong over here with their families," she
proclaimed strongly.

"Somebody gotta fight that war, Ma . . . defend
our country," he protested.

"Well, just not you then," she replied.

The room fell silent, mother and son in their
own thoughts for a short moment. Ms. Jones
broke the silence by saying, "I'll be downstairs
making you breakfast. Just keep your faith in
God and take it one day at a time and you'll be
okay, baby. You came home to something, a
family that loves you, a job and a warm home, so
thank your blessing and don't take it for granted."

Ms. Jones walked out of the bedroom and
closed the door behind her.

Samson stood up after his mother's exit and
reached for the school safety uniform, snatching
it from the hanger. He tossed it on the bed and
began getting dressed slowly. It was the closest
thing to law enforcement for him.

Chapter 1

Baby straddled her thick, juicy thighs around J. Rock's strapping frame, and the two were lost into each other's sexual perfection as she fucked him hard and fast. She felt his thick erection thrust into her like a vigorous drill, causing her body to vibrate and light up with pleasure from eight inches of experience. J. Rock was hardcore and played rough in the bedroom. He could be brutal in the bedroom. It was the way Baby liked it—rough and nasty. He would squeeze and smack her ass until it turned red. He would suck and bite on her nipples until it made Baby cringe. He would fuck her like he had complete authority over her pussy. And it was his alpha persona and notorious street reputation that Baby was attracted to.

Baby leaned forward and pressed her hands against J. Rocks' chest, with her nails digging into his flesh. She squirmed on top of J. Rock's hard-core physique; her legs came up and wrapped around him with her pussy dripping with excitement. He opened her pussy up wide like a doorway, causing Baby to pant in his ear and feeling a great heat rush through her as J. Rock forced himself deep inside of her.

"Ooooh, shit, fuck me, muthafucka . . . Ooooh, just like that . . . Damn it, just like that, my nigga!" she cooed.

"Ooh yeah, work that pussy, bitch. Oh shit . . . ooh, yeah," J. Rock moaned, staring up at Baby riding him like a race jockey with his hands against her bouncing tits.

They rattled the bed and Baby's nipples were hard as stones. J. Rock quickly switched Baby over and positioned her doggie style. He situated himself behind the young beauty. He gripped her soft figure from the back and admired her luscious backside and nice curves.

Baby was a phenomenal young woman. She was a goddess to many men, with long hair that was black as night, so black that it seemed to glow with the darkness. Her face was sculpted, as if it were chiseled out of marble, and Baby's eyes were set deep under perfectly shaped eyebrows. Her smooth caramel skin, full lips, ample breasts, and succulent, thick, and curvy figure made her the epitome of a bad bitch. She was wanted and envied by so many of her peers.

But Baby was, most times, nothing nice to play with. Her attitude was fierce; her tongue was sharp and her persona was brutal. She was a hood bitch, temperamental, and was known to easily cut a bitch or nigga with the razor or blade she carried on her person. Baby came out of the Baisley Projects off of Guy R. Brewer Boulevard, and she ran with a bunch of reckless girls who called themselves the Pussy Packin' Pound—the Triple P girls for short. They were a fifteen-deep female crew throughout their projects and were into everything including shoplifting, prostitution, drugs, fighting, and even murder if it came down to it. Baby sat high on the throne of the crew. She was well respected and loved by her homegirls. She clearly made it be known that she was not the bitch to fuck with.

It was Baby's eighteenth birthday, and she wanted to start out her day with some good dick before school. J. Rock was what she needed. He was her high for the moment. The way J. Rock would snake his dick inside of her, cup her tits, take control over her pussy, and massage her clit would cause Baby to become lost in a rapturous haze of mind-numbing orgasms that never seemed to end. She could recall almost losing consciousness a few times.

Baby gripped the bedroom banister firmly, trying to keep herself steady and prevent herself from tumbling off the bed as J. Rock had her legs spread, fucking her from the back vigorously. He was an animal. He palmed Baby's slim neck, pushed her face into the pillow, spread her ass cheeks wider, and thrust inside of Baby like an explosive discharge.

"Oh shit, I'm comin' . . . Ooooh, I'm comin' for you, baby," Baby cried out.

"That's right . . . come bitch, come on that dick," replied J. Rock with sweat dripping from his brow. "Ooh, back that sweet pussy up on a nigga!"

Baby twisted and turned. She howled in the bedroom and was about to reach the point of no return. J. Rock ravaged her pussy from behind, and it didn't take long until Baby reached her climax and exploded. Her mind spiraled into a touch of bliss as the strong orgasm rocked her into screams of more.

J. Rock soon came. Both parties looked spent. He pulled out of Baby's loving hole, and she collapsed on her side, looking exhausted. His big dick had invaded deep into her pussy and it instantly found her G spot.

"You good, Baby?" J. Rock asked.

"Shit, happy birthday to me," she replied with a delightful smile. Her body was glistening in sweat and her legs wobbly from the experience.

J. Rock didn't have time to relax after his nut; he stepped off the bed and began getting dressed, pulling up his jeans and donning his shirt. He looked at the time; it was almost 7:00 a.m.

"What time you gotta be in school?" he asked Baby.

"Whenever I get there. I ain't rushin' to get to that bitch. Shit, it's my fuckin' birthday, I need to stay home," Baby replied.

"A'ight, well, I need you to do me a favor."

"What?"

"Drop this package off for me," said J. Rock.

Baby sighed. "Where?"

"What the fuck you sighing for, Baby? Didn't you just enjoy yourself, right?"

Baby nodded.

"A'ight then . . . I'll hit you wit' fifty, just take this package to Mingles, that's all. I ain't got the time to see that nigga now," J. Rock said.

"A'ight, boo."

"Cool."

Baby stared at J. Rock as he continued to get dressed. He stood over six feet tall with an inviting, chiseled physique and long, twisting braids that reached down to his wide back. His

dark skin went well with his ink-black eyes.
J. Rock completed getting dressed. He then
opened one of his drawers, removed a small,
wrapped package, and tossed it over to Baby as
she lay on the bed.

"Hurry that shit over there, Baby. Don't have
this nigga waiting forever," J. Rock said.

"I got you, boo."

J. Rock then reached into his pocket and
pulled out a wad of bills. He peeled off a crisp
C-note and handed it to Baby, saying, "That's a
li'l somethin' extra for you to do it fast and right."

Baby smiled. She took the money without
any complaints. J. Rock tucked his 9 mm into
his waistband, concealed it with a jacket, and,
before he made his exit, he said to Baby, "Yo,
when you leave my shit, make sure my crib is
locked up tight . . . you hear me, Baby?"

"J, you know this isn't nothin' new to me. I got
you," Baby assured him.

"A'ight, just hurry up and leave."

J. Rock exited his place, leaving Baby sprawled
out across his bed buck naked and satisfied. She
loved spending time inside J. Rock's lavish apartment. It was a far better place and an escape from
her place. The large plasma TV, high-end stereo
system, the opulent leather furniture—including
the queen-sized bed that she just got fucked

on—the dope money and guns lying around, a few pictures of notorious rappers like B.I.G., Tupac, Scarface, and Goodfellas hanging on the walls—it was a gangster's paradise.

Baby lingered in bed for a few moments, savoring the aftermath of the sexual episode that was so fresh like rain in a desert. She could still feel her pussy throbbing. She didn't want to get up, but she knew that she couldn't spend her whole birthday cooped up in J. Rock's apartment. It was time to have fun. It was time to enjoy her eighteenth birthday. She was now legally an adult.

Baby got out of bed and put on her tight jean shorts, along with a tight shirt that highlighted her nice tits, and a pair of white Nikes. She let her hair flow down to her back and rocked her gleaming jewelry that was stolen from a few stores on Jamaica Avenue. She stared at herself in the bedroom mirror and smiled.

"Damn, I'm that bitch," she boasted to herself.

Baby felt she was pure perfection. She turned to look at her backside, and it was the perfect bubble for niggas to admire and drool over when she went passing by. Baby loved the attention, and loved knowing that niggas were thirsty to get inside of her panties. It was a thrill for her, but they could only look and couldn't touch. Only the privileged got to touch and then some.

Baby picked up her black book bag and stuffed J. Rock's package deep inside her bag. She slung it over her shoulder and left his apartment. She was ready to start her day. She stepped out of the building and footed it down Foch Boulevard toward Mingles's pad across the park. It was a ten-minute walk. Mingles was a hustler like J. Rock, moving product for the boss—hustling marijuana and crack out of his basement apartment off of 119th Road. It was on her way to school, so it was easy for her to carry out J. Rock's favor. Baby was far from worried about being caught with drugs or guns on her. She had been doing it for so long that it was an everyday thing for her. It came easy to her, like walking.

She arrived at Mingles's apartment and walked into a room full of wolves and thugs. Mingles was a chubby, high-yellow hustler with a nappy 'fro and bad hygiene. He had nasty habits and a nasty place to match. It was always dirty, stinking, and packed with niggas from the block. The hood thought of Mingles's place as looking like some type of refugee camp for lost thugs. He was sloppy with himself and his business. She hated going to see Mingles because she always felt that if she stayed in his place too long, then she would leave with some kind of stench, or nasty critter attached to her, and not knowing when the police might come to raid his place. He was reckless and careless. It was the last thing Baby wanted to get caught up in on her birthday.

"Baby, what's poppin' . . . ? You got somethin' for ya daddy?" Mingles greeted her with a smile. He had an afro pick pushed into his nappy 'fro, and was shirtless, exposing the funk and scars across his skin.

"I just came to drop this off for you. It's from J. Rock," she said, tossing Mingles the package she pulled from out of her book bag.

The room was crowded with niggas lingering around, smoking, playing Xbox, counting money, or packaging drugs. Everything and everyone was exposed, and there were too many unfamiliar faces to Baby. The minute she walked into the crib, all eyes were on her. She saw the lust in their eyes and felt their hunger to fuck her. But Baby stood with a deadpan stare and was focused on her business with Mingles.

"Damn, that's what's up. J. Rock always come through for a nigga," said Mingles.

"You good?" she asked.

"Yeah, we always good."

"Cool."

Baby turned and was ready to make her exit, but one of Mingles's goons decided to block the doorway. He was tall, shirtless, and ugly with missing teeth. "I'm sayin', why don't ya stay fo' a while? You ain't gotta rush to leave, ma," he said.

Baby instantly caught an attitude. "First off, nigga, I ain't ya fuckin' ma; I don't give birth to ugly babies. And second, nigga, you better get the fuck outta my way 'fore you get fucked up!"

The shirtless thug laughed. "I'm sayin', ma, you lookin' good. Stay around and chill for a minute. . . ."

"So you really wanna go there and dance wit' me right now, muthafucka!" Baby exclaimed through clenched teeth. "And you lookin' busted too; you just ugly, nigga!"

She locked eyes with the ugly thug. She showed no fear, and subtly had her blade gripped in her pocket and was ready to cut him.

"Bo, leave her alone before you have J. Rock comin' over here and fuckin' us up for fuckin' wit' his bitch," Mingles shouted.

"I was just playin' around wit' her, Mingles," he shouted back.

"She ain't that bitch to be fuckin' around wit'," replied Mingles.

"Listen to your friend, stupid," chimed Baby.

"Whatever," the thug shouted. He stepped to the side and allowed Baby to pass.

"Stupid muthafucka," Baby uttered loudly.

Baby stepped out of the basement apartment and exhaled. The funk in the basement was overwhelming. Baby hated that she had to endure that type of environment on her birthday. She took a quick whiff of her clothing to make sure she didn't smell funky like the basement. But she was okay. She continued her walk to school and couldn't wait to show off and show out on her birthday. She clearly wanted to make it known to everyone that she was eighteen and proud of it.

Chapter 2

Baby strutted through the doors with a smile and a sassy attitude. She walked through the metal detector without any incident from the alarm going off. She was clear for any weapons or contraband. She smiled at the tall guard with the security wand in his hand. He stared at Baby's racy attire. His eyes focused on the scanty shorts revealing the camel-toe imprint between her legs, and he lusted at her shapely and long legs. The petite and shapely high school student had him hypnotized for a short moment. Baby smiled at him and said, "Why you staring at me so hard, Marvin? You like what you see?"

Marvin waved her off and replied, "You know you're late, Baby."

"And?" Baby replied, rolling her eyes.

"Eighth time this month that you've been late."

"It's my birthday, Marvin. You ain't gonna wish me a happy birthday?"

"Happy birthday," Marvin replied dryly. "But you know after a certain time, I'm not allowed to let you into this school."

"But I'm here now, so what's the problem? And besides, you know you gonna let me in anyway; you like lookin' at all this. I be makin' ya fuckin' day when you see me move through these halls lookin' this fine," she commented harshly. "You wanna fuck me, Marvin?"

Marvin shook his head. He kept his composure. "You're a mess, Baby. But eighteen or not, you're still a little girl, and have a lot of growing up to do."

"Whatever, nigga . . . Let me just go to the office, get my late pass, and be on my way. You probably gay anyway, and can't handle this pussy even if I gave you a chance to hit it."

"This is my last warning to you, Baby. If you're late like this again, I'm not letting you into this school," he warned.

Baby smiled. "We'll see." She strutted by him, switching her hips and flaunting her sexuality in front of the safety officer. He took a quick glance and shook his head. Baby continued toward the main office to receive her late pass for class. The only reason she decided to come to school was because she wanted to flaunt for her birthday and see her girls. And, someone owed her money.

She pranced into the office and exclaimed, "I need a late pass."

The office staff stared at Baby with contempt. This was nothing new for them. Baby was one of a few problem students in the school, and they'd had their share of her wild antics over the years from the fights and attitude. They were still surprised that she was a student at August Martin. There were plenty of moments when she was at risk of being expelled. But, she had nine lives. It, supposedly, was her senior year, but graduation for her was still far off and farfetched.

One of the staff walked over to Baby. She had no words for the young child. Baby stared at her impatiently and said, "C'mon, Mrs. Jerry, I ain't got all day."

"Then why bother coming to school at all?" she asked.

"Shit, what else am I gonna do? I'm the life of this school."

Mrs. Jerry shook her head in shame and quickly wrote Baby a late pass to her second period class. Baby snatched the note from her hands without so much as saying a thank you to the lady. Mrs. Jerry watched her sashay out of the office and said, "That child is going to end up either pregnant or dead one day."

Baby stormed into her second period English class, handed the teacher her late pass, and marched toward the back of the classroom, interrupting Mr. Thompson's lecture on structuring a paragraph. For a short moment, all the attention was on her. She was rude. She looked around for her friends, but they weren't in the classroom. Baby figured that she was probably the only dumb one to come to school on her birthday. She didn't plan on staying long, though.

Mr. Thompson stared at Baby and exclaimed, "It's nice of you to finally join us, Ms. Rice."

"You know it's my birthday today, so I needed to make an entrance," she replied.

"Like you do every day, or on the days that you actually decide to show up to school," whipped Mr. Thompson.

"Ya funny, Mr. Thompson, I'm sayin' . . . Go on and teach; don't let me stop you. I'm here to learn, right . . ." she replied with sarcasm. "I'ma sit back here and look cute, but I'm still learning somethin' . . . but you should be learning from me."

There was an eruption of laughter from the class. Mr. Thompson didn't find her comment or humor funny. He glared at Baby and said, "Life is not a game, Ms. Rice. You need to understand that."

"Whatever, just teach somethin', Mr. Thompson, and I'ma sit here and pretend like I'm listening, a'ight!" Baby hissed back.

Mr. Thompson didn't want to spend too much time arguing with Baby. He didn't want to show her the attention that she always craved. He walked toward the chalkboard and continued with his lesson.

Baby slouched in her seat and looked around the classroom. She noticed a certain hard look trained on her. It was coming from Erica. The two hated each other. Baby cut her eyes back at Erica, smirked, and tossed up her middle finger, showing that she wasn't intimidated by the stare.

The two girls had had an ongoing beef for months. It was over J. Rock. He supposedly was Erica's man, but Baby had no problem fucking him occasionally—and J. Rock didn't have a problem showing Baby intimacy and splurging his ill-gotten wealth on her, when Erica was his girlfriend. Baby didn't hide the fact that she and J. Rock were fucking. Her mouth ran slick like oil throughout the hood, and she wanted to make Erica jealous. She hated how Erica flaunted herself, always bragging about her family being in the music business like they were the Jacksons.

Erica's older brother, Sean, used to be in a famous rap group back in the late nineties

and he became somewhat of a success with his
producing and acting in a few films. The family
came into some wealth, and Erica was living off
of her brother's success. She had everything she
needed: money, clothes, and even a car. She
walked around the school like she was a diva,
and Baby hated it. Baby always felt that Erica
was a fake bitch, and was too stuck-up to be with
a man like J. Rock. They came from two different
worlds; J. Rock was rugged, while Erica was the
Whitley Gilbert of the school when it came to
having money. But the difference was that Erica
knew how to throw down, and was able to hold
her own in a fight; she was nowhere like a Whitley Gilbert. She ran with a wild crew of girls who
called themselves Live Divas, or L.D. girls for
short. And, over the past few months, the Triple
P girls had bumped heads with the Live Divas,
and gotten into a few physical confrontations
inside and outside of the school.

Baby and Erica glared at each other. Baby
hated the way Erica was staring at her. She
became upset, and shouted, "Bitch, what the
fuck you lookin' at?"

"You, you stupid fuckin' bitch!" Erica shouted.
"You a fuckin' slut, bitch!"

"Bitch, that's why I just fucked ya man this
morning fo' my birthday. What the fuck you
gonna do about it?" Baby shouted.

Both girls jumped out of their seats and were ready to clash with each other. Mr. Thompson spun around and instantly got between the two girls. He knew about their history and had warned them many times about interrupting his class sessions. But the girls didn't care; they were ready to tear into each other with hatred and disrespect and were far from worried about a suspension from school.

"Sit down," Mr. Thompson screamed at both girls. "Not in my damn classroom. Do you two ladies hear me?"

The class had gotten riled up and was ready to see a fight take place. But Mr. Thompson quickly regained order. He wasn't having any disorder in his room. He stood over six feet tall and outweighed both girls easily. He was a black man from a poverty-stricken ghetto, also. He was able to relate to many of his students. He hated violence, was about unity with his kids, and he hated to see black students fight each other over foolishness. It really upset him that many of his students didn't take getting an education seriously.

"Fuck her, Mr. Thompson. I'm sick of that bitch," Baby exclaimed.

"You a dirty bitch, Baby. I swear, I'ma see you!" Erica retorted.

"See me then, bitch!"

Mr. Thompson had both girls sit down and then he shouted, "What is wrong with y'all? Y'all supposed to be sisters."

Baby sighed and retorted, "That bitch ain't no sister of mines. Mr. Thompson, save that family, African-pride shit for someone else who cares. Don't bring that shit my way."

"There's always a problem with y'all two, but I'm not having that nonsense in my classroom."

"Then we just gonna take it somewhere else," replied Baby.

"It's sickening . . . Two beautiful young women wanting to fight and destroy each other . . . and over what, a boy!" he exclaimed. "How twisted can y'all be?"

Baby sighed and averted her attention from her English teacher. She stared out the window with a scowl, having her arms folded across her chest. She was itching to fight Erica. The anxiety that was bubbling inside of her was ready to explode.

Mr. Thompson went on to teaching his class and the conflict between the two girls was only postponed. A fight between them was inevitable.

Chapter 3

August Martin High School was buzzing with students and staff. It was third period, and students swarmed the hallways with their loud chatter and laughter, and the teachers hurriedly prepared for their next class. The school sat across the street from Baisley Pond Park—giving it a serene view on the busy boulevard. The entrance to the school—with its towering stone pillars, gold doors, and iconic granite structure—was a sight for everybody to see, resembling the front of the Supreme Court building.

It was a Monday morning. Samson made his way toward the admissions office. He had new jack written all over his face. His eyes scanned every inch of the hallway; and the students noticed the new guard in their school immediately. Samson was tall and sturdy, and caught a few fleeting looks from female students and the staff. Samson's uniform fit him with style and class. The Marines taught him how to look sharp in any uniform. He wore it well with his build—it was identical to the uniform worn by police officers; the only exception was the color of the shirt, which was light blue in contrast to the dark blue shirt worn by police officers. His badge was oval with an eagle top, also in contrast to the shield worn by police officers.

Samson stood in the admissions office and waited to be greeted by his supervisor. The place was buzzing with activity: students in and out with schedules in their hands, the staff filing paperwork, and the phone ringing constantly. The aging ladies sitting in the office behind their desks glanced at Samson with smiles and admired his lean build and striking looks. He was eye candy to them—and he would be something or someone to talk about after his departure from the office.

"You're the new guy, huh?" Billy McDonald said to Samson. He emerged from the back office and walked up to Samson, greeting him with a smile and a handshake.

Samson nodded as they exchanged handshakes.

"I'm Billy McDonald, your supervisor. Welcome to the team," he said.

Samson remained quiet. Billy was a pudgy fellow with a protruding stomach and thinning hair. He was light skinned, clean shaven, and was always filled with trustworthy advice along with laughs and smiles for his coworkers. He was fun to be around. But he was the exact opposite of appearance when standing next to Samson. Samson towered over his supervisor by half a foot, and had a steady glance coming from the ladies in the office.

Billy was in his mid-forties and had been a security officer for over twenty years. He was married with children, and took his job seriously. He knew everything about the job and, most important, he knew everything about dealing with the students in his school.

"I heard you're a military man," Billy said.

"Yeah, Marines . . . Did two tours in Iraq," Samson mentioned.

Billy nodded and smiled. "My man . . . I'm a military man myself, army though. But didn't see much action . . . Wish I did, though. But, hey, the past is the past; it's the present day that matters now. You can't live your life wondering and thinking about the what-ifs, because if you start doing that, then you'll wake up from your daze and see that life done passed you by."

It was Billy's first good advice to Samson. Samson nodded.

"The uniform fits you well. I see you already got the ladies glued to you," Billy joked, slapping

Samson on the arm playfully. "But c'mon, take a walk with me. I'll show you around."

Samson followed his supervisor out of the office and into the lion's den. The hallway was clear of students. The next period bell sounded and the classes were filled with a diversity of freshmen to seniors.

"Now the first thing you must know: you're here to be alert and regulate the flow of students at entrances and from class to class, and to maintain order of the school interior. We check outer perimeters for unauthorized persons, and also check student ID, challenge visitors, and adhere to visitor control procedures. We also immediately report possible child abuse. I had plenty of those over the years. But, watch out for drugs, alcohol, gang participation, or psychological problems. On this job, we use minimal force necessary to effect arrest and so on and so on."

Billy's speech was textbook as they walked up the stairway to the second floor. Samson was quiet and listened intently.

"Now these kids are tough, most of them can be a handful . . . A few come from very broken homes, and unfortunately, the few bad apples make it hard for the rest of the students who want to learn in this school. They will test you, try you, make fun of you . . . basically, they're gonna try to break you, get under your skin. You can't let them. Remember, always remain professional on your job . . . You're the adult, and they're just children, so try to remember that at all times. Some of them might want to fight you; you don't hit back, no matter what they say or do to you. And some of these young girls will flirt with you; you keep your eyes and hands to yourself, because we take sexual harassment serious in this school and on this job. And you don't want to get caught up in that mess . . . Guilty or not, it will always leave a stigma on you," Billy proclaimed.

Samson listened. The two men were walking down the second floor corridor when suddenly a call erupted through Billy's radio. "We have a fight in the cafeteria . . . a fight between a group of girls."

Billy took off running and Samson followed him. As the men ran toward the cafeteria, Billy uttered, "Now you get to see the real thing."

The men bolted for the basement cafeteria. When they arrived on the chaotic scene, there were a bunch of girls fighting in the lunchroom. It was a four-on-one battle. The two officers already present tried to break it up, but the girls were brutal; there was hair pulling, kicking and screaming, and food being thrown everywhere.

"Fuck that bitch up! Fuck her up," one girl shouted.

The lunchroom was loud with excitement and riled up. The students around were encouraging the fight. There was blood spewing, clothing being torn, and weaves being ripped out. Erica tried to kick Baby in the face as she stumbled to the floor; she was being assaulted by three of the L.D. girls.

But, Baby wasn't going down easily. She grabbed one girl tightly by her long weave, knotting her fist around her hair, and yanked her hair back with such force that it felt like her neck had snapped. The girl screamed from the jolt of the rough hair pulling and Baby abruptly caught her with a strong right hook against her temple.

Erica jumped on Baby, striking her in the back of her head with her closed fist. Security tried to grab Erica off of Baby, but the young girl was stronger than they expected.

"Get the fuck off! Get the fuck off me!" Erica screamed. "I'ma fucked that bitch up! I'ma kill that slut bitch! She fucked my man . . ."

Baby spun around to lunge at Erica and punched her repeatedly in her face as security tried pulling Erica back from the group of girls fighting. Baby got off a few good hits until Billy and Samson rushed over. Samson immediately grabbed Baby from behind. His strong arms wrapped around Baby like a large cloth. He lifted her off her feet effortlessly and pulled Baby away from the assault on Erica. Baby struggled to break free from his strong grip, but it was fruitless. Samson was too strong.

"Get off me . . . Aaaahhh, nigga, get the fuck off me . . . I hate that bitch!" Baby shouted, squirming and trying to fight her way free from Samson's monstrous hold.

Samson refused to let her go until everything was cool. More safety officers rushed into the cafeteria, and the girls fighting were quickly broken apart and detained. The area was a mess. There was food everywhere and some blood. Lunch was over for everyone.

Billy walked over to where Samson was holding Baby. He glared at the brutal young student and shook his head. "Baby, there's always some problem with you. Just take her to the main office, Samson."

"Fuck you!" Baby spat. "That bitch started it!"

"And you had to finish it."

"They tried to jump me, and she got fucked up," growled Baby with the screw face.

Billy looked at Samson and said, "Just get her out of here."

Samson escorted Baby out of the cafeteria with
her still cursing and carrying on. But Samson
had her under control. He was forceful with the
young girl. When they'd exited the lunchroom,
Baby began to calm down somewhat. Her hair
was in disarray, and she had a few scratches
across her face, but everything else about Baby
was okay. Her pride and ego were more bruised
than anything.

Samson marched Baby up the stairs and into
the main office, doing as he was told. He pushed
Baby into the chair and stood over her.

"Damn, muthafucka . . . Why you gotta be so
rough?" Baby exclaimed.

Samson didn't respond. He just stood near
her to make sure she didn't go anywhere. Baby
started to size him up. She knew he was new.
Samson was built like stone and was almost
wide like a door. His muscles stretched all over
him. He wasn't smiling, but remained adamant.

"So, you like pushing me around like that, huh,
Conan?" Baby asked, giving him the name Conan
because of his overwhelming physique. "Did it
make you feel good to grab a bitch like me like
that, huh? I got ya dick hard, nigga? Let me see."

Samson didn't respond to her. When Baby
tried to grab his crotch, he took a step back and
said to her, "Don't go there."

"Why not?" She smiled.

Samson turned his attention away from her. Baby chuckled. "Whatever, faggot!"

But she found him impressive and mysterious. *He's different from the others,* Baby thought. She became calmer. She slouched in the chair and looked up at Samson. "You must be a military man," she continued.

Samson looked at her.

Baby smiled. "Yeah, now I got ya attention. Marines, right?" Baby continued with the questions. "But ya cute . . . damn, fuckin' sexy. You could touch on me if you like."

Before Samson could comment, the principal stormed into the main office. He stared harshly at Baby and said, "What is your damn problem, Monica?"

"My name isn't Monica, it's Baby," she corrected him with attitude.

"In my school, your name is Monica. Get inside my damn office," Principal Palmer exclaimed. "You're pushing my buttons, young lady. You seriously are!" Principal Palmer stormed off.

Baby jumped up from her chair and looked at Samson. "Well, it's been fun; see ya around, Marine," said Baby. She then coolly strutted toward the principal's office, following Palmer.

Samson stared at the girl longer than needed. He sighed and exited the office.

Principal Carson Palmer was a distinguished black man in his early fifties. He was educated with a few degrees in business and education from Harvard and Columbia. He grew up in Harlem during the seventies and was well respected in the school and in the community. He was a hands-on principal—always interacting with many of his students via programs, events, lingering in the hallways, and knowing many of his students by their names and personalities. He was also well acquainted with the teachers, staff, and officers. Palmer cared for everyone like they were his own family. He was a married man of fifteen years with three kids.

Baby walked into the principal's office and slumped down in the chair. Her face was still in a scowl with a nonchalant attitude. Principal Palmer sat behind his large desk opposite Baby and looked at her for a moment. His office was decorated with bowling and track trophies from his previous school days. There were pictures of his wife and kids situated on his desk, and many degrees from a few elite schools he graduated from were hanging up on his office walls in a proud display of accomplishments. It indicated how far he had come and how educated he was.

Palmer was dressed in a dark brown suit. He was handsome and tall, sporting a grayish goatee, and had a swag about him that preceded him.

He leaned back in his leather chair, stared at Baby and asked, "What am I going to do with you, young lady? What is wrong with you? Aren't you tired of coming to this office? And it's your birthday today . . . what a way to celebrate it."

"Why I'm the only one here? I wasn't fighting myself," she spat.

"Oh, they will be disciplined too. So you don't have to worry about them. But right now, we're here to talk about you," said Palmer.

"Then let's not," snapped Baby. "'Cause I really don't give a fuck right now!"

"You watch your mouth in this office and in my school."

Baby sucked her teeth.

Palmer let out an irate sigh. He leaned forward with his elbows resting on his desk and clasped his fingers together. He locked eyes with the young, rough Baby. He was very familiar with Baby's pedigree—knowing her history very well. He knew about her mother dying in prison when she was only fourteen, and that her father was killed overseas during his tour in Iraq a few years ago. Baby was alone. She felt abandoned.

She was staying with her elderly grandmother who had dementia. They had an in-house nurse living with them who was taking care of her sick grandmother. Baby was the only child, and the only person she had close to her who was like a sister to her was her cousin G.G. The two girls had been through thick and thin together. They started and ran the Pussy Packin' Pound crew jointly.

Palmer wanted to believe that Baby's wild and promiscuous ways were all a façade. He truly believed that she was hiding her pain of the loss of her parents by acting out—fighting and fucking whoever. She was a very pretty girl, so pretty that they said her beauty was able to hypnotize any man with a swinging penis. Baby's innocent look with her almond-shaped eyes, full, luscious lips, and butter-like complexion could stir any man's heart—but not everything that glitters is gold, and Baby was far from gold. She was poison.

"You want me to expel you from this school like your cousin, G.G.," said Palmer. "This beef with the L.D. girls needs to stop now, Monica, or I'll guarantee that you'll be gone from this school like your cousin."

"You act like G.G. give a fuck about this school. She out there gettin' money right now, somethin' that I need to be doin' too, instead of wasting my time in this bitch. But do what you gonna do, Principal Palmer. I'ma still be good, no matter what happens, 'cause I'm a hustler, and I'ma get mines," she proclaimed with attitude.

"Listen, Monica—"

"Baby . . . Stop callin' me that," she interrupted angrily.

"You know I will never call you that."

"Yeah, look," Baby started, standing up from her seat. "I need to go; we done here? Can I leave now?"

"Why did you show up to school in the first place?" he asked sympathetically.

"'Cause I wanted muthafuckas to sweat me up in here on my birthday," she returned. "You know how I do."

"You need to change your ways, Monica. I'm putting you on a three-day suspension. I'm going to help and pray for you," Palmer said.

Baby chuckled and replied with, "You is such a hypocrite nigga, fo' real, Principal Palmer. You better pray for yourself, 'cause you the one that's gonna need it."

Baby turned to exit his office, leaving the principal shaking his head and looking stunned. Everyone knew that he let her get away with too many things. Baby seemed almost untouchable in his school. They knew that Principal Palmer had a soft spot for Baby. He was known to care about his students, good or bad, but Baby had too many chances and they felt she had burned her bridges with everyone a long time ago.

Baby stormed out of the front entrance and right past Samson and Marvin.

"I'll see you in three days, Conan," she said to Samson with a pleasant smile.

The two safety officers watched Baby strut out of the building, their stares lingering on the perfect, round bubble formed in her shorts. Marvin shook his head, smiled, and said to Samson, "That young girl right there, she's nothing but a whirlwind of trouble. Stay far away from her, my man, 'cause that bitch right there can be a nigga's Delilah."

Samson didn't comment back. He just stood near the exit door and remained cool. His new job seemed more interesting in more ways than one.

Chapter 4

G.G. sat perched on the park bench in front of the baseball field, smoking a Newport and hanging out with the Pussy Packin' Pound girls. They passed around a burning blunt, along with a bottle of E&J—joking around and passing the day by getting high and talking shit. G.G. took a drag from the Newport, then took the blunt in her hand and took a long pull from it. She exhaled and laughed at T.T.'s comment.

"So I kicked that bird bitch dead in her ass, and heard the bitch howl and fart."

The group laughed. T.T. was the comedian. She was able to lighten up anyone's day with her wild antics and storytelling. She was both the rough and funny one in the group. T.T. was the one who would say something funny while whooping a bitch's ass or would be quick to clown on anyone who wasn't up to par, or if their wardrobe was whack. She didn't hold her tongue for anyone.

"You is dead wrong, T.T., but that's some funny shit. I hate that dumb bitch. You should'a cut that bitch, gave her ass a buck-fifty, fo' sure," said G.G.

"I let her be, G.G. I embarrassed that bitch enough already," T.T. replied. "But next time she look at me stupid like that again, I will cut that bitch like I'm Chef Boyardee."

"Shit, I'll do it for you. That bird bitch, Melissa, already know I don't like her trifling ass . . . Slut bitch," G.G. said.

G.G. took another pull from the blunt and passed it to the closet girl to her. G.G. was the dominant girl in her clique. She was just like her cousin, Baby—fierce and nothing nice to play with. She was also eighteen and a beautiful young woman. She was thick in the right places, with dark, penetrating eyes—but she carried a small scar across her right cheek: a clear indication of the numerous street battles she endured over the years. However, the scar didn't take away from her beauty or luscious figure; it only added to her assertive personality. Men still chased her, and females either envied or feared her.

G.G. was a hood bitch. She was always found fighting, selling drugs, fucking, or cursing somebody out. Her fierce reputation moved around like the wind in the air. She had no time for games or shit talking. G.G. was that bitch who wouldn't hesitate to hurt or even shoot someone when she felt disrespected or threatened. She carried a .25 for protection, and a razor. Sometimes it was concealed in her mouth, under her tongue, or on her person. Her record of arrests was as long as her arm. She had been tried in court for everything from felony assaults to drug possession, and even attempted murder. Her cases were all thrown out, dropped to lesser charges with a light plea, or she'd beaten the charges completely. G.G. had been a lucky woman over the years. She spent minimum time in Rikers Island.

G.G. was a young, beautiful girl, but one look in her young face and you were able to see the hardened image of someone who had been through enough hell. Her eyes told many stories of hardship and abuse. She had a sick mother at home, dying from cancer, and selling crack on the street corner or in the belly of the project stairway just wasn't cutting it for G.G. anymore. She was ready to look for means from a different hustle.

G.G.'s thick and long legs were clad in a pair of tight jeans along with a fitted T-shirt that highlighted her breasts. She sported a pair of fresh white Nikes, and a few trinkets around her wrist and neck. Her hair was styled into long, fine-looking dreadlocks that she'd been growing since she was thirteen. G.G. always took time out to take care of her appearance. She was a little rough around the edges, but her attire was always up to par, and her hair was always done.

The girls continued to smoke and talk. G.G. noticed young Meeka walking across the park. She stared at Meeka as the sixteen-year-old moved toward the clique with a sense of urgency. G.G. took a few more pulls from her cigarette and uttered, "What Meeka want? She rushing over like something happened."

The girls turned to see Meeka approaching. Everybody was quiet. Meeka ran over to G.G. and exclaimed, "Yo, G.G., fuckin' Erica and her crew just tried to jump on Baby."

"What?" G.G. shouted. "When?"

"I was there, this morning, in the cafeteria . . . They tried to go ham on your cousin."

G.G. jumped off the bench and walked toward Meeka. "Where my cousin at?"

"She got suspended."

"Yo, we gonna fuck that bitch up," G.G. exclaimed. "I swear, I hate that fuckin' bitch! She fuckin' wit' the wrong crew!"

Her girls had her back. They were six deep, and ready to storm up to the school and hunt Erica down. G.G. was ready to lead her pack into battle. They were quick to follow her lead. G.G. showed no hesitation. She marched toward the high school just as the afternoon classes were coming to an end. She wanted to find Baby.

The Triple P girls stood across the street from the school in a mob. The students who were exiting from their last period classes instantly knew something big was brewing—a fight. There were close to twenty people lingering in Baisley Pond Park, and the looks shown on the girls' faces indicated that they weren't at the school to laugh and mingle. G.G. stood among her girls, poised for battle with a scowl and trying to scan the crowd for Erica, or any one of her girls, to jump on. Baby wasn't around.

School safety officers were at the entrance of the school and they became on high alert when they noticed G.G. standing across the street with eight project girls standing behind her. They didn't want any problems, but they had seen this type of commotion before. They all were very aware of G.G.'s reputation. She was kicked out last year for assaulting a teacher and being caught with crack in her possession. She was arrested, charged, and had a court date pending, but she always was coming back for trouble.

G.G. stood with her mob of girls and searched the crowd for Erica. She was ready to fuck her

up. It was fifteen minutes past 3:00 p.m., and
the school grounds were flooded with students
on their way home, or to the nearest bus stops.
Many students decided to linger around, antici-
pating a fight or beat down to happen. There was
gossip—many knew about the incident earlier
in the cafeteria with Baby and Erica. They knew
the beef wasn't over; round two was expected
to happen sometime soon. School staff and
officers were on edge. Their school had become
a battleground for fights between warring gang
members like the Bloods, the Crips, the Triple P,
and the L.D. girls. They inundated the hallways
showing off their gang signs when it was not
allowed, tagging the bathrooms with their marks,
fighting each other, and threatening anyone who
came against them. It had become a serious
problem for the principal and his staff.

After a moment of waiting, G.G. finally saw
her rival.

Erica and her crew emerged from a side exit
of the school. Word had gotten back to her about
G.G. waiting outside to fight her. She was ready
to confront G.G. and tear her face apart.

"There go that bitch right there!" G.G. exclaimed.

G.G. and her crew ran over to where Erica
was seen approaching. They glared at each other

with their fists clenched, and a few razors and
knives in their possession. It was about to get
ugly. Security noticed the confrontation about to
take place, and a few ran over to try to prevent it
while 911 was being called.

"You try and jump my fuckin' cousin, bitch!"
G.G. shouted. "I swear, if you come near my
fuckin' cousin again, I'ma fuckin' body you,
bitch!"

"Fuck you and that bitch," retorted Erica. "Get
fucked up like she did earlier!"

"What, bitch?"

"You heard me, bitch! Step the fuck off, you
dumb slut!" shouted Erica. "Get the fuck out my
face!"

Tempers were flaring. The girls were harsh,
and soon up in each other's face like their skin
itself. A large crowd had formed around the
girls. It was getting ugly. The girls were ready to
kill each other. The harsh words aimed at both
groups were vile and threatening. But the two
groups didn't come to curse each other out. It
was inevitable for them to start clashing with fists
and blows at each other. Before security came to
break up the dispute, G.G. quickly swung on Erica,
striking her in the head a few times. Erica fought
back, grabbing G.G.'s shirt and ripping it from
her shoulders. Rapidly, both mobs of girls began

tearing into each other—a full-scale fight in front
of the school and in the middle of the street had
escalated.

The crowd that stood around watching were
yelling and screaming. It was an exciting episode. The vicious assaults happening in front of
their school had them wide eyed and some were
cheering for it to continue. The fighting was brutal—weaves were being ripped apart, girls were
being stomped on, and the yelling and cursing
was loud and obnoxious.

"Fuck that bitch up! Fuck that bitch up!" someone was heard shouting.

"You stupid bitch!"

A few camera phones were recording the
incident, following numerous fights among a
dozen or more ruthless girls, with some clothing
being ripped loosely and tits being exposed, with
some skin showing. It excited the young men.

"Yo, this shit is goin' on Worldstar, son . . .
YouTube and everything!" one young student
shouted out excitedly, as he followed the action
with his camera phone in hand.

The fight moved up the block away from the
school, and was stopping some traffic coming
down Baisley Boulevard. More people stopped to
witness the fighting. Security officers attempted
to break it up, but there were too many girls in
the conflict for them to handle at once.

G.G. had Erica on the ground. She stood over her with her fist clenched and wailed on Erica with a series of reckless blows, striking her in the face multiple times. "What, bitch, huh? What now, you stupid bitch?" G.G. screamed out.

Erica attempted to get up, but G.G. forcefully knocked her back down onto the pavement with a brutal kick across her face. "Touch my fuckin' cousin again!"

The Triple P girls were wreaking havoc on the L.D. girls; they had them outnumbered and were fierce in battle. Erica lay against the concrete pavement with a mouth full of blood and a bruised face along with a bruised ego. G.G. proved to be the victor of the fight. She continued assaulting Erica wickedly with kicks and punches to her face and body.

Police sirens were soon heard blaring from a distance. T.T. ran over to G.G. and pulled her friend off of Erica, shouting, "G.G., we gotta go! Let's get the fuck outta here."

G.G. glared down at the defeated Erica and shouted, "Lay there and fuckin' bleed, bitch!" She spat on Erica and ran off with T.T. and her crew.

The show was over, and many students quickly departed, leaving a few of the defeated L.D. girls lying on the ground, and licking their wounds.

Erica was seriously injured. She couldn't get up and needed medical assistance. Police were soon heavily on the scene, and Principal Palmer could only shake his head at the madness. He was clearly upset. He looked into the eyes of some of the students who lingered around after the fight and exclaimed, "What is going on with you kids? This hate and fighting among y'all needs to stop now!"

His students only looked at him nonchalantly. It was their world, and they felt that their principal didn't understand where they came from.

G.G. and T.T. walked toward their projects with pride and respect. They glorified the fight and ass-whooping they gave Erica and her weak crew by laughing and mocking the incident. G.G. felt victorious. It was a relief for her to beat those bitches down—revenge for them was refreshing. The day was still fresh and the two girls were like lionesses as they moved through their hood on a sunny October afternoon. G.G. and T.T. strutted into the lobby. The girls wanted to rest up and smoke some weed in G.G.'s apartment. But the minute G.G. and T.T. entered the lobby and headed toward the stairway, Young J stopped the girls in the lobby and warned G.G.

"Nah, don't go up there, G.G. You got cops up there right now knockin' on ya door and lookin' fo' you."

"What?" G.G. questioned. "Right now?"

"Yeah, they talkin' about tryin' to arrest you for some outstanding warrants on ya ass, and word is goin' around about that fight in front of Martin," Young J informed them.

Young J was fourteen. He was a sharp young kid who always had his ears and eyes open in the streets, knowing about people's business. He had the strongest crush on G.G.; whatever she needed he was willing to do, or go get for her.

T.T. looked at her friend and said, "You can come stay at my place, G.G."

G.G. looked lost for a moment. She refused to go back to jail. It wasn't her place. She spent some time in Rikers Island and hated her stay there. She vowed never to go back to jail. G.G. looked at T.T. and replied, "Nah, they probably gonna hit ya place too. I can't take that chance."

"So what you gonna do, G.G.?" Young J asked.

"Fuck it, let's bounce," G.G. said.

T.T. and G.G. quickly exited the lobby with Young J following them. They moved far away from G.G.'s building and walked toward Linden Boulevard. Young J was still following them. G.G. spun around and exclaimed, "Go home, J . . . We good."

"But I wanna chill wit' y'all," he said.

"No, not right now. You don't need to be around us," said T.T. "Besides, what can ya young ass do?"

Young J smirked, lifted up his shirt, and revealed the .25 handgun he had stuffed and concealed in his waistband. "I can do a lot, fo' real. I'ma be fifteen in two months. And fuck it, if 5-0 try to take you down, then I ain't scared to pop one of them pigs," he stated.

"It ain't that kind of party, boo," said G.G.

"Whatever!" he spat back.

"Just go home, J. I'ma be good, baby," G.G. said, giving Young J a warm smile. "I got somewhere to go. You don't have to worry about me."

Young J looked at G.G. "A'ight," he replied. G.G. was always able to warm his heart and talk sense into the young thug. Young J nodded. He turned around and went the opposite way.

The girls continued toward Linden Boulevard

"Damn, li'l nigga got it bad for you, G.G., fo' real," T.T. said.

"Young J got some heart." G.G. laughed.

"Yeah, he do . . . Shit, I probably fuck him . . . in like three more years when he's legal," T.T. joked.

"Bitch, you nasty."

"Yeah, but that li'l nigga is gonna grow up and be somethin' serious on these streets. And that young stallion gonna need a cougar to calm his wild ass down, and my pussy is gonna be that right thing for him to feed on," commented T.T. humorously.

The two girls laughed, forgetting about their earlier trouble with the police and the fight at August Martin. When they reached Linden Boulevard, they walked into the corner bodega and purchased a pack of Newports. The afternoon sun was fading with evening creeping above. They lit up on the corner and lingered on Linden and Guy Brewer Boulevard for a moment.

T.T. took a drag from the cancer stick and asked, "Yo, you spoke to Baby? You know where she at?"

G.G. shook her head. "Nah, I know she around, though . . . probably with J. Rock."

"She stay wit' that nigga . . . got that bitch Erica buggin' out over that shit."

"Fuck that bitch. My cousin better than that whack bitch. What J. Rock need to do is stop messing around wit' my cousin's feelings and just wife her up, and dump Erica to the fuckin' curb. She a trash-ass bitch anyway," G.G. proclaimed with conviction.

G.G. took another drag from her cigarette and exhaled. The corner was busy with traffic. With the local clinic and Gulf gas station across the street, the hood was bustling with activity with a few young teens milling about, people exiting the buses, coming home from work and stopping at the local bodega. The cool fall breeze was blowing in the air as the sun was about to cast away behind the horizon.

"I'm about to go see my boo, Jason. Shit, wit' all this shit happening, it got my pussy throbbing. I need him to tame my kitty cat," T.T. said. "You gonna be good, G.G.?"

"Bitch, I'm always good. Go do you. I'ma go check Dwight."

"A'ight."

The two girls said their good-byes and went their separate ways. T.T. walked back to the Baisley Projects and G.G. went the opposite way. Home wasn't an option for her at the moment. But she was worried about her sick mother. She had no one to care for her and G.G. was all she had. It sickened G.G. that cops were at her apartment looking for her. But it wasn't the first time they came looking for her. Her constant run-ins with the law had become a routine thing. And G.G. was used to being on the run. She knew the tricks and trades of the streets and the game.

G.G. walked toward 112th Road. When she got to the corner, a black Yukon with chrome rims and its system blaring came to a sudden stop near G.G. She already knew who was in the truck. She stopped in her tracks and watched the driver quickly exit his ride. He stormed over toward G.G. with a menacing stare and shouted, "Yo, G.G., where the fuck is my shit at?"

"I'll pay you back what I owe you, Echo," said G.G.

He approached G.G. harshly, pushed her against the wall, and towered over G.G. like a high rise. Echo stood six-two, and was wide like a doorway with a strapping physique. He was clad in sagging denim jeans, a black T-shirt, and fresh Timberlands. He sported a bulky, long white gold chain with a diamond 9 mm pendant. Echo was a cold-hearted, scheming, and wicked crack-dealing thug. G.G. worked under him moving or selling packages in the streets. She needed the money. It went to paying her rent and helping with her mother's medical bills. The last package she fucked up and got hit by stick up kids in her building, and her arrest a month ago didn't help her business relationship with Echo, either.

"You fucked up that package last week. That's two stacks you owe me, G.G.," Echo argued.

"You think I don't know that? I'ma get you your money," retorted G.G.

"You better, G.G. This ain't a game wit' me, fo' real," he warned.

"I got you, Echo, you ain't gotta fuckin' raise up on me like this. You know I'm always good wit' that paper. This is my one fuckup, and you actin' like a straight bitch," G.G. shouted.

"Bitch, who the fuck ya talkin' to like that!" Echo screamed, suddenly grabbing G.G. by her neck firmly and thrusting her against the wall. "You fuckin' cunt, you better fuckin' recognize, fo' real . . . I'll get deep in ya ass wit' no fuckin' Vaseline, G.G., if I don't get my money by next week. You hear me?"

G.G. gasped. He was too strong to fight off. G.G.'s eyes started to water with tears. She felt fear. It felt like a pair of vise grips was around her neck. Echo almost lifted her off of her feet with his strength and rage. G.G. managed to speak. "I'll get ya money."

He continued to choke her. Echo's cold black eyes stared into G.G.'s fading eyes as she struggled to breathe. She gripped and scratched at his thick wrist. She tried to fight him off, but it was like a puppy trying to attack a lion. He was crazy to commit a violent act on the corner in public. But Echo wasn't a sane person. He dominated the hood with pure fear. No one dared to fuck with him. He was crazy—a straight lunatic.

"Yeah, I can snatch ya fuckin' life right now, right here, bitch . . . snap ya fuckin' neck like a twig for fuckin' up my money," he growled.

He released his grip around her neck and pushed her in a hostile way to the pavement. G.G. fell on her side. She was hurt. She caught her breath, but the tears wouldn't stop flowing. Echo stood over her. He lifted his shirt to reveal the Glock 17 in his waistband.

"I don't give a fuck who you are or about ya pussy pack; I'll do them bitches too. You know I will, G.G. . . . So don't fuck around wit' me. Get me my fuckin' money," he warned through clenched teeth.

Echo walked back to his truck and jumped inside. He sped off, leaving G.G. picking herself up off the concrete. It was an embarrassing moment for her—just a few short hours ago, she was the domineering and feared one with the fight with Erica and her clique, and having the respect from her crew. But for that moment, G.G. felt weak, scared. She dried her tears, collected herself, and walked away.

Chapter 5

Baby's three-day suspension from school went by fast. She strutted into the school like everything was okay—acting like the fight with Erica never happened. She carried a book bag with a few books, but she wasn't there to learn. School had become a fashion show along with a business for her. Students owed her money—she was there to collect, and besides, it was fun to hang with a few of her homegirls and flirt with the boys in the classroom or the hallways.

Baby strutted by security in a pink, ruffled-edge skirt, a tight white shirt accentuating her tits, and a pair of fresh, new, white Nikes. Baby had her hair styled into two long pigtails, looking like the trashy and naughty schoolgirl. She had all the boys', and some grown men's, undivided attention as she walked down the hall and went into her first period class. Principal Palmer was there to warn her sternly about acting out or fighting. He said it was her last chance with him. If Baby was involved in any more serious incidents, then Palmer would expel her from his school like G.G. Baby took his warning lightly, but she promised to behave.

The first period class went by fast for Baby. She didn't pay any attention to Ms. Sunnier, who taught social studies. She slouched in her seat and messed around with her smart phone, texting friends and looking at pictures.

Ms. Sunnier didn't bother to disturb Baby as she sat in the back of the classroom. Baby had cursed her out a few times, and Ms. Sunnier didn't have the time or the courage to fight with the delinquent student. Baby made her class difficult to teach with her attitude and antics. Ms. Sunnier knew she was no match for the student. Ms. Sunnier was a middle-aged white woman from Long Island. The only time she saw the ghetto was when she was passing through it on her way to work. She didn't know what poverty was. She came from money, but loved teaching. It was her passion. While Ms. Sunnier taught her lessons, she avoided eye contact with Baby and focused on the kids who wanted to learn.

Baby smirked at Ms. Sunnier, knowing she had her teacher shaken.

The school day was going by in a blur for Baby. She remained low-key and quiet for the day. She mingled with her homegirls and tried to stay out of trouble. Baby had heard about the big fight with her cousin and Erica the day she got suspended. She loved how her cousin and her clique had wild out for her. It showed a sign of respect and love. Baby wished she'd been there when the brawl went down. Three days later, the students in school were still gossiping about it like it happened yesterday. A few friends showed Baby some video of the fight on their camera phones, and Baby got to witness the beat down that G.G. gave Erica in the middle of the street.

"Yo, G.G. went ham on that bitch, fo' real," said Tiny.

Baby smiled as she watched the video.

"Look, she wild on that bitch . . ."

It was fun to watch. Baby was happy to see Erica get fucked up. She wasn't in school and had been absent for a few days. The word on the streets was that Erica was staying home and re-covering from her injuries, but her brother and his goons were talking reckless about revenge on G.G. and Baby. Baby was far from worried about any get-back coming her way. She had goons who were ready to ride out for her too. Baby felt she rode too deep and was too well known to get caught out there. But her beef with Erica was escalating—niggas were talking about getting involved, and that meant things could soon get carried out of hand. That meant gunplay if the situation didn't get dissolved. Baby knew things were far from over, though. With the beat down that Erica received, she had to come back on her rivals just to salvage her reputation.

After watching the video, Baby left the cafeteria to head upstairs to the third floor. The hallways were quiet. It was sixth period. Baby lingered on the stairway for a moment, waiting and hoping security didn't come passing through. She kept a keen eye out. Soon, Tameka trotted up the stairway to greet Baby.

"You got that for me?" Baby asked.

"Yeah," Tameka replied.

Tameka handed Baby a knot of money—mostly wrinkled tens and twenties. Baby snatched it from Tameka's hand and started counting it.

"It's all there, Baby. You know I wouldn't fuck wit' you," said Tameka.

Baby didn't answer her. She quickly counted what was owed to her: $500. Baby was satisfied.

"We good," she said. "I got another package for you tomorrow after school."

Tameka nodded.

The transaction was quick and discreet. Tameka nervously went down the stairway. Baby picked up her book bag and was planning to stuff the cash inside. She unzipped it, but before she got the chance to conceal her money, she heard, "What the hell you doing?"

Baby looked up and saw that Samson had snuck up on her in the stairway. Baby clutched the cash in her fist behind her back, snatched up her book bag and tried to hide the money from Samson.

"I'm on my way to class. What the fuck you think I'm doing, Conan?" she spat.

Samson gave her a hard look. He approached closer; Baby took a few steps back.

"What's going on? What you trying to hide from me?" Samson asked.

"None of ya fuckin' business, nigga! Go toy cop somewhere else," Baby exclaimed.

Samson became upset. He hated to be disrespected. He was a military man. He refused to be slighted by a young teenage girl. Baby gripped her book bag firmly. She thought about running. She wanted to run and planned to. Before Baby could leap to her escape, Samson rushed forward, grabbing Baby by her arm with force, and snatched the book bag out of her hands.

"Give it back to me," Baby exclaimed, trying to snatch her bag back from him.

"What's in here?"

Samson unzipped the bag and removed the wad of bills from her bag. He was stunned by the contents inside—money and a few dime bags of weed.

Baby was furious. He was in her business.

"You selling drugs in this school?" he asked.

"No!"

"You think I'm stupid?"

"Look, you ain't gotta say shit to no one. I'll hook you up," she said. "I can take care of you. I promise. But I can't get caught out there. I can't get arrested and expelled right now."

"You didn't care about it a few days ago."

"That's different . . . Look, Conan—"

"My name is Samson," he interjected.

"Okay, Samson, I'm sorry, I didn't mean to offend you . . . but, just look the other way," she pleaded.

"I have a job to do. C'mon, you're coming with me," Samson said, grabbing Baby by her arm and pulling her toward the stairs.

Baby wasn't going to the office willingly. She jerked her arm free from Samson's strong grip and shouted, "Get the fuck off me! Please, don't do this to me . . . I'm sorry, a'ight? I'm begging you, don't turn me in."

Samson was surprised by how strong she was. Baby was reluctant to go anywhere with him.

She was ready to put up a fight, even though he outweighed her heavily and towered over her.

"I'm not playing with you, Baby."

"Look, if I get locked up, then there won't be anyone to care for my grandmother. She's sick, dying of cancer and, right now, I'm all she has. She can barely move, and I'm the only one that can go down to the pharmacy and get her medication. I do this 'cause we can't fuckin' afford it. Her medication is too expensive. And we don't have health insurance," Baby stated convincingly.

Samson stared at her. He had his doubts about her story. He figured her to be scheming and manipulative.

Baby had a few tears trickling from her eyes. It was the first time that anyone had seen her vulnerable. She was upset. She rarely cried. "Look, just let me go, and I promise you, I won't be a problem to anyone in this school. I'll be low-key," she said.

"Your reputation precedes you."

"You're new here; you don't know me. You don't even know this school. We can look out for each other."

Samson laughed.

"Ya a military man, right? What branch?"

Samson didn't answer her. Baby continued with, "My father was killed overseas when I was only thirteen . . . fighting an unjust war. And I look at you—"

"Look at me, what? I had nothing to do with your father's death."

"Please, just give me a second chance; I know you wish you had that yourself. I can see it in your eyes, the despair . . . not being able to do what you love, and I can look at you and tell that you loved the service. What was it, a medical or dishonorable discharge?" she asked. "I'll owe you, big time."

Samson sighed. He dwelled on the thought of letting her go. He knew he had a job to do, and he was being paid to do it correctly—not to cut corners or negotiate with students, but the look in Baby's eyes was captivating. She seemed convincing. She was cute and very well spoken for the hood-rat, evil young bitch the school portrayed her to be. There was a short moment of silence between them.

"I'll give you one chance . . . just this one chance," Samson said.

He still held on to her book bag and looked reluctant to give it back to her.

Baby reached for her bag and said, "Thank you. Can I have my bag back?"

"I don't wanna see you selling this shit in this school . . . not around me. I catch you again, and next time you will be taken in," he warned sternly. Samson handed Baby her book bag. He couldn't believe it.

Baby took her bag from him and stared at him for a moment. She smiled and said, "I owe you."

"No, just stay out of trouble."

Baby smiled, and then trotted down the stairway, leaving Samson in a look of semi bewilderment. He shook his head and lingered in the stairway for a moment. Doing security at a high school was going to be more difficult than he thought it would be. He just hoped that letting Baby off the hook didn't come back to bite him.

Chapter 6

G.G., T.T., and Baby were chilling in T.T.'s apartment on the fourth floor. The cluttered bedroom was teeming with weed smoke, as the girls got high from the potent Kush that G.G. had rolled up earlier. Baby took a much-needed drag from the blunt and passed it to G.G. G.G. unwound from the cannabis seeping into her system like her bloodstream. She slouched across T.T.'s bed, clad in a pair of basketball shorts and a T-shirt. She tried to forget about her troubles on the streets. G.G. kept her problems quiet. She was always seen as the tough and unbreakable one—able to hold her own whenever, and hard to knock down. She hadn't been home in three days, fearing the police were watching her crib. She stayed at a few friends' places, and tried to duck police and Echo simultaneously. Money was becoming tight, and the streets were too hot. G.G. got word that Erica's brothers were out for blood. Baby was on their hit list too. So the cousins had to watch their step and movements. Neither one showed any concern; they grew up around beef, gunplay, death, and gangsters. It was nothing new to them. They had problems before and always prevailed.

G.G. passed the burning blunt over to T.T., who sat by the window and peered outside. Her eyes were fixated on her little sister walking down Guy R. Brewer on her way home and heading into their building. T.T.'s little sister was the opposite of her and her friends. T.T.'s sister, Gina, was sixteen, and into her books and working hard on getting her education and graduating from high school. She would be the first in her family to go to college. Whereas T.T. was a high school dropout at sixteen, and heavily into the streets, Gina had a clean record and was far removed from her older sister's lifestyle. T.T. had so much love for her little sister. Gina was the good one, the one their parents would be proud of if they were still alive. But they died in a car accident when T.T. was fifteen. So, the sisters lived with their wild aunt, who was on welfare, Section 8, smoked like a chimney and cursed like a sailor, and got into as many fights as T.T., sometimes more. Now and again, the two women, auntie and niece, fought together on the streets to solidify their hood-rat status in the neighborhood. But T.T. was proud of Gina; she was different and doing something with her life. T.T. couldn't complain.

"Gina's on her way up," T.T. said to her friends.

G.G. and Baby had love for Gina too. She was nice and polite, smart, too. "That's my girl," said Baby. "She too quiet, though."

"Yeah, she doin' her thang," replied T.T.

"That's what's up. I haven't been seeing her around lately," G.G. chimed.

"She too busy with school and bein' in her books. She gonna come in here and head straight to her room and lock her door, probably studying or being online searching up shit," T.T. said.

"I ain't mad at that," said Baby.

The trio continued smoking, passing the blunt around the room and listening to Lil Wayne's CD. Baby took another pull, coughed, and suddenly mentioned, "Yo, we got this new school safety dude in my school, and he's a cutie. I think he's cool, too. Dude caught me slippin' in the hallway and let me slide. I mean, wit' a li'l persuasion, though."

"What, you fucked him?" T.T. joked.

"Nah, but he can get it," Baby returned with a smile. "I would fuck him."

"Slut," T.T. teased.

"Looks who's talkin' . . ."

The girls laughed. But G.G. looked deep in thought about something. She lay on the bed, and was aloof for a moment. Her mind was on too many things—too many issues that she was dealing with. Money was becoming tight. She owed Echo two grand, and barely had a hundred dollars her name. Her mother wasn't doing too well. G.G. was desperate for cash. Baby looked at her cousin and asked, "You okay, G.G.?"

"I'm good," G.G. replied matter-of-factly.

To ease her nerves, G.G. took one last pull from the potent Kush, savoring the high. She closed her eyes and chilled on T.T.'s soft bed like it was a temporary paradise somewhere. She curled up against the cotton pillows for comfort and looked like she was ready to go to sleep. Suddenly she uttered, "If sex was like smoking and this bed, I probably have eight kids right now."

"Your cousin is buggin', Baby," said T.T., laughing.

"She good," Baby said. "Bitch is stupid high right now, and talkin' some dumb shit."

"I know, right . . . Bitch, what you gonna do wit' eight kids? Keep ya legs closed," T.T. commented. "I'm not tryin' to even have one right now."

"I hear y'all bitches," replied G.G.

"And . . . we know you do, that's why we sayin' it," T.T. joked.

G.G. rested on the bed. She wanted to black out everything in her world for a moment. At eighteen years old, G.G. was an O.G. in the streets. She'd been putting in work since she was twelve years old, and wasn't planning on slowing down anytime soon.

T.T. heard the front door to the apartment open. She knew it was Gina coming in. T.T. took one last pull from the blunt and doused it in an ashtray. She left the room to greet her kid sister, while G.G. lay on the bed and Baby pulled out her cell phone to call J. Rock. The girls were in their own worlds at the moment.

Baby couldn't wait to hear J. Rock's voice. He picked up after the third ring. "Yo, who this?" he greeted in a rough and deadpan tone.

"It's Baby, where you at?"

"I'm comin' down Foch now. I'll be out front in like ten minutes," he said.

"A'ight, just hit me when you downstairs."

"A'ight, ma . . ."

Baby hung up with a smile on her face. She couldn't wait to see J. Rock again. Her pussy tangled and smiled when she heard his voice or when he came around. Baby was a helpless schoolgirl around J. Rock. She did whatever he wanted, but she hated that he was with Erica instead of her. She craved to be his number one wifey, and was ready to knock Erica out the box and become his main bitch. Baby wanted to prove to J. Rock that she could be his ride or die bitch. She had strength, street smarts, her crew, beauty, and her love. She was the total package.

Baby walked over to the window and looked outside. It was a nice fall afternoon. Everybody seemed to be outside enjoying the day. The fall breeze was comfortable, and the clear sky was welcoming. Baby couldn't wait to jump into J. Rock's black Dodge Charger. He had showy twenty-two-inch rims on his ride, with tinted windows, black and red leather interior, and an ear-piercing music system that could be heard from blocks away. The way J. Rock styled in his car—leaned back in his seat, profiling, and music blaring—was an immediate turn-on for her. She lost count of how many times J. Rock had fucked her in the back seat on late nights while parked somewhere secluded.

Baby looked over at her cousin resting on the bed. She walked over to G.G., nudged her gently and asked, "G.G., you okay?"

"I'm good, Baby. I'm just tired."

"A'ight . . . I'ma bounce, J. Rock's picking me up," Baby said.

"Don't get pregnant, bitch," G.G. stated.

"Like that would be a bad thang. Me and that nigga would have some fine-ass babies, fo' real," Baby replied.

"Well, I ain't babysitting."

"Whatever, bitch . . . You know you gonna be the godmother to our babies."

"I better," G.G. said faintly, with her eyes closed and taking pleasure in resting in T.T.'s bed with the pillow pressed to her head.

Baby walked out of the bedroom and was highly excited. She walked by T.T., who was coming out of the kitchen. "Bitch, you leaving?" T.T. asked.

"Yup, J. Rock is meeting me downstairs."

"Damn, don't get pregnant, bitch," T.T. clowned.

"What, you and my cousin in cahoots? She just told me the same shit in the bedroom," said Baby.

"'Cause ya fast ass love you some J. Rock. I hope you got that nigga strappin' up," T.T. said.

Baby sucked her teeth and replied with, "Shit, sometimes . . . but I love it when that nigga be running up in me natural . . . It ain't nothin' like the feel of hard skin running up in you."

"Bitch, you's a trip."

"I know . . . but y'all love a bitch anyway."

Baby strutted out the door in a fresh pair of skintight jeans, her ass forming a near perfect bubble in the fabric, with her T-shirt highlighting her curves and luscious tits, and her white Nikes the color of clouds. Baby rushed into the elevator and descended to the lobby. She walked out of the elevator and into the streets just in time to see J. Rock pulling up in his Charger. She rushed over with a smile. J. Rock was double-parked out front with his system blaring Rick Ross's "Maybach Music."

Baby jumped into his ride and leaned over to kiss her boo, but when she tried to press her lips against his, J. Rock avoided the intimate kiss she wanted to give him, and pulled away, saying, "You know I don't rock like that, Baby."

Baby sucked her teeth and straightened herself up in her seat. She was disappointed. She wanted to show J. Rock some affection, even though they weren't officially a couple. J. Rock was never with it. Baby knew that J. Rock was still upset with her because of what G.G. and her crew did to Erica the other day.

He had confronted her about it and had said, "Yo, why your cousin do that to my girl?"

"That bitch tried to jump me, J. Rock," Baby had said.

When J. Rock said that about his girl, butterflies and upset swam around Baby's stomach. She hated to hear him talk about Erica. In her mind, she was his boo and Erica was his dirty sidepiece.

"You know y'all got some heat over that shit with Erica outside of the school," J. Rock had mentioned.

"So, what you saying, J. Rock? You ain't got our back over this?"

"I'm just sayin' . . . that's my bitch, Baby. How the fuck you think I'm gonna feel! Your cousin put her in the fuckin' hospital."

Baby had felt disgusted. She glared at J. Rock and had asked, "So, you tryin' to go after my fuckin' cousin?"

J. Rock had remained silent. Baby was hurt. She didn't want to choose between J. Rock and her cousin. She loved them both. But her heart was with her cousin. Baby made up her mind that if J. Rock went after her cousin, then she would have her cousin's back, no matter what happened—family came first. But J. Rock had said to her, "Just tell your cousin to be careful out there. I ain't gonna put hands on her because of you. But if that bitch fucks wit' my bitch again, then we ain't gonna have this conversation anymore. I'll let you know that now. It will get ugly."

Baby felt some kind of way about his words and action, but she remained silent. She was definitely J. Rock's bitch. Baby thought it was love, but he used her for his own personal gains and gratifications. That conversation about G.G. was three days ago. Since then, things had somewhat smoothed over with them.

J. Rock drove off, with Baby looking a bit gloomy in the passenger seat. She wanted to love J. Rock with all of her heart. She wanted to become his ride or die bitch within every inch of her flesh and soul, but there were always limits with him. Why couldn't he love her completely? Erica was always getting in her way. Baby knew her place, but she wouldn't hesitate to express how she felt about J. Rock and tear down Erica's credibility.

J. Rock made a left on Linden Boulevard and drove toward the Van Wyck Expressway. Baby was quiet in her seat for a moment. When J. Rock merged onto the congested expressway, she finally asked, "Baby, where we goin'?"

"I gotta go take care of some business real fast. I wanted you to ride along," he said.

Baby didn't say anything else. She just went along with him like always. Any time that she got to spend with J. Rock was quality time for her, even when he put her life at risk with his treacherous lifestyle. But, her way of life was no different from his.

G.G. took a quick nap on T.T.'s bed. She woke up to the darkness engulfing outside the bedroom window. It was late evening. The bedroom was quiet. G.G. stretched and yawned, surprised that she slept for so long. Three hours had passed. She was tired. She had been on the go for a few days, trying to keep a low profile, and ducking her enemies.

G.G. stepped out of the bed just as T.T. was entering the bedroom.

"Damn, bitch . . . I see you finally woke ya tired ass up," T.T. said.

"Why you let me sleep so long?"

"You was tired. Shit, get ya rest, G.G. You know you're family here," T.T. said.

"What time is it?"

"Almost nine o'clock. I'm about to get dressed to go to work."

"You still dancing at the spot?" G.G. asked.

"Yeah, I get my paper there. It be a'ight some nights, when niggas ain't cheap. But I do me, I gets it in."

G.G. had a thought about something. She took a seat on the foot of the bed and lit up a cigarette. She took a deep drag and looked at T.T. T.T. was rummaging around in her closet, trying to put an outfit together for tonight. She had clothes thrown about everywhere, from the bed to the floor. She was very messy. Her room was a pigpen. T.T. didn't care about order; she didn't clean much.

G.G. took another pull from the cancer stick. Her face showed that she was uncertain to ask T.T. a question, but she had no other options or choice. She needed extra income. T.T. was stripping away her clothing in front of G.G., her body oozing with sex appeal from head to toe. T.T.'s sexiness was always hidden away in loose attire—baggy jeans or sweatpants, shapeless T-shirts, Timberlands, and sneakers. She carried herself as a tomboy or hood rat on the streets— but at nights, in the depths of the underground strip clubs where sex sold, T.T.'s curvy and nude body would glisten with exertion as she pranced around horny and hungry men looking for a good time, and making her ends in the course while grabbing their crotches and allowing them to touch and feel on her juicy booty and curves. For the right price, a man could have his own personal fun with T.T.

T.T. moved around her bedroom in her panties and bra. She picked up a few things off the floor and tossed them on the bed. Her bedroom looked like Macy's had exploded with clothing lying about everywhere.

"Damn, T.T., how come you never clean up?" G.G. asked.

"'Cause, I already know where everything is at
. . . I don't give a fuck, yeah, I'm a messy bitch."

G.G. shook her head.

"Anyway, G.G. . . . What you about to do? You
gonna chill here tonight?"

"I don't know. I was thinkin' 'bout rollin' wit'
you tonight."

"What, to the club, to see me dance tonight? I
thought that wasn't ya thang," said T.T.

"I'm sayin' . . . I ain't got shit else to do," G.G.
replied.

T.T. shrugged. "Hey, you know I don't give a
fuck. I've been tellin' you to come down and get
money wit' me for the longest. Shit, wit' ya body,
and ya looks, them niggas will go crazy over you.
But you always looked at me crazy, and shit."

"Things change."

"Mm-hmm . . . So, who you owe money to now,
bitch?" asked T.T. with a raised eyebrow.

"Why I gotta owe money to someone?"

"'Cause I know you, G.G. . . . The only time you
think about dancing wit' me is when you owe
some nigga out there some serious change."

"T.T., just stay the fuck out my business, a'ight?"
snapped G.G.

T.T. sucked her teeth. "A'ight, damn, you
ain't gotta get nasty wit' it. But if you wanna roll,
c'mon then . . . I got you."

G.G. looked reluctant at first. But she decided to roll with T.T. and see how things operated in the low-key clubs that T.T. danced in. She heard rumors of T.T. selling sex for cash. G.G. always thought she was above prostitution. It was a desperate act for cash for any woman, and G.G. would rather sell crack than give her body away for payment to some man she was not physically attracted to. The two friends had different views on the business.

"You comin'?" T.T. asked.

"Yeah," G.G. answered softly.

T.T. was excited to finally have her best friend come to work with her. She knew if G.G. got into dancing with her in the business, then they would kill it together. G.G. and T.T. started to get dressed at the same time, and then headed down to the club known for naked and willing women from all boroughs of the city, who were ready to expose their goodies from head to toe, and please their clientele at any lengths if the price was right.

Chapter 7

J. Rock's Charger sat parked under the thick, shaded tree on the darkened Queens Street with little traffic passing. It was almost midnight. J. Rock leaned back in his seat in a relaxed pose and enjoyed the blissful moment with Baby's sweet lips wrapped around his thick erection. His business in Queens Bridge went smoothly. In the trunk of his car was a small duffle bag filled with guns that he was ready to sell in the Carolinas—Charlotte and Greenville. Now, J. Rock wanted to unwind for a moment, and hinted that Baby should give him a blow job. She obliged. Baby wanted to please her man to the fullest. So she leaned forward into his lap as he undid his jeans and pulled out his growing erection. Baby didn't hesitate to wrap her lips around his dick and suck him off with pleasure.

Baby gently stroked J. Rock's cock, rendering his yearning lust in her grip, with his hard dick feeling like a steel pipe in the soft, warm palm of her hand. J. Rock moaned when Baby's lips touched the mushroom tip of his penis and her tongue coiled around it like a snake wrapping around prey. She then devoured him slowly, savoring every sugary taste of him. J. Rock was now thrusting into her mouth, his hand tangled in her hair.

"Ooooh, shit, baby . . . Ooooh that shit feels good. Ummm, do that shit," he cooed.

Baby's head bobbed up and down in his lap, deep throating him to perfection. J. Rock's grunts and moans were enough to let her know that he had no complaints about how she sucked his dick. Super Head had nothing on Baby. She massaged his balls and stroked his dick while sucking it simultaneously.

"Aaaahhh, shit," grunted J. Rock, as he looked down at the mass of black hair that was planted in his lap.

His eyes were opened a little bit, but they had a glassy look to them, as if he were possibly high on some really good shit. His body went rigid for just a moment while Baby moaned around his dick in her mouth. The sweet moaning vibrated J. Rock's dick inside Baby's mouth and he shoved her head hard against his dick repeatedly, as he felt the head of his dick sink past her tongue and into her throat. Baby didn't try to fight or pull away from J.

Rock's rough actions, she continued to suck and swallow—the motions in her throat were coaxing the orgasm out of J. Rocks balls. Baby was a freak. She wanted J. Rock to release himself down her throat, so she could taste his warm fluids in her mouth.

"Oh, shit . . . I'm gonna come," he exclaimed. "Damn, baby . . . just like that, don't stop . . . damn, don't fuckin' stop!"

It was so good for J. Rock that a single tear ran down from the side of his eye. He quickly wiped away the tear and grabbed the back of Baby's head and pushed her throat farther down his dick. Baby gagged momentarily, but she was a professional, and kept her lips wrapped around his dick. She moaned again, as J. Rock released himself deep into her esophagus, and tasting the white, thin liquid that trickled around in her mouth. J. Rock threw his head back and closed his eyes from the unbelievable orgasm.

Baby lifted her face from his lap, sat back in her seat and wiped her mouth of any evidence of her freaky actions. She smiled and asked, "You good, baby? You enjoyed yourself."

J. Rocks' actions were evident. "Damn, you did me good, Baby," he replied, buttoning up his jeans and collecting himself in the driver's seat.

"See, I take care of my boo," she said.

J. Rock started the ignition and drove off, leaving Baby's pussy still tingling. She wanted to fuck, but J. Rock just wanted some head. Baby's disappointment about not getting any dick was manifested on her face, but she kept her composure and didn't want to blow up about not getting any dick.

J. Rock cruised through Queens listening to Drake and Lil Wayne. He ignored Baby's upset and nodded to his favorite track, leaned back in his seat—gangsta lean—and clutching the steering wheel with his right hand.

Soon, he was pulling up to Baby's building in Baisley Park housing. He put the car in park, and looked over at Baby. She had been quiet for the duration of the ride home. Her mind was on so many things. She wanted to fuck just to relieve herself of some of the frustration she was feeling, but J. Rock clearly made it known that business came first, even when she treated him as a priority, and sucked his dick like a porn star—like she usually did.

"You okay?" he asked.

"I'm fine," she replied matter-of-factly.

"Yo, I need you to do me a favor," he mentioned.

Baby slowly twisted her direction at him with a look that said, "*He has some fuckin' nerve.*" She didn't curse him out, though. She found herself asking, "What?"

"Yo, I need to stash that duffle bag at your crib for a minute . . . a'ight?"

"Why?"

"'Cause I want you to . . . Damn, don't make this fuckin' difficult, Baby. Just do it, for me, a'ight?"

Baby let out an exasperated sigh. "A'ight."

"I'll be back around to get that shit next week."

"Why, where you goin?"

"I got some business in B-more," J. Rock stated.

"So I ain't gonna see you 'til next week, then?" Baby said, which meant she was going to be sexually frustrated for a fucking week. It was a nightmare.

"Yo, I'll be back . . . Why you fuckin' actin' like a bitch for? Don't I fuckin' take care of you?"

"Not tonight," she spat.

"What . . . 'cause you ain't get no dick? Bitch, please . . . You lucky I don't wild out on ya ass after what you and your cousin did to Erica," he argued.

Baby hated when he defended that bitch. She wanted nothing more than to wipe Erica clean from J. Rock's life and his mind, so she could be the only one concrete in his world.

"Whatever," she hissed, storming out of the car.

J. Rock popped open the truck so Baby could remove the duffle bag. Baby walked around to the back of the car, lifted open the trunk, and pulled out the small black duffle bag with the illegal handguns concealed inside. She slung it over her shoulder and strutted toward the lobby entrance without even turning to look back at J. Rock. She was upset. J. Rock smirked and pulled off, giving no thought about Baby's feelings.

Baby entered her apartment and called out for her grandmother. "Grandma, I'm home."

She knew her grandmother wouldn't answer. It was just something Baby liked to do. It made her think of the old days when her grandmother was normal and taking care of her with home-cooked meals and stories of her parents. The dementia came gradually—the deterioration of her brain cells was a painstaking process for both of them. Her grandmother's mental functioning was disappearing, such as concentration, memory, and the judgment that affected a person's ability to perform normal and daily activities.

Baby dropped the bag on the couch and walked down the corridor and stepped inside her grandmother's room. The door was ajar. The home attendant was sitting at the side of her grandmother's bed, trying to feed her grandmother peas and rice. Baby peered in the room. It was a sad sight. Her grandmother's frail body just lay there, looking like a skeleton with skin. Her graying hair was thin, and the wrinkles were plenty. The home attendant turned to look at Baby standing in the doorway.

"How she's doin' today?" Baby asked.

"She's the same."

Baby gazed at her sickly grandmother. She had nothing else to say. The lady in her late thirties had things under control in the apartment. Her name was Cindy Mathews. She was a Caribbean woman from St. Thomas. She was there night and day, taking care of her grandmother. She was good at her job and very well trusted.

"She's need her rest and medication. But she's fine, chil'," Cindy stated.

Baby wanted to yell out, "She's not fuckin' fine! She's fuckin' dying." But she held her tongue.

Baby turned and walked away, entering the living room. She picked up J. Rock's duffle bag of handguns and went into her bedroom, shutting the door behind her. She dropped his bag on the floor near the bed and walked over to her dresser mirror. She slowly began undressing herself, peeling her skintight jeans off, and removing her T-shirt. She then unhooked her bra and removed her panties and gazed at her curvy, luscious, and petite image in the mirror. Her reflection was a beautiful sight. Her ample breasts and womanly curves were hypnotizing to any man—but not hypnotizing enough to the man she desired. Baby let out a heavy sigh. She then locked on her own eyes in the mirror and solemnly asked, "What is wrong wit' me?" She had J. Rock on her mind when she asked the question.

Chapter 8

G.G. strutted behind T.T. into the dimly lit and bawdy underground Brooklyn club. Inside, the girls were met with the thunderous sounds of Lil Wayne and Drake's "She Will" blaring throughout the spot. The place was teeming with half-naked and some fully naked women wandering about in their stylish stilettos, and lustful, drinking men eager to play with some of the promiscuous women they came in contact with. The club was midsized; the stage and bar were makeshift. The dancers didn't need any resumes or an interview for the job. If you were a young girl looking to make some money, the only thing you needed was nerve, tip in or tip out money, and a willingness to tolerate being groped and lusted after by so many men—young and old.

G.G. looked around as she followed T.T. in the club. She was cool. The scene didn't bother her. She already knew what to expect. She already

caught attention inside the place. She immediately turned some heads. She was new and
beautiful. The small scar was a plus for some of
the fellows to see. They admired the way her hips
curved perfectly in the skintight jeans she wore,
and how her ass was like a bouncing bubble. She
wore heels and her long, exquisite dreads flowed
freely and framed her face and head perfectly.
She was the only lady in the club with dreads.

T.T. was a regular, and some of the men were
excited that she arrived. She greeted a few people,
and then introduced her friend G.G. to them. The
men stared at G.G. with such a strong hunger
that it was obvious in their eyes what they wanted
from her. She was like an Amazon to them in her
six-inch heels and long legs hidden away in tight
jeans.

G.G. and T.T. walked toward the back of the
club and headed down a narrow corridor that
led to VIP rooms for sex, and the changing room
for the ladies. As G.G. strutted down the hallway,
she could hear the moans and sexual sounds
coming from behind a few doors—indicating
some people were happy and having a good time.
T.T. carried a small bag around her shoulder.
G.G. carried nothing. She was still debating if
she should go through with this.

The girls walked into the small room made for changing. It was a windowless room, reeking of past girls before them, and was the size of a small ghetto bedroom. The eggshell walls were covered in graffiti and dirt, and the concrete floors were cold and scattered with a few garments from changing strippers. The girls were alone. The other girls were already on the floor bending over, dancing buck naked on stage, giving out lap dances, and showing their sweet goodies any which way and how for a few dollars.

T.T. dropped her bag and looked at G.G.

"You gonna do this? I mean, it's money out there, G.G.," said T.T. "Yo, you saw how them niggas was lookin' at you; they were already thirsty and shit."

G.G. still looked reluctant. She was reluctant only because of her reputation. She was from the block, hustled crack, and knew too many people, especially niggas. She didn't have any moral issue, and wasn't nervous about being buck naked in front of strangers. She just didn't want to be looked down on by niggas as a dumb, dancing slut, who was desperate for cash—which was the majority of the girls' reputations in the place. But her options were few—very few. And in reality, G.G. was desperate to make some extra cash and dancing was the only option she saw.

"How much do you usually make here?" G.G. asked.

"Shit, depends . . . A bitch could make an easy three to five hundred a night if she's doin' her fuckin' thang . . . But if you lookin' to make some more, you take that trick to one of the backrooms and fuck or suck that nigga off easily . . . have him break you wit' an easy hundred or more," T.T. proclaimed.

"You be doin' that shit, T.T.?"

"Bitch, it pays my fuckin' bills," she replied dryly. "Just try it, G.G. It's cool . . . Fuck you lookin' like it's beneath you?"

"'Cause it is," G.G. returned.

"Whatever, bitch! I'm tryin' to help you out wit' a job, and you burning bridges," snapped T.T. "All I know, I'm about to get dressed and go out there to make some money. Ya either wit' it, or you can leave, G.G. It ain't gonna hurt me none."

T.T. sat in the chair and began getting undressed. G.G. stood off in the corner contemplating. The door to the room swung open and two scantily clad young girls walked in. Both were clutching a fistful of money: singles and a few fives. One glanced at G.G. with a deadpan look, and the other greeted T.T., saying, "Hey, Spice." It was T.T.'s stage name.

G.G. wanted to snap and shout, "What the fuck you lookin' at?" But G.G. stood off to the side and watched everything. The girls came into the room to change into different outfits. They both were thick, hood-rat bitches in their early twenties. They began boasting about getting money, and turning tricks in the VIP rooms. T.T. removed her outfit from her bag and laid it across the back of the chair.

"She ya girl, Spice?" one of the dancers asked.

"Yeah."

The two strippers then proceeded to change into different outfits for the night. T.T. looked up at her friend with a questionable stare. G.G. looked back and asked, "What I'ma get dressed in?"

"That's what's up," T.T. replied.

T.T. started to remove a few outfits from her bag and said to G.G., "We about the same size, even though you got a little more ass than me."

Forty minutes later, both girls stepped out from the dressing room looking more like grown women in their raunchy attire and makeup than two eighteen-year-old teens. G.G. strutted behind T.T. toward the club floor, scantily clad in an elastic black halter baby-doll which was a Lycra net with elastic straps and wearing a matching thong underneath. The stilettos she wore made her shapely legs look stretched to the ceiling. T.T. wore a multi-colored striped fishnet long-sleeved dress. She had nothing on underneath, exposing her dark nipples and shaved pussy. She sported bright red stilettos. They walked into the lively club and numerous eyes were fixed on them.

T.T. and G.G. looked like divas, with their smooth skin glistening under their attire and their bodies releasing an intense sex appeal for the men to pick up. G.G. wasn't nervous. She went straight to the bar and ordered a drink to down quickly—a shot of vodka. Five minutes on the floor and G.G. already had men approaching her from every direction.

"Damn, beautiful . . . I like that; let me lick the crack of your ass," said one dude.

"What's your name, ma?"

"Can I get a dance wit' you?"

"Yo, shorty wit' the dreads, c'mere," said another.

"You lookin' good in that outfit."

G.G. was getting hit with questions and compliments left and right. She was bad and new. She lingered by the bar for a moment, talking to potential tippers and eager men who craved her attention. Drake and Jay-Z's "Light It Up" was blaring throughout the club. G.G. nodded to the track and looked around her newfound milieu. It screamed lust and sex from wall to wall. The young boys and thugs in the place were the most aggressive and loud ones, while the old heads were more laidback and chill—being gentler with the ladies.

G.G. strutted around the club, getting used to it. She gave out lap dances, and grinded on the fellows, feeling their hard-ons through their jeans poking against her. She drank and started making her ends.

T.T. got on the stage when the DJ started to play "Moment 4 Life" with Nikki Minaj and Drake. She strutted around the elevated platform with confidence. Her legs gleamed like the sun in the afternoon, and her swelled breasts jiggled like dangling fruit from a tree. She caught immediate attention from the fellows as she moved to the beat, and slowly raised her multi-colored, transparent fishnet dress up to her hips, exposing her shaved goodies clearly to the bright-eyed men in the crowd—their minds and attention becoming trapped in lust. T.T.'s pleasing hips swayed and gyrated on the stage like she was twirling with an invisible Hula-Hoop. She firmly gripped the pole centered on the stage and twirled around it like a young schoolgirl on the playground. Her legs were in the air like a joyful ride, exposing her

pussy to lively onlookers. She then dropped into
a rapid split across the floor, like a cheerleader,
and bounced her ass across the stage, leaning
forward, showing the crowd her flexibility.

"Damn," a man shouted.

"Yo, do that shit, ma . . . That's what the fuck
I'm talking about," another man shouted.

Money was tossed at her from everywhere;
some of it came floating down on T.T. like it
came from the heavens. She then rolled over on
her back, thrust and parted her legs up in the air
like a wide V and had her pussy in full view on
the stage. More money was thrown at her. T.T.
continued to move widely and seductively on
the stage, the transparent dress came off and
was tossed to the side, and she was buck naked
in some stilettos, giving the men a phenomenal
show. She made her ass bounce like a dribbling
ball, and worked the pole like a gymnast—showing off her upper body strength.

G.G. was stunned at T.T.'s skills. She showed
confidence. She watched her friend work magic
for the crowd around the stage and saw the
money she was making. There had to be a hundred dollars in singles and fives plastered across
the stage. She wasn't scared to flirt and get
extremely close with the men; they were able
to touch wherever they pleased. Their hands

groped her breasts and fondled between her legs.
G.G. saw that men had their hands everywhere
across T.T.'s skin.

G.G. downed another shot of vodka and had
already collected fifty dollars in tips. She quickly
adjusted to the scene and worked the crowd like
T.T. suggested. She was giving a local thug a wall
dance when she noticed T.T. talking to a young
local. They both were smiling, as he was whis-
pering something in her ear. She said something
back, smiled and then she collected her clothing
and strutted off the stage buck naked with her
cash and attire in her hands. She followed the
guy and walked toward the back where the VIP
rooms were. G.G. knew what type of business
was about to take place. It looked natural for T.T.
to disappear with a trick to fuck or suck.

The night progressed and G.G. had a handful
of dollar bills. The attention she was drawing
from everybody was causing jealousy among a
few of the other dancers in the building. G.G.
quickly became comfortable with exploiting her
curvaceous figure. She exposed her goodies, and
tolerated the many hands that touched her in
places where only previous lovers had that priv-
ilege, but the money she was making was cool. It
was less risk than selling crack, and G.G. figured
a few nights of doing this, then she would be able

to pay back Echo, and get that crazy nigga off her back. She didn't want any more dealings or problems with him.

T.T. had disappeared off to the back rooms to turn tricks a few times during the night. Every time, she would exit with a handful of money. G.G. had a few offers to sell her ass, but she turned them down. It wasn't her thing, but the men were thirsty to get between her thighs. One individual was willing to pay her $200 for sex with her. G.G. was appalled by him. T.T. thought she was stupid for turning him down. T.T. took the man up on his offer, and left with him for the back room. He was ugly and fat, and had a slight odor; G.G. didn't understand how T.T. could do it to herself, but to each his or her own.

G.G. was giving someone a lap dance to the sound of Rihanna. It was her third hour in the club. He touched on her succulent booty as she grinded her pussy into his lap. The aura of her sweat and thick skin against him had him extremely hard.

"Damn, you're so fuckin' sexy," he said to G.G.

"Thank you," she replied coolly.

G.G. arched her back, gripped his shoulders, and rotated her hips into his jeans, causing the boy to vibrate with excitement. She knew he would want to fuck, and it would be the umpteenth time someone asked her if she was doing VIP. She politely turned him down, and it looked like his whole world had crashed.

As G.G. seductively danced against him, she turned and noticed someone had been watching her for the longest time. Their eyes met, and G.G. couldn't turn away from him. He was very handsome in his brown skin, and his swag trickled off of him like sweat dripping. He was tall and beefy with chiseled cheekbones. His dark goatee edged his lips and chin perfectly, and his bald head gleamed like light. He was dressed in a pair of MEK boot-cut jeans, beige Timberlands, and a white T-shirt that hugged his beefy frame. He had little jewelry on—a long chain with a diamond cross, and a matching bracelet. His eyes sank into G.G. from little distance. She was instantly attracted to him.

After the dance, and the thirsty pleas for VIP from the boy, G.G. hopped off his lap and strutted near the bar where her handsome stranger stood, nursing a beer. She stood close to him, feeling his eyes burning into her scantily dressed and exposed flesh.

He smiled. "Can I buy you a drink, beautiful?" he asked, his voice booming with masculinity and confidence.

"Sure."

"What you drinking?"

"Grey Goose," she said.

"Straight?" he asked with a raised brow.

"Yup!"

"Ayyite . . ."

He turned to the female bartender and called her over. "Let me get a shot of Grey Goose and another beer."

She nodded and hurried to execute his order. The man turned to G.G., and asked, "So, what's your name?"

G.G. didn't know what name to give him. T.T. advised her to come up with a stage name—telling G.G. to always separate the club and your personal life. So G.G. quickly came up with the name Angel; her stage name.

"Angel," she told him.

He chuckled. "Cute. But your real name . . . not that stage name you give these other fools."

"Look at you, you ain't know a bitch but for one minute and already you asking my business. I hope the tip is right for all this," said G.G.

"Yeah, it's always right coming from me," he returned with a smile.

"Um huh . . ."

The female bartender approached them with their drinks in hand. She set down a beer and Goose. The man pulled out a huge wad from his pocket and peeled off twenty dollars, passed it to the bartender, and said, "Just keep the change, love."

"Thank you," she replied with a smile.

"Baller, huh?" G.G. stated.

"I do me."

"Thanks for the drink." G.G. took a sip from her Goose. Her eyes couldn't stray away from him. He was tall and definite eye candy. "What's your name?" she asked.

"Chubbs."

"Chubbs? That's ya real name?"

"It's what everybody calls me."

"So, Chubbs, you want a dance?"

"Yeah, bring that ass closer," he said, slightly tugging at G.G.'s outfit.

G.G. set her drink on the counter and pressed her soft, succulent backside against Chubbs. She began to grind her ass into his crotch, and could feel his dick indentation pressing against her ass. It felt like he had a big dick. G.G. was somewhat impressed. Chubbs wrapped his arm around her waist and hugged her close, as G.G. gyrated her sweetness against him.

"Damn, you're so fuckin' soft," he uttered.

"It's how a woman should be. I assume you like how my body feels?"

"Hells yeah."

G.G. turned around and pushed her tits against his chest. She could feel the muscles rippling from under the thin shirt he wore. His physique was phenomenal. Her pussy began dripping just by touching him. Chubbs gripped his wad of cash and slipped twenty dollars into her G-string. It was then followed by another twenty, and another. G.G. was ecstatic. It was good to know that he wasn't cheap. The other girls in the club looked on and jealousy soon stirred in their eyes watching the new bitch get money.

G.G. spent the majority of her time with Chubbs. He bought her drink after drink, and tipped her handsomely. She had his undivided attention, which was causing some animosity with the girls who wanted a piece of Chubbs themselves. The two were engaged in conversation, and soon Chubbs passed her his card and said, "I want you to holla at me."

"About what?" she asked, taking his card.

"You like what you do here?"

"Honestly, this is my first night here," she stated.

Chubbs was taken aback. "Oh word, you seem so cool and natural at this."

"'Cause I'm that bitch . . . But, what, you tryin' to pull my coat too?" she asked with concern.

"I like your style, Angel . . . Still didn't get that real name . . ."

"G.G.," she uttered.

"G.G. . . . cute. But as I was saying, you're beautiful, your skin, the dreads . . . you got the total package. You wanna make some real money?"

"Depends on doin' what?"

"Dancing in a rap video?"

"You serious? Whose video?"

Chubbs laughed. "Damn, you ask a lot of questions, G.G. But I feel you . . . you wanna know what you're getting into . . . understandable. But it's for this up-and-coming rapper named Johnny South Side. You heard of him?"

"Vaguely."

"Well, he's nice . . . coming up in the game. We need some girls like you that stand out to be in his video," Chubbs explained.

"How much ya paying . . . ?"

"Call me and find out."

G.G. looked at the card. It had his name, a business, and two numbers on it. She kept it in her hand and thought about it.

"Ask around about Chubbs, and you'll know what I'm about," he added.

Chubbs slipped G.G. an extra fifty dollars in her G-string and walked out. He left G.G. thinking about the proposal. Her first night dancing and she already got offered something better. It was luck. G.G. turned and noticed the hateful eyes watching. She was T.T.'s homegirl, and the other girls could only stare.

T.T. and G.G. exited the club at four in the morning. Both girls were content about tonight. They walked toward the idling cab parked outside the club talking and laughing. T.T. slid inside the back seat, and G.G. followed inside. They told the cab driver that they were going to Jamaica Queens, and he slowly pulled away from the curb.

As they rode toward Queens, T.T. counted her earnings for the night, totaling up $600. And G.G. made $400 for the night. G.G. looked at her friend and said, "Guess what."

"What?" T.T. asked without looking at her friend, her eyes still on the bills in her hands.

"I met this guy named Chubbs, and he offered me to dance in Johnny South Side's new video."

T.T. finally turned to look at her friend. "You serious?" she asked.

"Yeah, the nigga was fuckin' fine, T.T. He told me to give him a call for a job. Shit, I might just do that."

"That's what's up . . . cool," replied T.T. nonchalantly.

Chapter 9

Baby brushed by Samson and strutted into the cafeteria in her short skirt and white sneakers. She was too cute. She smiled at Samson and headed over to her group of girls seated at one of the tables near the entrance. Samson looked at her for a moment. He was nonchalant. The two locked eyes momentarily and then Samson swiftly diverted his attention elsewhere. Baby smirked and started talking to her friends at the table.

Marvin walked over toward Samson, playfully nudged him, and said, "Umm, that young girl needs a dress code in this school. But I see you looking, Samson. You better stay focus on what's important."

"I'm doing my job," Samson said dryly.

"I bet you are . . . Just make sure the job ain't doing you," he replied.

Samson cut his eyes at Marvin. He wasn't too fond of him. Marvin always had something stupid to say and he was a creep. Samson was quiet and low-key. Marvin was sometimes loud and boisterous. The two didn't bond at all.

Marvin glanced at Baby. His eyes traveled from her long, gleaming legs to her top area, and rested on her pretty face.

"Damn, if only I was ten years younger, then she would have been a problem for me. Damn, these young girls done definitely changed since I was in high school," Marvin said. "They're making the job much harder on a nigga. They say we can't touch, but shit, we can sure look . . . right, my nigga?"

He was contradictory.

Samson remained quiet. His military persona taught him to remain focused and alert at all times. He had no time for small, idiotic chitchat with Marvin. He looked around the cafeteria, observing the students and their activity. It was calm for the period. There weren't any indications of any problems brewing. So, Samson stood there relaxed.

Marvin kept talking, but soon took the hint when Samson didn't reply to anything he was saying. He walked away to the farther side of the cafeteria. Samson was happy that he was gone. He kept his composure and knew Marvin was stupid.

The lunch period ended, and the students began exiting the area. They poured out of the cafeteria like a massive herd. They were loud. Baby followed the exiting crowd. When she got close to Samson, she smiled at him and said, "You see, I've been a good girl for a week now . . . no contraband. You care to search me and find out?"

Samson remained stone-faced. He didn't comment back. He didn't even look her way. Baby laughed along with her girls and rushed out of the cafeteria. One of Baby's friends laughed and said, "Damn, that nigga's fuckin' fine."

"I know, right," Baby replied, looking back at Samson promptly.

Baby's look upon Samson showed she was very interested in getting to know him better. He was dogmatic a majority of the time. But Baby knew he had a soft spot. He could have turned her in and been an asshole; Baby knew there was an opening somewhere with him. She went on to her next class with Samson on her mind.

She was behaving herself in school, and everyone was shocked at her change of behavior during the past two weeks. But, unbeknownst to everyone, Baby had other motives. She had gotten caught once hustling in the stairway, and didn't want to get caught again. She had to change up. She had to substitute her demeanor. She was making money in the locker rooms, the cafeteria, and the classrooms and outside. Baby felt she had a foolproof system. She got her work from J. Rock and was moving it smoothly via the students in her school. She sold weed and E-pills (ecstasy). Baby was making a healthy profit. Some of the students were known to throw numerous cut parties during the week, and during these cut parties they wanted to lose themselves in a haze of sexual frenzy, having full-scale orgies in apartments or homes. To expedite things, the kids got high off of both mixtures. These parties became popular through word of mouth, and many wanted to attend, but the location was always kept a secret until the day of the party.

Baby was the main supplier for these parties. She sold weed by the ounces and the E-pills were always the first to go. The kids took them because it produced an intense pleasurable effect, enhancing a sense of self-confidence and energy. When they were high on pills, the kids felt a feeling of peacefulness, acceptance, and empathy. These users were experiencing the feeling of closeness with others and a strong desire to touch others and become intimate. The most close-minded and shy student instantly became a freak once on E-pills, and the girls found themselves indulged in overwhelming orgies with numerous boys all throughout the apartment, or homes they were hosted in. Because of them, teenage pregnancy and STDs were on the rise in the school.

Principal Palmer had gotten news of these scandalous cut parties, but he was powerless to stop them. They were happening outside of the school grounds at various locations, and the main perpetrators behind them were smart and cunning. He was also aware of the drugs in his school, and vowed a major crackdown on those responsible for making his high school into a shithole, but Baby had eyes and ears in much needed places. People always looked out for her. They had so much love for Baby, and, J. Rock taught her how to hustle and use people. Baby used her beauty and sex appeal to influence anyone. She was so street savvy and cunning, that when she came at you, most times, you didn't even see it coming then, instantly, you were caught up and tangled in her vicious web.

The school days continued and Baby and Samson were constantly running into each other in passing. Every time, Baby made it her business to tease or flirt with Samson, but, as always, he would ignore her and do his job with precision.

Baby saw that he was a tough nut to crack. She began to wonder if he would be able to crack at all, but she was persistent; when something or someone caught Baby's attention, she went after it until you became her undivided attention. Something about Samson caught her attention. She loved that he was a military man like her father. He was strong and a no-nonsense type of man. While the other school safety officers joked around and talked with the students on a regular basis, becoming friends, Samson kept to himself most times. He was introverted at times, but he was fair around the students. They would ask about his military background, but he would never talk about his experience in the Marines or the war in Iraq. He had seen some horrors overseas, and that's where he wanted to keep them: overseas.

Baby was attracted to him, and it was his introverted ways that she liked. He reminded her of a few gangsters around her way. They were quiet but deadly inside, just like Samson with his military training. His eyes were always alert, watching, and his demeanor was intense. He had all the qualities of a soldier that were still embedded into him. Baby was persistent with getting to know more about him.

She would come to school in her sexiest attire—sometimes, it would be too raunchy, stir-
ring up heated attention from the boys and male
staff she came across. She had been forewarned
before about some of the revealing clothing she
came to school in, and was immediately sent
home by the principal to change her clothing.
So, Baby pushed the limits. The things she wore
were somewhat revealing, but not too revealing
to get her sent home or kicked out. But, the boys'
eyes were still glued to everything on her—and
Samson would give her a fleeting look from time
to time, but it didn't linger on her long enough to
show that he was interested.

Baby decided to push the limits more. She
came to school in a pink tennis skirt. She strutted around school oozing sex and had the males'
minds fogged with lust and desire. She smiled
at them, and flirted with the cute ones, but her
focus was on Samson. There was something
about him that she craved. J. Rock had been
absent from her world for over a week. He was
in Baltimore conducting business and she hadn't
heard from him since she took his duffle bag
of guns into her grandmother's apartment. So,
Baby's attention needed to be elsewhere, and
indirectly, Samson was the chosen one. While
men lusted and chased after her, she subtly

hunted for Samson. She knew he would be useful to her in so many ways.

The school day was winding down. It was approaching eighth period and the hallways started to become lighter with students, as they were finishing up their classes and leaving the school. Baby had her eyes on Samson as she watched him walk down the hallway alone. He was heading toward the men's bathroom. She followed him at a distance. Samson went inside. Baby hesitated outside the men's bathroom for a short moment. She looked around, and the hallway was clear, silent like an empty room. She was bold. She hurried into the bathroom where Samson was pressed closely against one of the urinals taking a piss. When he felt the sudden presence of someone entering the bathroom, his head turned toward the entrance. He was shocked to see Baby in there with him.

"Hey," she greeted him with a smile.

"What are you doing here?" he exclaimed. "Get the hell out of here!"

"I wanna talk."

Samson was caught exposed. He quickly finished peeing and zipped up his trousers. Baby stood there with a smile. She tried to take a peek at his package, but he was pressed too close to the urinal to get a clear look at his dick. Samson became uncomfortable. Baby had put him in an awkward position, and she knew if they were caught together in the men's bathroom alone, it would raise questions, even if nothing happened. Baby loved the risk.

"I'm not playing with you, Baby . . . This is not a fucking game. Get the fuck outta here!" Samson barked.

It was the first time she heard him curse, or become hostile. Baby loved it. It was turning her on—it made her pussy ripple like a wave. She wasn't scared of him or his shouting. She looked at Samson with a daring look and said, "What, you scared I might see your dick? Shit, show me yours and I'll show you mines."

Baby became even more daring, lifting up her pink tennis skirt in front of Samson to reveal her secret: she came to school with no panties on, or had removed them earlier.

Samson was completely shocked. Her exposed pussy was completely shaved clean and fresh—dripping with her sweet nectar.

"See, I'm not shy," she added. "You like it?"

Samson was appalled more than turned on. She was risking his job, and he needed the income. He became speechless. The only thing Samson could do was rush out of the bathroom and hurry away from her.

Baby continued to smile and liked the reaction she created.

Chapter 10

Samson came home to find his mother asleep on the couch. She was still in her work uniform. It was late evening. The TV was on, playing reruns of *The Cosby Show*. The room was dimmed. The table was cluttered with open mail and magazines. It was a typical evening at home.

Samson was in plain clothes and he was hungry. His mother had leftover dinner on the table. He looked at his mother and knew she had another hard day at work. She had been working overtime every day, breaking her back to keep up with the bills and the mortgage. He rarely saw his mother and, when he did, she was either asleep, or coming and going from her two jobs. Samson hated to see his mother work so hard. She was fifty-five, and should be living in her golden years, taking it easy—reaching retirement. But instead, his mother was struggling to keep from going under in debt. Her savings was dwindling. While Samson was overseas, his mother had to take out a second mortgage on her home to pay for her doctor bills. She had become ill with cancer.

It had been rough for Samson since his return to the States and his discharge from the service. His job at the school was average and, he felt, was pointless. He was a soldier, and still carried himself as one, but he felt trapped. His world was guns and the Marines—protecting his country's freedom. At August Martin, he felt like a sap clad in a clown's uniform trying to protect young brats who didn't care about anything but themselves.

Samson thought about Baby, and was somewhat troubled by her shocking stunt in the bathroom. For some reason, he couldn't stop thinking about it. The way her body curved underneath the tennis skirt made him aroused for a moment. Her heavy beauty and curvy physique was stimulating to the point where Samson was almost paralyzed from it, but she was too young; Samson had her beat by ten years. He wanted to get the image out of his head. It had been a long while since he'd been with a woman. Most of his time was spent in the service, fighting in Iraq, and at home, dwelling over what his life had become.

Samson went into the kitchen to fix himself something to eat. He piled mounds of food onto his plate and stuffed it into the microwave. He pressed for five minutes. He then walked back into the living room and picked up a few pieces of mail from off the coffee table. He went through each piece seeing if anything had come for him, but everything was mostly bills and junk mail. Samson suddenly stopped at one piece of mail he came across in his hand. It caught his attention like a sharp pain inside of him. He was taken aback. His eyes burned into the bold, black letters stamped across the white envelope saying, FINAL WARNING, FORECLOSURE.

"What the fuck!" he mouthed to himself.

He didn't know what to expect. He removed the letter from the envelope and quickly read through it. They were about to lose their home. They were four months behind in paying the mortgage, and owed the bank, in total, $25,000. They didn't have that kind of money. Samson felt shaky. He had grown up there. It was his home—his foundation. He wanted to hold back the tears, but it was hard. His family was hurting. He had already been through so much. He knew his mother wanted to keep it a secret from him; that's why the letter was concealed under everything else, like a dirty little secret under the pile of bills.

Samson let out an exasperated sigh. He didn't know what to do. He looked down at his sleeping

mother, and felt he had let her down. She tried
to hide it from him. It was embarrassing. They
were being evicted from their own home. It was
something he wasn't going to allow to happen.
He planned on taking action. He was angry.
Samson felt that he'd put so much into protecting his country, and then adapting to become a
civilian, and now they wanted to put him out.

Samson placed the letter back into the envelope and situated it the same way he found it.
He heard the microwave beeping, indicating his
food was ready to be taken out. Samson walked
into the kitchen, removed his plate, sat down at
the table, and ate his meal silently in a somber
mood.

The next school day, Samson stood by the
cafeteria entrance with a stone-cold stare, and a
serious mood. The students were loud and lively
like always. His thoughts were heavy on the
foreclosure. He tried hard to keep his composure
and sanity, but he felt himself slipping gradually
the more he thought about it. He watched the
students in the cafeteria keenly. But he was
looking for one particular lady. She strutted into
the cafeteria ten minutes after the lunch period
started. She was lively and looking stunning in
her eye-catching attire like always.

Baby brushed by Samson with her usual smile and flirting. Samson remained himself with his deadpan gaze. Baby took a seat with her girls at the table and they began talking and laughing. She then glanced over at Samson and smiled once more. Samson looked her way and held her stare, lingering on her beauty. It was the longest Baby had ever seen him staring at her. She thought their encounter in the bathroom had finally had some strong effect on him.

Samson caught himself staring at her too long and quickly turned his direction elsewhere, but his lingering eyes upon her gave Baby the window she needed. She knew he was interested. It took awhile, but she figured that she finally hooked him. Baby continued conversing with her friends, while Samson surveyed the cafeteria making sure everything was okay.

The lunch period ended, and Baby moved closer to Samson and said to him, "I saw you staring earlier; you finally starting to like what you see?"

Samson kept his deadpan demeanor and didn't answer her. He focused on his job, watching the students leave the cafeteria. He wasn't in the mood, or didn't want to get caught frolicking with anyone. His soldier behavior made him a little aloof from the students, and even the staff,

and his coworkers. He didn't hang out after the
job like his coworkers. While they went to bars
and clubs to get drinks, mingle, and have a good
time, Samson was home. A few ladies had a
strong crush on him, and they wanted to get to
know him better, but Samson didn't want to get
to know them. The other school safety officers
started to think that he had internal issues—that
Iraq had fucked him up.

Baby stood by Samson closely and said, "It's
cool, daddy . . . I know how it is."

She strutted out of the cafeteria, leaving Samson pondering. He glanced at Baby, and thought
about the unthinkable—but then erased the
burdensome image from his mind and focused
on work.

It was after 5:00 P.M. when Samson exited the
school, coming underneath the rapidly graying
sky, and began making his way toward his truck
parked on the street. Samson walked briskly and
looked up at the sky. He could smell the rain
approaching. It had been a long day. He wanted
to go home and get some sleep. He crossed the
silent street. Removing the keys from his pocket,
he pressed to deactivate the alarm to his ride
and unlocked the doors. When he got near the

driver's side, he suddenly heard, "Can I get a ride home?"

Samson swiftly turned, and behind him stood Baby—only a few feet away. It appeared that she came out of nowhere. Samson was surprised. He looked around, and the street was clear. Everyone had gone home.

"What do you want from me?" he asked sternly.

"Just your time," she replied innocently. "We can talk."

"Listen, little girl, I ain't your damn peer," he barked, approaching Baby closely, trying to intimidate her.

"I'm not a little girl . . . Shit, look at me, nigga, do anything seem little on this body?" Baby said, stepping back from Samson, doing a 360, and showing him her ripe body. She was wearing a jean skirt with a jacket. Her eyes stayed glued to Samson.

"I gotta go," he said sharply, heading back to his truck.

"Give me a ride, then," she persisted. "You lookin' stressed or desperate about somethin' right now, yo! You can talk to me."

Samson turned once again to look at her. "Why you say that?" he asked her.

"I see it in your eyes . . . They never lie."

He shook his head and chuckled. "What the hell I'm gonna talk to you about? You're only eighteen."

"And? Age ain't nothin' but a number, and believe me, nigga . . . I got more wisdom inside of me than you think. You can talk to me about anything; I might surprise you," she said with conviction.

"You might . . . but I'm not with that. I don't socialize with students."

"We ain't in school right now. This is just two people talkin' on the block," replied Baby.

"What's so fuckin' special about me?"

"Ya different. I see it in your eyes, your mental, your demeanor . . . you keep to yourself, and you don't fuck wit' any of them clown-ass niggas in this school. I respect that about you."

"What you know about respect? You hardly give it to anybody," he returned.

"A muthafucka gotta earn my fuckin' respect from me."

"You gotta give respect first to get it."

"And don't I get it," she uttered. "They don't fuck wit' me."

"Look, Baby, right . . . That stunt in the bathroom the other day, it wasn't cute. And this right here, you and me, it ain't happening," Samson exclaimed.

"What ain't happening? What . . . you think I wanna fuck you?" She chuckled. "I just did that for a show. I like attention. And I wanted your attention at the time."

"I see," he said.

"I just wanna talk. You're a Marine, and my father was a Marine. I don't know too much about my father, he was always gone . . . but you remind me of him, somewhat. I just wanna talk to a soldier that did a tour overseas like my father did," she proclaimed.

Samson looked at her for a moment. He didn't know what to think or expect from her. She was intelligent. He knew by the way she spoke, that Baby could be very articulate. But she hid how smart she really was by her fierce attitude, foul language, fighting, and promiscuity. She also had charisma and beauty, two deadly ingredients for a woman. Samson sighed. He looked at Baby, and reluctantly said, "Just this one time."

Baby smiled. She rushed toward his truck and climbed inside the passenger seat. Samson looked uneasy about it, but he climbed into his truck and started the ignition. He didn't pull off right away. It looked like something was eating away at him. He gripped the steering wheel tightly and sighed heavily. He glanced at Baby, and couldn't believe he had her in the passenger seat of his truck. Samson knew it was a risk that he couldn't afford to take, but he was taking it.

"Somethin' wrong?" Baby asked.

"How far do you live from here?"

"Not far . . . I'm on Guy Brewer and Foch," she answered.

He knew the area. Samson hesitated to pull off, though. His mind drifted to someplace else for the moment. He looked straight ahead, at nothing in particular. He had been on the job for a month, and for him, it was a dead end.

"You miss it, don't you?" Baby suddenly stated.

"What?"

"The Marines. I could tell you miss it. You don't wanna be here, right?"

"It's a job."

"But you had a life, and they took that from you . . . just like they took my father away from me," she said.

Samson gazed at Baby. She hit the nail on the head; he went from having a life, a career with the Marines, to a local job at a school. It was eating away at him. He missed the excitement, his rank, and the traveling. He missed making a difference—protecting his country by any means necessary.

Before he knew it, Samson was engaged into a full conversation with Baby while still parked.

He poured out all of his feelings to Baby, and he didn't know why. He couldn't control himself. He was angry. Baby sat there and was willing to listen to him gripe. The frustration he felt was suddenly released like a flowing waterfall, and Baby was there to collect his sorrows like a puddle in her hands.

"Life is fucked up, that's all I can say . . . but sometimes a bad situation can put you in a good moment in life," she stated. "I used to hear my father say that all the time when I was young. I guess he used to say that to himself when he was fighting for his life in different countries."

They were words of wisdom coming from an eighteen-year-old.

Samson then changed his gloomy look to a questionable stare at Baby, and asked, "What's your story, huh? I look at you, and I see someone that's more than meets the eye. You're smart, Baby, so who you're fooling? Why you act the way you do? You got potential to do something with your life."

"Listen, you're not from my world, so you wouldn't understand," she replied.

"So, make me understand. But I done saw horrors that you can't even imagine."

"So have I," Baby matched. "So I guess we're both two peas in a pod, right?"

"I guess we are."

Samson found an unexpected comfort with Baby. The two sat for a half hour talking with time gradually passing by. Baby found herself leaning closer to him. Her eyes were strongly on Samson. Her thick legs gleamed from underneath the skirt she wore. Samson inadvertently stared at her long, defined legs and his mind abruptly was awash with waves of lust. He felt himself being pulled into a strong craving.

"I think it's time for us to go," he said suddenly, trying to snap himself out of the lustful thoughts.

"We can chill for a little longer. I'm in no rush to get home."

Samson looked at the time on the dashboard. It was five-thirty. The skies were getting darker and were soon about to burst open with rain and thunder. The two looked at each other heavily. Samson once again felt paralyzed from her beauty, and her conversation was on point. His mind told him to leave right now, and not to pursue the unthinkable, but his body had him trapped like a young stag in a lion's den.

"What you thinkin' about?" Baby asked him.

"Nothing," he said.

"You sure? I know you got a lot on ya mind." Baby leaned closer to him, and her hand rested on his leg naturally. She started to massage his thigh, and then her caresses slowly reached up to his strapping chest.

Samson found himself becoming aroused by her soft touch. He wanted to resist, but he didn't. Everywhere she touched him felt better than it ever had before. Each touch was alluring. Each caress was the most sensational caress that he could imagine, and then some. Samson felt his dick jump with hardness. It felt like it was ready to tear from his jeans. Baby rubbed his crotch tenderly and neared her lips against his. He opened his mouth for her tongue and let it plunder his mouth. They started to kiss fervently. Her lips were the softest lips he'd ever felt before.

With swiftness, Baby undid his jeans and pulled out his throbbing, hard dick. It was swelled with thickness and hard like concrete in Baby's soft grip. She stroked him lovingly. Her fingers wrapped around his cock with delight, putting Samson in bliss. Baby then suddenly attacked his dick, kissing the mushroom tip and wrapping her sweet lips around it. Samson's hand quickly went to her head. Her head bobbed back and forth in his lap. She had him weakened. His dick was at full staff down her throat, opening farther with each dip and swallow, hinting at a promise of taking every inch of him within. Baby sucked him off like a true porn star. She hummed at his balls, and would slip her lips back upward to his dripping tip.

Samson grunted. "Ugggh! Ugggh . . . shit."

Her pleasurable actions went on for fifteen minutes. Baby showed pure stamina when it came to sucking dick. She deep throated it, jerked him off, and was ready to have him come in her mouth if necessary. She had Samson squirming in his seat like his ass was on fire.

Baby pulled herself away from the dick abruptly and uttered, "I wanna fuck!"

Samson had to collect himself for a moment. His dick was still hard like calculus. His pants and boxers were lying around his ankles. He was completely exposed to her. The rain started; it came down heavy outside, and cascaded off the windshield like his truck was caught underneath a raging waterfall. It gave them the perfect cover.

Baby removed her skirt and top, and became buck naked in the front seat. Samson fastened his eyes to her nude body, and was almost in awe. Her shapely and flawless figure with her swelled tits and slender neck that was surrounded by her hair was hard to resist.

"You like what you see?" Baby asked.

He was caught up in the moment. She leaned toward him once more, stroking his long, thick shaft and getting his large member ready for action. Her eyes flared with a hungry lust. Baby climbed on top of him, sliding her bare hips down to his ready-to-burst organ, feeling his large member penetrate her slowly, and she began to ride his raw-boned dick, getting ready to drive. The soft flesh Samson felt caused him to pull Baby's hair roughly and grasp her ass, as her sweet nectar dripped against his balls.

His rhythm inside of her was driving upward as his dick head pierced her warm, tightening flesh. Baby clamped her legs around him and had Samson drowning in her scented, slick juices.

"Ooooh, you feel so fuckin' good. Ooooh, you feel so good . . . Ugggh . . . Uggh!" His feral grunts echoed inside of the truck.

They fucked hard. Baby wanted to relish the moment. It was what she expected. Samson had a lot of built-up frustration inside of him, and decided to release and express himself inside of Baby's tight pussy. Samson's hips thrust upward, as he impaled her with his dick.

"Aaah . . . Aaah, oh shit, oh my God . . ." she moaned, with her ass cheeks being spread apart by his strong grip, as her body arched upward, and opening her mouth in a moan of pleasure.

"Damn, your shit is tight, oh shit . . . so good . . . oh shit!" he growled as he stayed deep inside of her.

Baby's hands tensed into fists as her whole body went stiff as a board beneath Samson. Then she went limp like a wet noodle as he moved his dick in and out of her. Her nails dragged against his skin, and her eyes rolled to the back of her head. The heated flesh from his lap caused Baby to vibrate against him. Samson's body shook with a solid orgasm that raced through his whole body. His nut was heavy inside of her. He was lost in a rapturous haze of lust. Their bodies dripped with satisfaction.

The heated moment was quick and intense.

They both were breathless, but fulfilled. The rain continued to come down like a shower on the truck. Samson's truck reeked of sex and flesh. Baby climbed off his lap and collapsed in the passenger seat. Her naked flesh was sweaty and her breathing still remained shallow. Samson exhaled. He then slowly pulled up his jeans to his hips, but left them unfastened for a moment, and rested his head against the headrest. He had a sudden look of regret. *What the fuck did I just do?* he asked himself. She was only eighteen. *But,* he wondered, *who took advantage of who?*

"That was nice," Baby said, as she dressed herself.

Samson remained silent.

Baby was completely dressed and said, "You can take me home now."

Her smile aimed at him was conniving. Samson sat there, still lost in his thoughts, or regrets. He blew air out of his mouth and turned to face Baby. The pussy had him stagnant for a moment. Baby knew she had him caught up. It was what she was good at.

Samson knew it was time to take her home. He started the truck and drove off. They drove silently to Baisley Park Housing. When he reached his destination, Baby leaned over to give him a kiss, but Samson resisted. He pulled back from her and said, "You should go."

"Cool. See you tomorrow in school," Baby said coolly.

She jumped out of his truck and strutted toward her building. She felt she got what she needed. She didn't stress his sudden rejection.

Samson delayed driving off for a minute. His eyes followed Baby walking into her building. Once she was inside, Samson sighed. He thought about what he had done, and said to himself, "Never again."

Chapter 11

G.G. excitedly strutted toward the video shoot clad in a sexy, dirty-cop costume, which included a hat, badge, and the front button dress with handcuff garters, gloves, belt, tie, and a walkie-talkie. She sported clear stilettos, with her long dreads falling freely around her shoulders. Her body curved perfectly in the attire from head to toe. Her skin glistened with sex appeal. Her walk toward the video set attracted attention. She immediately turned heads left and right—men and women.

G.G. was excited to know that Chubbs was for real about his offer to be in Johnny South Side's video. She called him the next day, and the two spoke for an hour. Chubbs arranged everything for G.G., and she was being paid $2,500 for a day's shooting. It was the most legit money she ever made in her life.

So many things were on her mind. She was a little nervous, having butterflies swimming around in her stomach. She wanted to be on point. Her scene was simple. She had a few close-ups with Johnny South Side in the video, with one scene of her straddling the rapper on the hood of a police car. It was a sexy and raunchy video. The director wanted to push sex to the limit. G.G. wanted to be the sexiest bitch in the rap video. She was the youngest video girl on the set, and ready to express her sexuality in front of the camera by any means necessary.

G.G. hated that she came alone, though. She wanted T.T. to come and support her. But T.T. declined the invitation. Her excuse was lame, and G.G. knew it. G.G. suspected that T.T. became jealous of her unexpected opportunity because it wasn't her. The signs of jealousy were there. T.T. brought G.G. down to the club, and her first night dancing, she links up with Chubbs, a well-known player in the streets and in the music industry. What were the odds of that? The other dancers strived for the chance to get put on and be in a rapper's video or get with a baller. It gave them a reason to hate G.G. They all felt she stole something that belonged to one of them.

G.G. didn't give a fuck what T.T. or anyone felt about her. She wasn't going to take her chance for granted. She was a hood bitch with a chance, and she was ready to milk it 'til it was dry. It was only hate.

It was evening. The sun was slowly fading behind the horizon. There was a chill in the air. The video shoot was set to take place on a closed-off street and back alley in Brooklyn. It was a grimy location and perfect for what the director had in mind for his video. G.G. was the last girl to step on to the video set. There were numerous girls standing around, all of them wearing raunchy cop attire, but G.G.'s was a little raunchier. She showed more skin and cleavage, and her dark ebony skin shined as if recently oiled, or sweating after a long and hard workout.

She was ready to perform.

G.G. spotted Chubbs standing in the distance talking to the director. He looked handsome in a white V-neck T-shirt underneath a brown blazer, wearing a pair of Levi's jeans and fresh white Nikes. Chubbs looked over at G.G. and smiled. She smiled back. He finished talking to the director and walked over to G.G. He could tell that she was nervous. She stood alone, playing with her nails.

"How you holding up?" he asked.

"I'm okay."

"Nervous?" he asked her.

"A little," she admitted.

"You'll be okay, just be yourself out there . . . Let the camera do all the work, let them capture who G.G. is. Even though it's a small part, sometimes that three or five minutes on camera can change your life," he proclaimed.

G.G. nodded.

It was a different world for her, and G.G. seemed to be a completely different person for the moment. The confidence and hard persona she carried on the streets had dissipated while on the set. She was starting to look like a nervous young girl. She looked around her environment and took everything in—the 100,000-watt lights that were strategically placed on the street to brighten up the area of shooting, with stands and cords wrapped around the set, and multiple cameras situated near the tricked-out Impala cop car with the tinted windows and hydraulics underneath. Staff and crew people were bustling about, some jobs more important than others. Johnny South Side's entourage and goons stood in the background in their sagging designer jeans, and heavy jewelry, eyeing the luscious young video vixens who were ready to dance and perform their duties.

Johnny South Side stepped onto the set like an A-list movie star. His long diamond chain was swinging from around his neck with a diamond-encrusted pit bull pendent. His jeans sagged like his goons, exposing his boxers. He wore a wife beater over his slim physique. His Timberlands were fresh and a Yankees fitted was tilted to the left over his long cornrows. He was the epitome of a gangster rapper from Jamaica Queens. He'd been shot, locked up, and had an extensive criminal record. He was animated. He had a bottle of E&J in one grip and a cigarette in the other.

The first scene required all the scantily clad ladies to surround the cop car with Johnny standing atop the car being shirtless and rhyming with the bottle in his hand. Everyone took their position on set. G.G. stood at the hood of the car. She took a deep breath and waited.

"And . . . action!" the director shouted.

A heavy bass beat blared all of a sudden. It had a downbeat tempo with a piano melody. It was catchy. The girls started to move seductively to the beat—winding their hips, some groping their tits as Johnny started to rhyme. He was already hyped. He danced on the roof of the car and rhymed, "This is how we do, my niggas represent, South Road, Guy Brewer, we all over, so we gotta let these bitches know . . . we don't hug 'em or love 'em, just fuck 'em and chuck 'em, I love fuckin' wit' that round bubble, put my dick in her butt, now she can't strut. I luv to rub against them, no luv against 'em, dip down low, her backside crying, 'cause my dick is far from lying, she takes shots like she on the range, her mouth open wide for it like she ain't playin, like a doorway, my whole team comin' in, her pussy so good gotta put a grade-A seal on it . . ."

It was a derogatory rhyme. Johnny South Side let it flow without any shame. Everyone nodded to it. He jumped from the car and pulled one of the girls into his arms and fondled her big butt as he focused into the camera. She then bent over in front of him, pushing her ass back against his crotch and wiggled and jiggled her goodies for Johnny to enjoy. A second girl flanked Johnny, dropping down low to bounce her ass for the camera to pick up on. Johnny out of the blue doused two of the scantily clad girls with the liquor he had in his hand and they took his disrespectful action in stride.

G.G. looked on. She was shocked at what she saw. It was unbelievable. She remained focused and continued dancing against the Impala. She wanted the spotlight, too. Her nervousness disappeared the minute the director shouted, "Action!" Her neat, long dreads stood out. She noticed Johnny looking her way a few times as he poured liquor over the girls. She matched his passionate gaze upon her, and smiled.

A few girls started exposing themselves for the camera, flashing tits and nipples, thin G-strings and more skin. G.G. decided to be that bitch, and ripped open her shirt, having the buttons fly loose, exposing all her goodies. Her nipples were thick and dark like Hershey Kisses. She had some of the juiciest tits on the set. With her long dreads, and succulent figure, she definitely stood out. The scene went on for two minutes and the director shouted, "Cut!"

Everything stopped. The two girls Johnny doused with E&J were all smiles and playful. They stayed glued to Johnny like his hip, and it was obvious that they wanted more from him than a part in his rap video. The groupies were everywhere.

"That was nice, Johnny . . . really nice," the director complimented him.

"Yo, next scene, I wanna get really fuckin' raw wit' it, ya feel me, Mike? Make it fuckin' X-rated and shit. The girls are nice, though, fo' real," said Johnny in his long, rough drawl.

"I'll see what I can do, Johnny," replied Mike, the director.

Johnny walked back to his trailer with two groupies under his arms. It was evident what was going to take place. They had a fifteen-minute window before the next scene. Johnny's goons were ready to play too. When the scene was done, they approached the girls with only one thing on their minds, and it was transparent on their hungry faces. Two immediately went for G.G., but Chubbs intervened.

"I need to holla at her for a minute," said Chubbs, throwing his arm around G.G. and cock-blocking.

"Damn, Chubbs, why you gotta do it like that?" said one goon. "I know you saw a nigga tryin' to step to her."

"Step off, nigga, fo' real," barked Chubbs with authority in his tone.

The goon could only glare at them. He knew Chubbs's position, and dared not overstep his boundaries. He stepped away, and approached another young groupie. Chubbs led G.G. away from the set to talk privately.

"You did good for your first scene," he said.

"You think?"

"Yeah, you are a natural at this."

G.G. smiled. "I didn't overdo it, right?"

"Nah, this is a raunchy late-night video; you know this shit ain't gonna get any play on BET or MTV . . . it's something for the underground. The song is hot, and Johnny insisted that we do a video to it."

"I'm just happy to be down."

Chubbs smiled. He liked G.G.'s swag and appeal. Something about her had drawn him to her. She was young, but she was a sharp and rough girl. Chubbs liked everything about her. He was thirty-nine years old—twice her age.

"So, what's your plans for later on?" he asked.

"I don't know . . . I'll be back on the block wit' my crew," answered G.G.

Chubbs laughed. "Ya crew, huh . . . Yeah, I've heard about your crew."

"And what you heard?"

"Y'all don't play. Y'all rough . . . What y'all call yourselves? The Pussy packin' . . . what, or something . . ."

"The Pussy Packin' Pound . . . Triple P girls, fo' real . . . ride or die bitches," exclaimed G.G.

"That's what up, shorty. You fo' real wit' yours, I like that."

"That's the only way to be on these streets."

"Who you telling," said Chubbs. "But tonight, let's hang out, and do something. You down?"

"Hells yeah . . . I'm down."

"A'ight. I got spot where I wanna take you."

G.G. smiled.

The short break was soon over, and it was back to shooting the second scene for the video. Everyone was situated on the set, and G.G. had her one-on-one scene with Johnny. Johnny South

Side lay across the hood of the Impala and G.G. straddled him with her hands pressed against his chest. It was an intimate scene. Johnny gripped G.G.'s booty and peered up at the camera that was hovering above him for the aerial shot. A fog machine started to dispense smoke, giving the scene a mysterious haze. The other girls were situated around; some looked at G.G. with that green-eyed envy.

Johnny loved it. G.G. was soft in all places, and sat comfortably on top of him. He caught a slight erection as her hips grinded into his lap. He threw his hands up, and continued his rhyming.

"Yeah, you know I'm a freaky nigga, and gonna keep fuckin' a bitch in every freak kinda way. 'Cause when that pussy comes out, dat's when my freak comes out. Shit, I'll even fuck a bitch in the butt, if she don't front, make her huff and puff and then blow my nut out."

The girls moved to the song. G.G. continued her gyration motion against Johnny, swaying to the catchy beat. His lyrics were vulgar and it made some of the female crew uncomfortable, but they had a job to do. The scene went on for six minutes, and then the director shouted, "Cut!"

Johnny nodded. He looked up at G.G. still atop him and said, "I'm lovin' ya style, ma . . . fo' real. What's ya name?"

"G.G.," she said.

"That's what's up . . . You Chubbs' people, right?"

"Yup."

"A'ight . . . he cool peoples, that's my dude. He definitely got good taste," said Johnny.

"I know."

Chubbs walked over and interrupted their brief conversation. G.G. climbed off his lap and stood tall in her stilettos. Johnny looked at him and smiled. "We did good, right?"

"You did ya thang, Johnny," Chubbs said.

Johnny rose up from off the hood and gave Chubbs dap. The two had a mutual respect for each other. Chubbs looked at G.G. and said, "You can get dressed; we're done for the day."

G.G. nodded. She strutted toward the changing room behind a few other ladies and was happy that she was $2,500 richer. It was easy money for something she would have done for free. G.G. wished that Baby could have come out, too. She knew they would have loved her also. The cousins had that swag that made niggas thirsty for their attention—and people always confused them for sisters, rather than cousins. But Baby

was too caught up with running behind J. Rock
that she didn't know a good thing coming. G.G.
hated to see her favorite cousin chase behind a
nigga who wasn't trying to chase back.

It took G.G. twenty minutes to change. It had
been a good day. She couldn't wait to go out with
Chubbs that night. She knew he liked her; it was
in his eyes. She liked him too. He had that strong,
street swag and respect that she loved in a man.
Chubbs was a go-getter, a dreamer, but had
some serious thug in him. He had a checkered
past, too. She knew he was nobody to play with
when he checked Johnny's young goon earlier.

G.G. walked out of the dressing room and
stood in awe by what she saw. She was frozen for
a moment. Her sneakers felt rooted to the street
like concrete. She wondered how he knew she
was there. Her face went flush. Her day had suddenly turned upside down. Echo turned to face
her, and the scowl across his face was evidence
that he was done asking about his money.

Echo approached G.G. harshly. Her heart
began skipping beats. She knew he had the
gun tucked in his waistband. It seemed like he
was about to reach for it and blast her. She had
nowhere to run. He was blocking her exit.

"Bitch, you tryin' run from me? Huh?" Echo
shouted.

"I got your money, Echo," she returned. "I just got paid today."

But Echo was done reasoning with her. He never reasoned with anyone. It was always hurt or shoot first, and the person instantly got the message clearly—and if they survived, then they knew better not to fuck with him again. G.G. had pushed his last nerves. She was making him out to be a fool. Reputation was what Echo ran on. G.G. was about to become his next victim.

G.G. was ready to fight him if necessary. He was scary, but she refused to go out like a bitch. She regretted being weaponless. Her razor and .25 were left at home. She had rushed out of the apartment to meet with Chubbs. Echo towered over G.G. and was about to grab for her throat and start twisting and choking. He didn't care who saw the crime. He just wanted his money or her life.

G.G. poised herself for the attack. She locked eyes with the brutal savage and clenched her fist.

"I'ma fuck you up, bitch!" Echo exclaimed.

"Yo, is there a problem here?" a voice shouted out.

Echo turned to see who dared intervene with his business. He was known for assaulting anyone who got in his way with money or his reputation. He spun around with his hand near the Glock 17 that was tucked in his jeans, his eyes red with rage. His attention rested on Chubbs standing behind him. He was shocked.

"Chubbs . . . what's good, nigga?" Echo asked, his voice trailing a little.

"You tell me, Echo," Chubbs replied coolly.

"I'm just handling some business, that's all."

"With who, G.G.? What business you got with her?"

"Personal shit . . ."

"I see. But check this, she's with me, Echo, so don't bring that bullshit around here, you feel me?" Chubbs warned.

"Yeah, I do. But this bitch owes me two grand. She fucked up a package of mines, and she's been duckin' me for like three weeks now. You know how I do, Chubbs," said Echo.

"Yeah, I do. So for two grand, something that's pocket change for you, you ready to fuck up my business here and take her life."

"I gotta uphold my reputation," said Echo.

"Reputation." Chubbs chuckled slightly. Chubbs locked eyes with Echo and added, "Well, you know mines, right, Echo?"

"Yeah . . . so, what the fuck you gettin' at?" he growled.

"Check this, Echo, you let her be . . ."

"And my fuckin' money she owes me?"

Chubbs reached into his pocket, pulled out an enormous amount of big bills, and peeled off three grand. He then tossed it at Echo. The bills rained down and scattered at Echo's feet. Echo looked revolted by Chubb's disrespectful action.

"That's three grand, muthafucka; take it . . . And you're crying over two. So we good, right?"

Echo's face was twisted with upset. He turned to look at G.G., who had remained quiet during the conversation, then turned back to look at Chubbs. He said, "A'ight, we good, Chubbs . . . no problems."

"Cool. Pick up your money and get the fuck off my set," Chubbs exclaimed. "C'mon, G.G., let's go," he added, reaching out for G.G. to take his hand.

G.G. walked past Echo, who was squatted down and collecting the cash from off the ground. She didn't know what had happened, but it was brief, intense, and she never saw Echo back down from any man. It was a first.

G.G. walked away with Chubbs. They headed toward his silver Bentley Coupe parked on the street. G.G. wanted to ask questions. And she wanted to pay her own debts. She wasn't looking for any handouts.

"You didn't have to do that. I had the money to pay him," G.G. said.

"Nah, that's your money, G.G. You keep it. You earned it, so go celebrate with it," Chubbs said.

"So I'm in debt to you now?"

"Nah, that was just a favor. I can wipe my ass with three stacks. It's nothing for me. But I know Echo's reputation, never really liked the nigga anyway. He's brutal and vicious when he don't have to be. And I didn't want to see you get hurt. Compared to who I used to be back in the days, Echo is Mickey Mouse to me."

"I can hold my own."

"I know you can."

She smiled.

G.G. jumped into the passenger's side and Chubbs climbed behind the wheel of his lavish Bentley Coupe. It was the first time G.G. had ever been in an extravagant and pricy car. She felt like a queen against the plush, leather seats and feeling on the wood grain dashboard.

"Nice," she uttered.

"I only fuck with the best. And when you deal with me, you'll get the same treatment too."

"A'ight . . . we'll see."

Chubbs smiled and sped off.

Chapter 12

The school was quiet, the loud chats and perpetual traffic from students had gradually dissipated as the evening hours grew later. The hallways and classrooms were empty. Only a handful of teachers remained in some classrooms after hours going over study plans, having meetings, and grading papers. The high school had a totally different feeling after 3:00 p.m.

All the classrooms on the third floor, except for one, were vacant and ready to be cleaned by janitors working overtime. The empty halls and the late hours were perfect for Samson and Baby's sexual rendezvous. As 4:00 p.m. neared, they entered an empty classroom to fuck. It was their umpteenth encounter, and Samson couldn't get enough of the pussy. Baby had him strung, even though he wouldn't admit it. He promised himself never again, but the "never again" was substituted with "this is our last time together."

It had been two weeks since their first meeting, and since then, the two became a hush-hush item. They fucked in his truck, rented out motel rooms by the hour, fucked in the parking lot, and got nasty in vacant classrooms after school hours. Sometimes it got really risky between them; Baby would give him quick head in the locked stall in the men's bathroom during lunch periods. She loved taking risks, but, Samson wanted to be cautious. His job and, possibly, his freedom were at stake.

Samson found himself confiding in Baby a lot. They fucked but also talked. They were getting to know each other well. She knew about his situation at home—the foreclosure. He needed help, and she came up with a solution. Samson felt that his hand was forced into an inevitable situation. Life had delivered him a few blows, and he needed to start punching back. So, reluctantly, Baby's solution was helping her hustle drugs. He became a drug carrier and some muscle for her to earn some extra cash on the side. Baby knew he would be perfect for her operation. He was an ex-Marine—a trained killer, and desperate to keep his mother's home from going into foreclosure. It was ironic; a few weeks ago he was ready to turn her in for selling drugs in the stairway, now, he was in cahoots with her.

Baby followed behind Samson into the empty classroom. Everything was clear, the floor was quiet, and the majority of the staff had already gone home. Samson made sure the door was locked, and then the two positioned themselves out of sight from any view of the hallway. Samson stared at Baby with a strong craving that seeped inside of him. He quickly unbuckled his pants, slid them off, and stepped out of the pile. Baby shimmied out of her jeans, revealing her sweet, shaved nectar for Samson to ravage once more.

She held her arms out to him and said, "Fuck me, nigga!"

Samson was ready to oblige.

He neared her, dropped semi low in front of her, wrapped his arms around Baby's petite, juicy frame, and scooped her up into his masculine arms. He then plastered her against the wall as Baby straddled her legs around him. Their mouths hungrily devoured each other's lips—their tongues battled for dominance. Baby sucked on his tongue and could feel Samson's thick dick nearing her glorious hole getting ready for entry. She panted. He was strong. He was ready. Samson impaled himself inside of Baby while he still had her plastered against the wall.

"Ugh . . . Ugh!" she grunted, feeling the dick opening her up.

"Ugh shit . . . Ooooh, you feel so fuckin' good, Baby. Ooh, your pussy so good. Ooh so good," he moaned with his sturdy grip upon her.

They continued to kiss fervently. Baby sucked on his tongue, and easily pulled his wet muscle into her oral playground. Her nipples were hard as stones pressed against him. She could feel her juices escaping her, trickling down her legs as Samson wreaked havoc on her pussy with his long, periodic strokes inside of her.

"Ooooh, fuck me! Fuck me!" she cooed.

His dick thrust deep into her pink folds. And her heated, lively flesh wrapped around his hard shaft as he jerked his hips against her—causing her tight, hot walls to compress around his bulbous head. Her pussy pulsed nonstop. Their sexual and rough encounter was intense and nearly mind blowing. Baby's legs tightened around his upper thighs as she felt herself being pushed up the wall, which took higher learning to a whole new level.

"Ah shit, so good," he grunted once more.

They both felt their orgasms riding their course.

"I'm fuckin' comin'," he uttered.

"Come for me, baby . . . Ooooh, I feel you. I feel you!"

Samson's grip around Baby strengthened. His nut was brewing. Their bodies lit up with pleasure, and Samson discharged himself inside of Baby like a gusher. She hugged him closely still in his secure hold around her and rested her face against his skin. She exhaled. She got hers too. And it felt like she was coming down from her high. Her legs began to release around Samson's thighs and she was touching the floor again.

Samson looked spaced out for a moment. He sat in one of the chairs with his pants halfway pulled up and sighed. He looked ashamed for a moment. Baby quickly got dressed.

"What the fuck are we doing?" Samson asked.

Baby was used to his guilty conscience taking over after an intense fuck like that. She enjoyed it. He was becoming her puppet on a string.

"It's called having a good time," she said.

"Shit," he muttered. "This is crazy."

Samson stood up and started to fasten his pants and get himself organized. The pussy had him addicted. He had become a fiend for her in such a short time. It was unlike him. He was supposed to be disciplined. Drugs and sex had taken over his life. He was fucking Baby, running drugs for her, or getting high off of weed or E-pills. His world had drastically changed overnight.

They were dressed. Cautiously, they exited the classroom. Samson walked out first, inspected the area, and, when he was sure the hallway was clear, he signaled for her to step out. She strutted out and the two went their separate ways until next time.

Baby and T.T. walked into J. Rock's apartment and she couldn't wait to see her boo. He had just come back from Baltimore after doing a few runs. He was in the kitchen with a few of his goons getting much needed work ready for distribution in the streets. 2Pac's "Me Against the World" blared throughout the apartment. Heavy weed smoke lingered. Baby and T.T. walked into the kitchen. She was all smiles to finally see her boo after he'd been gone for weeks. J. Rock was seated at the table counting money. He was shirtless, his skin swathed with tattoos, and a long gold chain hung from his neck. Two thugs were seated at the table with him. A key of coke, a few liquor bottles, and an ashtray filled with cigarette butts, including blunt guts, and a few guns were spread out across the round kitchen table in front of J. Rock.

"Hey, baby," Baby greeted her boo.

She rushed toward him and was ready to jump into his arms to greet him with kisses. But J. Rock's gaze aimed at her wasn't so welcoming. J. Rock looked up at her. He wasn't thrilled like Baby was. He took a pull from his cigarette, and slowly stood up as Baby waited for her hug and kiss from him. He stood near Baby, calmly extinguished his cigarette into the ashtray, and then surprisingly struck Baby with a backhand slap across her face. The striking hit dropped Baby to the floor.

J. Rock stood over her and yelled, "Bitch, what the fuck is wrong wit' you . . . huh, bitch?"

Baby was shocked. She held the side of her face in anguish. T.T. approached J. Rock, ready to intervene and shouted, "Nigga, what the fuck is wrong wit' you?"

"T.T., stay the fuck outta this . . . this is between me and my bitch. Not you!" he sternly warned.

"You ain't gotta hit her like that, J. Rock," T.T. exclaimed. "And last time I checked, Erica was your bitch."

"T.T., shut the fuck up and leave," J. Rock exclaimed.

"That's my girl, J. Rock."

"And . . . me and your girl gonna have a little talk," he said. He then looked at his two thugs and said, "Yo, take that bitch into the living room and have her chill out."

424 Erick S. Gray

T.T. looked down at Baby still on the floor. Baby's eyes told her she was cool. T.T. nodded and walked out with the two men. Baby looked up at J. Rock and picked herself up off the floor. J. Rock stood next to her. He scowled, reaching out to grab Baby by her shirt and pulling her closer to him.

"What's this I hear about you fuckin' some other nigga, huh? Some security guard . . ."

Before Baby could answer him, he added, "And don't fuckin' lie to me, bitch. Or I'll fuckin' make it worse."

Baby was puzzled. *How did he find out about Samson?* He was the only man she was fucking while he was in B-more. J. Rock's angry look burned into her. He kept his tough grip around Baby's shirt and said, "Talk, 'cause I got eyes and ears everywhere."

"It's not what you think, J. Rock. It's only fuckin' business wit' him. I ain't got no feelings for the muthafucka."

"Business, huh . . ."

"Yes. I love you, baby," she strongly proclaimed.

"What kind of business? I hope you ain't got this muthafucka in my business."

"No, it's somethin' small time. I got this nigga open off of me, fo' real, baby. I can get him to do whatever I ask him to do. He's in a bad situation . . . desperate, so I just took advantage of it."

J. Rock looked at her. He loosened his grip around her shirt and relaxed his hard demeanor for the moment. "You always are scheming."

"But it always pays off, right, baby?"

"Maybe."

J. Rock was silent for a moment. He had a thought. He neared Baby, took her in his arms in a pleasant way this time, softened his look, and said to her, "Listen, I'm sorry, Baby . . . but you know how I get. I care for you a lot."

"I know, baby," she replied, becoming putty in his arms.

"I was thinking . . . I might cut that bitch off for good this time," he said, referring to Erica. "She fuckin' up."

It made Baby smile.

J. Rock continued with, "You ride or die wit' me fo' real all the time. I respect that, Baby. I do. I just be caught up in my moments."

"It's cool, daddy."

"But check this; you say this nigga is caught up on you like that?"

She nodded.

"A'ight . . . I got a proposition . . . me and crew, we doin' a serious come up, and you know it ain't never pretty wit' this shit. But I need a nigga got, and I need ya boy to do the deed. So, you think you could get this nigga to body a nigga for you?"

"Shit, I got my ways, baby," she said.

J. Rock smiled. "That's what I want to hear. But this shit is serious; I can't get none of my niggas to do it, 'cause it can't be traced back to me at all. And ya boy's a soldier, so I know he got the skills to kill this nigga."

"Who you want got, baby?" Baby asked.

"This nigga named Chubbs . . . It could be a new dawn wit' this nigga gone. You feel me, baby?"

"I do."

"A'ight . . . So set that up wit' ya soldier boy, and when Chubbs is toe-tagged, I'll do Erica the same, and it'll be you and me," J. Rock stated convincingly.

It made Baby smile once more. It felt like her dreams were finally coming to light. She couldn't wait for it to happen—especially for Erica to go. She was ready to set everything in motion, and knew the right type of persuasion to put on Samson to get him to kill for her.

Chapter 13

G.G. woke up in the Luxor platform bed with the sun beaming in her eyes. The shades were drawn and the morning sun lit up the well-furnished bedroom. She awakened with peace of mind for once and a lovely experience. She was naked underneath black satin sheets. The soothing texture of the black sheets against her skin put G.G. in a perpetual bliss. Last night had been remarkable—but the past week with Chubbs had been amazing. She lifted herself upright on the bed and rested her back against the headboard. Her pussy was still throbbing from last night. Chubbs fucked her like he had authority over her pussy, and ate her out like he was a hungry beast. They went at it like animals. They didn't hold anything back when it came to having sex with each other. She needed that.

The black satin sheets went with the room's décor—shimmering parquet floors, with a large designer throw rug situated at the foot of the

bed. Two grand emperor floor lamps flanked
the bed, with a Hikari cherry wood mirror with
walnut accents above the dresser, and there was
a Roma sleeper sofa near the door. A few Zen
paintings along with Japanese calligraphy hung
on the walls. There wasn't a TV in the room or a
radio, only numerous books to read about many
subjects.

G.G. knew Chubbs was different. He liked
to read a lot, and he had a fascination with
Japanese and Chinese culture. He was smart
and wealthy—two major pluses she liked. She
looked around the room and took everything in.
She slowly emerged from the bed in raw form
and walked over to the large floor-to-ceiling
windows. She peered out at Manhattan from the
twentieth floor, and it was a picturesque thing
to see. She went from the projects to a Midtown
high-rise. She didn't care about being naked in
the window; it was natural for her, and they were
so high up that hardly anyone could see into the
bedroom.

Chubbs entered the bedroom shirtless and
wearing basketball shorts. His physique was
beefy with a hairy chest, and a few tattoos. He
had qualities that the ladies ate up—a fierce
reputation, swag, and wealth. He looked at G.G.
and asked, "How did you sleep?"

"Good . . . I needed that shit."

"Good to hear."

Chubbs walked over toward the window to stand near G.G. He gently pulled G.G. into his arms and hugged her close. G.G. became lost in his sudden affection. They both peered out at the city together.

"You hungry?" he asked.

"I'm fuckin' starving . . . That dick got me hungry again."

Chubbs laughed. "Glad to know you enjoyed it."

"I loved it."

"C'mon, get dressed, I know a place where we can go and enjoy ourselves," said Chubbs.

"I'm wit' it."

G.G. quickly showered and got dressed, and left with Chubbs to have lunch in the city downtown. It was nearing late October, and the temperature was dropping gradually as the days trickled closer to November. G.G. strutted out of the high-rise in a black fall jacket, jeans, a pair of Nikes, and sporting hoop earrings. She was cute. She walked side by side with Chubbs toward his Bentley Coupe. It sat snuggly parked on the block among other lavish cars. He hit the alarm and they both climbed inside.

She was happy. Within the past week, her world had changed dramatically. She had been spending more time with Chubbs at his extravagant penthouse suite than being on the Queens block hanging with her crew. It was as if she forgot about them. Chubbs had her undivided attention, and he was exposing her to different venues and a diverse lifestyle.

They pulled up to a quaint spot that was nestled in the middle of the long city block. It was decades old—a popular café that was mostly frequented by the city's elite, and well-known athletes and celebrities. The place was well known for its sushi and exotic dishes, like strawberry sushi, kiwi sushi, and mango sushi. They were, by far, the best in the city. It was one of Chubbs's favorite spots to eat, and he wanted to expose G.G. to it. It would be something new for her.

They took a seat at the table and started sipping on beverages. G.G. was happy to be outside of Queens for once. She looked around the café jubilantly, but, she wasn't so sure about the choices from the menu. Chubbs sat opposite her and peered at the menu.

"I don't know about sushi, Chubbs . . . Ain't that raw fish? Is that healthy at all?" she asked with skepticism.

"It's cool. I eat here all the time. You don't have nothing to worry about," said Chubbs.

G.G. still looked skeptical. Chubbs laid down the menu on the table, looked at G.G., and assured her. "Look, just try it, and if you don't like it, then we'll go somewhere else. Okay?"

"A'ight." She smiled.

"But, you'll like it. I promise you that."

The waiter soon took down their orders, and G.G. was willing to try the strawberry sushi. She figured that something with strawberries in it couldn't be that bad. Chubbs ordered his usual, the mango sushi. He loved the way the taste lingered in his mouth after he bit into it. The waiter walked off and the conversation between the two of them was continuous.

"So what's your story?" G.G. asked him.

"What you mean?"

"I mean, the way you put Echo in check like that . . . I mean, I ain't never seen Echo back down to nobody . . . Even some of the hardest killers in my hood don't even fuck wit' Echo. So, for him to submit to you the way he did says somethin' about you," G.G. said.

Chubbs smiled. "I just have a reputation, that's all."

"I bet you do. I never heard of you, though," she admitted.

"And you don't need to. I move silently, and know the right people to know. But let's just say, I was a really bad man a few years ago," he acknowledged.

"Um, okay."

"But there's nothing else to tell. I've changed who I once was, and decided to take my risk with music now. It's better for me."

"Well, you ain't got no judgment comin' from my way, fo' sure . . . Shit, a bitch like me done seen my share of trouble too," G.G. said.

"I see. Tell me about your scar."

G.G. touched the side of her face where the minor scar showed, and it was a reminder of her mistake in the past. "It's nothing to tell, I just got caught slippin' one night wit' these bitches I had beef wit', and this is a reminder of how I'll never get caught slippin' again," she replied. "But the bitch that gave me this, look at that bitch now . . . this ain't nothin' compared to what I put on that bitch."

"You're impressive," said Chubbs.

"Yeah, I hear that a lot."

"But it fits you . . . I love a woman with an edge, beauty at that, too," Chubbs complimented her.

"You think I'm beautiful, huh . . ."

"I think you're amazing," he returned.

G.G. blushed, and that was a hard thing to get her to do. She was hard like stone, but being around Chubbs, she felt vulnerable and exposed. She was slightly overwhelmed by his comment. She was a hood-rat bitch from the projects—done seen violence, jail, gunplay, and death, but no man had ever taken the time out to show her something different—something like love. She was a quick fuck for niggas, and she didn't mind it. G.G. was that bitch who liked sex like any nigga, but the games niggas were playing were getting redundant for her.

It turned G.G. on that Chubbs was from her world, and they understood each other. He was able to escape and do quite well for himself. G.G. wanted to spend every moment with him. She was willing to learn and try something different in her life for once. Sitting down with Chubbs made G.G. open her eyes. The gang culture she was heavily involved in was wearing on her, but she was afraid to admit it to anyone, especially her peers. The last thing she wanted to come across as in the streets was being weak. She was only eighteen, but her eyes and soul gave off a different age. The experiences G.G. went through over the years had hardened her. She felt like a grown woman trapped inside a teenager's body sometimes.

Their food soon came. G.G. slowly tried the strawberry sushi, and to her surprise, she liked it. She devoured them like it was her last meal. She even tried some of Chubbs mango sushi and loved it.

"I told you," said Chubbs with a smile

"You was right . . . I'll give you that."

"See, you gotta trust me more. I ain't gonna steer you wrong."

"We'll see."

They continued to eat. G.G. took in the décor once more. The place was far different from the bodegas, dingy Chinese restaurants, and fast-food spots she would always eat from. She somewhat felt like oil in water, but Chubbs made it his business to make her feel really comfortable in the swanky spot. He took a sip from his drink. His cell phone ringing put a pause on their conversation. He looked at the number.

"Yo, I'm gonna have to excuse myself for a moment. I gotta take this," he said.

"I'm good. Go ahead, do you," G.G. said.

Chubbs pushed himself back from his chair and walked away with the phone to his ear. G.G. looked around the place again, and then continued to eat the sushi that had captivated her taste buds. She started to think about her cousin, Baby, and T.T. It felt like the tide was changing for all of them. T.T. and Baby were in their own worlds, while G.G. found someone new in her life she was starting to appreciate. G.G. felt she owed T.T. a huge favor. If it weren't for T.T. dragging her down to the club for a job stripping, then G.G. would have never met Chubbs. It felt like a match made in history.

But T.T.'s jealousy with G.G. had been escalating during the week. It started with ignoring G.G.'s calls. Afterward, T.T. had been going off at the mouth about how G.G. was fake and forgetting her crew and where she came from.

"That bitch caught up on some dick, fuck her," T.T. would say.

It bothered G.G., because T.T. was her best friend—her right-hand bitch. She didn't understand the sudden betrayal. They had each other's back since day one. T.T., G.G., and Baby were like the three amigos in the hood. It was very well known that if you fucked with one, then you fucked with them all, and they had a strong crew to back them. G.G., too, noticed that the minute Chubbs came into her life was when the drama started to unfold with T.T.

Chubbs came back to the table and took his seat.

"Everything okay?" G.G. asked.

"Yeah, just business, that's all," he responded.

But Chubbs's demeanor changed a little after the phone call. He had something on his mind and wasn't saying anything about it. G.G. knew it wasn't her business. The two continued to eat and talk.

Chapter 14

Samson glared at Baby and shouted, "You out your fuckin' mind!" He couldn't believe what Baby had just asked him to do. He had killed men before, but that was for his country. He was a soldier. He wasn't anymore. What Baby wanted him to do was straight murder—a civilian at that.

The two were shacked up in the motel room on the Conduit. It was late in the evening, and Baby had just finished riding his dick until he felt like he was about to deflate. The pussy was always good to him. Samson felt like a fiend. The way she would make him come was mind blowing. He couldn't get enough of it. He thought about Baby constantly. The sex had him open like a good book. The rush came suddenly and Samson knew he was in love with Baby. He couldn't pinpoint why—maybe it was because it had been a long time since he'd been with a woman. He was handsome, but the military had his time over the years, and the war overseas had his mind. He came back to the States feeling unsheltered. It took him awhile to fit into a normal society. He missed the action overseas. He missed his unit.

Baby walked up to him in her panties and bra. Her figure glistened like the afternoon sun. She neared Samson with her seductive eyes, holding his angry stare. He couldn't take his eyes away from her, though. The way she looked at him was almost paralyzing.

"You don't love me?" she questioned softy.

"Yeah, I do . . . but this is murder, Baby!" he spat.

"It needs to be done, baby. This nigga is a threat to me, and you," she exclaimed.

"How?" he asked.

"He's dangerous. He already threatened my life once, said he's gonna find me and kill me," she lied. "We need to act first. I know you don't wanna lose me, baby. And I don't wanna lose you. But this muthafucka name Chubbs, he's gonna come after us, and he will kill you and me in a heartbeat."

Samson sighed heavily. "Why?" he asked.

"'Cause he feels we're competition. He's not the type to talk, or negotiate. He'll come at us hardcore," Baby lied to him.

"This ain't right."

Baby placed her soft hand against his strong cheek, and started to caress his skin gently; her touch went from his cheek to his neck. She continued her stare into him. The man looked reluctant and torn from the decision. He averted his look from her, and was silent for a moment.

Baby continued to talk. "I love you, Samson," she lied. "But didn't I look out for you when you were in trouble? You was about to lose your home . . . your mother's home, and I gave you an opportunity to save it right. We made plenty of money in such a short period of time. And you got the best of both worlds being with me. You want that shit taken away? Huh, baby? You wanna lose every fuckin' thing that we worked hard for?"

Samson remained quiet. Baby placed her hands against his bare chest. She pressed him close, looking up at him. Her hand unhurriedly moved down his big and strong chest and slid into his boxers. She took a firm hold of his thick penis and stroked it up and down. Her thumb rolled across the top of the head, and she could feel the pre-come seeping out. She played with it like it was lubrication between her fingers.

Samson moaned from her touch. He closed his eyes and benefited from the way she always touched him. It was blissful. It was too enticing.

He didn't know how to resist her. He wanted to break off the affair, but she was magnetic. She suddenly became his world. Baby continued to stroke him into a growing hard-on.

"That feels good, right, baby?" she teased.

"You know it do."

"Do this for me. This nigga gotta go so you and me can live," she stated. "It's not like you never took a life before, this ain't new to you . . . just another enemy of war. Look at it like that."

Samson moaned when she massaged his mushroom tip so tenderly. He couldn't focus. She then started to massage his balls. She cupped them in her hand and soothingly rotated his nut sack in the palm of her hand, feeling his pubic hairs tickling her.

"Ugh!" he grunted.

"You a soldier, baby . . . become one for me," Baby tried to persuade him.

Samson wanted to fight the urge. He missed the action, but he didn't want to take a civilian's life. His mind was racing with thoughts. He had been surrounded by death and violence. He felt rejected, both by the military and the NYPD. Baby gave him a purpose. But he wanted to escape the madness.

Samson felt like he was about to reach the point of no return. She had him sucked into her world. Within the blink of an eye, he was tangled in her web. And every time he struggled to break free, the web got tighter and stronger around him. He yelled, "No!" and abruptly pushed himself away from Baby like she was fire burning him.

"You don't know what it's like, Baby, to see a man die . . . to see many men die. I've seen it done plenty of times . . . even the innocent that were caught in the crossfire. I killed because it was my job. It needed to be done. It was survival for me and my unit. The nightmares finally stopped awhile back. I'm getting some sleep now," he ranted.

"This is survival, too, Samson . . . Don't you fuckin' understand that? He will kill us if we don't kill him first!" Baby yelled. She was convincing.

She was frustrated. She didn't want to turn to her second option. She didn't want to force his hand. But Baby felt she had no other choice. He was being stubborn. And she promised J. Rock that she would get him to do the job. She didn't want to let J. Rock down. She loved him, and was ready to ride or die for her thug. Baby was determined to keep Samson as her pawn on the chessboard—by any means necessary.

"Look, I don't wanna die, Samson, and I'm not gonna die. You either do this for me . . . for us, or I'll tell," she protested.

"Tell what?"

"About us . . . I'll go to that school tomorrow and tell everybody how you was fuckin' a minor, and took advantage of me . . . maybe cry out rape. Yeah, it might be your word against mine . . . but you ready to take that chance? Huh? You ready to lose your job and maybe your freedom over this?" she announced harshly.

"Why would you do that? I love you."

"And I love you," she continued to lie. "But I'm scared; baby . . . this nigga Chubbs is dangerous. You know we can't go to the police; it will only open up an investigation. And we both can't afford the cops in our business. This is the only way."

Samson clenched his fist and was angry. "Why?" he screamed from the top of his lungs.

"Because, he needs to die so that you and I can truly live," Baby replied. "Understand that, Samson."

Baby approached Samson with her look changing from anger to softness. She tenderly wrapped her arms around his strapping physique and rested her head against his chest. She let herself linger in the moment, having Samson think about it once more. The decision was tearing him apart. Baby was ripping away his sanity.

"I love you, baby. I truly do . . . Just this one time, that's all. Please, for us," she whispered to him as her head remained against his chest, and her eyes casting down to the floor exposing her true look of deceit.

He wrestled with the thought while he held Baby close to him. Samson felt trapped. Baby wasn't giving him a choice. He had made his bed, now he needed to lie in it. He sighed heavily, finally coming up with his decision.

"Okay, I'll do it," he said faintly.

Baby smiled. She didn't look up at him right away, but continued to look down at the floor, saying to herself, *mission accomplished*.

"You saved my life, Samson. I fuckin' love you."

"I love you too," he replied halfheartedly.

Baby decided to seal the deal with pleasing him once more. She finally looked up to face Samson. His look was cold against her. She needed to change it. She dropped to her knees in front of him and slid his boxers down to his shins. She once again took his penis into her hands and stroked him nice and slow. Samson didn't fight it. Baby neared her precious lips to his throbbing tip and devoured him satisfactorily. He began to moan the second her lips became wrapped around his cock.

He was now thrusting into her mouth, once again, reaching the point of no return with her. Both his hands were wound through her hair and pressing into the back of her skull as he rammed his dick down her throat, and coming soon. He grunted. The sexual experiences with Baby were always the pleasant part, but the aftermath was the riskiest and most deadly.

Samson and Baby exited the motel after 10:00 P.M. They hurried to his truck in the cover of night and climbed inside. He started the ignition, looked around the parking lot, and slowly drove out of the motel parking lot. They thought it was the perfect meeting spot for their sexual rendezvous, but while Samson waited for the traffic on the Conduit to pass by so he could merge, they were being watched from a distance.

"Muthafucka," uttered the secret and keen eyes upon them from one of the parked cars in the motel parking lot. "I got you, Samson. I see you."

Chapter 15

G.G. strutted through the projects on a mission. She was back home. And she was ready to take care of business. She spotted her crew seated on the park bench by the baseball field. They were smoking and sipping on a small bottle of Henney. G.G. looked at T.T. perched on the bench surrounded by her clique like she was the queen bee bitch. G.G. had a few choice words for T.T. She didn't understand why T.T. was trying to drag her name through the mud. She didn't do anything to provoke T.T.'s behavior toward her.

G.G. marched over to her crew with her eyes trained on T.T. Her dreads were styled into one long ponytail and she was clad in sweatpants and a brown jacket over a large T-shirt. It looked like she was ready for battle. G.G. didn't tolerate anybody talking shit about her, not even her best friend. G.G. knew if she didn't confront her friend about it, then it would make her look weak and the other girls would question her authority.

The Triple P girls turned to see G.G. coming their way. Some were excited to finally see her after it'd been two weeks. They focused on G.G. marching up to them, and some of the girls knew the sudden tension between T.T. and G.G. They stood around T.T. cautiously.

G.G. went up to T.T. while she sat perched on the bench with a lit cigarette between her fingers. She didn't want to acknowledge G.G. at first. T.T. sucked her teeth and took a pull from her cancer stick then exhaled. She wanted to ignore G.G.

"T.T., let me holla at you fo' a minute," G.G. said.

"About what?" barked T.T.

"I just wanna talk to you, that's all, just c'mere . . ." G.G. said, becoming assertive.

T.T. sighed. "G.G., whatever you gotta say, you can say it in front the crew. I thought we was family, right? So, what you gotta say to me?"

G.G. became frustrated. T.T. was talking to her like she was some off-brand bitch. She took another pull from her cigarette and locked eyes with G.G. It was a stressful moment. G.G. couldn't hold her tongue any longer.

"Yo, why my name keep comin' out ya mouth on some hateful shit, huh? What's up wit' that? I thought you were my girl, T.T.," said G.G.

"What . . . Ain't nobody said shit about you, G.G. Step the fuck off wit' that bullshit. You rollin' up on a bitch over some gossip . . . bitch, please," T.T. replied roughly.

"So it's like that, T.T.? Huh? You hatin' on a bitch 'cause I bagged Chubbs? You wanted to fuck wit' that nigga too . . . That's why?"

"Bitch, you can have that nigga . . . He ain't shit, just like you," T.T. exclaimed, jumping up and stepping off the bench to confront G.G.

"You a fake fuckin' bitch, T.T.! I thought you was my girl!" G.G. shouted.

"Fuck you, G.G.! Always thinkin' you too good for everybody. Bitch, you ain't shit! I set that up for you . . . tryin' to be a friend and look out fo' you 'cause you needed some paper. You was a broke bitch, couldn't even pay Echo the two stack that you owed him!"

"Bitch, that's my fuckin' business, and he got his money."

"Yeah, because of Chubbs . . . Bitch, you think I don't know ya fuckin' business. You a fuckin' bird, G.G.," shouted T.T.

The bubble between them was about to burst. The other girls looked on. They were in awe. No one dared to intervene, though. It was T.T. and G.G.'s business. They were witnessing their crew being dismantled right before their eyes. T.T.

and G.G. were like the foundation for their crew. When they were together, nothing could stop them. They were both leaders. But now, it looked like a rivalry was brewing between them.

"Get the fuck out my face . . . Scarface!" T.T. shouted.

It was G.G.'s breaking point. G.G. clenched her fists, zeroed in on T.T. with the intent to destroy, and swung suddenly. The blow connected swiftly against T.T.'s jaw, followed by another hard hit by G.G. T.T. stumbled. And G.G. was all over her like white on rice. The other girls started hollering at the fight. It was hard to see two friends fight each other. If it had been an outsider, they would have jumped on that person until there was nothing left of the victim to beat on. But G.G. and T.T. were mutual friends—no one took sides.

T.T. tried to fight back. She got off a few good hits on G.G. She yanked at G.G.'s dreads and scratched her face a little. She refused to be beaten and humiliated in front of her friends. But G.G. was unstoppable. She hurled T.T. across the bench like she was a toy and jumped on her ex-friend's face with malice meaning.

"Fuck you, bitch . . . Come out ya fuckin' mouth again," shouted G.G., having T.T. in her strong grip as they tussled on the ground. She was overpowering T.T.

They were like savages, tearing into each other like a hungry lion shredding its prey apart. A crowd started to form around the fight. There was yelling.

"Yo, y'all need to chill. Fo' real, chill wit' that shit!" Meeka screamed. For her, it was like watching two big sisters fighting.

The fight was quick, but brutal. G.G. and T.T. were pulled apart from each other by their crew. But their rants and threats continued at each other. Their faces were bruised, scratched, and a little bloody. It was the end of their friendship.

"You a dumb bitch, T.T.!" G.G. shouted.

"I'ma see you G.G. I swear, you better watch ya fuckin' back, bitch!" T.T. screamed frantically while she was being held back by two girls.

"See me then, bitch. I'm here! You a jealous bitch! You always been a jealous bitch of what I got. My nigga is the shit; what the fuck you got, T.T.? You ain't got shit, bitch!"

G.G. hated that she had to beat down her best friend. But she had to protect her reputation. There was no other way around it—it had to get ugly. Before police showed up due to 911 being called about a dispute, the fight had broken up and the girls were leaving the scene with T.T. and G.G. going their separate ways, and licking their wounds.

***

Several days had passed, and G.G. found herself staying at Chubb's apartment in Midtown on a daily basis. She wanted to get her fight with T.T. from her mind. But it was hard to do. She tried to fight the depression she was sinking into. T.T., Baby, and her crew were all she had. They were who she loved. They all grew up together. They were her sisters, and within a split second, her family wasn't there anymore. *How did it get to this point?* G.G. asked herself. She had Chubbs, and he was the best thing that ever happened to her. He was teaching her new things, and taking her to so many different places in the city. But she wanted the best of both worlds, but that didn't seem possible.

Chubbs was there for her. He constantly tried to cheer her up, and it was working. The sex was phenomenal and the shopping sprees were extraordinary. He took her to malls, boutiques, and stores that she never knew existed. G.G. went from being a local hood rat to a baller's wifey. It was like her life had dramatically changed overnight. God had blessed her for some reason, and she didn't know why. G.G.'s entire life was gangs, violence, drugs, and sex. She didn't produce anything good. She was a menace to her society since she was twelve years old. G.G.

started to understand why T.T. was jealous. The bitch wanted to be her. They always dreamed of riches and success. T.T. wanted to escape from her harsh environment also. She wanted out. G.G. had gotten the opportunity, and T.T. felt that her best friend was leaving her behind. G.G. was starting to miss her girls, her family.

But she didn't want to harbor the thought. It was her life, and she couldn't feel sorry for T.T. The bitch did her dirty, and it was hard for G.G. to forgive her. Chubbs was showing her the time of her life, and she experienced the high-end nightlife, where they didn't have to wait in long lines, and everything for them was VIP.

But unbeknownst to G.G. and Chubbs, they were being followed closely. Wherever they went, a dark, looming threat followed them attentively. For the past week, he had become their shadow. He witnessed the good times the couple was experiencing, and the joy the woman was having. But he knew it all had to come to an abrupt end. He was willing, but reluctantly ready to kill off their happiness together so he could continue with his. It was only a job that he had to do. It was nothing personal.

Chubbs and G.G. exited the popular Midtown nightclub with smiles. They walked toward the parked Bentley Coupe. Chubbs had G.G. under

452 Erick S. Gray

his arm, and she was looking fantastic in a sexy, hot pink, cinched-front mini dress with the low cut and cowl neck, which was underneath her quarter-length black mink coat. The mink and the outfit were two of many gifts that came from Chubbs. G.G. was the center of attention. It seemed like her happiness was a pure fairytale, and she feared it would end soon.

The couple climbed into the Bentley. But Chubbs didn't start up the car right away. He relaxed in the driver seat and looked at G.G.

"You're beautiful, you know that, right?" he complimented her.

She blushed. "Thank you."

It was early November and the cool air outside was a clear reminder that fall would turn into winter within a few weeks. G.G. remembered that a year ago, today, she was being arrested for assault and battery on a young girl. The case was eventually dropped, and she was given a second chance once again—being with Chubbs made G.G. not want to become that girl anymore.

"What made you change your life around, Chubbs?" she asked.

Chubbs looked at her for a moment, holding on to to his answer.

G.G. didn't rush him, nor was she going to ask him again. If he didn't want to answer her, it was fine with her.

But the answer finally parted his lips. "I was a very bad man awhile back. I sold drugs in keys, had a direct link with the Colombians. I was big in Jersey and Brooklyn. I killed men just for the slightest infraction against me. I was torturous with brutality. Let's just say that twelve years in the feds and taking my own brother's life changes a man."

"Your brother?" G.G. questioned, thinking she must have heard him wrong.

"Yeah, he had stolen from me. And it wasn't even much . . . a thousand dollars. I could have wiped my ass with what he owed me. I could have let him be and live. But the mentality I had back then, I didn't care if it was ten dollars, I would have killed you for it, because you disrespected me. I was horrible. I was losing control, getting high off my own shit, too. I was facing, at one time, the death penalty for taking my brother's life and his friend, but my attorney was the best . . . I don't know how he did it, but I ended up with doing twelve years. I got a second chance.

"So, two years after my release, I took the money I had saved . . . that the feds didn't touch, and invested it into music and opening a few legit businesses. I got tired of that life. There was this feeling inside of me that said I needed to move on, and I did. I mean, I still got ties to the streets . . . my reputation precedes me, but I'm trying to let that be my past."

"And your sudden interest in me?" G.G. asked.

"You're like the female me . . . That's sexy," he joked.

G.G. chuckled. "I'm lovin' you, Chubbs, and I want this to be serious."

"It is serious," he let it be known, staring at G.G.'s lovely face.

She smiled.

"I know there's a tremendous age gap between us, but I don't look at it like that. I just see you, G.G. Eighteen or older, I like your fiery attitude," he proclaimed.

G.G. was happy. She felt the same way about her new man. It was the change she needed.

It was the first time Chubbs confided in a woman, and he felt good about it. The two lovers felt content, and Chubbs finally drove off to home. Chubbs pulled up to the high-rise in the city and parked a few cars down from the lobby entrance. The stretched city block was quiet under the towering buildings reaching the sky. The Midtown city bustle was gradually fading with the time nearing two in the morning. The loving couple both had naughty ideas for the bedroom. G.G. was ready to get frisky and do things to her newfound boyfriend that were only seen done in porno movies.

They walked toward the lobby arm in arm, enjoying the cool November breeze. They talked and laughed, enjoying the night together. As they strutted closer to the towering and remarkable glass high-rise building, their guard came down.

The shadowy threat slowly emerged from the darkened corner where he was hidden and trained his attention on Chubbs. The man had his back to him—he was defenseless. He was a few foot steps behind the walking couple, draped in a long black coat, and underneath it was a tool of death to get the job done.

Chubbs and G.G. were footsteps away from the lobby entrance. G.G. laughed and said, "You are silly. I love you, baby."

"I'm loving you too," replied Chubbs.

Suddenly the couple heard, "I'm so sorry!" It came from behind them. Chubbs spun around and was wide eyed. There was a man with an M16 pointed at them. Samson locked eyes with the once notorious kingpin and was silent. Chubbs could only smirk—thinking that this moment was inevitable, and knowing that his life was about to end. He thought it was his past finally catching up to him.

G.G. stood frozen. *It can't end like this,* she thought. "Please . . ." G.G. uttered.

Samson opened fire.

Bat! Bat! Bat! Bat! Bat! Bat! Bat! Bat! Bat! Bat!

He gunned down the couple where they stood. He didn't want to kill the woman, but she was a witness and had to fall also. Chubbs and G.G. dropped to the pavement violently, lying in the crimson blood pooling around their bullet-riddled bodies. Samson concealed the M16 back under his long coat and trotted off.

Chapter 16

The news of her cousin's death overwhelmed Baby with grief and it hit the hood like a ton of bricks. Everyone was shocked about it. They couldn't believe G.G. was dead. G.G.'s gruesome murder traveled like the wind through the streets. It seemed too unreal for everybody, and had Baisley Park Housing on standstill. There were many tearful eyes, and agony. G.G. was an icon—a rebel in their hood, and the founder of the Triple P girls. Her crew was angry, and wanted vengeance. Regardless of their sudden trouble, even T.T. was in grief. Her long-time friend was no more, and she regretted her spiteful actions toward G.G. It made T.T. sick to her stomach.

G.G.'s death made the evening news with several stations covering the couple who was gunned down in the city during the wee hours of the morning. The police and media associated the killings with Chubbs's checkered past. They figured it was a revenge killing with G.G. caught in the crossfire.

Baby was filled with anguish. She couldn't believe her cousin was gone. She couldn't believe Samson did them both. It wasn't part of the plan. It angered her. She sat in her still bedroom glued to the floor like an inanimate being. The tears flooded her face. The hurt seeped through her body and her skin like a plague devouring her slowly. She was bitter and regretful at the same time. She hated Samson. She hated him like he was a disease eating through her body.

The following school day, Baby marched through the halls on a mission. She ignored everybody she came in contact with and searched the crowded hallways for Samson. Her mind was on her dead cousin. She wasn't thinking rationally. The emotions and pain ate at her like a flesh-eating disease. People right away knew something was wrong. The school heard about G.G.'s death, and some were somber and shocked—but others thought that she had it coming. G.G. was a reckless girl, living a reckless life. Some of the students and teachers felt her violent and gang-banging ways finally caught up with her. But they wouldn't dare tell it to Baby's face. They already knew that she was suffering enough and was a firecracker ready to go off.

Baby spotted Samson standing by the cafeteria. It was his usual post during the lunch hours.

He had been absent for a moment—taking a few sick days after the murders and laying low—but now he was back to work like everything was fine.

Baby marched up to Samson with her fiery eyes trained at every part of him. His attention was turned toward another matter going on in the cafeteria. Baby clenched her fists tightly, so tightly that her nails were digging into the palms of her hands.

"You killed my fuckin' cousin!" she screamed madly.

Samson turned around and saw Baby charging for him at full throttle. She was filled with rage. He was taken aback suddenly. All attention in the cafeteria shifted toward Baby charging for Samson.

"You killed my fuckin' cousin!" Baby screamed again.

She lunged at Samson and punched him in the face with a mighty blow. He stumbled back. It was a striking hit from the petite, young girl. She tried to swing at him again, but other safety officers quickly intervened, grabbing Baby immediately and pulling her away from Samson.

"I hate you! You killed G.G.," she shouted.

The students were shouting and animated, and the adults were befuddled by Baby's wild statement. Samson could only stare at Baby—

watching as Pandora's Box was slowly opening and revealing his dirty little secret.

"I should never have fucked you. You a fuckin' killer . . . I hate you! I hate you!" Baby continued to scream.

She attempted to free herself from Billy's grip to continue her fight with Samson. But Billy overpowered the girl and dragged her out of the cafeteria with her screaming, crying, and throwing violence toward anyone around her. Samson was left standing there in the spotlight—exposed—with Baby's hard and revealing words lingering in everyone's heads that heard her say, "I should have never fucked you!"

"Is she telling the truth?" one lady security officer asked.

"She's crazy!" Samson responded.

Marvin walked up to Samson. He smirked at the rookie officer. He locked eyes with the fuming Samson and said to him, "No, she's not. You were fuckin' that young girl, weren't you?"

"I don't know what she's talking about. She's delusional," said Samson.

"No, she's not. I saw you, man. I saw you and her exiting from a motel room a few nights ago," Marvin let it be known.

Samson kept a deadpan look. Just like that, his life was spiraling out of control. The other officers didn't want to believe the scandal that was unfolding in their school. But it was happening. Samson tried to remain adamant about his innocence, but Marvin kept on pushing the subject.

"I told you to stay away from her, that she was bad news . . . but you a stupid muthafucka that couldn't keep your dick in your pants, huh," Marvin exclaimed.

It made Samson upset.

"She got you pussy whipped, nigga?" Marvin added.

Abruptly, Samson swung and punched Marvin in the jaw, throwing the slender man off his feet and onto his back, having him smashed against the floor.

"Fuck you!" Samson shouted.

He was quickly restrained by his coworkers and removed from the cafeteria. It took Marvin a moment to get back up on his feet. Samson had knocked the wind out of him. The students looked on in awe. His coworkers were disgusted. Samson quickly went from being the cute new school safety officer with the impressive military background in the school, to the shameful, perverted predator. He was called into the principal's office to meet with Principal Palmer about the incident. He knew his job was done for, and his freedom was at risk. He knew he had fucked his whole life for a piece of pussy.

Baby was devastated. She didn't know what to do or who to run to. She had been expelled from school. Principal Palmer had had enough of her out-of-control and reckless manners, and when she put her hands on Samson, even if it was for a good reason, she was still in the wrong. Palmer had sympathy for her, especially with the loss of G.G.—but he couldn't tolerate the behavior anymore. He couldn't put his other students at risk. The expulsion was a long time coming.

Baby stormed off the elevator and hurried toward J. Rock's apartment on the fifth floor. She was still emotional and grieving. She wanted Samson to pay for what he did to G.G. She wanted a hit out on him.

Baby approached J. Rock's door and banged heavily on it. She was impatient. She wanted to see her boo, and become wrapped in his arms— yearning for his roughneck affection. She needed some kind of comfort, and wanted J. Rock to take care of business. Baby banged continuously on J. Rock's door, attracting other neighbors to peek out their doors to see who was causing the loud commotion in the hallway.

"J. Rock, open the fuckin' door, baby. I need to see you," Baby hollered.

The door swung open abruptly, and J. Rock stood in the doorway shirtless with a cigarette dangling from his lips. It looked like Baby had interrupted him in action of something, but Baby didn't care.

"What the fuck is wrong wit' you, Baby. Huh? Fuck you bangin' on my goddamn door like you the muthafuckin' police?" screamed J. Rock.

"J. Rock, I need to see you, baby. I need ya help," pleaded Baby.

"I'm fuckin' busy right now, Baby."

Baby pushed passed J. Rock and stormed into the apartment. She wasn't taking no for an answer. J. Rock spun around on his heels and glared at Baby. "What the fuck, Baby! I told you I was fuckin' busy . . . Get the fuck out!"

"I want him killed, J. Rock. I want that mutha-fucka dead!" she shouted.

"Who? Ya soldier boy?"

"Yeah . . . He killed my cousin."

"Yeah, I heard about that . . . That's fucked up," J. Rock replied apathetically.

"So you gonna do it?"

"What . . . Fuck outta here, Baby. I ain't touchin' nowhere around that incident."

"But I did you that favor. He killed Chubbs for you . . . like you wanted him to."

"I don't know what the fuck you talkin' about, Baby," J. Rock replied with a deadpan stare focused on the emotional Baby.

"What? You told me, J. Rock, that once I could get him to kill Chubbs for you, we were goin' to officially be together. I'm your ride or die bitch, J. Rock," exclaimed Baby.

J. Rock looked at Baby like she was crazy. He didn't want anything to do with her. His harsh demeanor toward her was evident. He used her. Baby was teary eyed, and a train wreck waiting to happen. She came within reach of J. Rock in an attempt to get a hug from him. But she suddenly stopped in her tracks. Her eyes looked beyond J. Rock and were fixated on the threatening figure behind him.

"What the fuck is this, J. Rock?" Baby shouted.

J. Rock turned to see Erica standing behind him in her panties and bra. Her arm was outstretched, gripping a 9 mm that was aimed at Baby.

"Let me shoot this fuckin' bitch, J. Rock," Erica said through clenched teeth.

"Erica, chill the fuck out . . . not here, in this fuckin' place. You crazy?" said J. Rock.

"What the fuck, J. Rock! What the fuck is she doin' here?" screamed Baby.

"I hate this fuckin' bitch. I want her dead like her bitch cousin," spat Erica.

"Are you fuckin' serious, J. Rock? I thought you was done wit' that bitch!"

"Nah, I'm not. I lied to you," confessed J. Rock.

Erica's face had completely healed and she looked normal. The gun was shaky in her hands as she locked her hate and anger into Baby. She wanted to pull the trigger and kill off her rival so badly that her pussy was throbbing. Baby just stood there defenseless against Erica and J. Rock. She had experienced the ultimate betrayal, and the anguish that flowed through her was crippling her from head to toe. She couldn't move. She almost wanted to accept death to substitute the pain she felt.

"Get the fuck outta here, Baby . . . before I change my mind and have my bitch shoot you down," said J. Rock harshly.

"But I thought you loved me . . ."

"It was fun while it lasted, but you gotta go. You see, me and her got married yesterday, and she's pregnant wit' my seed. So I'ma stick wit' my true bitch," J. Rock informed her.

Erica smirked. She still had the gun pointed at Baby, and said, "Bitch, leave now, but it's definite I'ma see you again on the streets . . . And fuck your bitch cousin G.G. . . . That fuckin' ho got what she deserved."

It angered Baby to hear Erica disrespect her dead cousin. She snapped, and suddenly didn't care about the gun being in Erica's hand. She lunged for her foe, but J. Rock interfered with the attack. He snatched Baby into his arms roughly and started to drag her toward the exit.

"Get the fuck off me, J. Rock! I'ma kill that fuckin' bitch! I'ma kill her," Baby screamed madly, while trying to jerk and fight her way from his strong seize around her.

J. Rock dragged her to the door and pushed her out into the hallway forcefully. Baby was still screaming and yelling. She refused to go down silently. Her face was contorted with rage and tears, with her body trembling from tremendous upset.

"Bye, bitch!" Erica shouted.

The door was slammed shut, and Baby was left crying hysterically in the hallway. She dropped to the cold, dirty floor in defeat. She had lost everything—family, and her man. Her cries echoed in the hallway, disturbing the neighbors on the floor. Her reality hit her like lightening—everything about her life was a lie, and she was all alone.

Epilogue

Baby walked toward her building under the canopy of the stars. It was late, and she was still upset and crushed about G.G.'s death. Baby skipped her cousin's funeral. She couldn't bear the thought of seeing G.G. lying in a casket. It was too painful for her to witness. She felt responsible for everything that transpired, because she was. She felt bamboozled. J. Rock's betrayal had cut her soul deep to the core. She craved revenge and was willing to go to any lengths to kill those who did her wrong, starting with Samson.

It had been a week since she blew the whistle on their affair and let the cat out the bag about the murders. It caused much controversy and chaos in the school. The gossip spread like a virus through the high school and poured out into the streets like a popular trend. Everybody was talking about it. The scandal with Samson and Baby even made the evening news and headlined newspapers across the city. Samson was immediately terminated after the scandal surfaced of a school safety officer having a secret affair with a student, which led to drugs and murder. Reporters lay camped outside of August Martin searching for interviews and more dirt, and Samson had been arrested and charged with five counts of indictments. His bail was set at $200,000. It was a high bail. His mother had to attain a bondsman and put up her house for collateral to free her son from jail. Samson received bail because of a technicality in the case. His lawyer was a tearing apart the case against him. There was no solid evidence to link him to the two murders. Baby wasn't a reliable witness. The defense was able to shred her credibility during Samson's arraignment. The prosecutors were still pushing for a trial date and they fought to have his bail denied. It didn't happen. The judge would only set his bail really high. He had lost his job and his name was becoming mud. The ex-Marine was a disgrace to his country.

No one had heard or seen him since he was released from Rikers Island. The media was itching to get a statement from him, but he continued to hide and ignore the public.

Baby's name also was dragged through the streets of Queens. Her life was in turmoil. The detectives had picked her up numerous times for questioning, but she would become adamant and stubborn. She refused to cooperate with the authorities. They also had no case against her. The police investigation was still pending, but without a solid eyewitness, Samson was becoming a free man. It frustrated the NYPD.

Baby's mental state was deteriorating gradually from the tragedy she suffered. She entered the lobby and waited for the elevator to open up. She was alone in the litter-filled entrance. She was tired. She was frustrated. With the death of her cousin and a broken heart, it was enough to drive anyone suicidal.

The doors opened and Baby stepped into the elevator and pushed for her floor. It ascended, and shortly after, she got off on her floor and walked toward her door. She had her keys in her hand and was ready to enter the apartment. She felt a sudden chill coming from behind her while she was about to open the door into her apartment.

"Baby," she heard him call out.

Baby turned to see Samson coming out of the stairwell. He was clad in a dark hoodie draped over his head, and was wearing worn denim jeans and dirty white sneakers. He looked run-down and beaten. He wasn't the same handsome and strong Samson she remembered.

"Get the fuck away from me!" Baby screamed.

"I just wanna talk to you," said Samson, approaching closer with his eyes in a soft plea.

Baby turned from him and rushed to open her apartment door. She thrust the door open and turned to slam the door shut, but Samson was fast. Before the door could shut, he wedged his foot into the doorway and pushed open the door, forcing his way inside.

"I just want to talk to you," he said.

"Get outta here," she screamed.

No one was home. Baby's grandmother had to be admitted into the hospital a few days ago, and the home aid attendant was gone. Baby moved farther into her apartment trying to get away from Samson.

He came closer to her. "I'm sorry what happened with your cousin. It was a mistake. But I told you, I didn't want to do it. You gotta understand . . . it was an accident," he stated.

"Get the fuck away from me!"

"Come with me, Baby. I gotta leave this city. I can't stay here. I can't go to prison."

Baby thought he was sick and twisted. He had the audacity to ask her to leave with him. It made Baby want to throw up. She was outraged. "Are you fuckin' serious!"

"I did all this for you . . . so we can be together and happy. I forgive you. I do. I know you didn't mean to do what you did. You were emotional at the time. But you and I, we can go somewhere far and start over," Samson stated. "I know we were meant to be together. You understand me, Baby."

Baby looked at him, and took a few steps back. He was crazy.

Unbeknownst to her, one of the reasons he was discharged medically from the military was because he was diagnosed with a bipolar disorder. He suffered from severe manic episodes that could sometimes lead to psychotic symptoms such as delusions and hallucinations. It was the main reason the NYPD rejected him. The war in Iraq had disturbed Samson in so many ways. He was able to function normally most times, but then something would trigger his episodes, and he would fly off the edge.

"C'mon, pack your bags so we can get the fuck outta here, Baby. We ain't got much time," he exclaimed.

"No! I'm not goin' no fuckin' where wit' you. I fuckin' hate you! I hate you! I never loved you. Every damn thing about you repulses me. I used you, nigga . . . 'cause you was weak. I'm in love with another man," she sharply proclaimed. "I will never fuckin' love you! Ya sick and weak,

472 Erick S. Gray

nigga . . . Get the fuck outta here! You a stupid
fuckin' freak!"

Samson's face twisted into a sickening scowl.
Baby's words cut through him like a samurai
sword. He did everything for her, but he was
a fool. His mind thought it was love. However,
he never knew love from a woman. His whole
life had been to become a soldier—a killer. The
Marines trained him well, and taught him how
to become a fighter.

"How can you say that to me?" he screamed.
"After everything I did for you. I did it for our
love."

Baby inched herself closer to the kitchen. She
wanted to grab a weapon to protect her. The in-
sanity in Samson's eyes made her fear for her life.
His disturbing behavior sent a sharp, chilling
feeling down her spine. He was dangerous and
desperate—a lethal combination.

"Look, just leave, Samson . . . Leave!"

"No. You're coming with me. I'm not leaving
here without you. I love you."

Samson seemed transfixed by Baby. He was
serious. Baby glared at him and wanted him
dead. Her stomach churned with uneasiness.
Her mind filled with regrets. The situation in the
quiet, quaint apartment became intense. Baby
felt trapped. He was blocking the only way out.

There was no other way to get around his wide, muscular frame.

"Pack your bags, honey . . . we got a bus to catch," said Samson chillingly.

"Fuck you!" Baby screamed.

She bolted for the kitchen. Samson chased her. Baby ran for the kitchen drawer and snatched it open roughly, and in one act, reached for the kitchen knife inside and spun around with her arm outstretched, gripping the knife to protect herself. Samson swooped down on top of her, but felt the blade suddenly penetrate his side. He jolted for a moment, feeling the knife sink deeper into his flesh. He trained his eyes on Baby, feeling the blood ooze from the wound. The betrayal was costly.

"You fuckin' bitch!" he shouted.

Baby thought it would stop him, but the knife piercing his lower abdomen only made him stronger and madder. Samson hastily wrapped his powerful hands around Baby's slim neck and began to squeeze.

Baby gasped. Her grip around the handle of the knife weakened and she fought to live. She clawed and fought to free herself from his intense hold around her neck.

Samson's rage grew stronger. He picked her off her feet and continued to choke her. Baby's feet dangled like she was being hanged. Her fight to live was growing weaker.

"I loved you!" Samson screamed.

"Please . . . No . . ." Baby uttered faintly.

Samson's mind and anger were too far gone for him to stop. He squeezed tighter, restricting any air into her body.

Baby's eyes began to bulge. She felt her neck breaking. He was too strong. It felt like a machine had taken hold of her.

He looked into her eyes and saw the light and the life slowly fading away.

She gasped her last breath, and a minute later, she was dead.

Samson continued to squeeze, lifting her lifeless body in the air. Finally realizing she was gone, he let his compact grip go from around her neck. She dropped heavily to the kitchen floor with a thud, looking like a contorted, lifeless doll.

Samson looked aloof for a moment. He gazed down at his hideous feat and began to cry. He then tended to the knife in his lower abdomen. He slowly pulled it out. His wounds were ugly but he didn't care. He fell to the floor and rested against the kitchen cabinets. Baby's body was right next to him.

"I'm sorry, Baby. I'm sorry," he whined.

He was dying also. He reached for Baby's lifeless hand, took it into his and slowly felt his life also fading away. Soon, he was dead too.

The End